I0609394

A Certain Rich Man

William Allen White

Contents

A CERTAIN RICH MAN

BY

William Allen White

BOOK I

A CERTAIN RICH MAN

CHAPTER I

The woods were as the Indians had left them, but the boys who were playing there did not realize, until many years afterwards, that they had moved in as the Indians moved out. Perhaps, if these boys had known that they were the first white boys to use the Indians' playgrounds, the realization might have added zest to the make-believe of their games; but probably boys between seven and fourteen, when they play at all, play with their fancies strained, and very likely these little boys, keeping their stick-horse livery-stable in a wild-grape arbour in the thicket, needed no verisimilitude. The long straight hickory switches--which served as horses--were arranged with their butts on a rotting log, whereon some grass was spread for their feed. Their string bridles hung loosely over the log. The horsemen swinging in the vines above, or in the elm tree near by, were preparing a raid on the stables of other boys, either in the native lumber town a rifle-shot away or in distant parts of the woods. When the youngsters climbed down, they straddled their hickory steeds and galloped friskily away to the creek and drank; this was part of the rites, for tradition in the town of their elders said that whoever drank of Sycamore Creek water immediately turned horse thief. Having drunk their fill at the ford, they waded it and left the stumpy road, plunging into the underbrush, snorting and puffing and giggling and fussing and complaining--the big ones at the little ones and the little ones at the big ones--after the manner of mankind.

When they had gone perhaps a half-mile from the ford, one of the little boys, feeling the rag on his sore heel slipping and letting the rough woods grass scratch his raw flesh, stopped to tie up the rag. He was far in the rear of the pack when he stopped, and the boys, not heeding his blat, rushed on and left him at the edge of a thicket near a deep-rutted road. His cry became a whimper and his whimper a sniffle as he worked with the rag; but the little fingers were clumsy, and a heel is a hard place to cover, and the sun was hot on his back; so he took the rag in one hand and his bridle in the other, and limped on his stick horse into the thick shade of a lone oak tree that stood beside the wide dusty road. His sore did not bother him, and he sat with his back against the tree for a while, flipping the rag and making figures in the dust with the pronged tail of his horse. Then his hands were still, and as he ran from tune to tune with improvised interludes, he droned a song of his prowess. Sometimes he sang words and sometimes he sang thoughts. He sank farther and farther down and looked up into the tree and ceased his song, chirping instead a stuttering falsetto trill, not unlike a cricket's, holding his breath as long as he could to draw it out to its finest strand; and thus with his head on his arm and his arm on the tree root, he fell asleep.

The noon sun was on his legs when he awoke, and a strange dog was sniffing at him. As he started up, he heard the clatter of a horse's feet in the road, and saw an Indian woman trotting toward him on a pony. In an instant he was a-wing with terror, scooting toward the thick of the woods. He screamed as he ran, for his head was full of Indian stories, and he knew that the only use Indians had for little boys was to steal them and adopt them into the tribe. He heard the brush crackling behind him, and he knew that the woman had turned off the road to follow him. A hundred yards is a long way for a terror-stricken little boy to run through tangled underbrush, and when he had come to the high bank of the stream, he slipped down among the tree roots and tried to hide. His little heart beat so fast that he could not keep from panting, and the sound of breaking brush came nearer and then stopped, and in a moment he looked up and saw the squaw leaning over the bank, holding to the tree above him. She smiled kindly at him and said:--

"Come on, boy--I won't hurt you. I as scared of you as you are of me."

She bent over and took him by the arm and lifted him to her. She got on her pony and put him on before her and soothed his fright, as they rode slowly through the wood to the road, where they came to a great band of Indians, all riding ponies.

It seemed to the boy that he had never imagined there were so many people in the whole world; there was some parley among them, and the band set out on the road again, with the squaw in advance. They were but a few yards from the forks of the road, and as they came to it she said:--

"Boy--which way to town?"

He pointed the way and she turned into it, and the band followed. They crossed the ford, climbed the steep red clay bank of the creek, and filed up the hill into the unpainted group of cabins and shanties cluttered around a well that men, in 1857, knew as Sycamore Ridge. The Indians filled the dusty area between the two rows of gray houses on either side of the street, and the town flocked from its ten front doors before half the train had arrived. The last door of them all to open was in a slab house, nearly half a mile from the street. A washing fluttered on the clothes-line, and the woman who came out of the door carried a round-bottomed hickory-bark basket, such as might hold clothes-pins. Seeing the invasion, she hurried across the prairie, toward the town. She was a tall thin woman, not yet thirty, brown and tanned, with a strong masculine face, and as she came nearer one could see that she had a square firm jaw, and great kind gray eyes that lighted her countenance from a serene soul. Her sleeves rolled far above her elbows revealed arms used to rough hard work, and her hands were red from the wash-tub. As she came into the street, she saw the little boy sitting on the horse in front of the squaw. Walking to them quickly, and lifting her arms, as she neared the squaw's pony, the white woman said:--

"Why, Johnnie Barclay, where have you been?"

The boy climbed from the pony, and the two women smiled at each other, but exchanged no words. And as his feet touched the ground, he became conscious of the rag in his hand, of his bleeding heel, of his cramped legs being "asleep"--all in one instant, and went limping and whining toward home with his mother, while the Indians traded in the store and tried to steal from the other houses, and in a score of peaceful ways diverted the town's attention from the departing figures down the path.

That was the first adventure that impressed itself upon the memory of John Barclay. All his life he remembered the covered wagon in which the Barclays crossed the Mississippi; but it is only a curious memory of seeing the posts of the bed, lying flat beside him in the wagon, and of fingering the palm leaves cut in the wood. He was four years old then, and as a man he remembered only as a tale that is told the fight at Westport Landing, where his father was killed for preaching an abolition sermon from the wagon tongue. The man remembered nothing of the long ride that the child and the mother took with the father's body to Lawrence, where they buried it in a free-state cemetery. But he always remembered something of their westward ride, after the funeral of his father. The boy carried a child's memory of the prairie--probably his first sight of the prairie, with the vacant horizon circling around and around him, and the monotonous rattle of the wagon on the level prairie road, for hours keeping the same rhythm and fitting the same tune. Then there was a mottled memory of the woods--woods with sunshine in them, and of a prairie flooded with sunshine on which he played, now picking flowers, now playing house under the limestone ledges, now, after a rain, following little rivers down rocky draws, and finding sunfish and silversides in the deeper pools. But always his memory was of the sunshine, and the open sky, or the deep wide woods all unexplored, save by himself.

The great road that widened to make the prairie street, and wormed over the hill into the sunset, always seemed dusty to the boy, and although in after years he followed that road, over the hills and far away, when it was rutty and full of clods, as a child he recalled it only as a great bed of dust, wherein he and other boys played, now battling with handfuls of dust, and now running races on some level stretch of it, and now standing beside the road while a passing movers' wagon delayed their play. The movers' wagon was never absent from the boy's picture of that time and place. Either the canvas-covered wagon was coming from the ford of Sycamore Creek, or disappearing over the hill beyond the town, or was passing in front of the boys as they stopped their play. Being a boy, he could not know, nor would he care if he did know, that he was seeing one of God's miracles--the migration of a people, blind but instinctive as that of birds or buffalo, from old pastures into new ones. All over the plains in those days, on a hundred roads like that which ran through Sycamore Ridge, men and women were moving from east to west, and, as often has happened since the beginning of time, when men have migrated, a great ethical principle was stirring in them. The pioneers do not go to the wilderness always in lust of land, but sometimes they go to satisfy their souls. The spirit of God moves in the hearts of men as it moves on the face of the waters.

Something of this moving spirit was in John Barclay's mother. For often she paused at her work, looking up from her wash-tub toward the highway, when a prairie schooner sailed by, and lifting her face skyward for an instant, as her lips moved in silence. As a man the boy knew she was thinking of her long journey, of the tragedy that came of it, and praying for those who passed into the West. Then she would bend to her work again; and the washerwoman's child who took the clothes she washed in his little wagon with the cottonwood log wheels, across the commons into the town, was not made to feel an inferior place in the social system until he was in his early teens. For all the Sycamore Ridge women worked hard in those days. But there were Sundays when the boy and his mother walked over the wide prairies together, and she told him stories of Haverhill--of the wonderful people who lived there, of the great college, of the beautiful women and wise men, and best of all of his father, who was a student in the college, and they dreamed together--mother and child--about how he would board at Uncle Union's and work in the store for Uncle Abner--when the boy went back to Haverhill to school when he grew up.

On these excursions the mother sometimes tried to interest him in Mr. Beecher's sermons which she read to him, but his eyes followed the bees and the birds and the butterflies and the shadows trailing across the hillside; so the seed fell on stony ground. One fine fall day they went up the ridge far above the town where the court-house stands now, and there under a lone elm tree just above a limestone ledge, they spread their lunch, and the mother sat on the hillside, almost hidden by the rippling prairie grass, reading the first number of the

Atlantic Monthly, while the boy cleared out a spring that bubbled from beneath a rock in the shade, and after running for a few feet sank under a great stone and did not appear again. As the mother read, the afternoon waned, and when she looked up, she was astonished to see John standing beside the rock, waist deep in a hole, trying to back down into it. His face was covered with dirt, and his clothes were wet from the falling water of the spring that was flowing into the hole he had opened. In a jiffy she pulled him out, and looking into the hole, saw by the failing sunlight which shone directly into the place that the child had uncovered the opening of a cave. But they did not explore it, for the mother was afraid, and the two came down the hill, the child's head full of visions of a pirate's treasure, and the mother's full of the whims of the Autocrat of the Breakfast Table.

The next day school began in Sycamore Ridge,--for the school and the church came with the newspaper, *Freedom's Banner*,--and a new world opened to the boy, and he forgot the cave, and became interested in Webster's blue-backed speller. And thus another grown-up person, "Miss Lucy," came into his world. For with children, men and women generically are of another order of beings. But Miss Lucy, being John Barclay's teacher, grew into his daily life on an equality with his dog and the Hendricks boys, and took a place somewhat lower than his mother in his list of saints. For Miss Lucy came from Sangamon County, Illinois, and her father had fought the Indians, and she told the school as many strange and wonderful things about Illinois as John had learned from his mother about Haverhill. But his allegiance to the teacher was only lip service. For at night when he sat digging the gravel and dirt from the holes in the heels of his copper-toed boots, that he might wad them with paper to be ready for his skates on the morrow, or when he sat by the wide fireplace oiling the runners with the steel curly-cucs curving over the toes, or filing a groove in the blades, the boy's greatest joy was with his mother. Sometimes as she ironed she told him stories of his father, or when the child was sick and nervous, as a special favour, on his promise to take the medicine and not ask for a drink, she would bring her guitar from under the bed and tune it up and play with a curious little mouse-like touch. And on rare occasions she would sing to her own shy maidenly accompaniment, her voice rising scarcely higher than the wind in the sycamore at the spring outside. The boy remembered only one line of an old song she sometimes tried to sing: "Sleeping, I dream, love, dream, love, of thee," but what the rest of it was, and what it was all about, he never knew; for when she got that far, she always stopped and came to the bed and lay beside him, and they both cried, though as a child he did not know why.

So the winter of 1857 wore away at Sycamore Ridge, and with the coming of the spring of '58, when the town was formally incorporated, even into the boy world there came the murmurs of strife and alarms. The games the boys played were war games. They had battles in the woods, between the free-state and the pro-slavery men, and once--twice--three times there marched by on the road real soldiers, and it was no unusual thing to see a dragoon dismount at the town well and water his horse. The big boys in school affected spurs, and Miss Lucy brought to school with her one morning a long bundle, which, when it was unwrapped, disclosed the sword of her father, Captain Barnes, presented to him by his admiring soldiers at the close of the "Black Hawk War." John traded for a tin fife and learned to play "Jaybird" upon it, though he preferred the jew's-harp, and had a more varied repertory with it. Was it an era of music, or is childhood the period of music? Perhaps this land of ours was younger than it is now and sang more lustily, if not with great precision; for to the man who harks back over the years, those were days of song. All the world seemed singing--men in their stores and shops, women at their work, and children in their schools. And a freckled, barefooted little boy with sunburned curly hair, in home-made clothes, and with brown bare legs showing through the rips in his trousers, used to sit alone in the woods breathing his soul into a mouth-organ--a priceless treasure for which he had traded two raccoons, an owl, and a prairie dog. But he mastered the mouth-organ,--it was called a French harp in those days,--and before he had put on his first collar, Watts McHurdie had taught the boy to play the accordion. The great heavy bellows was half as large as he was, but the little chap would sit in McHurdie's harness shop of a summer afternoon and swing the instrument up and down as the melody swelled or died, and sway his body with the time and the tune, as Watts McHurdie, who owned the accordion, swayed and gyrated when he played. Mrs. Barclay, hearing her son, smiled and shook her head and knew him for a Thatcher; "No Barclay," she said, "ever could carry a tune." So the mother brought out from the bottom of the trunk her yellow-covered book, "Winner's Instructor on the Guitar," and taught the child what she could of notes. Thus music found its way out of the boy's soul.

One day in the summer of 1860, as he and his fellows were filing down the crooked dusty path that led from the swimming hole through the dry woods to the main road, they came upon a group of horsemen scanning the dry ford of the Sycamore. That was the first time that John Barclay met the famous Captain Lee. He was a great hulk of a man who, John thought, looked like a pirate. The boys led the men and their horses up the dry limestone bed of the stream to the swimming hole--a deep pool in the creek. The coming of the soldiers made a stir in the town. For they were not "regulars"; they were known as the Red Legs, but called themselves "The Army of the Border." Under Captain J. Lord Lee--whose life afterwards touched Barclay's sometimes--"The Army of the Border," being about forty in number, came to Sycamore Ridge that night, and greatly to the scandal of the decent village, there appeared with the men two women in short skirts and red leggins, who were introduced at Schnitzler's saloon as Happy Hally and Lady Lee. "The Army of the Border," under J. Lord and Lady Lee,--as they were known,--proceeded to get bawling drunk, whereupon they introduced to the town the song which for the moment was the national hymn of

Kansas:--

> "Am I a soldier of the boss,
> A follower of Jim Lane?
> Then should I fear to steal a hoss,
> Or blush to ride the same."

As the night deepened and Henry Schnitzler's supply of liquor seemed
exhaustless, the Army of the Border went from song to war and wandered
about banging doors and demanding to know if any white-livered
Missourian in the town was man enough to come out and fight. At
half-past one the Army of the Border had either gone back to camp, or
propped itself up against the sides of the buildings in peaceful
sleep, when the screech of the brakes on the wheels of the stage was
heard half a mile away as it lumbered down the steep bank of the
Sycamore, and then the town woke up. As the stage rolled down Main
Street, the male portion of Sycamore Ridge lined up before the Thayer
House to see who would get out and to learn the news from the
gathering storm in the world outside. As the crowd stood there, and
while the driver was climbing from his box, little John Barclay,
white-faced, clad in his night drawers, came flying into the crowd
from behind a building.

"Mother--" he gasped, "mother--says--come--mother says some one
come quick--there's a man there--trying to break in!" And finding
that he had made himself understood, the boy darted back across the
common toward home. The little white figure kept ahead of the men, and
when they arrived, they found Mrs. Barclay standing in the door of her
house, with a lantern in one hand and a carbine in the crook of her
arm. In the dark, somewhere over toward the highway, but in the
direction of the river, the sound of a man running over the ploughed
ground might be heard as he stumbled and grunted and panted in fear.
She shook her head reassuringly as the men from the town came into the

radius of the light from her lantern, and as they stepped on the hard clean-swept earth of her doorway, she said, smiling:

"He won't come back. I'm sorry I bothered you. Only--I was frightened a little at first--when I sent Johnnie out of the back door." She paused a moment, and answered some one's question about the man, and went on, "He was just drunk. He meant no harm. It was Lige Bemis--"

"Oh, yes," said Watts McHurdie, "you know--the old gang that used to be here before the town started. He's with the Red Legs now."

"Well," continued Mrs. Barclay, "he said he wanted to come over and visit the sycamore tree by the spring."

The crowd knew Lige and laughed and turned away. The men trudged slowly back to the cluster of lights that marked the town, and the woman closed her door, and she and the child went to bed. Instead of sleeping, they talked over their adventure. He sat up in bed, big-eyed with excitement, while his mother told him that the drunken visitor was Lige Bemis, who had come to revisit a cave, a horse thief's cave, he had said, back of the big rock that seemed to have slipped down from the ledge behind the house, right by the spring. She told the boy that Bemis had said that the cave contained a room wherein they used to keep their stolen horses, and that he tried to move the great slab door of stone and, being drunk, could not do so.

When the men of Sycamore Ridge who left the stage without waiting to see what human seed it would shuck out arrived at Main Street, the stage was in the barn, the driver was eating his supper, and the passenger was in bed at the Thayer House. But his name was on the dog-eared hotel register, and it gave the town something to talk about as Martin Culpepper was distributing the mail. For the name on the book was Philemon R. Ward, and the town after his name, Cambridge,

Massachusetts. Every man and woman and most of the children in
Sycamore Ridge knew who Philemon Ward was. He had been driven out of
Georgia in '58 for editing an abolition newspaper; he had been mobbed
in Ohio for delivering abolition lectures; he had been led out of
Missouri with a rope around his neck, and a reward was on his head in
a half-dozen Southern states for inciting slaves to rebellion. His
picture had been in **Harper's Weekly** as a General Passenger Agent of
the Underground Railway. Naturally to Sycamore Ridge, where more than
one night the town had sat up all night waiting for the stage to bring
the **New York Tribune**, Philemon R. Ward was a hero, and his presence
in the town was an event. When the little Barclay boy heard it at the
store that morning before sunrise, he ran down the path toward home to
tell his mother and had to go back to do the errand on which he was
sent. By sunrise every one in town had the news; men were shaken out
of their morning naps to hear, "Philemon Ward's in town--wake up,
man; did you hear what I say? Philemon Ward came to town last night on
the stage." And before the last man was awake, the town was startled
by the clatter of horses' hoofs on the gravel road over the hill south
of town, and Gabriel Carnine and Lycurgus Mason of Minneola came
dashing into the street and yelling, "The Missourians are coming, the
Missourians are coming!"

The little boy, who had just turned into Main Street for the second
time, remembered all his life how the news that the Minneola men
brought, thrilled Sycamore Ridge. It seemed to the boy but an instant
till the town was in the street, and then he and a group of boys were
running to the swimming hole to call the Army of the Border. The horse
weeds scratched his face as he plunged through the timber cross-lots
with his message. He was the first boy to reach the camp. What they
did or what he did, he never remembered. He has heard men say many
times that he whispered his message, grabbed a carbine, and came
tearing through the brush back to the town.

All that is important to know of the battle of Sycamore Ridge is that Philemon Ward, called out of bed with the town to fight that summer morning, took command before he had dressed, and when the town was threatened with a charge from a second division of the enemy, Bemis and Captain Lee of the Red Legs, Watts McHurdie, Madison Hendricks, Oscar Fernald, and Gabriel Carnine, under the command of Philemon Ward, ran to the top of the high bank of the Sycamore, and there held a deep cut made for the stage road,--held it as a pass against a half-hundred horsemen, floundering under the bank, in the underbrush below, who dared not file up the pass.

The little boy standing at the window of his mother's house saw this. But all the firing in the town, all the forming and charging and skirmishing that was done that hot August day in '60, either he did not see, or if he saw it, the memory faded under the great terror that gripped his soul when he saw his mother in danger. Ward in his undershirt was standing by a tree near the stage road above the bank. The firing in the creek bed had stopped. His back was toward the town, and then, out of some place dim in the child's mind--from the troop southwest of town perhaps--came a charge of galloping horsemen, riding down on Ward. The others with him had found cover, and he, seeing the enemy before him and behind him, pistol in hand, alone charged into the advancing horsemen. It was all confused in the child's mind, though the histories say that the Sycamore Ridge people did not know Ward was in danger, and that when he fell they did not understand who had fallen. But the boy--John Barclay--saw him fall, and his mother knew who had fallen, and the wife of the Westport martyr groaned in anguish as she saw Freedom's champion writhing in the dust of the road like a dying snake, after the troop passed over him. And even when he was a man, the boy could remember the woe in her face, as she stooped to kiss her child, and then huddling down to avoid the bullets, ran across the field to the wounded man, with dust in his mouth, twitching in the highway. Bullets were spitting in the dust about her as the boy saw his mother roll the bleeding man over, pick him up, get him on her back with his feet trailing on the earth beside her, and then rising to her full height, stagger under her limp burden back to the house. When she came in the door, her face and shoulders were covered with blood and her skirt ripped with a bullet.

That is all of the battle that John Barclay ever remembered. After that it seemed to end, though the histories say that it lasted all the long day, and that the fire of the invaders was so heavy that no one from the Ridge dared venture to the Barclay home. The boy saw his mother lay the unconscious man on the floor, while she opened the back door, and without saying a word, stepped to the spring, which was hidden from the road. She put her knee, her broad chest, and her strong red hand to the rock and shoved until her back bowed and the cords stood out on her neck; then slowly the rock moved till she could see inside the cave, could put her leg in, could squirm her body in. The morning light flooded in after her, and in the instant that she stood there she saw dimly a great room, through which the spring trickled. There were hay inside, and candles and saddles; in another minute she had the wounded man in the cave and was washing the dirt from him. A bullet had ploughed its way along his scalp, his body was pierced through the shoulder, and his leg was broken by a horse's hoof. She did what she could while the shooting went on outside, and then slipped out, tugged at the great rock again until it fell back in its place, and knowing that Philemon Ward was safe from the Missourians if they should win the day, she came into the house. Then as the mocking clouds of the summer drouth rolled up at night, and belched forth their thunder in a tempest of wind, the besiegers passed as a dream in the night. And in the morning they were not.

CHAPTER II

And so on the night of the battle of Sycamore Ridge, John Barclay
closed the door of his childhood and became a boy. He did not remember
how Ward's wounds were dressed, nor how the town made a hero of the
man; but he did remember Watts McHurdie and Martin Culpepper and the
Hendricks boys tramping through the cave that night with torches, and
he was the hero of that occasion because he was the smallest boy there
and they put him up through the crack in the head of the cave, and he
saw the stars under the elm tree far above the town, where he and his
mother had spent a Sunday afternoon three years before. He called to
the men below and told them where he was, and slipped down through,
the hole again with an elm sprout in his hand to prove that he had
been under the elm tree at the spring. But he remembered nothing of
the night--how the men picketed the town; how he sat up with them
along with the other boys; how the women, under his mother's direction
and Miss Lucy's, cared for the wounded man, who lapsed into delirium
as the night wore on, and gibbered of liberty and freedom as another
man would go over his accounts in his dreams.

His mother and Miss Lucy took turns nursing Ward night after night
during the hot dry summer. As the sick man grew better, many men came
to the house, and great plans were afloat. Philemon Ward, sitting up
in bed waiting for his leg to heal, talked much of the cave as a
refuge for fugitive slaves. There was some kind of a military
organization; all the men in town were enlisted, and Ward was their
captain, drums were rattling and men were drilling; the dust clouds
rose as they marched across the drouth-blighted fields. One night they
marched up to the Barclay home, and Ward with a crutch under his arm,

and with Mrs. Barclay and Miss Lucy beside him, stood in the door and made a speech to the men. And then there were songs. Watts McHurdie threw back his head and sang "Scots wha ha' wi' Wallace bled," following it with some words of his own denouncing slavery and calling down curses upon the slaveholders; so withal it was a martial occasion, and the boy's heart swelled with patriotic pride. But for a vague feeling that Miss Lucy was neglecting him for her patient, John would have begun making a hero of Philemon R. Ward. As it was, the boy merely tolerated the man and silently suspected him of intentions and designs.

But when school opened, Philemon Ward left Sycamore Ridge and John Barclay made an important discovery. It was that Ellen Culpepper had eyes. In Sycamore Ridge with its three hundred souls, only fifteen of them were children, and five of them were ten years old, and John had played with those five nearly all his life. But at ten sometimes the scales drop from one's eyes, and a ribbon or a bead or a pair of new red striped yarn stockings or any other of the embellishments which nature teaches little girls to wear casts a sheen over all the world for a boy. The magic bundle that charmed John Barclay was a scarlet dress, "made over," that came in an "aid box" from the Culpeppers in Virginia. And when the other children in Miss Lucy's school made fun of John and his ***amour***, the boy fought his way through it all--where fighting was the better part of valour--and made horsehair chains for Ellen and cut lockets for her out of coffee beans, and with a red-hot poker made a ring for her from a rubber button as a return for the smile he got at the sly twist he gave her hair as he passed her desk on his way to the spelling class. As for Miss Lucy, who saw herself displaced, she wrote to Philemon Ward, and told him of her jilting, and railed at the fickleness and frailty of the sex.

And by that token an envelope in Ward's handwriting came to Miss Lucy every week, and Postmaster Martin Culpepper and Mrs. Martin Culpepper and all Sycamore Ridge knew it. And loyal Southerner though he was, Martin Culpepper's interest in the affair between Ward and Miss Lucy was greater than his indignation over the fact that Ward had carried his campaign even into Virginia; nothing would have tempted him to disclose to his political friends at home the postmarks of Ward's letters. That was the year of the great drouth of '60, remembered all over the plains. And as the winter deepened and the people of Sycamore Ridge were without crops, and without money to buy food, they bundled up Martin Culpepper and sent him back to Ohio seeking aid. He was a handsome figure the day he took the stage in his high hat and his ruffled shirt and broad coat tails, a straight lean figure of a man in his early thirties, with fine black eyes and a shocky head of hair, and when he pictured the sufferings of the Kansas pioneers to the people of the East, the state was flooded with beans and flour, and sheeted in white muslin. For Martin Culpepper was an orator, and though he is in his grave now, the picture he painted of bleeding Kansas nearly fifty years ago still hangs in many an old man's memory. And after all, it was only a picture. For they were all young out here then, and through all the drouth and the hardship that followed--and the hardship was real--there was always the gayety of youth. The dances on Deer Creek and at Minneola did not stop for the drouth, and many's the night that Mrs. Mason, the tall raw-boned wife of Lycurgus, wrapped little Jane in a quilt and came over to the Ridge from Minneola to take part in some social affair. And while Martin Culpepper was telling of the anguish of the famine, Watts McHurdie and his accordion and Ezra Lane's fiddle were agitating the heels of the populace. And even those pioneers who were moved to come into the wilderness by a great purpose--and they were moved so--to come into the new territory and make it free, nevertheless capered and romped through the drouth of '60 in the cast-off garments of their kinsmen and were happy; for there were buffalo meat and beans for the needy, the aid room had flour, and God gave them youth.

Not drouth, nor famine, nor suffering, nor zeal of a great purpose can
burn out the sparkle of youth in the heart. Only time can do that, and
so John Barclay remembered the famous drouth of '60, not by his
mother's tears, which came as she bent over his little clothes, before
the aid box came from Haverhill, not by the long days of waiting for
the rain that never came, not even by the sun that lapped up the
swimming hole before fall, and left no river to freeze for their
winter's skating, not even by his mother's anguish when she had to go
to the aid store for flour and beans, though that must have been a
sorry day for a Thatcher; but he remembers the great drouth by Ellen
Culpepper's party, where they had a frosted cake and played kissing
games, and--well, fifty years is along time for two brown eyes to
shine in the heart of a boy and a man. It is strange that they should
glow there, and all memory of the runaway slaves who were sheltered in
the cave by the sycamore tree should fade, and be only as a tale that
is told. Yet, so memory served the boy, and he knew only at second
hand how his mother gave her widow's mite to the cause for which she
had crossed the prairies as of old her "fathers crossed the sea."

Before the rain came in the spring of '61 Martin Culpepper came back
from the East an orator of established reputation. The town was proud
of him, and he addressed the multitude on various occasions and wept
many tears over the sad state of the country. For in the nation, as
well as in Sycamore Ridge, great things were stirring. Watts McHurdie
filled *Freedom's Banner* with incendiary verse, always giving the
name of the tune at the beginning of each contribution, by which it
might be sung, and the way he clanked Slavery's chains and made love
to Freedom was highly disconcerting; but the town liked it.

In April Philemon R. Ward came back to Sycamore Ridge, and there was a
great gathering to hear his speech. Ward's soul was aflame with anger.
There were no Greek gods and Roman deities in what Ward said, as there
were in Martin Culpepper's addresses. Ward used no figures of speech

and exercised no rhetorical charms; but he talked with passion in his
voice and the frenzy of a cause in his eyes. Martin Culpepper was in
the crowd, and as Ward lashed the South, every heart turned in
interrogation to Culpepper. They knew what his education had been.
They understood his sentiments; and yet because he was one of them,
because he had endured with them and suffered with them and ministered
to them, the town set him apart from its hatred. And Martin Culpepper
was sensitive enough to feel this. It came over him with a wave of
joy, and as Ward talked, Culpepper expanded. Ward closed in a low
tone, and his face was white with pent-up zeal as he asked some one to
pray. There was a silence, and then a woman's voice, trembling and
passionate, arose, and Sycamore Ridge knew that Mrs. Barclay, the
widow of the Westport martyr, was giving sound to a voice that had
long been still. It was a simple halting prayer, and not all those in
the room heard it clearly. The words were not always fitly chosen; but
as the prayer neared its close,--and it was a short prayer at the
most,--there came strength and courage into the voice as it asked for
grace for "the brother among us who has shared our sufferings and
lightened our burdens, and who has cleaved to us as a brother, but
whose heart is drawn away from us by ties of blood and kinship"; and
then the voice sank lower and lower as though in shame at its
boldness, and hushed in a tremulous Amen.

No one spoke for a moment, and as Sycamore Ridge looked up from the
floor, its eyes turned instinctively toward Martin Culpepper. He felt
the question that was in the hearts about him, and slowly, to the
wonder of all, he rose. He had a beautiful deep purring voice, and
when he opened his eyes, they seemed to look into every pair of eyes
in the throng. There were tears on his face and in his voice as he
spoke. "Entreat me not to leave thee, or to return from following
after thee: for whither thou goest, I will go; and where thou lodgest,
I will lodge: thy people shall be my people, and thy God my God: where
thou diest, I will die, and there will I be buried: the Lord do so to

me, and more also, if aught but death part thee and me." And then he sank to his chair and hid his face, and for a moment a hundred wet-eyed men were still.

Though John Barclay was at the meeting, he remembered only his mother's prayer, but in his heart there was always a picture of a little boy trying to walk home with a little girl, and when he came up with her she darted ahead or dropped back. At the Culpepper gate she stood waiting fully a minute for him to catch her, and when he came up to her, she laughed, "Huh, Mr. Smarty, you didn't, did you?" and ran up the walk, scooted into the house, and slammed the door. But he understood and went leaping down the hill toward home with happiness tingling in his very finger-tips. He seemed to be flying rather than walking, and his toes touched the dirt path so lightly that he rounded the corner and ran plump into Miss Lucy and Philemon Ward standing at the gate. And what he saw surprised him so that he let out a great "haw-haw-haw" and ran, trying to escape his shame and fear at his behaviour. But the next morning Miss Lucy smiled so sweetly at him as he came into the schoolroom, that he knew he was forgiven, and that thrill was lost by the thump of joy that startled his heart when he saw a bunch of dog-tooth violets in his ink bottle, and in his geography found a candy heart with a motto on it so fervent that he did not eat it for three long abstemious days of sheer devotion, in which there were eyes and eyes and eyes from the little girl in the scarlet gown.

It is strange that the boy did not remember how Sycamore Ridge took the call to arms for the war between the states. All he remembered of the great event in our history as it touched the town was that one day he heard there was going to be a war. And then everything seemed to change. A dread came over the people. It fell upon the school, where every child had a father who was going away.

And it was because Madison Hendricks, the first man to leave for the war, was father of Bob and Elmer Hendricks that John's first associations of the great Civil War go back to the big black-bearded man. For Madison Hendricks, who was a graduate of West Point, and a veteran of the Mexican War, was called to Washington in May, and his boys acquired a prestige that was not accorded to them by the mere fact that their father was president of the town company, and was accounted the first citizen of the town. Madison Hendricks, who owned the land on which the town was built, Madison Hendricks, scholar and gentleman, veteran of the Mexican War, first mayor of Sycamore Ridge upon its incorporation,--his sons had no standing. But Madison Hendricks, formally summoned to go to Washington to put down the rebellion, and leaving on the stage with appropriate ceremonies, --there was a man who could bequeath to his posterity in the boy world something of his consequence.

So in the pall that came upon the school in Sycamore Ridge that spring of '61, Bob and Elmer Hendricks were heroes, and their sister--who was their only guardian in their father's absence--had to put them in her dresses and send them to bed, and punish them in all the shameful ways that she knew to take what she called "the tuck out of them." And the boy of all the boys who gave the Hendricks boys most homage was little Johnnie Barclay. There was no dread in his hero-worship. He had no father to go to the war. But the other children and all the women were under a great cloud of foreboding, and for them the time was one of tension and hoping against hope that the war would soon pass.

How the years gild our retrospect. It was in 1903 that Martin Culpepper, a man in his seventies, collected and published "The Complete Poetical and Philosophical Works of Watts McHurdie, together with Notes and a Biographical Appreciation by Martin F. Culpepper." One of the earlier chapters, which tells of the enlistment of the volunteer soldiers for the Civil War in '61, devotes some space to the recruiting and enlistment in Sycamore Ridge. The chapter bears the heading "The Large White Plumes," and in his "introductory remarks" the biographer says, "To him who looks back to those golden days of heroic deeds only the lines of Keats will paint the picture in his soul:--

"'Lo, I must tell a tale of chivalry,
For large white plumes are dancing in mine eyes.'"

And so the "large white plumes" blinded his eyes to the fear and the dread that were in the hearts of the people, and he tells his readers nothing of the sadness that men felt who put in crops knowing that their wives must cultivate and harvest them. He sees only the glory of it; for we read: "Hail to the spirit of mighty Mars. When he strode through our peaceful village, he awoke many a war song in our breasts. As for our hero, Mars, the war god forged iron reeds for his lute, and he breathed into it the spirit of the age, and all the valour, all the chivalry of a golden day came pouring out of his impassioned reeds." Such is the magic of those large white plumes on Martin Culpepper's memory. Although John Barclay in that latter day bought a thousand copies of the Biography and sent them to public libraries all over the world, he smiled as he read that paragraph referring to Watts McHurdie's accordion as the "impassioned reeds." When he read it, John Barclay, grown to a man of fifty-three, sitting at a great mahogany table, with a tablet of white paper on a green blotting pad before him, and a gorgeous rose rising from a tall graceful green vase on the shining table, looked out over a brown wilderness of roofs and chimneys across a broad river into the hills that were green afar off, and there, rising out of yesterday, he saw, not the bent little old man in the harness shop with steel-rimmed spectacles and greasy cap, whom you may see to-day; but instead, the boy in John Barclay's soul looked through his eyes, and he saw another Watts McHurdie,--a dapper little fellow under a wide slouch hat, with a rolling Byronic collar, and fancy yellow waistcoat of the period, in exceedingly tight trousers. And then, flash! the picture changed, and Barclay saw Watts McHurdie under his mushroom hat; Martin Culpepper in his long-tailed coat; Philemon Ward, tall, fair-skinned, blue-eyed, slim, and sturdy; skinny, nervous Lycurgus Mason and husky Gabriel Carnine from Minneola; Jake Dolan in his shirt sleeves, without adornment of any kind, except the gold horseshoe pinned on his shirt bosom; Daniel Frye, the pride of an admiring family, in his best home-made clothes; Henry Schnitzler, Oscar Fernald, and nearly a hundred other men, to the boy's eyes so familiar then, now forgotten, and all their faces blurred in the crowd that stood about the recruiting officer by the town pump in Sycamore Ridge that summer day of '61. A score or so of men had passed muster. The line on the post at the wooden awning in front of Schnitzler's saloon was marked at five feet six. All had stood by it with their heads above the line. It was Watts McHurdie's turn. He wore high-heeled boots for the occasion, but strut as he would, his roached hair would not touch the stick that came over the line. "Stretch your neck--ye bantam," laughed Jake Dolan. "Walk turkey fashion, Watts," cried Henry Schnitzler, rushing up behind Watts and grabbing his waistband. The crowd roared. Watts looked imploringly at the recruiting officer and blubbered in wrath: "Yes, damn you--yea; that's right. Of course; you won't let me die for my bleedin' country because I ain't nine feet tall." And the little man turned away trying to choke his tears and raging at his failure. And because the recruiting officer was considerable of a man, Watts McHurdie's name was written in the muster roll, and he went out.

Many days must have passed between the time when the men were mustered
in and the day they went away to the war. But to the man who saw those times through the memory of the boy in blue jeans forever playing bugle-calls upon his fife, it was all one day. For that crowd dissolved, and another picture appeared upon the sensitized plate of

his memory. There is a crowd in the post-office--mostly men who are
going away to war. The stage has come in, and a stranger, better
dressed than the men of Sycamore Ridge, is behind the letter-boxes of
the post-office. The boy is watching his box; for it is the day when
the ***Springfield Republican*** is due. Gradually the hum in front of the
boxes quiets, and two loud voices have risen behind the screen. Then
out walks great Martin Culpepper, white of face, with pent-up fury.
His left hand is clutched like a talon in the shoulder of the
stranger, whom Martin is holding before him. "Gentlemen, your
attention," demands Culpepper. The stranger swallows his Adam's apple
as if to speak; Martin turns to him with, "Don't you say that word
again, sir, or I'll wring your neck." Then he proceeds:--

"Gentlemen, this busybody has come all the way from Washington here to
tell me I'm a thief. I wrote to his damn Yankee government that I was
needing the money last winter to go East on the aid committee and
would replace it, and now that I'm going out to-morrow to die for his
damn Yankee government, he has the impertinence to come in here and
say I stole that money. Now what I want to ask you, gentlemen, is
this: Do I go out to-morrow to die on the field of glory for my
country, or does this here little contemptible whippersnapper take me
off to rot in some Yankee jail? I leave it to you, gentlemen. Settle
it for yourselves." And with that Culpepper throws the man into the
crowd and walks behind the screen in solemn state.

The boy never knew how it was settled. But Martin Culpepper went to
"the field of glory," and all the boy knew of the incident is here
recorded. However, in the Biography of Watts McHurdie above-mentioned
and aforesaid occur these words, in the same chapter--the one
entitled "The Large White Plumes": "Let memory with gentle hand cover
with her black curtain of soft oblivion all that was painful on that
glorious day. Let us not recall the bickerings and the strifes, let
the grass watered by Lethe's sweet spring creep over the scars in the

bright prospect which lies under our loving gaze. Let us hold in our heart the tears in beauty's eyes; the smile that curls her crimson lips, and the hope that burns upon her brow. Let us fondle the sacred memory of every warm hand clasp of comrade and take to the silent grave the ever green garland of love that adorned our hearts that day. For the sordid thorns that pierced our bleeding hearts--what are they but ashes to-day, blown on the winds of yesterday?"

What indeed, Martin Culpepper--what indeed, smiled John Barclay as he reached for the rose on his broad mahogany desk across forty long years, and looking through a wide window, saw on the blank wall of a great hulk of a building half a mile away, the fine strong figure of a man with black shaggy hair on his young leonine head rise and wave his handkerchief to a woman with tears running down her face and anguish in her eyes, standing in a swarm of children. What indeed are sordid thorns when the "large white plumes are dancing"--what indeed?

That was a busy night in Sycamore Ridge--the night before the men left for war in the summer of '61. And the busiest man in all the town was Philemon R. Ward. Every man in the town was going, and most of the men were going who lived in the county--an area as large as a New England state, and yet when they were all gathered in Main Street, there were less than fivescore of them. They had agreed to elect Ward captain, Martin Culpepper first lieutenant, Jake Dolan second lieutenant. It was one of the diversions of the occasion to call out "Hello, Cap," when Ward hustled by a loitering crowd. But his pride was in his work, and before sundown he had it done. The Yankee in him gave him industry and method and foresight. At sunset the last of the twenty teams and wagons he had ordered came rattling down the hill west of town, driven by Gabriel Carnine of Minneola, with Mrs. Lycurgus Mason sitting like a war goddess on the back seat holding Lycurgus, a spoil of battle, while he held their daughter on his lap, withal a martial family party. Mrs. Barclay and Miss Lucy went to the

aid store-room and worked the long night through, getting breakfast
for the men. Mary Murphy and Nellie Logan came from the Thayer House
to the aid room when the hotel dishes were washed, and helped with the
work. And while they were there the Culpeppers walked in, returning
from a neighbourly visit to Miss Hendricks; John Barclay in an apron,
stirring a boiling pot of dried apples, turned his back on the eyes
that charmed him, but when the women sent him for a bucket of water,
he shook the handle at Ellen Culpepper and beckoned her with a finger,
and they slipped out into the moonlight together. She had hold of the
handle of the bucket with him, and they pulled and hauled and laughed
as boy and girl will laugh so long as the world turns round. The
street was deserted, and only the bar of light that fell across the
sidewalk from Schnitzler's saloon indicated the presence of human
beings in the little low buildings that pent in the highway. The boy
and the girl stood at the pump, and the boy stuck a foot in the horse
trough. He made a wet silhouette of it on the stone beneath him, and
reached for the handle of the pump. Then he said, "I got somepin I
won't tell."

"Three little niggers in a peanut shell," replied the girl.

"All right, Miss Cuteness. All right for you; I was going to tell you
somepin, but I won't now." He gave the pump-handle a pull. It was limp
and did not respond with water. "Ellen--" the boy repeated as he
worked the handle, "I got somepin to tell you. Honest I have."

"I don't care, Mr. Smarty," the girl replied; she made a motion as if
to walk away, but did not. The boy noticed it and said, "Yes,
sir--it's somepin you'd like to know." The girl did not turn round.
The boy, who had been working with the wheezy pump, was holding the
handle up, and water was gurgling down the well. And before she could
answer he said, "Say, Ellen--don't be mad; honest I got somepin."

"Who's it about?" she asked over her shoulder.

"Me."

"That's not much--who else?"

"Elmer Hendricks!"

"Who else?" The girl was halfway turned around when she spoke.

"Bob--Bob Hendricks," replied the boy.

"Aw--Bob Hendricks--" returned the girl, in contempt. Then she faced the boy and said, "What is it?"

"Come here 'n' I'll tell you."

"I'll come this far." The girl took two steps.

"I got to whisper it, and you can't hear."

"Well, 'tain't much." The girl dangled one bare foot hesitatingly.

"I'll come halfway," she added.

The boy made a mark in the dust of the road a few feet from him with his toe, and said, "Come to there."

The girl shook her head, and spoke. "Tell me part--'n' I'll see if it's good."

"Me and Elmer an' Bob are goin' to run away!" The girl stepped to the toe mark and cried, "What?"

"Yes, sir--in the mornin'." He caught hold of the girl's arm awkwardly and swung her around to the opposite side of the pump-handle, and put her hands on it and began to pump. She pumped with him as he puffed between the strokes, "Um' huh--we're going to hide in the provision wagons, under some saddles they is there and go--to--war!" The water was pouring into the bucket by the time he had got this out. Their hands touched on the pump-handle. It was the boy who drew his hand away. The girl gasped:--

"Why, John Barclay,--it ain't no such thing--does your ma know it?"

He told her that no one knew it but her, and they pumped in silence until the bucket was full, and walking back carrying the bucket between them, he told her another secret: that Watts McHurdie had asked John to get his guitar after midnight, and play an accompaniment to the accordion, and that Watts and Ward and Jake Dolan and Gabriel Carnine were going out serenading. Further he told her that Watts was going to serenade Nellie Logan at the Thayer House, and that Gabriel Carnine was going to serenade Mary Murphy, and that Philemon Ward was going to serenade Miss Lucy, and that he, John Barclay, had suggested that it would be fine to serenade Mrs. Culpepper, because she was such a nice woman, and they agreed that if he would bring his guitar, they would!

When the boy and girl returned to the store, Ward and Miss Lucy went to the Barclay home for the guitar. When they came back, Mrs. Barclay noted a pink welt on one of Ward's fingers where his cameo ring had been, and she observed that from time to time Miss Lucy kept feeling of her hair as if to smooth it. It was long after midnight before the girls from the hotel went home, and Miss Lucy and Mrs. Barclay lay on the counter in the store, trying to sleep. They awoke with the sound of music in their ears, and Miss Lucy said, "It's Captain Ward--and the other boys, serenading us." They heard the high tenor voice of Watts McHurdie and the strong clear voice of Ward rising above the accordion and guitar:--

"For her voice is on the breeze,
Her spirit comes at will,
At midnight on the seas
Her bright smile haunts me still."

And underneath these high voices was the gruff bass voice of Gabriel Carnine and the baritone of Jake Dolan. And when Mrs. Barclay heard the piping treble of her son, and the tinkle of his guitar, her eyes filled with tears of pride.

The serenaders waked the chickens, and the crowing roosters roused Mrs. Barclay, and in the hurry of the hour she forgot to look for her son. As "the gray dawn was breaking," a hundred men came into the room, and found the smoking breakfast on the table. It was a good breakfast as breakfasts go when men are hungry. But they sat in silence that morning. The song was all out of them; the spring of youth was crushed under the weight of great events. And as they rose--they who had been so merry the day before, and had joked of the things the soldier fears, they were all but mute, and left their breakfasts scarcely tasted.

The women remember this,--the telltale sign of the untouched breakfast,--and their memory is better than that of Martin Culpepper, who wrote in that plumy chapter of the Biography, before mentioned:--

"The soldiers left their homes that beautiful August morning as the sun was kissing the tips of the sycamore that gave the magnificent little city its name. They had partaken abundantly of a bountiful breakfast, and as they satisfied their inner man from a table groaning with good things prepared by the fair hands of the gentler sex, the gallant men rose with song and cheer, and went on their happy way where duty and honour called them."

But the women who scraped the plates that morning knew the truth. One wonders how much of history would be thrown out as worthless, like Martin Culpepper's fine writing, if the women who scraped the plates might testify. For those "large white plumes" do not dance in women's eyes!

After breakfast the men tumbled into the wagons, and as one wagon after another rattled out of Fernald's feed lot and came down the street, the men waved their hats and the women waved their aprons, and a great cloud of dust rose on the highway, and as the wagons ducked down the bank to the river, only the tall figure of Martin Culpepper, waving his handkerchief, rose above the cloud. At the end of the line was a provision wagon, and on it rode Philemon Ward--Yankee in his greatest moment, scorning the heroic place in the van, and looking after the substantials. In the feed lot, just as the reins were in his hands, Ward saw Elmer Hendricks' foot peeping from under a saddle. Ward dragged the boy out, spanking him as he came over the end gate, and noted the sheepish smile on his face. Ten days later, as Ward, marching in the infantry, was going up a hill through the timber at the battle of Wilson's Creek, that same boy rode by with the cavalry, and seeing Ward, waved a carbine and smiled as he charged the brow of the hill. That night, going back under the stars, Ward stumbled over a body, and stooping, saw the smile still on the boy's face, and the carbine clutched in his hand. But for the hole through the boyish brow, the eyes might still have been laughing.

CHAPTER III

A few years ago, in the room of the great mahogany table, with its clean blotting pad, its writing tablet, and its superb rose rising from a green vase in the midst of the shining unlittered expanse, there was a plain, heavy mahogany wainscoting reaching chin-high to the average man. A few soft-toned pictures adorned the dull gray walls above the wainscoting, and directly over a massive desk that never was seen open hung a framed letter. The letter was written on blue-lined paper in red pokeberry ink. At the top of the letter was the advertisement of a hotel, done in quaint, old-fashioned, fancy script with many curly-cues and printers' ornaments. The advertisement set forth that the Thayer House at Sycamore Ridge was "First class in every particular," and that "Especial attention was paid to transient custom." On a line in the right-hand corner the reader was notified that the tavern was founded by the Emigrant Aid Society, and balancing this line, in the left-hand corner, were these words: "The only livery-stable west of Lawrence." John Barclay's eyes have read it a thousand times, and yet he always smiled when he scanned the letter that followed the advertisement. The letter read:--

"Dear Ma I am going to war. Doan crye. Iff father was here he wood go; so why should not I. I will be very caerfull not to get hurt & stay by Cap Ward all the time. So godby yours truly J. Barclay Jr."

It was five hours after the soldiers had gone when Mrs. Barclay came home from her work in the aid room, and the first thing that attracted her attention was her son's letter, lying folded on the table. When she read it, she ran with the open letter across the common to the

town. It was a woman's town that morning,--not a man was left in
it,--for Ezra Lane, the only old man living in the Ridge, had left
Freedom's Banner to shift for itself while he rode to Leavenworth
with the soldiers to bring back the teams; and when Mrs. Barclay came
into the street, she found some small stir there, made by Miss
Hendricks--the only mother the Hendricks boys remembered--who was
inquiring for her lost boys. Mrs. Barclay displayed her note, and in a
moment the whole population of Sycamore Ridge, with hands under its
aprons, was standing in front of the post-office. Then Ellen Culpepper
found her tongue, and Mrs. Barclay began to look for a horse. Elmer
Hendricks' pony in the pasture was the only horse Ward had left within
twenty miles. When Ellen Culpepper and her little sister Molly came
back from the pasture and announced that Elmer's pony was gone also,
the women surmised that he had taken it with him, for they could not
know that after he was spanked from the provision wagon, he had
slipped out to the pasture and ridden by a circuitous route to the
main road.

It was Captain Ward, dismounting from his driver's seat on the
provision wagon at noon, who discovered two boys: a little boy eleven
years old in a dead faint, and a bigger boy panting with the heat.
They threw cold spring water on John Barclay's face, and finally his
eyes opened, and he grinned as he whispered, "Hullo, Captain," to the
man bending over him. The man held water to the boy's lips, and he
sipped a little and swam out into the blackness again, and then the
man reappeared and the boy tried to smile and whispered, "Aw--I'm all
right." They saw he was coming out of his faint, and one by one the
crowd dropped away from him; but Ward stayed, and when the child could
speak, he replied to Ward's question, "'Cause I wanted to." And then
again when the question was repeated, the boy said, "I tell you 'cause
I wanted to." He shook his head feebly and grinned again and tried to
rise, but the man gently held him down, and kept bathing his temples
with cold water from the spring beside them. Finally, when the man

seemed a little harsh in his questions, the boy's eyes brimmed and he said: "Whur'd my pa be if he was alive to-day? I just guess I got as much right here as you have." He made a funny little picture lying on the lush grass by the spring in the woods; his browned face, washed clean on the forehead and temples, showed almost white under the dirt. There were tear-stained rings about the eyes, and his pink shirt and blue trousers were grimy with dust, and the red clay of the Sycamore still was on the sides of his dust-brown bare feet. Around a big toe was a rag which showed a woman's tying--neat and firm, but red with clay.

Ward left, and Bob Hendricks came and stood over the prostrate boy. Bob was carrying a bucket of water to the cook as a peace offering.

"What did they do?" asked the boy on the ground.

"Just shook me--and then said father'd tend to me for this." The boys exchanged comments on the situation without words, and then Bob said as he drew the dripping bucket from the spring, "We're going clear on to Leavenworth, and they say then we've got to come back with Ezra Lane and the teams."

The boy on the ground raised himself by rolling over and catching hold of a sapling. He panted a moment, and "I'll bet y' I don't." The other boy went away with a weak "Me neither," thrown over his shoulder.

During that long afternoon, and all the next day and the next, the boys ran from wagon to wagon, climbing over end gates, wriggling among the men, running with the horses through the shady woods, paddling in the fords, and only refusing to move when the men got out of the wagons and walked up the long clay hills that rise above the Kaw River. At night they camped by the prairie streams, and the men sang and wondered what they were doing at home, and Philemon Ward took

John
Barclay out into the silence of the woods and made him say his
prayers. And Ward would look toward the west and say, "Well,
Johnnie,--there's home," and once they stood in an open place in the
timber, and Ward gazed at a bright star sinking in the west, and said,
"I guess that's about over Sycamore Ridge." They went on, and the boy,
looking back to see why the man had stopped, caught him throwing a
kiss at the star. And they could not know, as they walked back
together through the woods abashed, that two women sitting before a
cabin door under a sycamore tree were looking at an eastern star, and
one threw kisses at it unashamed while the other wept. And on other
nights, many other nights, the two, Miss Lucy and Mrs. Barclay, sat
looking at their star while the terror in their hearts made their lips
mute. God makes men brave who stand where bullets fly, yet always they
can run away. But God seems to give no alternative to women at home
who have to wait and dread.

Forty years later John Barclay took from a box in a safety vault back
of his office in the city a newspaper. It was the Sycamore Ridge
Banner, yellow and creased and pungent with age. "This," he said to
Senator Myton, spreading the wrinkled sheet out on the mahogany table,
"this is my enlistment paper." He smiled as he read aloud:--

"At noon of our first day out we came across two stowaways. Hendricks,
aged twelve, son of our well-known and popular Mayor, and J. Barclay,
aged eleven, son of Mrs. M. Barclay, who, owing to the suddenness of
the departure of our troops for the seat of war in Missouri, and
certain business delays made necessary in ye editor's return, were
slipped out with our company rather than left in the rough and
uncertain city of Leavenworth. They are called by the boys of 'C'
company respectively 'the little sergeant and the little corporal,
Good Luck boys.'"

A little farther down the column was this paragraph:

"Aug. 2nd we went into camp on Sugar Creek, and some sport was had by the men who went in bathing, taking the horses with them."

"Ever go in swimming with the horses, Senator?" asked Barclay. The senator shook his head doubtfully.

"Well--you haven't. For if you had you'd remember it," answered Barclay, and a hundred naked young men and two skinny, bony boys splashed and yelled and ducked and wrestled and locked their strong wet arms about the necks of the plunging horses and dived under them, and rolled across them and played with them like young satyrs in the cool water under the overhanging elms with the stars twinkling in the shining mahogany as Barclay folded the paper and put it away. He thrummed the polished surface a moment and looked back into the past to see Philemon Ward straight, lean, and glistening like a god standing on a horse ready to dive, and as he huddled, crouched for the leap, Barclay said, "Well, come on, Senator, we must go to lunch now."

It was late in the afternoon of their third day's journey that the men from Sycamore Ridge rode in close order, singing, through the streets of Leavenworth. Watts McHurdie was playing his accordion, and the people turned to look at the uncouth crowd in civilian's clothes that went bellowing "O My Darling Nellie Gray," across the town and out to the Fort. Ezra Lane promised to call at the Fort for the two boys and with drivers for the teams early the next morning--but to Sycamore Ridge, Leavenworth in those days was the great city with its pitfalls, and when Ezra Lane, grizzled though he was, came to a realizing sense of his responsibilities, the next day was gone and the third was waning. When he went to the Fort, he found the Sycamore Ridge men had been hurried into Missouri to meet General Price, who was threatening Springfield, and no word had been left for him about the boys. As he

left the gate at the Fort, a troop of cavalry rode by gaily, and a
boy, a big overgrown fourteen-year-old boy in a blue uniform, passed
and waved his hand at the befuddled old man, and cried, "Good-by, Mr.
Lane,--tell 'em you saw me." He knew the boy was from Sycamore Ridge,
but he knew also that he was not one of the boys who had come with the
soldiers; and being an old man, far removed from the boy world, he
could not place the child in his blue uniform, so he drove away
puzzled.

The afternoon the men from Sycamore Ridge came to Leavenworth they
were hurriedly examined again, signed the muster rolls, and were sent
away without uniforms all in twenty-four hours. But not before they
had found time to have their pictures taken in borrowed regimentals.
For twenty years after the war the daguerreotypes of the soldiers
taken at Leavenworth that day were the proudest adornments of the
centre-tables of Sycamore Ridge, and even now on Lincoln Avenue, in a
little white cottage with green blinds, that sits in a broad smooth
lawn with elm trees on it, stands an easel. On the easel is a
picture--an enlarged crayon drawing of a straight, handsome young
fellow in a captain's uniform. One hand is in his coat, and the other
at his hip. His head is thrown back with a fierce determination into
the photographer's iron rest and all together the picture is marked
with the wrinkled front of war. For over one corner of the easel hangs
a sword with an ivory handle, and upon it is an inscription
proclaiming the fact that the sword was presented to Captain Philemon
R. Ward by his company for gallant conduct on the field of battle on
the night of August 4, 1861. Above the easel in the corner hangs
another picture--that of a sweet-faced old man of seventy, beaming
rather benignly over his white lawn necktie. The forty-five years that
have passed between the two faces have trimmed the hair away from the
temples and the brow, have softened the mouth, and have put patience
into the eyes--the patience of a great faith often tried but never
broken. The five young women of the household know that the crayon

portrait on the bamboo easel is highly improper as a parlour ornament--for do they not teach school, and do they not take all the educational journals and the crafty magazines of art? But the hand that put it there was proud of its handiwork, and she who hung the sword upon the easel is gone away, so the girls smile at the fierce young boyish face in the picture as they pass it, and throw a kiss at the face above it, and the easel is not moved.

And the man,--the tall old man with a slight stoop in his shoulders, the old man who wears the alpaca coat and the white lawn tie seen in the upper picture,--sometimes he wanders into the stately front room with a finger in a census bulletin as a problem in his head creases his brow--and the sight of the sword always makes him smile, and sometimes the smile is a chuckle that stirs the cockles of his heart.

For his mind goes back to that summer night of August 4, 1861, and he sees himself riding on a horse with a little boy behind with his arms in the soldier's belt. It is dusk, and "C" Company on foot is filing down a Missouri hill. It is a muddy road, and the men are tired and dirty. There is no singing now. A man driving an ox team has turned out of the road to let the soldiers pass. Some one in the line asks the man, "Where's Price?"

"Over the hill yonder," replies the man, pointing with his hickory whip-stock. The word buzzes up and down the line. The captain on his horse with the boy clutching at his belt does not hear it. But the line lags and finally halts. The men have been only two days under military discipline. That day last week Phil Ward--who was he, anyway? Henry Schnitzler and Oscar Fernald could have bought him and sold him twice over. So the line halted. Then the captain halted. Then he called Second Lieutenant Dolan and asked to know what was the matter. "They say they are going to camp," responded Dolan, touching his cap. Captain Ward's face flushed. He told Dolan to give the order to march. There were shouts and laughter, and Gabriel Carnine cried, "Say, Phil, this here Missourian we passed says old General Price is over that hill." The boys laughed again, and Ward saw that trouble was before him. The men stood waiting while he controlled his rage before he spoke. Dolan said under his breath from the ground beside the horse, "They're awful tired, Cap, and they don't want to tackle Price's army all by their lonelies." Some one in the company called out, "We've voted on this thing, Cap. Don't the majority rule in this country?"

A smile twitched at Ward's mouth and the boy in him pricked a twinkle in his eyes, for he was only twenty-six, and he laughed--threw his head back and then leaned over and slapped the horse's neck and finally straightened up and said, "Gentlemen, I bow to the will of the people."

And so it happened that when they drew their first month's pay, Martin Culpepper and Jake Dolan suggested to the company that they buy Ward a sword to commemorate the victory of the people. And Martin Culpepper made a great presentation speech in which he said that to the infantry, cavalry, and artillery arms of military service, "C" Company had added the "vox populi." But the night after the presentation Oscar Fernald and Watts McHurdie crawled under the captain's tent and stole the sword and pawned it for beer, and there was a sound of revelry by night.

When they found the great camp near Springfield, it seemed to John Barclay that all the soldiers in the world were gathered. It is difficult for a boy under a dozen years to remember things consecutively; because boys do not do things consecutively. They flit around like butterflies, and so the picture that they make of events jumps from scene to scene. One film on a roll of John's memory showed a hot August day in the camp of "C" Company; the men are hurrying about the place. The tents are down; the boys--John and Bob--are kicking around the vacant camp looking for trophies. But there the film broke and did not record the fact that Captain Ward put Bob and John on a commissary wagon that stood in a side street as the soldiers moved out. John remembered looking into a street filled with marching soldiers. First the regulars and the artillery came swinging down the street. At their head the boy saw General Lyon, the commanding officer, and around him was a bodyguard whose plumed hats, with the left brim pinned up, caught the boys' eyes. The regulars marched by silently. It was part of their day's work; but following them came a detachment of Germans singing "Marchen Rote," and then the battery of six guns and then the Kansans. Small wonder Captain Gordon Granger told Colonel Mitchel that the Kansas soldiers were only an armed mob. They filed out of Springfield, some in rags and some in tags and some in velvet gowns. They carried guns; but they looked like delegates to a convention, and as the boys saw their own company, they waved their hands, but they were almost ashamed of the shabby clothes of the men from Sycamore Ridge; for a boy always notices clothes on others. When the Germans stopped singing "Marchen Rote," the boys heard Watts McHurdie's high tenor voice start up "The Dutch Companee," and the crowd that was lining the street cheered and cheered. A Missouri regiment followed and more regulars, and then a battery of four guns passed, and then came more Kansans still going to that everlasting convention. And a band came roaring by,--with its crashing brass and rumbling drums,--and then after the band had turned the corner, came Iowa in gray blouses and such other garments as the clothes-lines of the country afforded. They were singing as they passed--a song the boy had never heard, being all about the "happy land of Canaan." And before the sun had set again, after that night, hundreds of those who sang of the happy land were there. In the rear were the ambulances and the ammunition and the hospital vans, and the wagon which held the boys wheeled into the line. After they had passed, the streets were clogged with carts and drays and wagons of all sorts, for the citizens were moving to places of safety.

As a man, the boy's memory did not tell him how the boys fared, but he does remember that it was dark in the timber where they camped that night, and that they slipped away into the woods to lie down together. The chirping of the birds at dawn wakened them, and as John sat up rubbing his eyes, he heard a rifle's crack. They were at the edge of a field, and half a mile from him, troops were marching by columns across a clearing. The rifle-shot was followed by another, and another, and then by a half-dozen. "Wake up, Bob--wake up--they's a battle," he cried, and the two boys stumbled to their feet. The shots were far in front of the marching soldiers, and the boys could not make out what the firing meant. The line formed and ran up the hill, and the boys saw the morning sun flashing on the guns of the enemy. The battery roared, and the boys were filled with terror. They ran through the woods like dogs until they came to the soldiers from Sycamore Ridge. The boys crawled on their bellies to their friends, and lay with their faces all but buried in the ground. The men were lying at the edge of the timber talking, and Watts McHurdie was on his back.

"What's the matter with you, Watts?" asked Oscar Fernald.

"Os," replied Watts, "I got a presentiment I'm goin' to be shot in the rear. It will kill me to be shot in the back, and I've got a notion that's how I am goin' to die."

The line laughed. Captain Ward, who was sitting a few paces in the rear of the men, went over to Watts, and scuffled the man over with his foot. A bullet went through Ward's hat before he got back to his place. The men were sticking up ramrods and betting on the number of minutes they would last. No ramrod stood more than ten minutes. Martin Culpepper threw up his hat five times before a bullet hit it; but he went bareheaded the rest of the day, and John Barclay, in sheer fear, began to dig a hole under him. After he had been on his belly for an hour, Henry Schnitzler got tired and rose. The men begged him to lie down. But his only reply when they told him he was a fool was, "Vell, vot of it?" And when they said he would be shot, he answered again, "Vell, vot of it?" And when Jake Dolan cried, "You pot-gutted Dutchman, sit down or there'll be a sauer-kraut shower in hell pretty quick," Henry shook his fat sides a moment and laughed, "Vell, vot of dot--altzo!" For an hour, that seemed ten, he moved back and forth on the line, firing and joking, and then the spell broke and a bullet took part of his jaw. As he dropped to his position, with the blood gushing from his face, his eyes blazed, and he spat out, "By hell-tam, now I vos mad," and he fought the day out and died that night. But as he sank to his place when the bullet hit him, Watts McHurdie saw Schnitzler stagger, and through the smoke, knew that he was wounded. Watts rushed to Schnitzler and bent over him, when a ball hit Watts and went ripping through the fleshy part of his hip. "Shot in the back--damn it, shot in the back!" he screamed, as he jumped into the air. "What did I tell you, boys, I'm shot in the back." And he crawled bleeding to the rear.

All the long forenoon the camp of the enemy continued to belch out men. The battery mowed them down, and once the Kansans were ordered to charge the hill, and the boys were left alone. It was there that the two were separated. John saw men sink in awful silence, and the blood ooze from their heads. He saw men cramp in agony and choke with blood, and he saw Martin Culpepper, perhaps with the large white plumes still dancing in his eyes, dash out of the line and pick up a Union banner that Sigel's men had lost, and that the enemy was flaunting just before the artillery mowed the gray line down. He heard the hoarse men cheer Martin, and as the tall swart figure came running back waving the flag, the boy prayed to his father's God to save the man.

When the battle lulled, the boy found himself parted from "C" Company, and fled back through the woods to the rear. There he came upon a smell that was familiar. He had known it in the slaughter-house at home. It was the smell of fresh blood, and with it came the sickening drone of flies. In an instant he stood under a tree where men were working smeared with blood. He stumbled over a little pile of dismembered legs and hands. A man with a bloody knife was bending over a human form stretched on a bloody and, it seemed to the boy, a greasy table. Another was helping the big man. They were cutting the bullet out of Watts McHurdie, who was lying white and unconscious and with flies crawling over him, half naked and blood-smeared, on the table. The boy screamed, and the man turned his head and snarled through his clenched teeth that held the knife, "Get out of here--no--go get me a bucket of water from the creek." Some one handed the boy a bucket, and he ran where he was told to go, with the awful sight burned on his brain, with the sickening smell in his nose, and with the drone of flies in his ears. When he came back the firing had begun again. The surgeon was saying, "Well, that's all that's waiting--now I'm going for a minute." He grabbed a gun standing by the table and ran toward the front; he did not take off his blood-splotched apron, and the boy fled from the place in terror. In a few moments the firing ceased; but the boy ran on, hunting for a hiding-place. He saw a troop of Alabamians plunge over a log in a charge, and roll in an awful, writhing, screaming pile of dying men and horses, and in the heap he saw the terror-stricken face of a youth, who was shrieking for help; John carried that fear-distorted face in his memory for years, until long afterwards it appeared in Sycamore Ridge.

But that day John fled from the death-trap almost mad with fear. Rushing farther into the woods, he came upon General Lyon and his staff. The plumed hats of the bodyguard told the boy that the sandy-haired man before him was in command, though the man's face was bloody from a wound in his head, and though his clothes were stained with blood and he was hatless. He sat upright on his horse, and as the boy turned, he heard the voices of Captain Ward and his soldiers, begging to be sent into the fight. It was a clamour fierce and piteous, and the general had turned his head to the Kansans, when something at the left startled him. There was no firing, and a column of soldiers was approaching. Doubt paralyzed the group around Lyon for a moment. The men wore gray blouses strangely like those the Iowans wore. The men might be Sigel's men, coming back from their artillery duel. The general plainly was puzzled. He rode out from the bodyguard a few paces. The boy was staring at him, when the bodyguard with their gay plumed hats came up, and he saw wrath flash into the general's face as he recognized the enemy. "Shoot them--shoot them--" he shouted. But the gray line vomited its smoke first, and the boy felt his foot afire. The general dropped from his horse, and as the boy looked down, he saw a red blot coming out on his instep. In the same instant he saw Captain Ward rush to the falling general, and saw the bodyguard gather about him, and then the blackness came over the child and he fell. He did not see them bear General Lyon's body into the brush, nor hear Ward moan his sorrow. But when Ward returned from the thicket, he saw the child lying limp on the grass.

As Ward ran toward the hospital van carrying the limp little body, he could see that a ball had pierced the boy's foot. Also he saw the men in retreat who had shot Lyon, and all over the field the firing had ceased. As he hurried through the underbrush, Ward ran into Bob Hendricks hiding in the thicket. Ward took the child's hand and he began to sob: "I saw Elmer go up that hill, Captain; I saw him go up with the horses and he ain't come back." But Ward did not understand him, and hurried the little fellow along with John to the surgeon.

Then Ward left them, and when John Barclay opened his eyes, Bob Hendricks was sitting beside him. A great lint bandage was about John's foot, and they were in a wagon jolting over a rutty road. He did not speak for a long time, and then he asked, "Did we whip 'em?"

And Bob nodded and said, "Cap says so!"

The children clasped hands and talked of many things that passed from the boy's mind. But his mind recorded that the next day in the hospital Martin Culpepper said, "Bob can't come to-day, Johnnie; you know he's tendin' Elmer's funeral." The boy must have opened his eyes, for the man said, "Why, Johnnie, I thought you knew; yes; they found him dead that night--right under the reb--under the enemies' guns on the brink of the hill."

The child's eyes filled with tears, but he did not cry. His emotion was spent. The two sat together for a time, and the little boy said, "Why didn't you go, Mr. Culpepper?" And the man replied: "Me? Oh--why--Oh, yes, I got a little scratch here in my leg, and they won't let me out of here. There's Watts over there in the next cot; he got a little scratch too--didn't you, Watts?" Watts and the boy smiled at each other, but John did not see Bob again for years. Miss Hendricks came and took him to their father's people in Ohio.

One day some one came in the hospital where John and Watts and Martin Culpepper were lying, and began to call out mail for the men, and the third name the corporal called was "Captain Martin Culpepper"; and when they brought him a long official envelope with General Fremont's name on it, Martin Culpepper held it in his hands, looked at the inscription, read the word "captain" again and again, and could not speak for choked joy. And tears so dimmed his eyes that he could not see the "large white plumes" of chivalry, but the men in the beds cheered as they heard the words the corporal read.

With such music as that in his ears, and with his soul stirred by the events about him, Watts McHurdie, lying in the hospital, wrote the song that made him famous. They know in Sycamore Ridge that Watts is not much of a poet, that his rhymes are sometimes bad and his metre worse. But once his heart took fire and burned for a day sheer white, and in that day he wrote words that a nation sang, and now all the world is singing. And they are proud of him, and when people come to Sycamore Ridge on pilgrimages to see the author of the song, men do not smile in wonder; they show the visitors his shop, and point out the bowed little man bending over his bench, stretching his arms out as he sews, and they point him out with pride. Not even John Barclay with all his millions, or Bob Hendricks, who once refused a place in the President's cabinet, are more esteemed in Sycamore Ridge than the little harness maker who set the world to singing.

And curiously enough, John Barclay was with Watts McHurdie when he wrote the song. They brought him an accordion one day while he was getting well, and the two sat together. Watts droned along and shut his eyes and mumbled some words, and then burst out with the chorus. Over and over he sang it and exclaimed between breaths: "Say--ain't that fine? I just made it up." He was exalted with his performance, and some women came loitering down the corridor where the wounded man and the boy were lying. The visitors gazed compassionately at them--little Watts not much larger than the boy. A woman asked, "And where were you wounded, son?" looking at Watts with his accordion. His face flushed up at the thought of his shame, and he could not keep back the tears that always betrayed him when he was deeply moved. "Ten--ten miles from Springfield, madam, ten miles from Springfield." And to hide his embarrassment he began sawing at his accordion, chanting his famous song. But being only a little boy, John Barclay tittered.

A few days after the battle Captain Ward wrote to Miss Lucy telling her that some soldiers slightly wounded would go home on a furlough to

Lawrence, and that they would take John with them and put him on the stage at Lawrence for Sycamore Ridge. Then Ward's letter continued: "It is all so horrible--this curse of war; sometimes I think it is worse than the curse of slavery. There is no 'pomp and circumstance of glorious war.' Men died screaming in agony, or dumb with fear. They were covered with dirt, and when they were dead they merged into the landscape like inanimate things. What vital difference is there between a living man and a dead man, that one stands out in a scene big and obtrusive, and the other begins to fade into the earth as soon as death touches the body? The horror of death is upon me, and I cannot shake it off. It is a fearful thing to see a human soul pass 'in any shape, in any mood.' And I have seen so many deaths--we lost one man out of every three--that I am all unnerved. I saw General Lyon die--the only abolitionist in the regular army, they say. He died like a soldier--but not as the soldiers die in pictures. He sank off his horse so limp, and so like an animal with its death wound, and gasped so weakly, 'I'm killed--take care of my body,' that when we covered his face and bore him away, we could not realize we were carrying a man's body. And now, my dear, if I should go as these men go, I have neither kith nor kin to mourn me--only you, and you must not mourn, for I shall be near you always and always, without sign or token, and when you feel my presence near, know that it is real, and not a seeming. For the great force of life that moves events in this world has but one symbol, but one vital manifestation, and that is love, and when a soul is touched with that, it is immortal."

But Martin Culpepper, with his dancing plumes, saw things in another light. Perhaps we always see things in another light when forty years have passed over them. But in his chapter "The Shrill Trump," in the Biography, he writes: "'O you mortal engines, whose rude throats the immortal Jove's dread clamours counterfeit,' O for the 'spirit-stirring drum, and the ear-splitting fife' 'in these piping times of peace.' Small wonder it was that with the clang and clank of sabre and artillery

in his ears, with the huzzas of comrades and the sparkle of the wine of
war in his eyes, our hero wrote the never dying words that made him
famous. How the day comes back with all its pageantry, the caparisoned
horses, the handsome men stepping to the music of inspiring melody, the
clarion commands of the officers, and the steady rumble of a thousand
feet upon the battle ground, going careless whether to death or
immortality in deathless fame."

A curious thing is that deathless fame which Martin speaks of--a
passing curious thing; for when word came of Henry Schnitzler's death,
Mary Murphy, of the Thayer House, put off Gabriel Carnine's ring, and
wept many tears in the stage driver's coffee and wore black in her hat
for a year, and when Gabriel came home, she married him and all went
as merrily as a wedding-bell. What covert tenderness or dream of gauzy
romance was in her memory, the town could never know; but the
Carnines' first boy was named Henry, and for many years after the war,
she was known among the men, who do not understand a woman's heart, as
the "War widow by brevet." Yet that was Henry's "deathless fame" in
Sycamore Ridge, for the town has long since forgotten him, and even
his name means nothing to our children, who see it on the bronze
statue set up by the rich John Barclay to commemorate our soldier
dead.

But John was our first war hero. And when he brought his battle scars
home that September night in '61, for hours before the stage drove
across Sycamore Creek the boy was filled with a nameless dread that he
might be spanked.

They carried him on a cot to his mother's house, and put him in the
great carved four-poster bed, and in the morning Miss Lucy came and
hovered over him, and they talked of Captain Ward to her heart's
content, and the boy told Miss Lucy the gossip of the hospital,--that
Captain Ward was to be made a major,--and she kissed him and petted

him until he was glad none of the boys was around to see the sickening spectacle. And then Miss Lucy and Mrs. Barclay told the child of their plans,--that Miss Lucy was going to war as a nurse, and that Mrs. Barclay was to teach the Sycamore Ridge school during the winter. And in a few weeks John was out of the hero business, working in Culpepper's store after school, and getting used to a limp that stayed with him all his life.

The next spring he traded a carbine that he brought home from the army for an Indian pony, and then he began business for himself. He organized the cows of the town into a town herd and took them every morning to pasture on the prairie. All day he rode in the open air, and the town boys came out to play with him, and they explored the cave by his mother's house, and with their sling-shots killed quails and prairie chickens and cooked them, and they played war through the long summer days. But John did not grow as the other boys grew; he remained undersized, and his limp put him at a disadvantage; so he had few fights, but he learned cunning, and got his way by strategy rather than by force--but he always had his way. He was strong; the memory of what he had seen and what he had been that one awful day in the battle made lines on his face; sometimes at night he would wake screaming, when he dreamed he was running away from the surgeon with the bloody knife in his teeth and that the man was going to throw an arm at him. And when he wished to bring Ellen Culpepper to time he would begin in a low terrorful voice, "And I saw--the man--take--a--g-r-e-a-t l-o-n-g knife d-r-i-p-p-i-n-g with r-e-d-b-l-o-o-d out of his t-e-e-t-h and go slish, k-slish," but he never got farther than this, for the girl would begin shaking, and if they were alone, would run to him and grab him and put her hand to his mouth to make him stop.

And so his twelfth year passed under the open sky in the sunshine in summer and in winter working after school in town where men were wanting, and where a boy could always find work. He grew brown and lean, and as his voice grew squeaky and he sang alto in the school, he became more and more crafty and masterful. The fact that his mother was the teacher, did not give him more rights in school than other boys, for she was a sensible woman, but it gave him a prestige on the playground that he was not slow to take. He was a born trader; and he kept what he got and got more. His weakness was music. He kept two cows in his herd in the summer time in return for the use of the melodeon at the Thayer House, and moved it to his own home and put it in the crowded little room, and practised on it at night when the other boys were loafing at the town pump. For a consideration in marbles he taught Buck Culpepper the chords in "G" on the guitar, and for further consideration taught him the chords in "D" and "C," and with the aid of Jimmy Fernald, aged nine, and Molly Culpepper, aged eleven, one with a triangle and the other with a pumpkin reed pipe, John organized his Band, which he led with his mouth-organ, and exhibited in Culpepper's barn, appropriating to himself as the director the pins charged at the door. Forty years afterward, when Molly called his attention to his failure to divide with the children, John Barclay smiled as he lifted his lame foot to a fat leather chair in front of him and said, "That was what we call the promoter's profit." And then the talk ran to Ellen, and John opened his great desk and from a box without a mark on it he brought out a tintype picture of Ellen at fourteen, a pink-cheeked child in short sleeves, with the fringe of her pantalets showing above her red striped stockings and beneath her bulging skirts, and with a stringy, stiff feather rising from the front of her narrow-rimmed hat.

During the time when he was going to school by day and working evenings and caring for the town herd through the summer, the war was dragging wearily on. Sometimes a soldier came home on a furlough and there was news of the Sycamore Ridge men, but oftener it was a season of waiting and working. The women and children cared for the farms and the stores as best they could and lived, heaven only knows how, and opened every newspaper with horror and dread, and glanced down the long list of names of the dead, the missing and the wounded, fearful of what they might see. Mrs. Barclay heard from Miss Lucy and through her kept track of Philemon Ward, who was transferred to another regiment after he was made major. And when he was made a colonel at Shiloh, there were tear blots on Miss Lucy's letter that told of it, and after Appomattox he was brevetted a general. As for Captain Culpepper, he came home a colonel, and Jake Dolan came home a first lieutenant. But Watts McHurdie came home with a letter from Lincoln about his song, and he was the greatest man of all of them.

It is odd that Sycamore Ridge grew during the war. Where the people came from, no one could say--yet they came, and young Barclay remembered even during the war of playing in the foundations and running over the rafters of new houses. But when the war closed, the great caravan that had lagged while the war was raging, began to trail itself steadily in front of Mrs. Barclay's door, through the streets of Sycamore Ridge and out over the western hills. Soldiers with their families passed, going to the free homesteads, and the line of movers' wagons began with daybreak and rumbled by far into the night. But hundreds of wagons stopped in Sycamore Ridge, and the stage came crowded every night. Brick buildings, the town's mortal pride, began showing their fronts on Main Street, and other streets in the town began to assert themselves. Mrs. Barclay's school grew from a score of children in 1864 to three rooms full in '65, and in '66 the whole town turned out to welcome General and Mrs. Ward, she that was Miss Lucy Barnes, and there was a reunion of "C" Company that night, and a camp-fire in Culpepper Hall, and the next day Lige Bemis was painting a sign which read "Philemon R. Ward, Attorney-at-Law, Pension Matters Promptly Attended To." And the first little Ward was born at the Thayer House and named Eli Thayer Ward.

The spring that found John Barclay sixteen years old found him a

browned, gray-eyed, lumpy sort of a boy, big at the wrong places, and
stunted at the wrong places, with a curious, uneven sort of an
education. He knew all about Walden Pond; and he knew his
Emerson--and was mad with passion to see the man; he had travelled
over the world with Scott; had crossed the bridge with Caesar in his
father's books; had roamed the prairie and the woods with Cooper's
Indians; had gone into the hearts of men with Thackeray and Dickens,
holding his mother's hand and listening to her voice; but he knew
algebra only as a name, and rhetoric was a dictionary word with him.
Of earthly possessions he had two horses, a bill of sale for his
melodeon, a saddle, a wagon, a set of harness; four mouth-organs, one
each in "A," "D," "E," and "C," all carefully rolled in Canton flannel
on a shelf above his bed; one concertina,--a sort of German
accordion,--five pigs, a cow, and a bull calf. Moreover, there were
two rooms in the Barclay home; and the great rock was gone from the
door of the cave, and a wooden door was in its place and the Barclays
were using it for a spring-house. The boy had a milk route and sold
butter to the hotel. But the chiefest treasure of the household was
John's new music book. And while he played on his melodeon, Ellen
Culpepper's eyes smiled from the pages and her voice moved in the
melodies, and his heart began to feel the first vague vibration with
the great harmony of life. And so the pimples on his chin reddened,
and the squeak in his voice began to squawk, and his big milky eyes
began to see visions wherein a man was walking through this vain
world. As for Ellen Culpepper, her shoe tops were tiptoeing to her
skirts, and her eyes were full of dreams of the warrior bold, "with
spurs of gold," who "sang merrily his lay." And rising from these
dreams, she always stepped on her feet. But that was a long time ago,
and men and women have been born and loved, and married and brought
children into the world since then. For it was a long time ago.

CHAPTER IV

The changes of time are hard to realize. One knows, of course, that
the old man once was young. One understands that the tree once was a
sapling, and conversely we know that the child will be a man and the
gaunt sapling stuck in the earth in time will become a great spreading
tree. But the miracle of growth passes not merely our understanding,
but our imagination.

So though men tell us, and grow black in the face with the vehemence
of telling, that the Sycamore Ridge of the sixties--a gray smudge of
unpainted wooden houses bordering the Santa Fe trail, with the street
merging into the sunflowers a block either way from the pump,--is the
town that now lies hidden in the elm forest, with its thirty miles of
paving and its scores of acres of wide velvet lawns, with its parks
wherein fountains play, guarded by cannon discarded by the pride of
modern war, with the court-house on the brink of the hill that once
was far west of the town and with twenty-two thousand people whizzing
around in trolleys, rattling about in buggies or scooting down the
shady avenues in motor-cars--whatever the records may show, the real
truth we know; the towns are not the same; the miracle of growth
cannot fool us. And yet here is the miracle in the making. Always in
John Barclay's eyes when he closed them to think of the first years
that followed the war between the states, rose visions of yellow pine
and red bricks and the litter and debris of building; always in his
ears as he remembered those days were the confused noises of wagons
whining and groaning under their heavy loads, of gnawing saws and
rattling hammers, of the clink of trowels on stones, of the swish of

mortar in boxes, and of the murmur of the tide of hurrying feet over board sidewalks, ebbing and flowing night and morning. In those days new boys came to town so rapidly that sometimes John met a boy in swimming whom he did not know, and, even in 1866, when Ellen and Molly
Culpepper were giving a birthday party for Ellen, she declared that she "simply couldn't have all the new people there."

And so in the sixties the boy and the town went through their raw, gawky, ugly adolescence together. As streets formed in the town, ideas took shape in the boy's mind. As Lincoln Avenue was marked out on the hill, where afterward the quality of the town came to live, so in the boy's heart books that told him of the world outlined vague visions. Boy fashion he wrote to Bob Hendricks once or twice a month or a season, as the spirit moved him, and measured everything with the eyes of his absent friend. For he came to idealize Bob, who was out in the wonderful world, and their letters in those days were curious compositions--full of adventures by field and wood, and awkward references to proper books to read, and cures for cramps and bashfully expressed aspirations of the soul. Bob's father had become a general, and when the war closed, he was sent west to fight the Indians, and he took Lieutenant Jacob Dolan with him, and Bob sent to John news of the Indian fighting that glorified Bob further.

And when a letter came to the Ridge from Dolan announcing that he and the Hendricks family were coming back to the Ridge to live,--the general to look after his neglected property, and Dolan to start a livery-stable,--John heard the news with a throb of great joy. When a letter from Bob confirmed the news, John began to count the days. For the love of boys is the most unselfish thing in a selfish world. They met awkwardly and sheepishly at the stage, and greeted each other with grunts, and became inseparable. Bob came back tall, lanky, grinny, and rather dumb, and he found John undersized, wiry, masterful, and rather mooney, but strong and purposeful, for a boy. But each accepted the other as perfect in every detail.

Nothing Bob did changed John's attitude, and nothing John did made Bob waver in his faith in John. Did the boys come to John with a sickening story that Bob's sister made him bring a towel to the swimming hole, John glared at them a moment and then waved them aside with, "Well, you big brutes,--didn't you know what it was for?" When they reported to John that Bob's father was making him tip his hat to the girls, they got, instead of the outbreak of scorn they expected, "Well--did the girls tip back?" And when Bob's sister said that the Barclay boy--barefooted, curly-headed, dusty, and sunburned--looked like something the old cat had dragged into the house, the boy-was impudent to his sister and took a whipping from his father.

That fall the children of Sycamore Ridge assembled for the first time in their new seven-room stone schoolhouse, and the two boys were in the high school. The board hired General Philemon Ward to teach the twenty high school pupils, and it was then he first began to wear the white neckties which he never afterwards abandoned. Ward's first clash with John Barclay occurred when Ward organized a military company. John's limp kept him out of it, so he broke up the company and organized a literary society, of which he was president and Ellen Culpepper secretary, and a constitution was adopted exempting the president and secretary from work in the society. It was natural enough that Bob Hendricks should be made treasurer, and that these three officers should be the programme committee, and then a long line of vice-presidents and assistant secretaries and treasurers and monitors was elected by the society.

So John became the social leader of the group of boys and girls who were just coming out of kissing games into dances at one another's homes in the town. John decided who should be in the "crowd" and who

might be invited only when a mixed crowd was expected. Fathers
desiring trade, and mothers faithful to church ties, protested; but
John Barclay had his way. It was his crowd. They called themselves the
"Spring Chickens," and as John had money saved to spend as he pleased,
he dictated many things; but he did not spend his money, he lent it,
and his barn was stored with, skates and sleds and broken guns and
scrap-iron held as security, while his pockets bulged with knives
taken as interest.

As the winter waned and the Spring Chickens waxed fat in social
honours, Bob Hendricks glanced up from his algebra one day, and
discovered that little Molly Culpepper had two red lips and two
pig-tail braids of hair that reached below her waist. Then and there
he shot her deftly with a paper wad, chewed and fired through a cane
pipe-stem, and waited till she wiped it off her cheek with her apron
and made a face at him, before he plunged into the mysteries of $x2 +$
$2xy + y2$. And thus another old story began, as new and as fresh as
when Adam and Eve walked together in the garden.

John Barclay was so busy during his last year in the Sycamore Ridge
school that he often fancied afterwards that the houses on Lincoln
Avenue in Culpepper addition must have come with the grass in the
spring, for he has no memory of their building. Neither does he
remember when General Madison Hendricks built the brick building on
the corner of Main Street and Fifth Avenue, in which he opened the
Exchange National Bank of Sycamore Ridge. Yet John remembered that his
team and wagon were going all winter, hauling stone for the foundation
of the Hendricks home on the hill--a great brick structure, with
square towers and square "ells" rambling off on the prairie, and
square turrets with ornate cornice pikes pricking the sky. For years
the two big houses standing side by side--the Hendricks house and the
Culpepper house, with its tall white pillars reaching to the roof, its
double door and its two white wings spreading over the wide green

lawn--were the show places of Sycamore Ridge, and the town was always divided in its admiration for them. John's heart was sadly torn between them. Yet he was secretly glad to learn from his mother that his Uncle Union's house in Haverhill had tall columns, green blinds on the white woodwork, and a wide hall running down the centre. For it made him feel more at home at the Culpeppers'. But when the Hendricks' piano came, after they moved into the big house, the boy's heart was opened afresh; and he spent hours with Bob Hendricks at the piano, when he knew he would be welcome at the Culpeppers'. He leased his town herd in the summer to Jimmie Fernald--giving him the right to take the cows to the commons around town upon the payment of five dollars a month to John for keeping out of the business, and passing Jimmie good-will. In the meantime, by day, John worked his team, and hired two others and took contracts for digging cellars. At nights he went to the country with his concertina and played for dances, making two dollars a night, and General Hendricks for years pointed with pride to the fact that when the Exchange National Bank of Sycamore Ridge opened for business the first morning, standing at the head of the line of depositors was John Barclay, with his concertina under his arm, just as he had returned from a country dance at daylight, waiting to be first in line, with $178.53 in his pocket to deposit. That deposit slip, framed, still hangs over the desk in the office of the president of the bank, and when John Barclay became famous, it was always a part of the "Art Loan Exhibit," held by the women in Barclay Memorial Hall.

That summer of '67 John capitulated to life, held his hands up for the shackles and put on shoes in summer for the first time. Also, he only went swimming twice--both times at night, and he bought his first box of paper collars and his mother tried to make his neckties like those in Dorman's store; but some way she did not get the hang of it, and John bought a Sunday necktie of great pride, and he and his mother agreed that it was off the tail of Joseph's coat of many colours. But he wore it only on state occasions. At work, he made an odd figure limping over the dirt heaps and into the excavations bossing men old enough to be his father. He wore a serious face in those days,--for a boy,--and his mouth was almost hard, but something burned in his eyes that was more than ambition, though that lighted his face like a flame, and he was always whistling or singing. At night he and Bob Hendricks wandered away together, and sometimes they walked out under the stars and talked as boys will talk of their little world and the big world about them, or sometimes they sat reading at one or the other's home, and one would walk home with the other, and the other walk a piece of the way back. They read poetry and mooned; "Lalla Rookh" appealed to John because of its music and melody, and both boys devoured Byron, and gobbled over the "Corsair" and the "Giaour" and "Childe Harold" with the book above the table, and came back from the barn on Sundays licking their chops after surreptitiously nibbling "Don Juan." But they had Captain Mayne Reid and Kingsley as an antidote, and they soon got enough of Byron.

The two boys persuaded each other to go away to school, and John chose the state university because it was cheap and because he heard he could get work in Lawrence to carry him through. He did not recollect that his mother had any influence in the matter; but in those days she always seemed to be sitting by the lamp in their little home, sewing, with his shirts and underwear strewn about her. She had a permanent place in the town schools, and the Barclay home had grown to a kitchen and two bedrooms as well as the big room with its fireplace. His mother's hair was growing gray at the temples, but her clear, firm, unwrinkled skin and strong broad jaw kept youth in her countenance, and as Martin Culpepper wrote in the Biography, where he names the pioneers of Sycamore Ridge whose lives influenced Watts McHurdie's, "the three graces, Faith, Hope, and Charity, were mirrored in her smile."

One night when the boy came in tired after his night's ramble, he left his mother, as he often did those last nights before he went away to school, bending over her work, humming a low happy-noted song, even though the hour was late. He lay in his bed beside the open window looking out into the night, dreaming with open eyes about life. Perhaps he actually dreamed a moment, for he did not hear her come into the room; but he felt her bend over him, and a tear dropped on his face from hers. He turned toward her, and she put her arms about his neck. Then she sobbed: "Oh, good-by, my little boy--good-by. I am coming here to bid you good-by, every night now." He kissed her hand, and she was silent a moment, and then she spoke: "I know this is the last of it all, John. You will never come back to me again--not you, but a man. And you will seem strange, and I will seem strange." She paused a moment to let the cramp in her throat leave, then she went on: "I was going to say so many things--when this time came, but they're all gone. But oh, my boy, my little tender-hearted boy--be a good man--just be a good man, John." And then she sobbed for an unrestrained minute: "O God, when you take my boy away, keep him clean, and brave, and kind, and--O God, make him--make him a good man." And with a pat and a kiss she rose and said as she left him, "Now good night, Johnnie, go to sleep."

        *   *   *   *   *

In the Sycamore Ridge **Banner** for September 12, 1867, appeared some verses by Watts McHurdie, beginning:--

"Hail and farewell to thee, friend of my youth,
Pilgrim who seekest the Fountain of Truth,
Hail and farewell to thy innocent pranks,
No more can I send thee for left-handed cranks.
Farewell, and a tear laves the ink on my pen,
For ne'er shall I 'noint thee with strap-oil again."

It was a noble effort, and in his notes to the McHurdie poems following the Biography published over thirty years after those lines were written, Colonel Culpepper writes: "This touching, though somewhat humorous, poem was written on the occasion of the departure for college of one who since has become listed with the world's great captains of finance--none other than Honourable John Barclay, whose fame is too substantial to need encomium in these humble pages. Suffice it to say that between these two men, our hero, the poet, and the great man of affairs, there has always remained the closest friendship, and each carries in his bosom, wrapped in the myrrh of fond memory, the deathless blossom of friendship, that sweetest flower in the conservatory of the soul."

The day before John left for Lawrence he met Lieutenant Jacob Dolan.

"So ye're going to college--ay, Johnnie?"

"Yes, Mr. Dolan," replied the boy.

"Well, they're all givin' you somethin', Johnnie: Watts here has given a bit of a posey in verse; and my friend, General Hendricks, I'm told, has given you a hundred-dollar note; and General Philemon Ward has given you Wendell Phillips' orations; and your sweetheart--God bless her, whoever she is--will be givin' ye the makins' of a broken heart; and your mother'll be givin' you her blessin'--and the saints' prayers go with 'em; and me, havin' known your father before you and the mother that bore you, and seein' her rub the roses off her cheeks tryin' to keep your ornery little soul in your worthless little body, I'll give you this sentiment to put in your pipe and smoke: John Barclay, man--if they ever be's a law agin damn fools, the first raid the officers should make is on the colleges. And now may ye be struck blind before ye get your education and dumb if it makes a fool of ye."

And so slapping the boy on the back, Jake Dolan went down the street winding in and out among the brick piles and lumber and mortar boxes, whistling "Tread on the Tail of me Coat."

For life was all so fine and gay with Lieutenant Dolan in those days. And he whistled and sang, and thought what he pleased, and said what he pleased, and did what he pleased, and if the world didn't like it, the world could picket its horses and get out of Jacob Dolan's livery barn. For Mr. Dolan was thinking that from the livery-stable to the office of sheriff is but a step in this land of the free and home of the brave; so he carried his head back and his chest out and invited insult in the fond hope of provoking assault. He was the flower of the times,--effulgent, rather gaudy, and mostly red!

CHAPTER V

Good times came to Sycamore Ridge in the autumn. The dam across the creek was furnishing power for a flour-mill and a furniture factory. The endless worm of wagons that was wriggling through the town carrying movers to the West, was sloughing many of its scales in Sycamore Ridge. Martin Culpepper had been East with circulars describing the town and adjacent country. He had brought back three stage loads of settlers, and was selling lots in Culpepper's addition faster than they could be surveyed. The Frye blacksmith shop had become a wagon shop, and then a hardware store was added; the flag fluttered from the high flagstaff over the Exchange National Bank building, and all day long farmers were going from the mill to the bank. General Philemon Ward gave up school-teaching and went back to his law office; but he was apt to take sides with President Andrew Johnson too vigorously for his own good, and clients often avoided his office in fear of an argument. Still he was cheerful, and being only in his early thirties, looked at the green hills afar from his pasture and was happy. The Thayer House was filled with guests, and the Fernalds had money in the bank; Mary Murphy and Gabriel Carnine were living happily ever after, and Nellie Logan was clerking in Dorman's Dry Goods store and making Watts McHurdie understand that she had her choice between a preacher and a drummer. Other girls in the dining room of the Thayer House were rattling the dinner dishes and singing "Sweet Belle Mahone" and "Do you love me, Molly Darling?" to ensnare the travelling public that might be tilted back against the veranda in a mood for romance. And as John and Bob that hot September afternoon made the round of the stores and offices bidding the town good-by, it seemed to them that perhaps they were seizing the shadow and letting the substance fade. For it was such a good-natured busy little place that their hearts were heavy at leaving it.

But that evening John in his gorgeous necktie, his clean paper collar, his new stiff hat, his first store clothes, wearing proudly his father's silver watch and chain, set out to say good-by to Ellen Culpepper, and his mother, standing in the doorway of their home, sighed at his limp and laughed at his strut--the first laugh she had enjoyed in a dozen days.

John and Bob together went up the stone walk leading across a yard, still littered with the debris of building, to the unboxed steps that climbed to the veranda of the Culpepper house. There they met Colonel Culpepper in his shirt-sleeves, walking up and down the veranda admiring the tall white pillars. When he had greeted the boys, he put his thumbs in his vest holes and continued his parade in some pomp.

The boys were used to this attitude of the colonel's toward themselves and the pillars. It always followed a hearty meal. So they sat respectfully while he marched before them, pointing occasionally, when he took his cigar from his mouth and a hand from his vest, to some feature of the landscape in the sunset light that needed emphatic attention.

"Yes, sir, young gentlemen," expanded the colonel, "you are doing the right and proper thing--the right and proper thing. Of all the avocations of youth, I conceive the pursuit of the sombre goddess of learning to be the most profitable--entirely the most profitable. I myself, though a young man,--being still on the right side of forty,--have reaped the richest harvest from my labours in the classic shades. Twenty years ago, young gentlemen, I, like you, left my ancestral estates to sip at the Pierian spring. In point of fact, I attended the institution founded by Thomas Jefferson, the father of the American democracy--yes, sir." He put his cigar back in his mouth and added, "Yes, sir, you are certainly taking a wise and, I may say, highly necessary step--"

Mrs. Culpepper, small, sprightly, blue-eyed, and calm, entered the veranda, and cut the colonel off with: "Good evening, boys. So you are going away. Well--we'll miss you. The girls will be right out."

But the colonel would not be quenched; his fires were burning deeply. "As I was saying, Mrs. Culpepper," he went on, "the classic training obtained from a liberal education such as it was my fortune--"

Mrs. Culpepper smiled blandly as she put in, "Now, pa, these boys don't care for that."

"But, my dear, let me finish. As I started to say: the flowers of poetry, Keats and his large white plumes, the contemplation of nature's secrets, the reflective study of--"

"Yes,--here's your coat now, pa," said the wife, returning from a dive into the hall. "John, how's your ma going to get on without you? And, pa, be sure don't forget the eggs for breakfast. I declare since we've moved up here so far from the stores, we nearly starve."

The colonel waited a second while a glare melted into a smile, and then backed meekly into the arms stretched high to hold his alpaca coat. As he turned toward the group, he was beaming. "If it were not," exclaimed the colonel, addressing the young men with a quizzical smile, "that there is a lady present--a very important lady in point of fact,--I might be tempted to say, 'I will certainly be damned!'" And with that the colonel lifted Mrs. Culpepper off her feet and kissed her, then lumbered down the steps and strode away. He paused at the gate to gaze at the valley and turned to look back at the great unfinished house, then swung into the street and soon his hat disappeared under the hill.

As he went Mrs. Culpepper said, "Let them say what they will about Mart Culpepper, I always tell the girls if they get as good a man as their pa, they will be doing mighty well."

Then the girls appeared bulging in hoops, and ruffles, with elbow sleeves, with a hint of their shoulders showing and with pink ribbons in their hair. Clearly it was a state occasion. The mother beamed at them a moment, and walked around Molly, saying, "I told you that was all right," and tied Ellen's hair ribbon over, while the young people were chattering, and before the boys knew it, she had faded into the dusk of the hall, and the clattering of dishes came to them from the rear of the house. John fancied he felt the heavy step of Buchanan Culpepper, and then he heard: "Don't you talk to me, Buck Culpepper, about woman's work. You'll do what I tell you, and if I say wipe dishes--" the voice was drowned by the rattle of a passing wagon. And soon the young people on the front porch were so busy with their affairs that the house behind them and its affairs dropped to another world. They say, who seem to know, that when any group of boys and girls meet under twenty-five serious years, the recording angel puts down his pen with, a sigh and takes a needed nap. But when the group pairs off, then Mr. Recorder pricks up his ears and works with both hands, one busy taking what the youngsters say, and the other busy with what they would like to say. And shame be it upon the courage of youth that what they would like to say fills the larger book. And marvel of marvels, often the book that holds what the boys would say is merely a copy of what the girls would like to hear, and so much of the work is saved to the angel.

It was nine o'clock when the limping boy and the slender girl followed the tall youth and the plump little girl down the walk from the Culpepper home through the gate and into the main road. And the couple that walked behind took the opposite direction from that which they took who walked ahead. Yet when John and Ellen reached the river and were seated on the mill-dam, where the roar of the falling water drowned their voices, Ellen Culpepper spoke first: "That looks like them over on the bridge. I can see Molly, and Bob's hat about three feet above her."

"I guess so," returned the boy. He was reaching behind him for clods and pebbles to toss into the white foaming flood below them. The girl reached back and got one, then another, then their hands met, and she pulled hers away and said, "Get me some stones." He gave her a handful, and she threw the pebbles away slowly and awkwardly, one at a time. There was a long gap in their talk while they threw the pebbles. The girl closed it with, "Ma made old Buck wipe the dishes." Then she giggled, "Poor Buckie."

John managed to say, "Yes, I heard him." Then he added, "What does your mother think of Bob?"

"Oh, she likes him fine. But she's glad you're all going away."

The boy asked why and the girl returned, "Watch me hit that log." She threw, and missed the water.

"Why?" persisted the boy.

The girl was digging in a crevice for a stone and said, "Can you get that out?"

John worked at it a moment and handed it to her with, "Why?"

She threw it, standing up to give her arm strength. She sat down and folded her hands and waited for another "why." When it came she said, "Oh, you know why." When he protested she answered, "Ma thinks Molly's too young."

"Too young for what?" demanded the boy, who knew.

"Too young to be going with boys."

There was a long pause, then he managed to say it, "She's no younger than you were--nor half as old."

"When?" returned the girl, giving him the broadside of her eyes for a second, and letting them droop. The eyes bewitched the boy, and he could not speak. At length the girl shivered, "It's getting cold--I must go home."

The boy found voice. "Aw no, Bob and Molly are still up there."

She started to rise, he caught her hand, but she pulled it away and resigned herself for a moment. Then she looked at him a long second and said, "Do you remember years ago at the Frye boy's party--when we were little tots, and I chose you?"

The boy nodded his head and turned full toward her with serious eyes. He devoured her feature by feature with his gaze in the starlight. The moon was just rising at the end of the mill-dam behind them, and its light fell on her profile. He cried out, "Yes, Ellen, do you--do you?"

She nodded her head and spoke quickly, "That was the time you got your hands stuck in the taffy and had to be soaked out."

They laughed. John tried to get the moment back. "Do you remember the rubber ring I gave you?"

She grew bold and turned to him with her heart in her face: "Yes--yes, John, and the coffee-bean locket. I've got them both in a little box at home." Then, scampering back to her reserve, she added, "You know ma says I'm a regular rat to store things away." She felt that the sudden reserve chilled him, for in a minute or two she said, looking at the bridge: "They're going now. We mustn't stay but a minute." She put her hand on the rock between them, and said, "You remember that night when you went away before?" Before he answered she went on: "I was counting up this afternoon, and it's six years ago. We were just children then."

Again the boy found his voice: "Ellen Culpepper, we've been going together seven years. Don't you think that's long enough?"

"We were just children then," she replied.

The boy leaned awkwardly toward her and their hands met on the rock, and he withdrew his as he asked, "Do you--do you?"

She bent toward him, and looked at him steadily as she nodded her head again and again. She rose to go, saying, "We mustn't stay here any longer."

He caught her hand to stop her, and said, "Ellen--Ellen, promise me just one thing." She looked her question. He cried, "That you won't forget--just that you won't forget."

She took his hand and stood before him as he sat, hoping to stay her. She answered: "Not as long as I live, John Barclay. Oh, not as long as I live." Then she exclaimed: "Now--" and her voice changed, "we just must go, John; Molly's gone, and it's getting late." She helped him limp over the rocks and up the steep road, but when they reached the level, she dropped his hand, and they walked home slowly, looking back at the moon, so that they might not overtake the other couple. Once or twice they stopped and sat on lumber piles in the street, talking of nothing, and it was after ten o'clock when they came to the gate. The girl looked anxiously up the walk toward the house. "They've come and gone," she said. She moved as if to go away.

"I wish you wouldn't go right in," he begged.

"Oh--I ought to," she replied. They were silent. The roar of the water over the dam came to them on the evening breeze. She put out her hand.

"Well," he sighed as he rested his lame foot, and started, "well--good-by."

She turned to go, and then swiftly stepped toward him, and kissed him, and ran gasping and laughing up the walk.

The boy gazed after her a moment, wondering if he should follow her, but while he waited she was gone, and he heard her lock the door after her. Then he limped down the road in a kind of swoon of joy. Sometimes he tried to whistle--he tried a bar of Schubert's "Serenade," but consciously stopped. Again and again under his breath as loud as he dared, he called the name "Ellen" and stood gazing at the moon, and then tried to hippety-hop, but his limp stopped that. Then he tried whistling the "Miserere," but he pitched it too high, and it ran out, so he sang as he turned across the commons toward home, and that helped a little; and he opened the door of his home singing, "How can I leave thee--how can I bear to part?" The light was burning in the kitchen, and he went to his mother and kissed her. His face was aglow, and she saw what had happened to him. She put him aside with, "Run on to bed now, sonny; I've got a little work out here." And he left her. In the sitting room only the moon gave light. He stood at the window a moment, and then turned to his melodeon. His hands fell on the major chord of "G," and without knowing what he was playing he began "Largo." He played his soul into his music, and looking up, whispered the name "Ellen" rapturously over and over, and then as the music mounted to its climax the whole world's mystery, and his personal thought of the meaning of life revelled through his brain, and he played on, not stopping at the close but wandering into he knew not what mazes of harmony. When his hands dropped, he was playing "The Long and Weary Day," and his mother was standing behind him humming it. When he rose from the bench, she ran her fingers through his hair and spoke the words of the song, "'My lone watch keeping,' John, 'my lone watch keeping.' But I think it has been worth while."

Then she left him and he went to bed, with the moon in his room, and the murmur of waters lulling him to sleep. But he looked out into the sky a long time before his dream came, and then it slipped in gently through the door of a nameless hope. For he wished to meet her in the moon that night, but when they did meet, the white veil of the falling waters of the dam blew across her face and he could not brush it away. For one is bold in dreams.

A little after sunrise the next morning John rode away from his mother's door, on one of his horses, leading the other one. He was going up the hill to get Bob Hendricks, and the two were to ride to Lawrence. He had been promised work, carrying newspapers, and the Yankee in him made him believe he could find work for the other horse. As the boy turned into Main Street waving his mother good-by, he saw the places where he and Ellen Culpepper had stopped the night before, and they looked different some way, and he could not realize that he was in the same street.

As he climbed the hill, he passed General Ward, working in his flower garden, and the man sprang over the fence and came into the road, and put his hand on the horse's bridle, saying, "Stop a minute, John: I just wanted to say something." He hesitated a moment before going on: "You know back where I came from--back in New England--the name of John Barclay stands for a good deal--more than you can realize, John. Your father was one of the first martyrs of our cause. I guess your mother never has told you, but I'm going to--your father gave up a business career for this cause. His father was rich--very rich, and your grandfather was set on your father going into business." John looked up the hill toward the Hendricks home, and Ward saw it, and mistook the glance for one of impatience. "Johnnie," said the man, his fine thin, features glowing with earnestness, "Johnnie--I wish I could get to your heart, boy. I want to make you hear what I have to say with your soul and not with your ears, and I know youth is so deaf. Your grandfather was angry when your father entered the ministry and came out here. He thought it was folly. The old man offered to give fifty thousand dollars to the Kansas-Nebraska cause, and that would have sent a good many men out here. But your father said no. He said money wouldn't win this cause. He said personal sacrifice was all that would win it. He said men must give up themselves, not their money, to make this cause win--and so he came; and there was a terrible quarrel, and that is why your mother has stayed. She had faith in God, too--faith that her life some way in His Providence would prove worth something. Your father and mother, John, believed in God--they believed in a God, not a Moloch; your father's faith has been justified. The death he died was worth millions to the cause of liberty. It stirred the whole North, as the miserable little fifty thousand dollars that Abijah Barclay offered never could have done. But your mother's sacrifice must find its justification in you. And she, not your father, made the final decision to give up everything for human freedom. She has endured poverty, Johnnie--" the man's voice was growing tense, and his eyes were ablaze; "you know how she worked, and if you fail her, if you do not live a consecrated life, John, your mother's life has failed. I don't mean a pious life; God knows I hate sanctimony. But I mean a life consecrated to some practical service, to an ideal--to some actual service to your fellows--not money service, but personal service. Do you understand?" Ward leaned forward and looked into the boy's face. He took hold of John's arm as he pleaded, "Johnnie--boy--Johnnie, do you understand?"

The boy answered, "Yes, General--I think I get your meaning." He picked up his bridle, and Ward relaxed his hold on the boy's arm. The man's hand dropped and he sighed, for he saw only a boy's face, and heard a boy's politeness in the voice that went on, "Thank you, General, give my love to Miss Lucy." And the youth rode on up the hill.

In a few minutes the boys were riding down the steep clay bank that led to the new iron bridge across the ford of the Sycamore, and for half an hour they rode chattering through the wood before they came into the valley and soon were Climbing the bluff which they had seen the night before from the Culpepper home. On the brow of the bluff Bob said, "Hold on--" He turned his horse and looked back. The sun was on the town, and across on the opposite hill stood the colonel's big house with its proud pillars. No trees were about it in those days, and it and the Hendricks house stood out clearly on the horizon. But on the top of the Culpepper home were two little figures waving handkerchiefs. The boys waved back, and John thought he could tell Ellen from her sister, and the night and its joy came back to him, and he was silent.

They had ridden half an hour without speaking when Bob Hendricks said, "Awful fine girls--aren't they?"

"That's what I've always told you," returned John.

After another quarter of a mile Bob tried it again. "The colonel's a funny old rooster--isn't he?"

"Well, I don't know. That day at the battle of Wilson's Creek when he walked out in front of a thousand soldiers and got a Union flag and brought it back to the line, he didn't look very funny. But he's windy all right."

Again, as they crossed a creek and the horses were drinking, Bob said: "Father thinks General Ward's a crank. He says Ward will keep harping on about those war bonds, and quarrelling because the soldiers got their pay in paper money and the bondholders in gold, until people will think every one in high places is a thief."

"Oh, Ward's all right," answered John. "He's just talking; he likes an argument, I guess. He's kind of built that way."

It was a poor starved-to-death school that the boys found at Lawrence in those days; with half a dozen instructors--most of whom were still in their twenties; with books lent by the instructors, and with appliances devised by necessity. But John was happy; he was making money with his horses, doing chores for his board, and carrying papers night and morning besides. The boy's industry was the marvel of the town. His limp got him sympathy, and he capitalized the sympathy. Indeed, he would have capitalized his soul, if it had been necessary. For his Yankee blood was beginning to come out. Before he had been in school a year he had swapped, traded, and saved until he had two teams, and was working them with hired drivers on excavation contracts. In his summer vacations he went to Topeka and worked his two teams, and by some sharp practice got the title to a third. He was rollicking, noisy, good-natured, but under the boyish veneer was a hard indomitable nature. He was becoming a stickler for his rights in every transaction.

"John," said Bob, one day after John had cut a particularly lamentable figure, gouging a driver in a settlement, "don't you know that your rights are often others' wrongs?"

John was silent a moment. He looked at the driver moving away, and then the boy's face set hard and he said: "Well--what's the use of blubbering over him? If I don't get it, some one else will. I'm no charitable institution for John Walruff's brewery!" And he snapped the rubber band on his wallet viciously, and turned to his books.

But on the other hand he wrote every other day to his mother and every other day to Ellen Culpepper with unwavering precision. He told his mother the news, and he told Ellen Culpepper the news plus some Emerson, something more of "Faust," with such dashes of Longfellow and

Ruskin as seemed to express his soul. He never wrote to Ellen of money, and so strong was her influence upon him that when he had written to her after his quarrel with the driver, he went out in the night, hunted the man up, and paid him the disputed wages. Then he mailed Ellen Culpepper's letter, and was a lover living in an ethereal world as he walked home babbling her name in whispers to the stars. Often when this mood was not upon him, and a letter was due to Ellen, he went downstairs in the house where he lived and played the piano to bring her near to him. That never failed to change his face as by a miracle. "When John comes upstairs," wrote Bob Hendricks to Molly, "he is as one in a dream, with the mists of the music in his eyes. I never bother him then. He will not speak to me, nor do a thing in the world, until that letter is written, sealed, and stamped. Then he gets up, yawns and smiles sheepishly and perhaps hits me with a book or punches me with his fist, and then we wrestle over the room and the bed like bear cubs. After the wrestle he comes back to himself. I wonder why?"

And Ellen Culpepper read those letters from John Barclay over and over, and curiously enough she understood them; for there is a telepathy between spirits that meet as these two children's souls had met, and in that concord words drop out and only thoughts are merchandized. Her spirit grew with his, and so "through all the world she followed him."

But there came a gray dawn of a May morning when John Barclay clutched his bedfellow and whispered, "Bob, Bob--look, look." When the awakened one saw nothing, John tried to scream, but could only gasp, "Don't you see Ellen--there--there by the table?" But whatever it was that startled him fluttered away on a beam of sunrise, and Bob Hendricks rose with the frightened boy, and went to his work with him.

Two days later a letter came telling him that Ellen Culpepper was dead.

Now death--the vast baffling mystery of death--is Fate's strongest lever to pry men from their philosophy. And death came into this boy's life before his creed was set and hard, and in those first days while he walked far afield, he turned his face to the sky in his lonely sorrow, and when he cried to Heaven there was a silence.

So his heart curdled, and you kind gentlemen of the jury who are to pass on the case of John Barclay in this story, remember that he was only twenty years old, and that in all his life there was nothing to symbolize the joy of sacrifice except this young girl. All his boyish life she had nurtured the other self in his soul,--the self that might have learned to give and be glad in the giving. And when she went, he closed his Emerson and opened his Trigonometry, and put money in his purse.[1]

There came a time when Ellen Culpepper was to him as a dream. But she lived in her mother's eyes, and through all the years that followed the mother watched the little girl grow to maturity and into middle life with the other girls of her age. And even when the little headstone on the Hill slanted in sad neglect, Mrs. Culpepper's old eyes still saw Ellen growing old with her playmates. And she never saw John Barclay that she did not think of Ellen--and and what she would have made of him.

And what would she have made of him? Maybe a poet, maybe a dreamer of dreams--surely not the hard, grinding, rich man that he became in this world.

NOTE:

[1] To the Publisher.--"In returning the Mss. of the life of John Barclay, which you sent for my verification as to certain dates and

incidents, let me first set down, before discussing matters pertaining
to his later life, my belief that your author has found in the death
of Ellen Culpepper an incident, humble though it is, that explains
much in the character of Mr. Barclay. The incident probably produced a
mental shock like that of a psychological earthquake, literally
sealing up the spring of his life as it was flowing into consciousness
at that time, and the John Barclay of his boyhood and youth became
subterranean, to appear later in life after the weakening of his
virility under the strain of the crushing events of his fifties. Yet
the subterranean Barclay often appeared for a moment in his life,
glowed in some kind act and sank again. Ellen Culpepper explains it
all. How many of our lives are similarly divided, forced upward or
downward by events, Heaven only knows. We do not know our own souls. I
am sure John never knew of the transformation. Surely 'we are
fearfully and wonderfully made.'... The other dates and incidents are
as I have indicated.... Allow me to thank you for your kindness in
sending me the Mss., and permit me to subscribe myself,

"Yours faithfully,

"Philemon R. Ward."

CHAPTER VI

John Barclay returned to Sycamore Ridge in 1872 a full-fledged young man. He was of a slight build and rather pale of face, for five years indoors had rubbed the sunburn off. During the five years he had been absent from Sycamore Ridge he had acquired a master's degree from the state university, and a license to practise law. He was distinctly dapper, in the black and white checked trousers, the flowered cravat, and tight-fitting coat of the period; and the first Monday after he and his mother went to the Congregational Church, whereat John let out his baritone voice, he was invited to sing in the choir. Bob Hendricks came home a year before John, and with Bob and Watts McHurdie singing tenor at one end of the choir, and John and Philemon Ward holding down the other end of the line, with Mrs. Ward, Nellie Logan, Molly Culpepper, and Jane Mason of Minneola,--grown up out of short dresses in his absence,--all in gay colours between the sombre clothes of the men, the choir in the Congregational Church was worth going miles to see--if not to hear.

Now you know, of course,--or if you do not know, it is high time you were learning,--that when Fate gives a man who can sing a head of curly hair, the devil, who is after us all, quits worrying about that young person. For the Old Boy knows that a voice and curly hair are mortgages on a young man's soul that few young fellows ever pay off. Now there was neither curly head nor music in all the Barclay tribe, and when John sang "Through the trees the night winds murmur, murmur low and sweet," his mother could shut her eyes and hear Uncle Leander, the black sheep of three generations of Thatchers. So that the fact that John had something over a thousand dollars to put in General Hendricks' bank, and owned half a dozen town lots in the various additions to the town, made the mother thankful for the Grandfather Barclay's blood in him. But she saw a soul growing into the boy's face that frightened her. What others admired as strength she feared, for she knew it was ruthlessness. What others called shrewdness she, remembering his Grandfather Barclay, knew might grow into blind, cruel greed, and when she thought of his voice and his curly hair, and recalled Uncle Leander, the curly-headed, singing ne'er-do-well of her family, and then in the boy's hardening mouth and his canine jaw saw Grandfather Barclay sneering at her, she was uncertain which blood she feared most. So she managed it that John should go into partnership with General Ward, and Bob Hendricks managed it that the firm should have offices over the bank, and also that the firm was made attorneys for the bank,--the highest mark of distinction that may come to a law firm in a country town. The general realized it and was proud. But he thought the young man took it too much as a matter of course.

"John," said the general, one day, as they were dividing their first five-hundred-dollar fee, "you're a lucky dog. Everything comes so easily with you. Let me tell you something; I've figured this out: if you don't give it back some way--give it back to the world, or society, or your fellows,--or God, if you like to bunch your good luck under one head,--you're surely going to suffer for it. There is no come-easy-go-easy in this world. I've learned that much of the scheme of things."

"You mean that I've got to pay as I go, or Providence will keep books on me and foreclose?" asked John, as he stood patting the roll of bills in his trousers pocket.

"That's the idea, son," smiled the elder man.

The younger man put his hand to his chin and grinned. "I suppose," he replied, "that's why so many men keep the title to their religious proclivities in their wife's name." He went out gayly, and the elder man heard the boyish limp almost tripping down the stairs. Ward walked to the window, straightening his white tie, and stood looking into the street at the young man shaking hands and bowing and raising his hat as he went. Ward's hair was graying at the temples, and his thin smooth face was that of a man who spends many hours considering many things, and he sighed as he saw John turn a corner and disappear.

"No, Lucy, that's not it exactly," said the general that afternoon, as he brought the sprinkler full of water to the flower bed for the eighth time, and picketed little Harriet Beecher Ward out of the watermelon patch, and wheeled the baby's buggy to the four-o'clocks, where Mrs. Ward was working. "It isn't that he is conceited--the boy isn't that at all. He just seems to have too little faith in God and too much in the ability of John Barclay. He thinks he can beat the game--can take out more happiness for himself than he puts in for others."

The wife looked up and put back her sunbonnet as she said, "Yes, I believe his mother thinks something of the kind."

One of the things that surprised John when he came home from the university was the prominence of Lige Bemis in the town. When John left Sycamore Ridge to go to school, Bemis was a drunken sign-painter married to a woman who a few years before had been the scandal of half a dozen communities. And now though Mrs. Bemis was still queen only of the miserable unpainted Bemis domicile in the sunflowers at the edge of town, Lige Bemis politically was a potentate of some power. General Hendricks consulted Bemis about politics. Often he was found in the back room of the bank, and Colonel Culpepper, although he was an unterrified Democrat, in his campaign speeches referred to Bemis as "a diamond in the rough." John was sitting on a roll of leather one day in Watts McHurdie's shop talking of old times when Watts recalled the battle of Sycamore Ridge, and the time when Bemis came to town with the Red Legs and frightened Mrs. Barclay.

"Yes--and now look at him," exclaimed John, "dressed up like a gambler, and referred to in the *Banner* as 'Hon. E. W. Bemis'! How did he do it?"

McHurdie sewed two or three long stitches in silence. He leaned over from his bench to throw his tobacco quid in the sawdust box under the rusty stove, then the little man scraped his fuzzy jaw reflectively with his blackened hand as if about to speak, but he thought better of it and waxed his thread. He showed his yellow teeth in a smile, and motioned John to come closer. Then he put his head forward, and whispered confidentially:--

"What'd you ruther do or go a-fishing?"

"But why?" persisted the young man.

"Widder who?" returned Watts, grinning and putting his hand to his ear.

When John repeated his question the third time, McHurdie said:--

"I know a way you can get rich mighty quick, sonny." And when the boy refused to "bite," Watts went on: "If any one asks you what Watts McHurdie thinks about politics so long as he is in the harness business, you just take the fellow upstairs, and pull down the curtain, and lock the door, and tell him you don't know, and not to tell a living soul."

With Bob Hendricks, John had little better success in solving the mystery of the rise of Bemis. "Father says he's effective, and he would rather have him for him than against him," was the extent of Bob's explanation.

Ward's answer was more to the point. He said: "Lige Bemis is a living example of the power of soft soap in politics. We know--every man in this county knows--that Lige Bemis was a horse thief before the war, and that he was a cattle thief and a camp-follower during the war; and after the war we know what he was--he and the woman he took up with. Yet here he has been a member of the legislature and is beginning to be a figure in state politics,--at least the one to whom the governor and all the fellows write when they want information about this county. Why? I'll tell you: because he's committed every crime and can't denounce one and goes about the country extenuating things and oiling people up with his palaver. Now he says he is a lawyer--yes, sir, actually claims to be a lawyer, and brought his diploma into court two years ago, and they accepted it. But I know, and the court knows, and the bar knows it was forged; it belonged to his dead brother back in Hornellsville, New York. But Hendricks downstairs said we needed Lige in the county-seat case, so he is a member of the bar, taking one hundred per cent for collecting accounts for Eastern people, and giving the country a black eye. A man told me he was on over fifty notes for people at the bank; he signs with every one, and Hendricks never bothers him. He managed to get into all the lodges, right after the war when they were reorganized, and he sits up with the sick, and is pall-bearer--regular professional pall-bearer, and I don't doubt gets a commission for selling coffins from Livingston." Ward rose from the table his full six feet and put his hands in his pocket and stretched his legs as he added, "And when you think how many Bemises in the first, second, or third degree there are in this government, you wonder if the Democrats weren't right when they declared the war was a failure."

The general spoke as he did to John partly in anger and partly because he thought the youth needed the lesson he was trying to implant. "You know, Martin," explained the general, a few days later, to Colonel Culpepper, "John has come home a Barclay--not a Barclay of his father's stripe. He has taken back, as they say. It's old Abijah--with the mouth and jaw of a wolf. I caught him palavering with a juror the other day while we had a case trying."

The colonel rested his hands on his knees a moment in meditation and smiled as he replied: "Still, there's his mother, General. Don't ever forget that the boy's mother is Mary Barclay; she has bred most of the wolf out of him. And in the end her blood will tell."

And now observe John Barclay laying the footing stones of his fortune. He put every dollar he could get into town lots, paying for all he bought and avoiding mortgages. Also he joined Colonel Culpepper in putting the College Heights upon the market. "For what," explained the colonel, when the propriety of using the name for his addition was questioned, when no college was there nor any prospect of a college for years to come--"what is plainer to the prophetic eye than that time will bring to this magnificent city an institution of learning worthy of our hopes? I have noticed," added the colonel, waving his cigar broadly about him, "that learning is a shy goddess; she has to be coaxed--hence on these empyrean heights we have provided for a seat of learning; therefore College Heights. Look at the splendid vista, the entrancing view, in point of fact." It was the large white plumes dancing in the colonel's prophetic eyes. So it happened that more real estate buyers than clients came to the office of Ward and Barclay. But as the general that fall had been out of the office running for Congress on the Greeley ticket, still protesting against the crime of paying the soldiers in paper and the bondholders in gold, he did not miss the clients, and as John saw to it that there was enough law business to keep Mrs. Ward going, the general returned from the canvass overwhelmingly beaten, but not in the least dismayed; and as Jake Dolan put it, "The general had his say and the people had their choice so both are happy."

As the winter deepened John and Colonel Culpepper planted five hundred elm trees on the campus on College Heights, lining three broad avenues leading from the town to the campus with the trees. John rode into the woods and picked the trees, and saw that each one was properly set. And the colonel noticed that the finest trees were on Ellen Avenue and spoke of it to Mrs. Culpepper, who only said, "Yes, pa--that's just like him." And the colonel looked puzzled. And when the colonel added, "They say he is shining up to that Mason girl from Minneola, that comes here with Molly," his wife returned, "Yes, I expected that sooner than now." The colonel gave the subject up. The ways of women were past his finding out. But Mrs. Culpepper had heard Jane Mason sing a duet in church with John Barclay, and the elder woman had heard in the big contralto voice of the girl something not meant for the preacher. And Mrs. Culpepper heard John answer it, so she knew what he did not know, what Jane Mason did not know, and what only Molly Culpepper suspected, and Bob Hendricks scoffed at.

As for John, he said to Bob: "I know why you always want me to go over with you and Molly to get the Mason girl--by cracky, I'm the only fellow in town that will let you and Molly have the back seat coming home without a fuss! No, Robbie--you don't fool your Uncle John." And so when there was to be special music at the church, or when any other musical event was expected, John and Bob would get a two-seated buggy, and drive to Minneola and bring the soloist back with them. And there would be dances and parties, and coming from Minneola and going back there would be much singing. "The fox is on the hill, I hear him calling still," was a favourite, but "Come where the lilies bloom" rent the midnight air between the rival towns many times that winter and spring of '73. And never once did John try to get the back seat. But there came a time when Bob Hendricks told him that Molly told him that Jane had said that Molly and Bob were pigs--never to do any of the driving. And the next time there was a trip to Minneola, John said as the young people were seated comfortably for the return trip, "Molly, I heard you said that I was a pig to do all the driving, and not let you and Bob have a chance. Was that true?"

"No--but do you want to know who did say it?" answered Molly, and Jane Mason looked straight ahead and cut in with, "Molly Culpepper, if you say another word, I'll never speak to you as long as I live." But she glanced down at Barclay, who caught her eye and saw the smile she was swallowing, and he cried: "I don't believe you ever said it, Molly,--it must have been some one else." And when they had all had their say,--all but Jane Mason,--John saw that she was crying, and the others had to sing for ten minutes without her, before they could coax away her temper. And crafty as he was, he did not know it was temper--he thought it was something entirely different.

For the craft of youth always is clumsy. The business of youth is to fight and to mate. Wherever there is young blood, there is "boot and horse," and John Barclay in his early twenties felt in him the call for combat. It came with the events that were forming about him. For the war between the states had left the men restless and unsatisfied who had come into the plain to make their homes. They had heard and followed in their youth the call John Barclay was hearing, and after the war was over, they were still impatient with the obstacles they found in their paths. So Sycamore Ridge and Minneola, being rival towns, had to fight. The men who made these towns knew no better settlement than the settlement by force. And even during his first six months at home from school, when John sniffed the battle from afar, he was glad in his soul that the fight was coming. Sycamore Ridge had the county-seat; but Minneola, having a majority of the votes in the county, was trying to get the county-seat, and the situation grew so serious for Sycamore Ridge that General Hendricks felt it necessary to defeat Philemon Ward for the state senate so that Sycamore Ridge could get a law passed that would prevent Minneola's majority from changing the county-seat. This was done by a law which Hendricks secured, giving the county commissioners the right to build a court-house by direct levy, without a vote of the people,--a court-house so large that it would settle the county-seat matter out of hand.

The general, however, took no chances even with his commissioners. For
he had his son elected as one, and with the knowledge that John was
investing in real estate in the Ridge and had an eye for the main
chance, the general picked John for the other commissioner. The place
was on the firing-line of the battle, and John took it almost
greedily. As the spring of '73 opened, there were alarms and rumours
of strife on every breeze, and youth was happy and breathed the fight
into its nostrils like a balsam. For all the world of Sycamore Ridge
was young then, and all the trees were green in the eyes of the men
who kept up the town. Each town had its hired desperadoes, and there
were pickets about each village, and drills in the streets of the two
towns, and a martial spirit all over the county. And as John limped
about his tasks in those stirring spring days, he felt that he was
coming into his own. But it was all a curious mock combat,--that
between the towns,--for though the pickets drilled, and the bad men
swaggered on the streets, and the bullies roared their anathemas, the
social relations between the towns were not seriously disturbed.
Youths and maidens came from Minneola to the Ridge for parties and
dances, and from the Ridge young men went to Minneola to weddings and
festivals of a social nature unmolested, for it takes a real war--and
sometimes more than that--to put a bar across the mating ground of
youth. So Bob and Molly and John drove to Minneola time and again for
Jane Mason, and other boys and girls came and went from town to town,
while the bitterness and the bickering and the mimic war between the
rival communities went on.

Dolan was made sheriff, and Bemis county attorney, and with those two
officers and a majority of the county commissioners the Ridge had the
forces of administration with her. And so one night Minneola came with
her wrinkled front of war; viz., forty fighting men under Gabriel
Carnine and an ox team, prepared to take the county records by force
and haul them home by main strength. But Lycurgus Mason, whose wife

had locked him in the cellar that night to keep him from danger, was the cackling goose that saved Rome; for when, having escaped his wife's vigilance, he came riding down the wind from Minneola to catch up with his fellow-townsmen, his clatter aroused the men of the Ridge, and they hurried to the court-house and greeted the invaders with half a thousand armed men in the court-house yard. And in a crisis where craft and cunning would not help him, courage came out of John Barclay's soul for the first time and into his life as he limped through the guns into the open to explain to the men from Minneola when they finally arrived that Lycurgus Mason had not betrayed them, but had rushed into the town, thinking his friends were there ahead of him. It was a plucky thing for John to do, considering that his death would stop the making of the levy for the court-house that was to be recorded in a few days. But the young man's blood tingled with joy as he jumped the court-house fence and went back to his men. There was something like a smile from Jane Mason in his joy, but chiefly it was the joy that youth has in daring, that thrilled him. And the next day, or perhaps it was the next,--at any rate, it was a Sunday late in June,--when an armed posse from Minneola came charging down on the town at noon, John ran from his office unseen, over the roofs of buildings upon which as a boy he had romped, and ducking through a second-story window in Frye's store, got two kegs of powder, ran out of the back door, under the exposed piling supporting the building, put the two kegs of powder in a wooden culvert under the ammunition wagons of the Minneola men, who were battling with the town in the street, and taking a long fuse in his teeth, crawled back to the alley, lit the fuse, and ran into the street to look into the revolver of J. Lord Lee--late of the Red Legs--and warn him to run or be blown up with the wagons. And when the explosion came, knocking him senseless, he woke up a hero, with the town bending over him, and Minneola's forces gone.

And so John and the town had their fling together. And we who sit among our books or by our fire--or if not that by our iron radiator exuding its pleasance and comfort--should not sniff at that day when blood pulsed quicker and joy was keener, and life was more vivid than it is to-day.

Thirty-five years later--in August, 1908, to be exact--the general, in his late seventies, sat in McHurdie's harness shop while the poet worked at his bench. On the floor beside the general was the historical edition of the Sycamore Ridge **Banner**--rather an elaborate affair, printed on glossy paper and bedecked with many photogravures of old scenes and old faces. A page of the paper was devoted to the County Seat War of '73. The general had furnished the material for most of the article,--though he would not do the writing,--and he held the sheet with the story upon it in his hand. As he read it in the light of that later day, it seemed a sordid story of chicanery and violence--the sort of an episode that one would expect to find following a great war. The general read and reread the old story of the defeat of Minneola, and folded his paper and rolled it into a wand with which he conjured up his spirit of philosophy. "Heigh-ho," he sighed. "We don't know much, do we?"

McHurdie made no reply. He bent closely over his work, and the general went on: "I was mighty mad when Hendricks defeated me for the state senate in '72, just to get that law passed cheating Minneola out of a fair vote on the court-house question. But it's come out all right."

The harness maker sewed on, and the general reflected. Finally the little man at the bench turned his big dimmed eyes on his visitor, and asked, "Did you think, General, that you knew more than the Lord about making things come out right?" There was no reply and McHurdie continued, "Well, you don't--I've got that settled in my mind."

There was silence for a time, and Ward kept beating his leg with the paper wand in his hand. "Watts," said the general, finally, "I know what it was--it was youth. John Barclay had to go through that period. He had to fight and wrangle and grapple with life as he did. Do you remember that night the Minneola fellows came up with their ox team and their band of killers to take the county records--" and there was more of it--the old story of the town's wild days that need not be recorded, and in the end, in answer to some query from the general on John's courage, Watts replied, "John was always a bold little fice--he never lacked brass."

"Was he going with Jane Mason then, Watts,--I forget?" queried the general.

"Yes--yes," replied McHurdie. "Don't you remember that very next night she sang in the choir--well, John had brought her over from Minneola two days before, and that Sunday when the little devil went in the culvert across Main Street and blew up the Minneola wagons, Jane was in town that day--I remember that; and man--man--I heard her voice say things to him in the duet that night that she would have been ashamed to put in words."

The two old men were silent. "That was youth, too, Watts,--fighting and loving, and loving and fighting,--that's youth," sighed the general.

"Well, Johnnie got his belly full of it in his day, as old Shakespeare says, Phil--and in your day you had yours, too. Every dog, General--every dog--you know." The two voices were silent, as two old men looked back through the years.

McHurdie put the strap he was working upon in the water, and turned with his spectacles in his hands to his comrade. "Maybe it's this way: with a man, it's fighting and loving before we get any sense; and with

a town it's the same way, and I guess with the race it's the same
way--fighting and loving and growing sensible after it's over. Maybe
so--maybe so, Phil, comrade, but man, man," he said as he climbed on
his bench, "it's fine to be a fool!"

CHAPTER VII

In Sycamore Ridge every one knows Watts McHurdie, and every one takes
pride in the fact that far and wide the Ridge is known as Watts
McHurdie's town, and this too in spite of the fact that from Sycamore
Ridge Bob Hendricks gained his national reputation as a reformer and
the further fact that when the Barclays went to New York or Chicago or
to California for the winter in their private car, they always
registered from Sycamore Ridge at the great hotels. One would think
that the town would be known more as Hendricks' town or Barclay's
town; but no--nothing of the kind has happened, and when the rich and
the great go forth from the Ridge, people say: "Oh, yes, Sycamore
Ridge--that's Watts McHurdie's town, who wrote--" but people from
the Ridge let the inquirers get no farther; they say: "Exactly--it's
Watts McHurdie's town--and you ought to see him ride in the open
hack with the proprietor of a circus when it comes to the Ridge and
all the bands and the calliope are playing Watts' song. The way the
people cheer shows that it is really Watts McHurdie's town." So when
Colonel Martin Culpepper wrote the "Biography of Watts McHurdie" which
was published together with McHurdie's "Complete Poetical and
Philosophical Works," there was naturally much discussion, and the

town was more or less divided as to what part of the book was the best. But the old settlers,--those who, during the drouth of '60, ate mince pies with pumpkins as the fruit and rabbit meat as the filling and New Orleans black-strap as the sweetening, the old settlers who knew Watts before he became famous,--they like best of all the chapters in the colonel's Biography the one entitled "At Hymen's Altar." And here is a curious thing about it: in that chapter there is really less of Watts and considerably more of Colonel Martin Culpepper than in any other chapter.

But the newcomers, those who came in the prosperous days of the 70's or 80's, never could understand the partiality of the old settlers for the "Hymen's Altar" chapter. Lycurgus Mason also always took the view that the "Hymen" chapter was drivel.

"Now, John, be sensible--" Lycurgus insisted one night in 1903 when the two were eating supper in Barclay's private car on a side-track in Arizona; "don't be like my wife--she always drools over that chapter, too. But you know my wife--" Lycurgus always referred to Mrs. Mason with a grand gesture as to his dog or his horse, which were especially desirable chattels. "My wife,--it's just like a woman,--she sits and reads that, and laughs and weeps, and giggles and sniffs, and I say, 'What's the matter with you, anyway?'"

John Barclay pushed a button. To the porter he said, "Bring me that little red book in my satchel." The book had been published but a few weeks, and John always carried a copy around with him in those days to give to a friend. When the porter brought the book, Barclay read aloud, "Ah, truly hath the poet said, 'Marriages are made in heaven.'"

But Lycurgus Mason pulled his napkin from under his chin and moved back from the table, dusting the crumbs from his obviously Sunday clothes. "There you go--that's it; 'as the poet says.' John, if you

heard that 'as the poet says' as often as I do--" He could not finish
the figure. But he sniffed out his disgust with "as the poet says."
"It wasn't so bad when we were in the hotel, and she was busy with
something else. But now--but now--" he repeated it the third time,
"but now--honest, every time that woman goes to get up a paper for
the Hypatia Club, she gets me in the parlour, and rehearses it to me,
and the dad-binged thing is simply packed full of 'as the poet
sayses.' And about that marriages being made in heaven, I tell my wife
this: I say, 'Maybe so, but if they are, I know one that was made on a
busy day when the angels were thinking of something else.'"

And John Barclay, who knew Mrs. Mason and knew Lycurgus, knew that he
would as soon think of throwing a bomb at the President as to say such
a thing to her; so John asked credulously: "You did? Well, well! Say,
what did she say to that?"

"That's it--" responded Lycurgus. "That's it. What could she say? I
had her." He walked the length of the room proudly, with his hands
thrust into his pockets.

Barclay moved his chair to the rear of the car, where he sat smoking
and looking into the clear star-lit heavens above the desert. And his
mind went back thirty years to the twilight in June after he had set
off the powder keg in the culvert under Main Street in Sycamore Ridge,
and he tried to remember how Jane Mason got over from Minneola--did
he bring her over the day before, or was she visiting at the
Culpeppers', or did she come over that day? It puzzled him, but he
remembered well that in the Congregational choir he and Jane sang a
duet in an anthem, "He giveth his beloved sleep." And he hummed the
old aria, a rather melancholy tune, as he sat on the car platform in
Arizona that night, and her voice came back--a deep sweet contralto
that took "G" below middle "C" as clearly as a tenor, and in her lower
register there was a passion and a fire that did not blaze in the

higher notes. For those notes were merely girlish and untrained. That June night in '73 was the first night that he and Jane Mason ever had lagged behind as they walked up the hill with Bob and Molly. And what curious things stick in the memory! The man on the rear of the car remembered that as they left the business part of Main Street behind and walked up the hill, they came to a narrow cross-walk, a single stone in width, and that they tried to walk upon it together, and that his limp made him jostle her, and she said, "We mustn't do that."

"What?" he inquired.

"Oh--you know--walk on one stone. You know what it's a sign of."

"Do you believe in signs?" he asked. She kept hold of his arm, and kept him from leaving the stone. She was taller than he by a head, and he hated himself for it. They managed to keep together until they crossed the street and came into the broader walk. Then she drew a relieved breath and answered: "Oh, I don't know. Sometimes I do." They were lagging far behind their friends, and the girl hummed a tune, then she said, "You know I've always believed in my 'Star light--star bright--first star I've seen to-night,' just as I believe in my prayers." And she looked up and said, "Oh, I haven't said it yet." She picked out her star and said the rhyme, closing with, "I wish I may, I wish I might, have the wish I wish to-night."

And sitting on the car end in Arizona thirty years after, he tried to find her star in the firmament above him. He was a man in his fifties then, and the night she showed him her star was more than thirty years gone by. But he remembered. We are curious creatures, we men, and we remember much more than we pretend to. For our mothers in many cases were women, and we take after them.

As Barclay stood in the door of his car debating whether or not to go

in, the light from the chimney of the sawmill on the hill attracted
his attention, and because he was in a mood for it, the flying sparks
trailing across the night sky reminded him of the fireworks that
Fourth of July in 1873, when he and Jane Mason and Bob and Molly spent
the day together, picnicking down in the timber and coming home to
dance on the platform under the cottonwood-bough pavilion in the
evening. It was a riotous day, and Bob and Molly being lovers of long
acceptance assumed a paternal attitude to John and Jane that was
charming in the main, but sometimes embarrassing. And of all the
chatter he only remembered that Jane said: "Think how many years these
old woods have been here--how many hundred years--maybe when the
mound-builders were here! Don't you suppose that they are used to--to
young people--oh, maybe Indian lovers, and all that, and don't you
suppose the trees see these young people loving and marrying, and
growing old and ugly and unhappy, and that they some way feel that
they are just a little tired of it all?"

If any one replied to her, he had no recollection of it, for after
that he saw the dance and heard the music, and then events seemed to
slip along without registering in his memory. There must have been the
fifth and the sixth of July in 1873, for certainly there was the
seventh, and that was Sunday; he remembered that well enough, for in
the morning there was a council in his office to discuss ways and
means for the week's work in the county-seat trouble. Tuesday was the
day which the new law designated as the one when the levy must be made
for the court-house improvements that would hold the county-seat in
Sycamore Ridge. At four o'clock, after the Sunday council, John and
Bob drove out of Sheriff Jake Dolan's stable with his best two-seated
buggy, and told him they would be back from Minneola at midnight or
thereabout after taking Jane Mason home, and the two boys drove down
Main Street with the girls, waving to every one with their hats, while
the girls waved their parasols, and the town smiled; for though all
the world loves a lover, in Sycamore Ridge it has been the custom,

since the days when Philemon Ward first took Miss Lucy out to drive, for all the town to jeer at lovers as they pass down street in buggies and carriages! And so thirty years slipped from Barclay as he stood in the doorway of his car looking at the Arizona stars. A flicker of light high up in the sky-line seemed to move. It was the headlight of a train coming over the mountain. A switchman with a lantern was passing near the car, and Barclay called to him, "Is that headlight No. 2?" And when the man affirmed Barclay's theory, he asked, "How long does it take it to get down here?"

"Oh, she comes a-humming," replied the man. "If she doesn't jump the track, she'll be down in eight minutes."

Inside the car Barclay heard a watch snap, and knew that Lycurgus Mason didn't believe anything of the kind and proposed to get at the facts. So Barclay sat down on the platform; but his mind went back to the old days, and the ride through the woods along the Sycamore that Sunday night in July came to him, with all its fragrance and stillness and sweetness. He recalled that they came into the prairie just as the meadow-lark was crying its last plaintive twilight trill, and the western sky was glowing with a rim of gold upon the tips of the clouds. The beauty of the prairie and the sky and the calm of the evening entered into their hearts, and they were silent. Then they left the prairie and went into the woods again, on the river road. And before they came out of that road into the upland, Fate turned a screw that changed the lives of all of them. For in a turn of the road, in a deep cut made by a ravine, Gabriel Carnine, making the last stand for Minneola, stepped into the path and took the horses by the bridles. The shock that John felt that night when he realized what had happened came back even across the years. And as the headlight far up in the mountain above the desert slipped into a tunnel, though it flashed out again in a few seconds, while it was gone, all the details of the kidnapping of the young people in the buggy hurried across his mind.

Even the old anxiety that he felt lest Sycamore Ridge would think him
a traitor to their cause, when they should find that he was not there
to sign the tax levy and save the court-house and the county-seat,
came back to him as he gazed at the mountain, waiting for the
headlight, and he remembered how he made a paper trail of torn bits
from a Congregational hymn-book, left in Bob's pocket from the morning
service, dropping the bits under the buggy wheels in the dust so that
the men from the Ridge would see the trail and follow the captives. In
his memory he saw Jake Dolan, who had followed the trail where it led
to Carnine's farm, come stumbling into the farm-house Tuesday where
they were hidden, and John, in memory, heard Jake whisper that he had
left his dog with the rescuing party to lead the rescuers to him if he
was on the right trail and did not return.

And then as Barclay's mind went back to the long Tuesday, when he
should have been at the Ridge to sign the tax levy, the headlight
flashed out of the tunnel. But these were fading pictures. The one
image that was in his mind--clear through all the years--was of a
wood and a tree,--a great, spreading, low-boughed elm, near Carnine's
house where the young people were held prisoners, and Jane Mason
sitting with her back against the tree, and lying on the dry grass at
her feet his own slight figure; sometimes he was looking up at her
over his brow, and sometimes his head rested on the roots of the tree
beside her, and she looked down at him and they talked, and no one was
near. For through youth into middle life, and into the dawn of old
age, That Day was marked in his life. The day of the month--he forgot
which it was. The day of the week--that also left him, and there came
a time when he had to figure back to recall the year; but for all
that, there was a radiance in his life, an hour of calm joy that never
left him, and he called it only--That Day. That Day is in every
heart; in yours, my dear fat Mr. Jones, and in yours, my good dried-up
Mrs. Smith; and in yours, Mrs. Goodman, and in yours, Mr. Badman;
maybe it is upon the sea, or in the woods, or among the noises of some

great city--but it is That Day. And no other day of all the thousands
that have come to you is like it.

Why should he remember the ugly farm-yard, the hard faces of the men,
the straw-covered frame they called a barn, and the unpainted house?
All these things passed by him unrecorded, as did the miserable fare
of the table, the hard bed at night, and the worry that must have
gnawed at his nerves to know that perhaps the town was thinking him
false to it, or that his mother, guessing the truth, was in pain with
terror, or to feel that a rescuing party coming at the wrong time
would bring on a fight in which the girls would be killed. Only the
picture of Jane Mason, fine and lithe and strong, with the pink cheeks
of twenty, and the soft curves of childhood still playing about her
chin and throat as he saw it from the ground at her feet,--that
picture was etched into his heart, and with it the recollection of her
eyes when she said, "John,--you don't think I--I knew of
this--beforehand, do you?" Just that sentence--those were the only
words left in his memory of a day's happiness. And he never heard a
locust whirring in a tree that it did not bring back the memory of the
spreading tree and the touch--the soft, quick, shy touch of her
fingers in his hair, and the fire that was in her eyes.

It was in the dusk of Tuesday evening that Jake Dolan's dog came into
the yard where the captives were, and Jake disowned him, and joined
the men who stoned the faithful creature out to the main road. But the
prisoners knew that their rescuers would follow the dog, so at supper
the three men from the Ridge sat together on a bench at the table
while Mrs. Carnine and the girls waited on the men--after the fashion
of country places in those days. Dolan managed to say under his breath
to Barclay, "It's all right--but the girls must stay in the house
to-night." And John knew that if he and Bob escaped with horses before
ten o'clock, they could reach the Ridge in time to sign the levy
before midnight. Darkness fell at eight, and a screech-owl in the wood

complained to the night. Dolan rose and stretched and yawned, and then
began to talk of going to bed, and Gabriel Carnine, whose turn it was
to sleep because he had been up two nights, shuffled off to the
straw-covered stable to lie down with the Texan who was his bunk mate,
leaving half a dozen men to guard the prisoners. An hour later the
screech-owl in the wood murmured again, this time much closer, and
Dolan rose and took off his hat and threw it in the straw beside him.
He was looking at the time anxiously toward the wood. But the next
moment from behind the barn in the opposite direction something
attracted them. It was a glare of light, and the guards noticed it at
the same time. A last year's straw stack next to the barn was afire.
Jane Mason was standing in the back door of the house, and in the
hurried blur of moving events John divined that she had slipped out
and fired the stack. In an instant there was confusion. The men were
on their feet. They must fight fire, or the barn would go. Dolan ran
with the men to the straw stack. "We'll help you," he cried. "I'll
wake Gabe." There was hurrrying for water pails. The women appeared,
crying shrilly, and in the glare that reddened the sky the yard
seemed, full of mad men racing heedlessly.

"John," whispered Jane, coming up to him as he drew water from the
well, "let me do this. There are two horses in the pasture. You and
Bob go--fly--fly." The Texan came running from the barn, which was
beginning to blaze. Dolan and Carnine still were in it. Then from the
wood back of the camp fifty men appeared, riding at a gallop. Lige
Bemis and General Ward rode in front of the troop of horsemen. Carnine
was still in the burning barn asleep, and there was no leader to give
command to the dazed guards. Ward and Bemis ran up, motioning the men
back, and Ward cried, "Shall we help you save your stock and barn, or
must we fight?" It was addressed to the crowd, but before they could
answer, Dolan stumbled out of the barn through the smoke and flames
crying, "Boys,--boys,--I can't find him." He saw the rescuing party
and shouted, "Boys,--Gabe's in there asleep and I can't find him."

The wind had suddenly veered, and the crackling flames had reached the straw roof of the barn. The fire was gaining headway, and the three buckets that were coming from the well had no effect on it. As the last horse was pulled out of the door, one side of the straw wall of the barn fell away on fire and showed Gabriel Carnine sleeping not ten feet from the flames. Lige Bemis soused his handkerchief in water, tied it over his mouth, and ran in. He grabbed the sleeping man and dragged him through, the flames; but both were afire as they came into the open.

Now in this story Elijah Westlake Bemis is not shown often in a heroic light. Yet he had in his being the making of a hero, for he was brave. And heroism, after all, is only effective reliance on some virtue in a crisis, in spite of temptations to do the easy excusable thing. And when Lige Bemis sneaks through this story in unlovely guise, remember that he has a virtue that once exalted even him.

"Gabe Carnine," said Ward, as the barn fell and there was nothing more to fear, "we didn't fire your haystack; I give you my word on that. But we are going to take these boys home now. And you better let us alone."

That John Barclay remembered, and then he remembered being in the front yard of the farm-house a moment--alone with Jane Mason, his bridle rein over his arm. IIer hair was down, and she looked wild and beautiful. The straw was still burning back of the house, and the glow was everywhere. He always remembered that she held his hand and would not let him go, and there two memories are different; for she always maintained that he did, right there and then, and he recollected that as he mounted his horse he tried to kiss her and failed. Perhaps both are right--who knows? But both agree that as he sat there an instant on his horse, she threw kisses at him and he threw them back. And when the men rode away, she stood in the road, and he could see her in the

light of the waning fire, and thirty years passed and still he saw
her.

As the headlight of the train lit up the cinder yard, and brought the
glint of the rails out of the darkness, John Barclay, a thousand miles
away and thirty years after, fancied he could see her there in the
railroad yards beside him waving her hands at him, smiling at him with
the new-found joy in her face. For there is no difference between
fifty-three and twenty-three when men are in love, and if they are in
love with the same woman in both years, her face will never change,
her smile will always seem the same. And to John Barclay there on the
rear platform of the car, with the crash of the great train in his
ears, the same face looked out of the night at him that he saw back in
his twenties, and he knew that the same prayer to the same God would
go up that night for him that went up from the same lips so long ago.
The man on the car platform rose from his chair, and went into the
car.

"Well," he said to Lycurgus Mason as the old man reached for his
watch, "how about it?"

Lycurgus replied as he put it back in his pocket, "Just seven minutes
and a half. She's covered a lot of track in those seven minutes!"

And John Barclay looked back over the years, and saw a boy riding like
the wind through the night, changing horses every half-hour, and
trying to tell time from his watch by a rising moon, but the moon was
blown with clouds like a woman's hair, and he could not see the hands
on the watch face. So as he looked at the old man sitting crooked over
in the great leather chair, John Barclay only grunted, "Yes--she's
covered a long stretch of country in those seven minutes." And he
picked the Biography off the table and read to himself: "I sometimes
think that only that part of the soul that loves is saved. The rest is

dross and perishes in the fire. Whether the love be the love of woman or the love of kind, or the love of God that embraces all, it matters not. That sanctifies; that purifies--that marks the way of the only salvation the soul can know, and he who does not love with the fervour of a passionate heart some of God's creatures, cannot love God, and not loving Him, is lost in spite of all his prayers, in spite of all his aspirations. Therefore, if you would live you must love, for when love dies the soul shrivels. And if God takes what you love--love on; for only love will make you immortal, only love will cheat death of its victory."

And looking at Lycurgus Mason fidgeting in his chair, John Barclay wondered when he would die the kind of a death that had come to the little old man before him, and then he felt the car move under him, and knew they were going back to Sycamore Ridge.

"Day after to-morrow," said Barclay, meditatively, as he heard the first faint screaming of the heavily laden wheels under him, "day after to-morrow, Daddy Mason, we will be home with Colonel Culpepper and his large white plumes."

CHAPTER VIII

This chapter might have had in it "all the quality, pride, pomp, and circumstance of glorious war" if it had not been for the matters that came up for discussion at the meeting of the Garrison County Old

Settlers' Association this year of our Lord Nineteen Hundred and Eight. For until that meeting the legend of the last hour of the County-seat War of '73 had flourished unmolested; but there General Philemon Ward rose and laid an axe at the root of the legend, and while of course he did not destroy it entirely, he left it scarred and withered on one side and therefore entirely unfitted for historical purposes. It seems that Gabriel Carnine was assigned by President John Barclay of the Association to prepare and read a paper on "The Rise, Decline, and Fall of Minneola." Certainly that was a proper subject considering the fact that corn has been growing over the site of Minneola for twenty years. And surely Gabriel Carnine, whose black beard has whitened in thirty years' faithful service to Sycamore Ridge, whose wife lies buried on the Hill, and whose children read the Sycamore Ridge *Banner* in the uttermost parts of the earth,--surely Gabriel Carnine might have been trusted to tell the truth of the conflict waged between the towns a generation ago. But men have curious works in them, and unless one has that faith in God that gives him unbounded faith in the goodness of man, one should not open men up in the back and watch the wheels go 'round. For though men are good, and in the long run what they do is God's work and is therefore acceptable, no man is perfect. There goes Lige Bemis past the post-office, now, for instance; when he was in the legislature in the late sixties, every one knows that Minneola raised twenty thousand dollars in cash and offered it to Lige if he would pretend to be sick and quit work on the Sycamore Ridge county-seat bill. He could have fooled us, and could have taken the money, which was certainly more than he could expect to get from Sycamore Ridge. Did he take it? Not at all. A million would not have tempted him. He was in that game; yet ten days after he refused the offer of Minneola, he tried to blackmail his United States senator out of fifty dollars, and sold his vote to a candidate for state printer for one hundred dollars and flashed the bill around Sycamore Ridge proudly for a week before spending it.

So Gabriel Carnine must not be blamed if in that paper on Minneola, before the Old Settlers' Association, he let out the pent-up wrath of thirty years; and also if in the discussion General Ward unsealed his lips for the first time and blighted the myth that told how a hundred Minneola men had captured the court-house yard on the night that John Barclay and Bob Hendricks rode home from their captivity to sign the tax levy. Legend has always said that Lige Bemis, riding half a mile ahead of the others that night, came to the courtyard; found it guarded by Minneola men, rode back, met John and Bob and the general crossing the bridge over the old ford of the Sycamore, and told them that they could not get into the court-house until the men came up who had ridden out to rescue the commissioners,--perhaps a quarter of an hour behind the others,--and that even then there must be a fight of doubtful issue; and further that it was after eleven o'clock, and soon would be too late to sign the levy. The forty thousand people in Garrison County have believed for thirty years that finding the court-house yard in possession of the enemy, Bemis suggested going through the cave by the Barclays' home, which had its west opening in the wall of the basement of the court-house; and furthermore, tradition has said that Bemis led John and Bob through the cave, and with crowbars and hammers they made a man-sized hole in the wall, crawled through it, mounted the basement stairs, unlocked the commissioners' room, held their meeting in darkness, and five minutes before twelve o'clock astonished the invading forces by lighting a lamp in their room, signing the levy that Bemis, as county attorney, had prepared the Sunday before, and slipping with it into the basement, through the cave and back to the troop of horsemen as they were jogging across the bridge on their way back from Carnine's farm. And here are the marks of General Ward's axe--verified by Gabriel Carnine: first, that there were no Minneola invaders in possession of the court-house, but only a dozen visitors loafing about town that night to watch developments; second, that the regular pickets were out as usual, and an invading force could not have stolen in; and third,

that Bemis knew it, but as his political fortunes were low, he rode
ahead of the others, hatched up the cock-and-bull story about the
guarded court-house, and persuaded the boys to let him lead them into
a romantic adventure that would sound well in the campaign and help to
insure his reelection the following year. In view of the general's
remarks and Gabriel Carnine's corroborative statement, and in view of
the bitterness with which Carnine assailed the whole Sycamore Ridge
campaign, how can a truthful chronicler use the episode at all?
History is a fickle goddess, and perhaps Pontius Pilate, being human
and used to human errors and human weakness, is not so much to blame
for asking, "What is truth?" and then turning away before he had the
answer.

Walking home from the meeting through Mary Barclay Park, Barclay's
mind wandered back to the days when he won his first important
lawsuit--the suit brought by Minneola to prevent the collection of
taxes under the midnight levy to build the court-house. It was that
lawsuit which brought him to the attention of the legal department of
the Fifth Parallel Railroad Company, and his employment by that
company to defeat the bonds of its narrow-gauged competitor, that was
seeking entrance into Garrison County, was the beginning of his
career. And in that fight to defeat the narrow-gauged railroad, the
people of Garrison County learned something of Barclay as well. He and
Bemis went over the county together,--the little fox and the old
coyote, the people called them,--and where men were for sale, Bemis
bought them, and where they were timid, John threatened them, and
where they were neither, both John and Bemis fought with a ferocity
that made men hate but respect the pair. And so though the Fifth
Parallel Railroad never came to the Ridge, its successor, the Corn
Belt Road, did come, and in '74 John spoke in every schoolhouse in the
county, urging the people to vote the bonds for the Corn Belt Road,
and his employment as local attorney for the company marked his first
step into the field of state politics. For it gave him a railroad

pass, and brought him into relations with the men who manipulated state affairs; also it made him a silent partner of Lige Bemis in Garrison County politics.

But even when he was county commissioner, less than two dozen years old, he was a force in Sycamore Ridge, and there were days when he had four or five thousand dollars to his credit in General Hendricks' bank. The general used to look over the daily balances and stroke his iron-gray beard and say: "Robert, John is doing well to-day. Son, I wish you had the acquisitive faculty. Why don't you invest something and make something?" But Bob Hendricks was content to do his work in the bank, and read at home one night and slip over to the Culpeppers' the next night, and so long as the boy was steady and industrious and careful, his father had no real cause for complaint, and he knew it. But the town knew that John was getting on in the world. He owned half of Culpepper's second addition, and his interest in College Heights was clear; he never dealt in equities, but paid cash and gave warranty deeds for what he sold. It was believed around the Ridge that he could "clean up," for fifteen or twenty thousand dollars, and when he called Mrs. Mason of the Mason House, Minneola, into the dining room one afternoon to talk over a little matter with her, he found her most willing. It was a short session. After listening and punctuating his remarks with "of courses" and "yeses" and "so's," Mrs. Mason's reply was:--

"Of course, Mr. Barclay,"--the Mr. Barclay he remembered as the only time in his life he ever had it from her,--"of course, Mr. Barclay, that is a matter rather for you and Mr. Mason to settle. You know," she added, folding her hands across her ample waist, "Mr. Mason is the head of the house!" Then she lifted her voice, perhaps fearing that matters might be delayed. "Oh, pa!" she cried. "Pa! Come in here, please. There's a gentleman to see you."

Lycurgus Mason came in with a tea towel in his hands and an apron on.
He heard John through in a dazed way, his hollow eyes blinking with
evident uncertainty as to what was expected of him. When Barclay was
through, the father looked at the mother for his cue, and did not
speak for a moment. Then he faltered: "Why, yes,--yes,--I see! Well,
ma, what--" And at the cloud on her brow Lycurgus hesitated again,
and rolled his apron about his hands nervously and finally said,
"Oh--well--whatever you and her ma think will be all right with me,
I guess." And having been dismissed telepathically, Lycurgus hurried
back to his work.

It was when John Barclay was elected President of the Corn Belt
Railway, in the early nineties, that Lycurgus told McHurdie and Ward
and Culpepper and Frye, as the graybeards wagged around the big brown
stove in the harness shop one winter day: "You know ma, she never saw
much in him, and when I came in the room she was about to tell him he
couldn't have her. Now, isn't that like a woman?--no sense about men.
But I says: 'Ma, John Barclay's got good blood in him. His grandpa
died worth a million,--and that was a pile of money for them days;'
so I says, 'If Jane Mason wants him, ma,' I says, 'let her have him.
Remember what a fuss your folks made over me getting you,' I says;
'and see how it's turned out.' Then I turned to John--I can see the
little chap now a-standing there with his dicky hat in his hand and
his pipe-stem legs no bigger than his cane, and his gray eyes lookin'
as wistful as a dog's when you got a bone in your hand, and I says,
'Take her along, John; take her along and good luck go with you,' I
says; 'but,' I says, 'John Barclay, I want you always to remember Jane
Mason has got a father.' Just that way I says. I tell you, gentlemen,
there's nothing like having a wife that respects you." The crowd in
the harness shop wagged their heads, and Lycurgus went on: "Now, they
ain't many women that would just let a man stand up like that and, as
you may say, give her daughter right away under her nose. But my wife,
she's been well trained."

In the pause that followed, Watts McHurdie's creaking lever was the only sound that broke the silence. Then Watts, who had been sewing away at his work with waving arms, spoke, after clearing his throat, "I've heard many say that she was sich." And the old man cackled, and it became a saying-among them and in the town.

One who goes back over the fifty years that have passed since Sycamore Ridge became a local habitation and a name finds it difficult to realize that one-third of its life was passed before the panic of '78, which closed the Hendricks' bank. For those first nineteen years passed as the life of a child passes, so that they seem only sketched in; yet to those who lived at all, to those like Watts McHurdie and Philemon Ward, who now pass their happiest moments mooning over tilted headstones in the cemetery on the Hill, those first nineteen years seem the longest and the best. And that fateful year of '73 to them seems the most portentous. For then, perhaps for the first time, they realized the cruel uncertainty of the struggle for existence. With the terrible drouth of '60 this realization did not come; for the town was young, and the people were young; only Ezra Lane was a graybeard in all the town in the sixties; and youth is so sure; there is no hazard under thirty. In the war they fought and marched and sang and starved and died, and were still young. But when the financial panic of '73 spread its dread and its trouble over the land, youth in Sycamore Ridge was gone; it was manhood that faced these things in the Ridge, and manhood had cares, had given hostages to fortune, and life was serious and hard; and big on the horizon was the fear of failure. General Hendricks swayed in the panic of '73; and the time marked him, took the best of the light from his eye, and put the slightest perceptible hobble on his feet. To Martin Culpepper and Watts McHurdie and Philemon Ward and Jacob Dolan and Oscar Fernald, the panic came in their late thirties and early forties, a flash of lightning that prophesied the coming of the storm and stress of an inexorable fate.

The wedding of John Barclay and Jane Mason occurred in September, 1873, two days after he had stood on the high stone steps of the Exchange National Bank and made a speech to the crowd, telling them he was the largest depositor in the bank, and begging them to stop the run. But the run did not stop, and the day before John's wedding the bank did not open; the short crop and the panic in the East were more than Garrison County people could stand. But all the first day of the bank's closing and all the next day John worked among the people, reassuring them. So that it was five o'clock in the evening before he could start to Minneola for his wedding.

And such a wedding! One would say that when hard times were staring every one in the face, social forms would be observed most simply. But one would say so without reckoning with Mrs. Lycurgus Mason. As the groom and the bridesmaid and best man rode up from Sycamore Valley, two miles from Minneola, in the early falling dusk that night, the Mason House loomed through the darkness, lighted up like a steamboat. "You'll have to move along, John," said Bob Hendricks; "I think I heard her whistle."

On the sidewalk in front of the hotel they met Mrs. Mason in her black silk with a hemstitched linen apron over it. She ushered them into the house, took them to their rooms, and whirled John around on a pivot, it seemed to him, with her interminable directions. His mother, who had come over to Minneola the day before, came to his room and quieted her son, and as he got ready for what he called the "ordeal," he could hear Mrs. Mason swinging doors below stairs, walking on her heels through the house, receiving belated guests from Sycamore Ridge and the country,--for the whole county had been invited,--and he heard her carrying out a dog that had sneaked into the dining room.

The groom missed the bride, and as he was tying his necktie,--which reminded him of General Ward by its whiteness,--he wondered why she did not come to him. He did not know that she was a prisoner in her room, while all the young girls in Sycamore Ridge and Minneola were looking for pins and hooking her up and stepping on each other's skirts. For one wedding is like all weddings--whether it be in the Mason House, Minneola, or in Buckingham Palace. And some there are who marry for love in Minneola, and some for money, and some for a home, and some for Heaven only knows what, just as they do in the chateaux and palaces and mansions. And the groom is nobody and the bride is everything, as it was in the beginning and as it shall be ever after. Probably poor Adam had to stand behind a tree neglected and alone, while Lilith and girls from the land of Nod bedecked Eve for the festivities. Men are not made for ceremonies. And so at all the formal occasions of this life--whether it be among the great or among the lowly, in the East or the West, at weddings, christenings, and funerals--man hides in shame and leaves the affairs to woman, who leads him as an ox, even a muzzled ox, that treadeth out the corn. "The doomed man," whispered John to Bob as the two in their black clothes stood at the head of the stair that led into the parlour of the Mason House that night, waiting for the wedding march to begin on the cabinet organ, "ate a hearty supper, consisting of beefsteak and eggs, and after shaking hands with his friends he mounted the gallows with a firm step!"

Then he heard the thud of the music book on the organ, the creak of the treadle,--and when he returned to consciousness he was Mrs. Mason's son-in-law, and proud of it. And she,--bless her heart and the hearts of all good women who give up the joy of their lives to us poor unworthy creatures,--she stood by the wax-flower wreath under the glass case on the whatnot in the corner, and wept into her real lace handkerchief, and wished with all the earnestness of her soul that she could think of some way to let John know that his trousers leg was wrinkled over his left shoe top. But she could not solve the

problem, so she gave herself up to the consolation of her tears. Yet
it should be set down to her credit that when the preacher's amen was
said, hers was the first head up, and while the others were rushing
for the happy pair she was in the kitchen with her apron on dishing up
the wedding supper. Well might the Sycamore Ridge **Weekly Banner**
declare that the "tables groaned with good things." There were not
merely a little piddling dish of salad, a bite of cake, and a dab of
ice-cream. There were turkey and potatoes and vegetables and fruit and
bread and cake and pudding and pie--four kinds of pie, mark you--and
preserves, and "Won't you please, Mrs. Culpepper, try some of that
piccalilli?" and "Oh, Mrs. Ward, if you just would have a slice of
that fruit cake," and "Now, General,--a little more of the gravy for
that turkey dressing--it is such a long ride home," or "Colonel, I
know you like corn bread, and I made this myself as a special
compliment to Virginia."

And through it all the bride sat watching the door--looking always
through the crowd for some one. Her face was anxious and her heart was
clouded, and when the guests had gone and the house was empty, she
left her husband and slipped out of the back door. There, after the
glare of the lamps had left her eyes, she saw a little man walking
with his head down, out near the barn, and she ran to him and threw
her arms about him and kissed him, and when she led Lycurgus Mason,
who was all washed and dressed, back through the kitchen to her
husband, John saw that the man's eyelids were red, and that on the
starched cuffs were the marks of tears. For to him she was only his
little girl, and John afterward knew that she was the only friend he
had in the world. "Oh, father, why didn't you come in?" cried the
daughter. "I missed you so!" The man blinked a moment at the lights
and looked toward his wife, who was busy at a table, as he said: "Who?
Me?" and then added: "I was just lookin' after their horses. I was
coming in pretty soon. You oughtn't to bother about me. Well, John,"
he smiled, as he put out his hand, "the seegars seems to be on

you--as the feller says." And John put his arm about Lycurgus Mason, as they walked out of the kitchen, and Jane reached for her gingham apron. Then life began for Mr. and Mrs. John Barclay in earnest.

CHAPTER IX

Forty thousand words--and that is the number we have piled up in this story--is a large number of words to string together without a heroine. That is almost as bad as the dictionary, in which He and She are always hundreds of pages apart and never meet,--not even in the "Z's" at the end,--which is why the dictionary is so unpopular, perhaps. But this is the story of a man, and naturally it must have many heroines. For you know men--they are all alike! First, Mrs. Mary Barclay was a heroine--you saw her face, strong and clean and sharply chiselled with a great purpose; then Miss Lucy--black-eyed, red-cheeked, slender little Miss Lucy--was a heroine, but she married General Ward; and then Ellen Culpepper was a heroine, but she fluttered out of the book into the sunlight, and was gone; and then came Jane Mason,--and you have seen her girlish beauty, and you will see it develop into gentle womanhood; but the real heroine,--of the real story,--you have not seen her face. You have heard her name, and have seen her moving through these pages with her back consciously turned to you--for being a shy minx, she had no desire to intrude until she was properly introduced. And now we will whirl her around that you may have a good look at her.

Let us begin at the ground: as to feet--they are not too small--say three and a half in size. And they support rather short legs--my goodness, of course she has legs--did you think her shoes were pinned to her over-skirt? Her legs carry around a plump body,--not fat--why, certainly not--who ever heard of a fat heroine (the very best a heroine can do for comfort is to be plump)--and so beginning the sentence over again, being a plump little body, there is a neck to account for--a neck which we may look at, but which is so exquisite that it would be hardly polite to consider it in terms of language. Only when we come to the chin that tips the oval of the face may we descend to language, and even then we must rise and flick the red mouth with, but a passing word. But this much must be plainly spoken. The nose does turn up--not much--but a little (Bob used to say, just to be good and out of the way)! That, however, is mere personal opinion, and of little importance here. But the eyes are brown--reddish brown, with enough white at the corners to make them seem liquid; only liquid is not the word. For they are radiant--remember that word, for we may come back to it, after we are done with the brow--a wide brow--low enough for Dickens and Thackeray and Charlotte Bronte, and for Longfellow and Whittier and Will Carleton in his day, and high enough for Tennyson at the temples, but not so high but that the gate of the eyes has to shut wearily when Browning would sail through the current of her soul. As to hair--Heaven knows there is plenty of that, but it had rather a checkered career. As she clung to her mother's apron and waved her father away to war, she was a tow-headed little tot, and when he came back from the field of glory he thought he could detect a tendency to red in it, but the fire smouldered and went out, and the hair turned brown--a dark brown with the glint of the quenched fires in it when it blew in the sun. Now frame a glowing young face in that soft waving hair, and you have a picture that will speak, and if the picture should come to life and speak as it was in the year of our Lord 1873, the first word of all the words in the big fat dictionary it would utter would be Bob. And so you may lift up your face and take your name and place in this story--Molly Culpepper, heroine.

And when you lift your face, we may see something more than its pretty features: we shall see a radiant soul. For scientists have found out that every material thing in this universe gives off atomic particles of itself, and some elements are more radiant than others. And there is a paralleling quality in the spiritual world, and some souls give off more of their colour and substance than others, though what it is they radiate we do not know. Even the scientists do not know the material things that the atoms radiate, so why should we be asked to define the essence of souls? Yet from the soul of Molly Culpepper, in joy and in sorrow, in her moments of usefulness and in her deepest woe, her soul glowed and shed its glory, and she grew even as she gave her substance to the world about her. For that is the magic of God's mystery of life.

And now having for the moment finished our discussion on the radio-activity of souls, let us go back to the story.

Mary Barclay rode home from her son's wedding that night with Bob Hendricks and Molly Culpepper. They were in a long line of buggies that began to scatter out and roam across fields to escape the dust of the roads. "Well," said Mrs. Barclay, as they pulled up the bank of the Sycamore for home, "I suppose it will be you and Molly next, Bob?"

It was Molly who replied: "Yes. It is going to be Thanksgiving."

"Well, why not?" asked Mrs. Barclay.

"Oh--they all seem to think we shouldn't, don't you know, Mrs. Barclay--with all this hard times--and the bank closing. And hasn't John told you of the plan he's worked out for Bob to go to New York this winter?"

The buggy was nearing the Barclay home. Mrs. Barclay answered, "No," and the girl went on.

"Well, it's a big wheat land scheme--and Bob's to go East and sell the stock. They worked it out last night after the bank closed. He'll tell you all about it."

Mrs. Barclay was standing by the buggy when the girl finished. The elder woman bade the young people good night, and turned and went into the yard and stood a moment looking at the stars before going into her lonely house. The lovers let the tired horses lag up the hill, and as they turned into Lincoln Avenue the girl was saying: "A year's so long, Bob,--so long. And you'll be away, and I'm afraid." He tried to reassure her; but she protested: "You are all my life,--big boy,--all my life. I was only fourteen, just a little girl, when you came into my life, and all these long seven years you are the only human being that has been always in my heart. Oh, Bob, Bob,--always."

What a man says to his sweetheart is of no importance. Men are so circumscribed in their utterances--so tongue-tied in love. They all say one thing; so it need not be set down here what Bob Hendricks said. It was what the king said to the queen, the prince to the princess, the duke to the lady, the gardener to the maid, the troubadour to his dulcinea. And Molly Culpepper replied, "When are you going, Bob?"

The young man picked up the sagging lines to turn out for Watts McHurdie's buggy. He had just let Nellie Logan out at the Wards', where she lived. After a "Hello, Watts; getting pretty late for an old man like you," Hendricks answered: "Well, you know John--when he gets a thing in his head he's a regular tornado. There was an immense crowd in town to-day--depositors and all that. And do you know, John went out this afternoon with a paper in his hand, and five hundred dollars he dug out of his safe over in the office, and he got options to lease their land for a year signed up by the owners of five thousand acres of the best wheat land in Garrison County. He wants twenty thousand acres, and pretty well bunched down in Pleasant and Spring townships, and I'm going in four days." The young man was full of the scheme. He went on: "John's a wonder, Molly,--a perfect wonder. He's got grit. Father wouldn't have been able to stand up under this--but John has braced him, and has cheered up the people, and I believe, before the week is out, we will be able to get nearly all the depositors to agree to leave their money alone for a year, and then only take it out on thirty days' notice. And if we can get that, we can open up by the first of the month. But I've got to go on to Washington to see if I can arrange that with the comptroller of the currency."

They were standing at the Culpepper gate as he spoke. A light in the upper windows showed that the parents were in. Buchanan came ambling along the walk and went through the gate between them without speaking. When he had closed the door, the girl came close to her lover. He took her in his arms, and cried, "Oh, darling,--only four more days together." He paused, and in the starlight she saw on his face more than words could have told her of his love for her. He was a silent youth; the spoken word came haltingly to his lips, and as often happens, words were superfluous to him in his moments of great emotion. He put her hands to his lips, and moaned, for the hour of parting seemed to be hurrying down upon him. Finally his tongue found liberty. "Oh, sweetheart--sweetheart," he cried, "always remember that you are bound in my soul with the iron of youth's first love--my only love. Oh, I never could again, dear,--only you--only you. After this it would be a sacrilege."

They stood silent in the joy of their ecstacy for a long minute, then he asked gently: "Do you understand, Molly,--do you understand? this is forever for us, Molly,--forever. When one loves as we love--with our childhood and youth welded into it all--whom God hath joined--" he stammered; "oh, Molly, whom God hath joined," he whispered, and his voice trembled as he sighed again, and kissed her, "whom God hath joined. Oh, God--God, God!" cried the lover, as he closed his eyes with his lips against her hair.

The restless horses recalled the lovers to the earth. It was Molly who spoke. "Bob--Bob--I can't let you go!"

Molly Culpepper had no reserves with her lover. She went on whispering, with, her face against his heart: "Bob--Bob, big boy, I am going to tell you something truthy true, that I never breathed to any one. At night--to-night, in just a few minutes--when I go up to my room--all alone--I get your picture and hold it to me close, and holding it right next to my very heart, Bob, I pray for you." She paused a moment, and then continued, "Oh, and--I pray for us--Bob--I pray for us." Then she ran up the stone walk, and on the steps she turned to throw kisses at him, but he did not move until he heard the lock click in the front door.

At the livery-stable he found Watts McHurdie bending over some break in his buggy. They walked up the street together. At the corner where they were about to part the little man said, as he looked into the rapturous face of the lanky boy, "Well, Bob,--it's good-by, John, for you, I suppose?"

"Oh--I don't know," replied the other from his enchanted world and then asked absently, "Why?"

"Well, it's nature, I guess. She'll take all his time now." He rubbed his chin reflectively, and as Bob turned to go Watts said: "My Heavens, how time does fly! It just seems like yesterday that all you boys were raking over the scrap-pile back of my shop, and slipping in and nipping leather strands and braiding them into whips, and I'd have to douse you with water to get rid of you. I got a quirt hanging up in the shop now that Johnnie Barclay dropped one day when I got after him with a pan of water. It's a six-sided one, with eight strands down in the round part. I taught him how to braid it." He chewed a moment and spat before going on: "And now look at him. He's little, but oh my." Something was working under McHurdie's belt, for Bob could hear it chuckling as he chewed: "Wasn't she a buster? It's funny, ain't it--the way we all pick big ones--we sawed-offs"? The laugh came--a quiet, repressed gurgle, and he added: "Yes--by hen, and you long-shanks always pick little dominickers. Eh?" He chewed a meditative cud before venturing, "That's what I told her comin' home to-night." Bob knew whom he meant. The man went on: "But when she saw them--him so little she'll have to shake the sheet to find him--and her so big and busting, I seen *her*--you know," he nodded his head wisely to indicate which "her" he meant. "I saw her a-eying me, out of the corner of her eye, and looking at him, and then looking at the girl, and looking at herself, and on the way home to-night I'm damned if I didn't have to put off asking her another six months." He sighed and continued, "And the first thing I know the drummer or the preacher'll get her." He chewed for a minute in peace and chuckled, "Well--Bob, I suppose you'll be next?" He did not wait for an answer, but spoke up quickly, "Well, Bob, good night--good night," and hurried to his shop.

The next day the people that blackened Main Street in Sycamore Ridge talked of two things--the bank failure and the new Golden Belt Wheat Company. Barclay enlisted Colonel Culpepper, and promised him two dollars for every hundred-acre option to lease that he secured at three dollars an acre the cash on the lease to be paid March first. Barclay's plan was to organize a stock company and to sell his stock in the East for enough to raise eight dollars an acre for every acre he secured, and to use the five dollars for making the crop. He believed that with a good wheat crop the next year he could make money and buy as much land as he needed. But that year of the panic John

capitalized the hardship of his people, and made terms for them, which they could not refuse. He literally sold them their own want. For the fact that he had a little ready money and could promise more before harvest upon which the people might live--however miserably was no concern of his--made it possible for him to drive a bargain little short of robbery. It was Bob's part of the business to float the stock company in the East among his father's rich friends. John was to furnish the money to keep Bob in New York, and the Hendricks' connections in banking circles were to furnish the cash to float the proposition, and the Hendricks' bank--if John could get it opened again--was to guarantee that the stock subscribed would pay six per cent interest. So there was no honeymoon for John Barclay. When he dropped the reins and helped his bride out of the buggy the next morning in front of the Thayer House, he hustled General Ward's little boy into the seat, told him to drive the team to Dolan's stable, and waving the new Mrs. Barclay good-by, limped in a trot over to the bank. In five minutes he was working in the crowd, and by night had the required number of the depositors ready to agree to let their money lie a year on deposit, and that matter was closed. He was a solemn-faced youth in those days, with a serious air about him, and something of that superabundance of dignity little men often think they must assume to hold their own. The town knew him as a trim little man in a three-buttoned tail-coat, with rather extraordinary neckties, a well-brushed hat, and shiny shoes. To the country people he was "limping Johnnie," and General Ward, watching Barclay hustle his way down Main Street Saturday afternoons, when the sidewalk and the streets were full of people, used to say, "Busier 'n a tin pedler."
And he said to Mrs. Ward, "Lucy, if it's true that old Grandpa Barclay got his start carrying a pack, you can see him cropping out in John, bigger than a wolf."

But the general had little time to devote to John, for he was state organizer of a movement that had for its object the abolition of

middlemen in trade, and he was travelling most of the time. The dust
gathered on his law-books, and his Sunday suit grew frayed at the
edges and shiny at the elbows, but his heart was in the cause, and his
blue eyes burned with joy when he talked, and he was happy, and had to
travel two days and nights when the fourth baby came, and then was too
late to serve on the committee on reception, and had to be satisfied
with a minor place on the committee on entertainment and amusements of
which Mrs. Culpepper was chairman. But John turned in half of a fee
that came from the East for a lawsuit that both he and Ward had
forgotten, and Miss Lucy would have named the new baby Mary Ward, but
the general stood firm for Elizabeth Cady Stanton. Sitting at Sunday
dinner with the Wards on the occasion of Elizabeth Cady Stanton Ward's
first monthly birthday, John listened to the general's remarks on the
iniquity of the money power, and the wickedness of the national banks,
and kept respectful and attentive silence. The worst the young man did
was to wink swiftly across the table at Watts McHurdie, who had been
invited by Mrs. Ward with malice prepense and seated by Nellie Logan.
The wink came just as the general, waving the carving knife, was
saying: "Gentlemen, it's the world-old fight--the fight of might
against right. When I was a boy like you, John, the fight was between
brute strength and the oppressed; between slaves and masters. Now it
is between weakness and cunning, between those who would be
slaveholders if they could be, and those who are fighting the
shackles." And Mrs. Ward saw the wink, and John saw that she saw it,
and he was ashamed.

So before the afternoon was over, Mr. and Mrs. John Barclay went over
to Hendricks's, picking up Molly Culpepper on the way, and the three
spent the evening with the general and Miss Hendricks--a faded mousy
little woman in despairing thirties; and before the open fire they sat
and talked, and John played the piano for an hour, and thought out an
extra kink for the Golden Belt Wheat Company's charter. He jabbered
about it to Jane as they walked home, and the next day it became a

fact.

"That boy," said the colonel to his assembled family one evening as they dined on mush and dried peaches, and coffee made of parched corn, "that John Barclay certainly and surely is a marvel. Talk about drawing blood from a turnip,--why, he can strike an artery in a pumpkin." The colonel smiled reflectively as he proceeded: "Chicago lawyer came in on the stage this afternoon,--kinder getting uneasy about a little interest I owed to an Ohio man on that College Heights property, and John took that Chicago lawyer up to his office, and talked him into putting the interest in a second mortgage with all the interest that will fall due till next spring, and then traded him Golden Belt Wheat Company stock for the mortgage and a thousand dollars besides."

"Well, did John give you back the mortgage, father?" asked Molly.

"No, sis,--that wouldn't be business," replied the colonel, as he stirred his dried peaches into his third dish of mush for dessert; "business is business, you know. John took the mortgage over to the bank and discounted it for some money to buy more options with. John surely does make things hum."

"Yes, and he's made Bob resign from the board of commissioners, and won't let him come home Christmas, and keeps him on fifty dollars a month there in New York--all the same," returned the girl.

The colonel looked at his daughter a moment in sympathetic silence; then he put his thumbs in the armholes of his vest and tilted back in his chair and answered: "Oh, well, my dear,--when you are living in a brown-stone house on Fifth Avenue down in New York, stepping on a nigger every which way you turn, you'll thank John that he did keep Bob at work, and not bring him back here to pin on a buffalo tail,

drink crick water, eat tumble weeds, and run wild. I say, and I fear
no contradiction when I say it, that John Barclay is a marvel--a
living wonder in point of fact. And if Bob Hendricks wants to come
back here and live on the succulent and classic bean and the luscious,
and I may say tempting, flapjack, let him come, Molly Farquhar
Culpepper, let him come." The colonel, proud of his language, looked
around the family circle. "And we at our humble board, with our plain
though--shall I say nutritive--yes, nutritive and wholesome fare,
should thank our lucky stars that John Barclay keeps the Golden Belt
Wheat Company going, and your husband and father can make a more or
less honest dollar now and then to supply your simple wants."

The colonel had more in his mind, for he rose and began to pace the
floor in a fine frenzy. But Mrs. Culpepper looked up for an instant
from her tea, and said, "You know you forgot the mail to-day, father,"
and he replied, "Yes, that's so." Then added: "Molly dear, will you
bring me my overcoat--please?"

The girl bundled her father into his threadbare blue army overcoat
with the cape. He stood for a moment absently rattling some dimes in
his pocket. Then the faintness of their jingle must have appealed to
him, for he drew a long breath and walked majestically away. He was a
tall stout man in the midst of his forties, with a military goatee and
black flowing mustaches, and he wore his campaign hat pinned up at the
side with the brass military pin and swayed with some show of swagger
as he walked. His gift of oratory he did not bring to the flower of
its perfection except at lodge. He was always sent as a delegate to
Grand Lodge, and when he came home men came from all over the county
to see the colonel exemplify the work. But as he marched to funerals
under his large white plume and with his sword dangling at his side,
Colonel Martin Culpepper, six feet four one way and four feet two the
other, was a regal spectacle, and it will be many years before the
town will see his like again.

The colonel walked over to the post-office box and got his mail, then took a backless chair and drew it up to the sand box in which the stove sat, and the conversation became general in its nature, ranging from Emerson's theory of the cosmos and the whiskey ring to the efficacy of a potato in the pocket for rheumatism. Finally when they had come to their "don't you remembers" about the battle of Wilson's Creek, General Ward, with his long coat buttoned closely about him, came shivering into the store to get some camphor gum and stood rubbing his cold hands by the stove while the clerk was wrapping up the package. His thin nose was red and his eyes watered, and he had little to say. When he went out the colonel said, "What's he going to run for this year?"

"Haven't you heard?" replied McHurdie, and to the colonel's negative Watts replied, "Governor--the uprising's going to nominate him."

"Yes," said Frye, "and he'll go off following that foolishness and leave his wife and children to John or the neighbours."

"Do you suppose he thinks he'll win?" asked the Colonel.

"Naw," put in McHurdie; "I was talking to him only last week in the shop, and he says, 'Watts, you boys don't understand me.' He says, 'I don't want their offices. What I want is to make them think. I'm sowing seed. Some day it will come to a harvest--maybe long after I'm dead and gone.' I asked him if a little seed wouldn't help out some for breakfast, and he didn't answer. Then he said: 'Watts--what you need is faith--faith in God and not in money. There are no Christians; they don't believe in God, or they'd trust Him more. They don't trust God; they trust money. Yet I tell you it will work. Go ahead--do your work in the world, and you won't starve nor your children beg in the streets.'" McHurdie stopped a moment to gnaw his plug of tobacco. "The general's gitting kind of a crank--and I told him so."

"What did he say?" inquired the colonel.

"Oh, he just laughed," replied McHurdie; "he just laughed and said if he was a crank I was a poet, and neither was much good at the note window of the bank, and we kind of made it up."

And so the winter evening grew old, and one by one the cronies rose and yawned and went their way. Evening after evening went thus, and was it strange that in the years that came, when the sunset of life was gilding things for Watts McHurdie, he looked through the golden haze and saw not the sand in the pit under the stove, not the rows of drugs on the wall, not the patent medicine bottles in their faded wrappers, but as he wrote many years after in "Autumn Musing":--

"Those nights when Wisdom was our guide
And Friendship was the glow,
That warmed our souls like living coals,
Those nights of long ago."

Nor is it strange that Martin Culpepper, his commentator, conning those lines through the snows of many winters, should be a little misty as to details, and having taken his pen in hand to write, should set down this note:--

"These lines probably refer to the evenings which the poet passed in a goodly company of choice spirits during the early seventies. E'en as I write, Memory, with tender hand, pushes back the sombre curtain, and I see them now--that charmed circle; the poet with the brow of Jove and Minerva's lips; the rugged warrior at his side, with the dignity of Mars himself; perhaps some Croesus with his gold, drawn by the spell

of Wisdom's enchantment into the magic circle; and this your humble
disciple of Thucydides, sitting spellbound under the drippings of the
sacred font, getting the material for these pages. That was the Golden
Age; there were giants in those days."

And so there were, Colonel Martin Culpepper of the Great Heart and the
"large white plumes"--so there were.

CHAPTER X

It was a cold raw day in March, 1874. Colonel Culpepper was sitting in
the office of Ward and Barclay over the Exchange National Bank waiting
for the junior member of the firm to come in; the senior member of the
firm, who had just brought up an arm load of green hickory and dry
hackberry stove wood, was standing beside the box-shaped stove,
abstractedly brushing the sawdust and wormwood from his sleeves and
coat front. The colonel was whistling and whittling, and the general
kept on brushing after the last speck of dust had gone from his shiny
coat. He walked to the window and stared into the ugly brown street.

Two or three minutes passed, and Colonel Culpepper, anxious for the
society of his kind, spoke. "Well, General, what's the trouble?"

"Nothing in particular, Martin. I was just questioning the reality of
matter and the existence of the universe as you spoke; but it's not
important." The general shivered, and turned his kind blue eyes on his

friend in a smile, and then bethought him to put the wood in the stove.

While he was jamming in a final stick, Colonel Culpepper inquired, "Well, am I an appearance or an entity?"

The general put the smoking poker on the floor, and turned the damper in the pipe as he answered: "That's what I can't seem to make out. You know old Emerson says a man doesn't amount to much as a thinker until he has doubted the existence of matter. And I just got to thinking about it, and wondering if this was a real world after all--or just my idea of one." The two men smiled at the notion, and Ward went on: "All right, laugh if you want to, but if this is a real world, whose world is it, your world or my world? Here is John Barclay, for instance. Sometimes I get a peek at his world." Ward picked up the poker and sat down and hammered the toe of a boot with it as he went on: "John's world is the Golden Belt Wheat Company, wheat pouring a steady stream into boundless bins, and money flowing in golden ripples over it all. Sometimes Bob Hendricks' head rises above the tide long enough to gasp or cry for help and beg to come home, but John's golden flood sweeps over him again, and he's gone. And here's your world, Martin, wherein every one is kind and careless, and generous and good, and full of smiles and gayety. And there's Lige Bemis' world, full of cunning and hypocrisy, and meanness and treachery and plotting--a hell of a world it is, with its foundations on hate and deceit--but it's his world, and he has the same right to it that I have to mine. And there's old Watts' world--" The general sighted along the poker over his toe to the stove side whereon a cornucopia wriggled out of nothing and poured its richness of fruit and grain into nothing. "There's Watts' world, full of stuffed Personifications, Virtue, Pleasure, Happiness, Sin, Sorrow, and God knows what of demigods, with the hay of his philosophy sticking out of their eyeholes. You know about his maxims, Mart; he actually lives by 'em, and no matter how common sense yells at him to get off the track, old Watts just goes on following his maxims, and gets butted into the middle of next week."

The colonel was making a hole in the stick in his hands, and his attention was fixed on the whittling, but he added, "And your own world, General--how about your own world?"

"My world," replied the general, as he pulled at the bows of his rather soiled white tie, and evened them, "My world--" the general jabbed the poker spear-like into the floor, "I guess I'm a kind of a transcendentalist!"

The colonel blew the chips through the hole in his stick; he bored it round in the pause that followed before he spoke.

"A transcendentalist, eh? Well, pintedly, General, that is what I may call a soft impeachment, as the poet says--a mighty soft impeachment. I've heard you called a lot worse names than that--and I may say," here the crow's-feet began scratching for a smile around the colonel's eyes, "proved, sir, with you as the prosecuting witness."

The two men chuckled. Then the general, balancing himself, with the poker point on the floor, as he tilted back went on: "My world, Mart Culpepper, is a world in which the ideal is real--a world in a state of flux with thoughts of to-day the matter of to-morrow; my world is a world of faith that God will crystallize to-day's aspirations into to-morrow's justice; my world," the general rose and waved his poker as if to beat down the forces of materialism about him, "my world is the substance of things hoped for, and the evidence of things not seen." He paused. "As I was saying," he continued at last, "if this is a real world, if matter actually exists and this world is not a dream of my consciousness, whose world is it, my world, your world, Watts McHurdie's world, Lige's world, or John's world? It can't be all of 'em." He put the poker across the stove hearth, and sank his hands deeply into his pockets as he continued: "The question that philosophy never has answered is this: Am I a spectre and you an essence, or are you a spectre and am I an essence? Is it your world or mine?"

The two men looked instinctively at the rattling doorknob, and John Barclay limped into the room. His face was red with the cold and the driving mist. He walked to the stove and unbuttoned his ulster, while the colonel put the subject of the debate before him. The general amended the colonel's statement from time to time, but the young man only smiled tolerantly and shook his head. Then he went to his desk and pulled a letter from a drawer.

"Colonel, I've got a letter here from Bob. The thing doesn't seem to be moving. He only sold about a thousand dollars' worth of stock last month--a falling off of forty per cent, and we must have more or we can't take up our leases. He's begging like a dog to come home for a week, but I can't let him. We need that week." He limped over to the elder and put his hand on the tall man's arm as he said: "Now, Colonel, that was what I sent for you about. You kind of speak to Molly and have her write him and tell him to hold on a little while. It's business, you know, and we can't afford to have sentiment interfere with business."

The colonel, standing by the window, replied, after a pause: "I can see where you are right, John. Business is business. You got to consider that." He looked into the street below and saw General Hendricks come shuddering into the cold wind. "How's he getting on?" asked Culpepper, nodding towards Hendricks, who seemed unequal to the gale.

"Oh, I don't know, Colonel,--times are hard."

"My, how he's aging!" said the colonel, softly.

After a silence Barclay said: "There's one thing sure--I've got it into his hard old head that Bob is doing something back there, and he couldn't earn his salt here. Besides," added Barclay, as if to justify himself against an accusing conscience, "the old man does all the work in the bank now, with time to spare."

It was the day of army overcoats, and the hard times had brought hundreds of them from closets and trunks. General Hendricks, fluttering down the street in his faded blue, made a rather pathetic figure. The winter had whitened his hair and withered his ruddy face. His unequal struggle with the wind seemed some way symbolical of his life, and the two men watched him out of sight without a word. The colonel turned toward his own blue overcoat which lay sprawling in a chair, and Barclay said as he helped the elder man squeeze into it, "Don't forget to speak to Molly, Colonel," and then ushered him to the door. For a moment Colonel Culpepper stood at the bottom of the stairs, partly hesitating to go into the windy street, and partly trying to think of some way in which he could get the subject on his mind before his daughter in the right way. Then as he stood on the threshold with his nose in the storm, he recalled General Ward's discourse about the different worlds, and he thought of Molly's world of lovers' madness, and that brought up his own youth and its day-dreams, and Molly flew out of his mind and her mother came in, and he saw her blue-eyed and fair as she stood before him on their wedding-day. With that picture in his heart he breasted the storm and went home whistling cheerfully, walking through his world like a prince.

When the colonel left the office of Ward and Barclay, the partners retired into their respective worlds and went sailing through space, each world upon its own axis. The general in a desultory way began writing letters to reformers urging them to prepare for the coming struggle; but John was head over heels in the business of the Golden Belt Wheat Company, and in an hour had covered two sheets of foolscap with figures and had written a dozen letters. The scratch, scratch of his pen was as regular as the swish of a piston. On the other hand, the general often stopped and looked off into space, and three times he got up to mend the fire. At the end of the afternoon Mrs. Ward came in, her cheeks pink with the cold; she had left the seven-year-old to care for the one-year-old, and the five-year-old to look after the three-year-old, and had come scurrying through the streets in a brown alpaca dress with a waterproof cape over her shoulders. She and the general spoke for a few moments in their corner, and she hurried out again. The general finished the letter he was writing and wrote another, and then backed up to the stove with his coat tails in front of him and stood benignly watching Barclay work. Barclay felt the man's attention, and whirling about in his chair licking an envelope flap, he said, "Well, General--what's on your mind?"

"I was just thinking of Lucy--that's all," replied the general. Barclay knew that the Wards had gone through the winter on less than one hundred dollars, and it occurred to the younger man that times might be rather hard in the Ward household. So he asked, "Are you worried about money matters, General?"

The general's smile broadened to a grin. "Well, to be exact, Lucy and I just counted cash--it's in her pocketbook, and we find our total cash assets are eight dollars and thirty-nine cents, and it's got to tide us over till grass." He stroked his lean chin, and ran his hands through his iron-gray hair and went on, "That's plenty, the way we've figured it out--Lucy and I only eat one meal a day anyway, and the children seem to eat all the time and that averages it up." He smiled deprecatingly and added: "But Lucy's got her heart set on a little matter, and we've decided to spend eighty-seven cents, as you might say riotously, and get it. That's what we were talking about."

Barclay entered into the spirit of Ward's remarks and put in: "But the National debt, General--if you have all that money to spare, why don't you pay it off? Practise what you preach, General."

The smile faded from Ward's face. He was not a man to joke on what he regarded as sacred things. He replied: "Yes, yes, that's just it. My share of the interest on that debt this winter was just seventy-five cents, and if it wasn't for that, we would have had enough to get them; as it is, we are going to cut out meat for a week--we figured it all out just now--and get them anyway. She's down at the store buying them."

"Buying what?" asked Barclay.

The general's face lighted up again with a grin, and he replied: "Now laugh--dog-gone you--buying flower seeds!" They heard a step at the bottom of the stairs, and the general strode to the door, opened it, and called down, "All right, Lucy--I'm coming," and buttoning up his coat, he whisked himself from the room, and Barclay, looking out of the window, watched the two forms as they disappeared in the dusk. But appearances are so deceptive. The truth is that what he saw was not there at all, but only appeared on his retina; the two forms that he seemed to see were not shivering through the twilight, but were walking among dahlias and coxcombs and four-o'clocks and petunias and poppies and hollyhocks on a wide lawn whereon newly set elm trees were fluttering their faint green foliage in the summer breeze. Yet John Barclay would have sworn he saw them there in the cold street, with the mist beating upon them, and curiously corroborative of this impression is a memory he retained of reflecting that since the general's blue overcoat had disappeared the winter before, he had noticed that little Thayer had a blue Sunday suit and little Elizabeth

Cady Stanton had appeared wrapped in a blue baby coat. But that only shows how these matter-of-fact people are fooled. For though the little Wards were caparisoned in blue, and though the general's blue overcoat did disappear about that time, the general and Lucy Ward have no recollection of shivering home that night, but instead they know that they walked among the flowers.

And John, looking into the darkening street, must have seen something besides the commonplace couple that he thought he saw; for as he turned away to light his lamp and go to work again, he smiled. Surely there was nothing to smile at in the thing he saw. Perhaps God was trying to make him see the flowers. But he did not see them, and as it was nearly an hour before six o'clock, he turned to his work under the lamp and finished his letter to Bob Hendricks. When it was written, he read it over carefully, crossing his "t's" and dotting his "i's," and as no one was in the room he mumbled it aloud, thus:--

"DEAR BOB:--Don't get blue; it will be all right. Stick to it. I am laying a wire that will get you an audience with Jay Gould. Make the talk of your life there. You may be able to interest him--if just for a few dollars. Offer him anything. Give him the stock if he will let us use his name.

"Don't get uneasy about Molly, Bob. Jane and I see that she goes to everything, and we've scared her up a kind of brevet beau--an old rooster named Brownwell--Adrian Pericles Brownwell, who has blown in here and bought the *Banner* from Ezra Lane. Brownwell is from Alabama. Do you remember, Bob, that day at Wilson's Creek after we got separated in the Battle I ran into a pile of cavalry writhing in a road? Well, there was one face in that awful struggling mass that I always remembered--and I never expect to see such a look of fear on a man's face again--he was a young fellow then, but now he's thirty-five or so. Well--that was this man Brownwell. I asked him about it the other day. How he ever got out alive, I don't know; but the fact that he should turn up here proves that this is a small world. Brownwell also is a writer from Writersville. You should see the way he paints the lily in the **Banner** every week. You remember old Cap Lee--J. Lord Lee of the Red Legs--and Lady Lee, as they called her when she was a sagebrush siren with the 'Army of the Border' before the War? Well, read this clipping from the **Banner** of this week: 'The wealth, beauty, and fashion of Minneola--fairest village of the plain--were agog this week over the birth of a daughter to Lord and Lady Lee, whose prominence in our social circles makes the event one of first importance in our week's annals. Little Beatrix, for so they have decided to christen her, will some day be a notable addition to our refined and gracious circles. Welcome to you, little stranger.'

"Now you know the man! You needn't be jealous of him. However, he has frozen to the Culpeppers because they are from the South, and clearly he thinks they are the only persons of consequence in town. So he beaus Molly around with Jane and me to the concerts and sociables and things. He is easily thirty-five, walks with a cane, struts like a peacock, and Molly and Jane are having great sport with him. Also he is the only man in town with any money. He brought five thousand dollars in gold, real money,--his people made it on contraband cotton contracts during the War, they say,--and he has been the only visible means of support the town has had for three months. But in the meantime don't worry about Molly, Bob, she's all right, and business is business, you know, and you shouldn't let such things interfere with it. But in another six months we'll be out of the woods and on our way to big money."

Now another strange thing happened to John Barclay that evening, and this time it was what he saw, not what he failed to see, that puzzled him. For just as he sealed the letter to his friend, and thumped his lean fist on it to blot the address on the envelope and press the mucilage down, he looked around suddenly, though he never knew why, and there, just outside the rim of light from his lampshade, trembled the image of Ellen Culpepper with her red and black checked flannel dress at her shoe tops and his rubber button ring upon her finger. She smiled at him sweetly for a moment and shook her head sadly, and her curls fluttered upon her shoulders, and then she seemed to fade into the general's desk by the opposite wall. John was pallid and frightened for a moment; then as he looked at the great pile of letters before him he realized how tired and worn he was. But the face and the eyes haunted him and brought back old memories, and that night he and Jane and Molly Culpepper went to Hendricks', and he played the piano for an hour in the firelight, and dreamed old dreams. And his hands fell into the chords of a song that he sang as a boy, and Molly came from the fire and stood beside him while they hummed the words in a low duet:--

"Let me believe that you love as you loved
   Long, long ago--long ago."

But when he went out into the drizzling night, and he and Jane left Molly at home, he stepped into the whirling yellow world of gold and grain, and drafts and checks, and leases and mortgages, and Heaven knows what of plots and schemes and plans. So he did not heed Jane when she said, "Poor--poor little Molly," but replied as he latched the Culpepper gate, "Oh, Molly'll be all right. You can't mix business and pleasure, you know. Bob must stay."

And when Molly went into the house, she found her mother waiting for her. The colonel's courage had failed him. The mother took her daughter's hand, and the two walked up the broad stairs together.

"Molly," said the mother, as the girl listlessly went about her preparations for bed, "don't grieve so about Bob. Father and John need him there. It's business, you know."

The daughter answered, "Yes, I know, but I'm so lonesome--so lonesome." Then she sobbed, "You know he hasn't written for a whole week, and I'm afraid--afraid!"

When the paroxysm had passed, the mother said: "You know, my dear, they need him there a little longer, and he wants to come back. Your father told me that John sent word to-day that you must not let him come." The girl's face looked the pain that struck her heart, and she did not answer. "Molly dear," began the mother again, "can't you write to Bob to-morrow and urge him to stay--for me? For all of us? It is so much to us now--for a little while--to have Bob there, sending back money for the company. I don't know what father would do if it wasn't for the company--and John."

The daughter held her mother's hand, and after gasping down a sob, promised, and then as the sob kept tilting back in her throat, she cried: "But oh, mother, it's such a big world--so wide, and I am so afraid--so afraid of something--I don't know what--only that I'm afraid."

But the mother soothed her daughter, and they talked of other things until she was quiet and drowsy.

But when she went to sleep, she dreamed a strange dream. The next day she could not untangle it, save that with her for hours as she went about her duties was the odour of lilacs, and the face of her lover, now a young eager face in pain, and then, by the miracle of dreams, grown old, bald at the temples and brow, but fine and strong and clean--like a boy's face. The face soon left her, but the smell of the lilacs was in her heart for days--they were her lilacs, from the bushes in the garden. As days and weeks passed, the dream blurred into the gray of her humdrum life and was gone. And so that day and that night dropped from time into eternity, and who knows of all the millions of stars that swarmed the heavens, what ones held the wandering souls of the simple people of that bleak Western town as they lay on their pillows and dreamed. For if our waking hours are passed in worlds so wide apart, who shall know where we walk in dreams?

It is thirty years and more now since John Barclay dreamed of himself as the Wheat King of the Sycamore Valley, and in that thirty years he had considerable time to reflect upon the reasons why pride always goeth before destruction. And he figured it out that in his particular case he was so deeply engrossed in the money he was going to make that first year, that he did not study the simple problem of wheat-growing as he should have studied it. In those days wheat-growing upon the plains had not yet become the science it is to-day, and many Sycamore Valley farmers planted their wheat in the fall, and failed to make it pay, and many other Sycamore Valley farmers planted their wheat in the spring, and failed, while many others succeeded. The land had not been definitely staked off and set apart by experience as a winter wheat country, and so the farmers operating under the Golden Belt Wheat Company, in the spring of 1874, planted their wheat in March.

That was a beautiful season on the plains. April rains came, and the great fields glowed green under the mild spring sun. And Bob Hendricks, collecting the money from his stock subscriptions, poured it into the treasury of the company, and John Barclay spent the money for seed and land and men to work the land, and so confident was he of the success of the plan that he borrowed every dollar he could lay his hands on, and got leases on more land and bought more seed and hired more men, in the belief that during the summer Hendricks could sell stock enough to pay back the loans. To Colonel Culpepper, Barclay gave a block of five thousand dollars' worth of the stock as a bonus in addition to his commission for his work in securing options, and the colonel, feeling himself something of a capitalist, and being in funds from the spring sale of lots in College Heights addition, invested in new clothes, bought some farm products in Missouri, and went up and down the earth proclaiming the glories of the Sycamore Valley, and in May brought two car-loads of land seekers by stages and wagons and buggies to Sycamore Ridge, and located them in Garrison County. And in his mail when he came home he found a notice indicating that he had overdrawn his account in the bank five hundred dollars, and that his note was due for five hundred more on the second mortgage which he had given the previous fall.

For two days he was plunged in gloom, and Barclay, observing his depression and worming out of the colonel the cause, persuaded General Hendricks to put the overdraft and the second mortgage note into one note for a thousand dollars plus the interest for sixty days until the colonel could make a turn, and after that the colonel was happy again. He forgot for a moment the responsibility of wealth and engaged himself in the task of making the Memorial Day celebration in Sycamore Ridge the greatest event in the history of the town. Though there were only five soldiers' graves to decorate, the longest procession Garrison County had ever known wound up the hill to the cemetery, and Colonel Martin Culpepper in his red sash, with his Knights Templar hat on, riding up and down the line on an iron-gray stallion, was easily the most notable figure in the spectacle. Even General Hendricks, revived by the pomp of the occasion, heading the troop of ten veterans of the Mexican War, and General Ward, in his regimentals, were inconsequential compared with the colonel. And his oration at the graves, after the bugles had blown taps, kept the multitude in tears for half an hour. John Barclay's address at the Opera House that afternoon--the address on "The Soldier and the Scholar"--was so completely overshadowed by the colonel's oratorical flight that Jane teased her husband about the eclipse for a month, and never could make him laugh. Moreover, the **Banner** that week printed the colonel's oration in full and referred to John's address as "a few sensible remarks by Hon. John Barclay on the duty of scholarship in times of peace." But here is the strange thing about it--those who read the colonel's oration were not moved by it; the charm of the voice and the spell of the tall, handsome, vigorous man and the emotion of the occasion were needed to make the colonel's oratory move one. Still, opinions differ even about so palpable a proposition as the ephemeral nature of the colonel's oratory. For the **Banner** that week pronounced it one of the classic oratorical gems of American eloquence, and the editor thereof brought a dozen copies of the paper under his arm when he climbed the hill to Lincoln Avenue the following Sunday night, and presented them to the women of the Culpepper household, whom he was punctilious to call "the ladies," and he assured Miss Molly and Mistress Culpepper--he was nice about those titles also--that their father and husband had a great future before him in the forum.

It may be well to pause here and present so punctilious a gentleman as Adrian Pericles Brownwell to the reader somewhat more formally than he has been introduced. For he will appear in this story many times. In the first place he wore mustaches--chestnut-coloured mustaches--that drooped rather gracefully from his lip to his jaw, and thence over his coat lapels; in the second place he always wore gloves, and never was without a flower in his long frock-coat; and thirdly he clicked his cane on the sidewalk so regularly that his approach was heralded, and the company was prepared for the coming of a serious, rather nervous, fiery man, a stickler for his social dues; and finally in those days, those sombre days of Sycamore Ridge after the panic of '73, when men had to go to the post-office to get their ten-dollar bills changed, Brownwell had the money to support the character he assumed. He had come to the Ridge from the South,--from that part of the South that carried its pistol in its hip pocket and made a large and serious

matter of its honour,--that was obvious; he had paid Ezra Lane two
thousand dollars for the ***Banner***, that was a matter of record; and he
had marched with some grandeur into General Hendricks' bank one
Saturday and had clinked out five thousand dollars in gold on the
marble slab at the teller's window, and that was a matter attested to
by a crowd of witnesses. Watts McHurdie used to say that more people
saw that deposit than could be packed into the front room of the bank
with a collar stuffer.

But why Adrian Brownwell had come to the Ridge, and where he had made
his money--there myth and fable enter into the composition of the
narrative, and one man's opinion is as good as another's. Curiously
enough, all who testify claim that they speak by the authority of Mr.
Brownwell himself. But he was a versatile and obliging gentleman
withal, so it is not unlikely that all those who assembled him from
the uttermost parts of the earth into Sycamore Ridge for all the
reasons in the longer catechism, were telling the simple truth as they
have reason to believe it. What men know of a certainty is that he
came, that he hired the bridal chamber of the Thayer House for a year,
and that he contested John Barclay's right to be known as the glass of
fashion and the mould of form in Garrison County for thirty long
years, and then--but that is looking in the back of the book, which
is manifestly unfair.

It is enough to know now that on that Sunday evening after Memorial
Day, in 1874, Adrian P. Brownwell sat on the veranda of the Culpepper
home slapping his lavender gloves on his knee by way of emphasis, and
told the company what he told General Beauregard and what General
Beauregard told him, at the battle of Shiloh; also what his maternal
grandfather, Governor Papin, had said to General Jackson, when his
grandmother, then Mademoiselle Dulangpre, youngest daughter of the
refugee duke of that house, had volunteered to nurse the American
soldiers in Jackson's hospital after the battle of New Orleans; also,

and with detail, what his father, Congressman Brownwell, had said on the capitol steps in December, 1860, before leaving for Washington to resign his seat in Congress; and also with much greater detail he recounted the size of his ancestral domain, the number of the ancestral slaves and the royal state of the ancestral household, and then with a grand wave of his gloves, and a shrug of which Madam Papin might well have been proud, "But 'tis all over; and we are brothers--one country, one flag, one God, one very kind but very busy God!" And he smiled so graciously through his great mustaches, showing his fine even teeth, that Mrs. Culpepper, Methodist to the heart, smiled back and was not so badly shocked as she knew she should have been.

"Is it not so?" he asked with his voice and his hands at once. "Ah," he exclaimed, addressing Mrs. Culpepper dramatically, "what better proof would you have of our brotherhood than our common bondage to you? However dark the night of our national discord--to-day, North, South, East, West, we bask in the sunrise of some woman's eyes." He fluttered his gloves gayly toward Molly and continued:--

"'O when did morning ever break,
And find such beaming eyes awake.'"

And so he rattled on, and the colonel had to poke his words into the conversation in wedge-shaped queries, and Mrs. Culpepper, being in due and proper awe of so much family and such apparent consequence, spoke little and smiled many times. And if it was "Miss Molly" this and "Miss Molly" that, when the colonel went into the house to lock the back doors, and "Miss Molly" the other when Mrs. Culpepper went in to open the west bedroom windows; and even if it was "Miss Molly, shall we go down town and refresh ourselves with a dish of ice-cream?" and even if still further a full-grown man standing at the gate under the May moon deftly nips a rose from Miss Molly's hair and holds the rose in both hands to his lips as he bows a good night--what then? What were roses made for and brown eyes and long lashes and moons and May winds heavy with the odour of flowers and laden with the faint sounds of distant herd bells tinkling upon the hills? For men are bold at thirty-five, and maidens, the best and sweetest, truest, gentlest maidens in all the world, are shy at twenty-one, and polite to their elders and betters of thirty-five--even when those elders and betters forget their years!

As for Adrian P. Brownwell, he went about his daily task, editing the *Banner*, making it as luscious and effulgent as a seed catalogue, with rhetorical pictures about as florid and unconvincing. To him the town was a veritable Troy--full of heroes and demigods, and honourables and persons of nobility and quality. He used no adjective of praise milder than superb, and on the other hand, Lige Bemis once complained that the least offensive epithet he saw in the *Banner* tacked after his name for two years was miscreant. As for John Barclay, he once told General Ward that a man could take five dollars in to Brownwell and come out a statesman, a Croesus or a scholar, as the exigencies of the case demanded, and for ten dollars he could combine the three.

Yet for all that Brownwell ever remained a man apart. No one thought of calling him "Ade." Sooner would one nickname a gargoyle on a tin cornice. So the editor of the *Banner* never came close to the real heart of Sycamore Ridge, and often for months at a time he did not know what the people were thinking. And that summer when General Hendricks was walking out of the bank every hour and looking from under his thin, blue-veined hand at the strange cloud of insects covering the sky, and when Martin Culpepper was predicting that the plague of grasshoppers would leave the next day, and when John Barclay was getting that deep vertical crease between his eyes that made him look forty while he was still in his twenties, Adrian P. Brownwell was chirping cheerfully in the *Banner* about the "salubrious climate of Garrison County," and writing articles about "our phenomenal prospects for a bumper crop." And when in the middle of July the grasshoppers had eaten the wheat to the ground and had left the corn stalks stripped like beanpoles, and had devoured every green thing in their path, the *Banner* contained only a five-line item referring to the plague and calling it a "most curious and unusual visitation." But that summer the *Banner* was filled with Brownwell's editorials on "The Tonic Effect of the Prairie Ozone," "Turn the Rascals Out," "Our Duty to the South," and "The Kingdom of Corn." As a writer Brownwell was what is called "fluent" and "genial." And he was fond of copying articles from the Topeka and Kansas City papers about himself, in which he was referred to as "the gallant and urbane editor of the *Banner*."

But then we all have our weaknesses, and be it said to the everlasting credit of Adrian Brownwell that he understood and appreciated Watts McHurdie and Colonel Culpepper better than any other man in town, and that he printed Watts' poems on all occasions, and never referred to him as anything less than "our honoured townsman," or as "our talented and distinguished fellow-citizen," and he never laughed at General Ward. But the best he could do for John Barclay--even after John had become one of the world's great captains--was to wave his gloves resignedly and exclaim, "Industry, thy name is Barclay." And Barclay in return seemed never to warm up to Brownwell. "Colonel," replied John to some encomium of his old friend's upon the new editor, "I'll say this much. Certainly your friend is a prosperous talker!"

CHAPTER XI

The twenty-fifth of July, 1874, is a memorable day in the life of John Barclay. For on that day the grasshoppers which had eaten off the twenty thousand acres of wheat in the fields of the Golden Belt Wheat Company, as though it had been cropped, rose and left the Missouri Valley. They will never come back, for they are ploughed under in the larva every year by the Colorado farmers who have invaded the plains where once the "hoppers" had their nursery; but all this, even if he had known it, would not have cheered up John that day. For he knew that he owed one hundred and fifty thousand dollars to Eastern stockholders of the company, and he had not a dollar to show for it. He had expected to borrow the money needed for the harvesting in the fall, and over and over and over again he had figured with paper and pencil the amount of his debt, and again and again he had tried to find some way to pay even the interest on the debt at six per cent, which the bank had guaranteed. While the locusts were devouring the vegetation, he walked the hemp carpet that ran diagonally across his office, and chased phantom after phantom of hope that lured him up to the rim of a solution of the problem, only to push him back into the abyss. He walked with his hands deep in his trousers pockets and his head down, and as General Ward was out organizing the farmers in a revolt against the dominant party in the state, Barclay was alone most of the time. The picture of that barren office, with its insurance chromos, with its white, cobweb-marked walls, with its dirty floor partly covered with an "X" of red-bordered hemp carpet reaching from the middle to the four corners, the picture of the four tall unwashed windows letting in the merciless afternoon sun to fade the grimy black and white lithograph of William Lloyd Garrison above the general's desk, never left John Barclay's memory. It was like a cell on a prisoner's mind.

As he paced the room that last day of the visit of the grasshoppers, General Hendricks came in. His hair had whitened in the summer. The panic and the plague of the locusts had literally wrung the sap out of his nerves. Old age was pressing inexorably upon him, palsying his hands on its rack, tripping his feet in its helpless mazes. His dimmed eyes could see only ruin coming, coming slowly and steadily toward him. In the panic, it came suddenly and inspired fight in him. But this year there was something diabolical in its resistless approach. So he shrank from his impending fate as a child trembles at some unknown terror. But Barclay did not swerve. He knew the affairs of the bank fairly well. He was a director who never signed the quarterly statement without verifying every item for himself. He had dreaded the general's visit, yet he knew that it must come, and he pulled toward the general a big hickory chair. The old man sank into it and looked helplessly into the drawn hard face of the younger man and sighed, "Well, John?"

Barclay stood before him a second and then walked down one arm of the "X" of the carpet and back, and up another, and then turned to Hendricks with: "Now, don't lose your nerve, General. You've got to keep your nerve. That's about all the asset we've got now, I guess."

The general replied weakly: "I--I, I--I guess you're right, John. I suppose that's about it."

"How do you figure it out, General?" asked Barclay, still walking the carpet.

The general fumbled for a paper in his pocket and handed it to Barclay. He took it, glanced at it a moment, and then said: "I'm no good at translating another man's figures--how is it in short?--Right down to bed-rock?"

Hendricks seemed to pull himself together and replied: "Well, something like ten thousand in cash against seventy thousand in deposits, and fifty thousand of that time deposits, due next October, you know, on the year's agreement. Of the ten thousand cash, four thousand belongs to Brownwell, and is on check, and you have two thousand on check."

"All right. Now, General, what do you owe?"

"Well, you know that guarantee of your and Bob's business--that nine thousand. It's due next week."

"And it will gut you?" asked Barclay.

The old man nodded and sighed. Barclay limped carefully all over his "X," swinging himself on his heels at the turns; his mouth was hardening, and his eyes were fixed on the old man without blinking as he said: "General--that's got to come. If it busts you--it will save us, and we can save you after. That has just absolutely got to be paid, right on the dot."

The old man could not have turned paler than he was when he entered the room, but he rose halfway in his chair and shook his leonine head, and then let his hands fall limply on his knees as he cried: "No--no, John--I can't. I can't."

Barclay put his hand on the back of the old man's chair, and he could feel the firm hard grip of the boy through his whole frame. Then after a moment's pause Barclay said: "General, I'm in earnest about that. You will either mail those dividend certificates according to your guarantee on the first, or as sure as there is a God in heaven I'll see that you won't have a dollar in your bank on the night of the second."

The old man stood gasping. The eyes of the two men met. Barclay's were bold and green and blazing.

"Boy! Boy! Boy!--" the old man faltered. "Don't ruin me! Don't ruin me--" he did not finish the sentence, but sank into his chair, and dropped his face to his breast and repeated, "Don't, don't, don't," feebly for a few times, without seeming to realize what he was saying. From some outpost of his being reinforcements came. For he rose suddenly, and shaking his haggard fist at the youth, exclaimed in a high, furious, cracking voice as he panted and shook his great hairy head: "No--by God, no, by God, no! You damned young cut-throat--you can break my bank, but you can't bulldoze me. No, by God--no!" He started to leave the room. Barclay caught the old man and swung him into a chair. The flint that Barclay's nature needed had been struck. His face was aglow as with an inspiration.

"Listen, man, listen!" Barclay cried. "I'm not going to break your bank, I'm trying to save it." He knew that the plan was ripe in his head, and as he talked it out, something stood beside him and marvelled at its perfection. As its inherent dishonesty revealed itself, the old man's face flinched, but Barclay went on unfolding his scheme. It required General Hendricks to break the law half a dozen ways, and to hazard all of the bank's assets, and all of its cash. And it required him to agree not to lend a dollar to any man in the county except as he complied with the demands of the Golden Belt Wheat Company and mortgaged his farm to Barclay. The plan that Barclay set forth literally capitalized the famine that had followed the grasshopper invasion, and sold the people their own need at Barclay's price. Then for an hour the two men fought it out, and at the end Barclay was saying: "I am glad you see it that way, and I believe, as you do, that they will take it a little better if we also agree to pay this year's taxes on the land they put under the mortgage. It would be a great sweetener to some of them, and I can slip in an option to sell the land to us outright as a kind of a joker in small type." His brassy eyes were small and beady as his brain worked out the details of his plan. He put his hands affectionately on General Hendricks' shoulders as he added, "You mustn't forget to write to Bob, General; hold him there whatever comes."

At the foot of the stairs the two men could hear the heavy tread of Colonel Culpepper. As Hendricks went down the stairs John heard the colonel's "Mornin', General," as the two men passed in the hallway.

"Mornin', Johnnie--how does your corporocity sagashiate this mornin'?" asked the colonel.

Barclay looked at the colonel through little beady green eyes and replied,--he knew not what. He merely dipped an oar into the talk occasionally, he did not steer it, and not until he emerged from his calculations twenty minutes after the colonel's greeting did Barclay realize that the colonel was in great pain. He was saying when Barclay's mind took heed: "And now, sir, I say, now, having forced his unwelcome and, I may say, filthy lucre upon me, the impudent scalawag writes me to-day to say that I must liquidate, must--liquidate, sir; in short, pay up. I call that impertinence. But no matter what I call it, he's going to foreclose." Barclay's eyes opened to attention. The colonel went on. "The original indebtedness was a matter of ten thousand--you will remember, John, that's what I paid for my share of the College Heights property, and while I have disposed of some,--in point of fact sold it at considerable profit,--yet, as you know, and as this scoundrel knows, for I have written him pointedly to that effect, I have been temporarily unable to remit any sum substantial enough to justify bothering him with it. But now the scamp, the grasping insulting brigand, notifies me that unless I pay him when the mortgage is due,--to be plain, sir, next week,--he proposes to foreclose on me."

The colonel's brows were knit with trouble. His voice faltered as he added: "And, John--John Barclay, my good friend--do you realize that that little piece of property out on the hill is all I have on earth now, except the roof over my head? And may--" here his voice slid into a tenor with pent-up emotion--"maybe the contemptible rapscallion will try to get that." The colonel had risen and was pacing the floor. "What a damn disreputable business your commerce is, anyway! John, I can't afford to lose that property--or I'd be a pauper, sir, a pauper peddling organs and sewing-machines and maybe teaching singing-school." The colonel's face caught a rift of sunshine as he added, "You know I did that once before I was married and came West--taught singing-school."

"Well, Colonel--let's see about it," said Barclay, absently. And the two men sat at the table and figured up that the colonel's liabilities were in the neighbourhood of twelve thousand, of which ten thousand were pressing and the rest more or less imminent. At the end of their conference, Barclay's mind was still full of his own affairs. But he said, after looking a moment at the troubled face of the big black-eyed man whose bulk towered above him, "Well, Colonel, I don't know what under heavens I can do--but I'll do what I can."

The colonel did not feel Barclay's abstraction. But the colonel's face cleared like a child's, and he reached for the little man and hugged him off his feet. Then the colonel broke out, "May the Lord, who heedeth the sparrow's fall and protects all us poor blundering children, bless you, John Barclay--bless you and all your household." There were tears in his eyes as he waved a grand adieu at the door, and he whistled "Gayly the Troubadour" as he tripped lightly down the stairs. And in another moment the large white plumes were dancing in his eyes again. This time they waved and beckoned toward a subscription paper which the colonel had just drawn up when the annoying letter came from Chicago, reminding him of his debt. The paper was for the relief of a farmer whose house and stock had been burned. The colonel brought from his hip pocket the carefully folded sheet of foolscap which he had put away when duty called him to Barclay. He paused at the bottom of the stair, backed the paper on the wall, and wrote under the words setting forth the farmer's destitution, "Martin Culpepper--twenty-five dollars." He stood a moment in the stairway looking into the street; the day was fair and beautiful; the grasshoppers were gone, and with them went all the vegetation in the landscape; but the colonel in his nankeen trousers and his plaited white shirt and white suspenders, under his white Panama hat, felt only the influence of the genial air. So he drew out the subscription paper again and erased the twenty-five dollars and put down thirty-five dollars. Then as Oscar Fernald and Daniel Frye came by with long faces the colonel hailed them.

"Boys," he said, "fellow named Haskins down in Fairview, with nine children and a sick wife, got burnt out last night, and I'm kind of seeing if we can't get him some lumber and groceries and things. I want you boys," the colonel saw the clouds gathering and smiled to brush them away, "yes, I want you boys to give me ten dollars apiece."

"Ten dollars!" cried Fernald.

"Ten dollars!" echoed Frye. "My Lord, man, there isn't ten dollars in cash between here and the Missouri River!"

"But the man and his children will starve, and his wife will die of neglect."

"That's the Lord's affair--and yours, Mart," returned Fernald, as he broke away from the colonel's grasp; "you and He brought them here." Frye went with Oscar, and they left the colonel with his subscription paper in his hand. He looked up and down the street and then drew a long breath, and put the paper against the wall again and sighed as he erased the thirty-five dollars and put down fifty dollars after his name. Then he started for the bank to see General Hendricks. The large white plumes were still dancing in his eyes.

But so far as Barclay is concerned the colonel never reached the bottom of the stairs, for Barclay had his desk covered with law-books and was looking up contracts. In an hour he had a draft of a mortgage and option to buy the mortgaged land written out, and was copying it for the printer. He took it to the *Banner* office and asked Brownwell to put two men on the job, and to have the proof ready by the next morning.

Brownwell waved both hands magnificently and with much grace, and said: "Mr. Barclay, we will put three men on the work, sir, and if you will do me the honour, I will be pleased to bring the proof up Lincoln Avenue to the home of our mutual friend, Colonel Culpepper, where you may see it to-night." Barclay fancied that a complacent smile wreathed Brownwell's face at the prospect of going to the Culpeppers', and the next instant the man was saying: "Charming young lady, Miss Molly! Ah, the ladies, the ladies--they will make fools of us. We can't resist them." He shrugged and smirked and wiggled his fingers and played with his mustaches. "Wine and women and song, you know--they get us all. But as for me--no wine, no song--but--" he finished the sentence with another flourish.

Barclay did what he could to smile good-naturedly and assent in some sort of way as he got out of the room. That night, going up the hill, he said to Jane: "Brownwell is one of those fellows who regard all women--all females is better, probably--as a form of vice. He's the kind that coos like a pouter pigeon when he talks to a woman."

Jane replied: "Yes, we women know them. They are always claiming that men like you are not gallant!" She added, "You know, John, he's the jealous, fiendish kind--with an animal's idea of honour." They walked on in silence for a moment, and she pressed his arm to her side and their eyes met in a smile. Then she said: "Doubtless some women like that sort of thing, or it would perish, but I don't like to be treated like a woman--a she-creature. I like to be thought of as a human being with a soul." She shuddered and continued: "But the soul doesn't enter even remotely into his scheme of things. We are just bodies."

The Barclays did not stay late at the Culpeppers' that night, but took the proofs at early bedtime and went down the hill. An hour later they heard Molly Culpepper and Brownwell loitering along the sidewalk. Brownwell was saying:--

"Ah, but you, Miss Molly, you are like the moon, for--

  "'The moon looks on many brooks,
  The brook can see no moon but this.'

"And I--I am--"

The Barclays did not hear what he was; however, they guessed, and they guessed correctly--so far as that goes. But Molly Culpepper did hear what he was and what he had been and what he would be, and the more she parried him, the closer he came. There were times when he forgot the "Miss" before the "Molly," and there were other times when she had to slip her hand from his ever so deftly. And once when they were walking over a smooth new wooden sidewalk coming home, he caught her swiftly by the waist and began waltzing and humming "The Blue Danube." And at the end of the smooth walk, she had to step distinctly away from him to release his arm. But she was twenty-one, and one does not always know how to do things at twenty-one--even when one intends to do them, and intends strongly and earnestly--that one would do at forty-one, and so as they stood under the Culpepper elm by the gate that night,--under the elm, stripped gaunt and naked by the locusts,--and the July moon traced the skeleton of the tree upon the close-cropped sod, we must not blame Molly Culpepper too much even if she let him, hold her hand a moment too long after he had kissed it a formal good night; for twenty-one is not as strong as its instincts. It is such a little while to learn all about a number of important things in a big and often wicked world that when a little man or a little woman, so new to this earth as twenty-one years, gets a finger pinched in the ruthless machinery, it is a time for tears and mothering and not for punishment. And so when Adrian Brownwell pulled the little girl off her feet and kissed her and asked her to marry him all in a second, and she could only struggle and cry "No, no!" and beg him to let her go--it is not a time to frown, but instead a time to go back to our twenty-ones and blush a little and sigh a little, and maybe cry and lie a little, and in the end thank God for the angel He sent to guard us, and if the angel slept--thank God still for the charity that has come to us.

The next day John Barclay had Colonel Martin Culpepper and Lige Bemis in his office galvanizing them with his enthusiasm and coaching them in their task. They were to promise three dollars an acre, August 15, to every farmer who would put a mortgage on his land for six dollars an acre. The other three dollars was to cover the amount paid by Barclay as rent for the land the year before. They were also to offer the landowner a dollar and a half an acre to plough and plant the land by September 15, and another dollar to cultivate it ready for the harvest, and the company was to pay the taxes on the land and furnish the seed. Barclay had figured out the seed money from the sale of the mortgages. The man was a dynamo of courage and determination, and he charged the two men before him until they fairly prickled with the scheme. He talked in short hard sentences, going over and over his plan, drilling them to bear down on the hard times and that there would be no other buyers or renters for the land, and to say that the bank would not lend a dollar except in this way. Long after they had left his office, Barclay's voice haunted them. His face was set and his eyes steady and small, and the vertical wrinkle in his brow was as firm as an old scar. He limped about the room quickly, but his strong foot thumped the floor with a thud that punctuated his words.

They left, and he sat down to write a letter to Bob Hendricks telling him the plan. He had finished two pages when General Hendricks came in a-tremble and breathless. The eyes of the two men met, and Hendricks replied:--

"It's Brownwell--the fat's in the fire, John. Brownwell's going!"

"Going--going where?" asked the man at the desk, blankly.

"Going to leave town. He's been in and given notice that he wants his money in gold day after to-morrow."

"Well--well!" exclaimed Barclay, with his eyes staring dumbly at nothing on the dingy white wall before him. "Well--don't that beat the Jews? Going to leave town!" He pulled himself together and gripped his chair as he said, "Not by a damn sight he ain't. He's going to stay right here and sweat it out. We need that four thousand dollars in our business. No, you don't, Mr. Man--" he addressed a hypothetical Brownwell. "You're roped and tied and bucked and gagged, and you stay here." Then he said, "You go on over to the bank, General, and I'll take care of Brownwell." Barclay literally shoved the older man to the door. As he opened it he said, "Send me up a boy if you see one on the street."

In ten minutes Brownwell was running up the stairs to Barclay's office in response to his note. He brought a copy of the mortgage with, him, and laid it before Barclay, who went over it critically. He found a few errors and marked them, and holding it in his hands turned to the editor.

"Hendricks says you are going to leave town. Why?" asked Barclay, bluntly. He had discovered even that early in life that a circuitous man is generally knocked off his guard by a rush. Brown well blinked and sputtered a second or two, scrambling to his equilibrium. Before he could parry Barclay assaulted him again with: "Starving to death, eh? Lost your grip--going back to Alabama with the banjo on your knee, are you?"

"No, sir--no, sir, you are entirely wrong, sir--entirely wrong, and scarcely more polite, either." Brown well paused a minute and added: "Business is entirely satisfactory, sir--entirely so. It is another matter." He hesitated a moment and added, with the ghost of a smirk, "A matter of sentiment--for--

"'The heart that is soonest awake to the flowers,
Is always the first to be touched by the thorns.'"

Brownwell sat there flipping his gloves, exasperatingly; Barclay screwed up his eyes, put his head on one side, and suddenly a flash came into his face and he exclaimed, "Come off, you don't mean it--not Molly!"

The rejected one inclined his head. Barclay was about to laugh, but instead he said, "Well, you are not a quitter; why don't you go ahead and get her?" He glanced instinctively at his letter to Bob Hendricks, and as if to shield what he was going to say, put a paper over the page, and then the seriousness of the situation came over him. "You know women; cheer up, man--try again. Stick to it--you'll win," cried Barclay. The fool might go for so small a reason. It was no time for ribaldry. "Let me tell you something," he went on. His eyes opened again with a steady ruthless purpose in them, that the man before him was too intent on his own pose to see. Barclay put a weight upon the white sheet of paper that he had spread over his letter to Bob Hendricks and then went on. "Say, Brownwell, let me tell you something. This town is right in the balance; you can help." Something seemed to hold Barclay back, but he took the plunge. "You can stay here and help. We need men like you." Then he took a blind shot in the dark before going on--perhaps to give himself another chance. "Have you got any more of that buried money--I mean more than you gave General Hendricks--the kind that you dug up after the war and scratched the mould off the eagles?"

Brownwell flushed and replied, as he put one hand in his coat and the other, with his stick and hat and gloves, behind him: "That is my affair, sir. However, I will say that I have."

"I thought so," retorted Barclay. "Now look here, bring it to the Ridge. Here's the place to invest it and now's the everlasting time. You jump in here and help us out, help build up the town, and there's nothing too good for you." Barclay was ready for it now. He did not flinch, but went on: "Also here's your chance to help Colonel Culpepper. He's to be closed out, and ten thousand would save him. You know the kind of a man the colonel is. Stay with the game, Mr. Man, stay with the game." He saw Brownwell's eyes twitch. Barclay knew he had won. He added slowly, "You understand?"

Brownwell smiled benignly. Barclay looked nervously at the unfinished letter on the table. Brownwell waved his arms again dramatically, and replied: "Ah, thank you--thank you. I shall play my hand out--and hearts are trumps--are they not?" And he went out almost dancing for joy.

When the man was gone Barclay shuddered; his contempt for Brownwell was one of the things he prided himself on, and the intrigue revolted him. He stood a moment at the window looking into the street absently. He became conscious that some one was smiling at him on the crossing below. Then automatically he heard himself say, "Oh, Molly, can you run up a minute?" And a moment later she was in the room. She was a bewitching little body in her wide skirts and her pancake of a hat with a feather in it as she sat there looking at her toes that morning, with her bright eyes flashing up into his like rockets. But there were lines under the eyes, and the rims of the eyelids were almost red--as red as pretty eyelids ever may be. Barclay went right to the midst of the matter at once. He did not patronize her, but told her in detail just the situation--how the Golden Belt Wheat Company's interest must be met by the bank under its guarantee, or Bob and his father would be worse than bankrupts, they would be criminals. He put Bob always in the foreground. Barclay unfolded to her all the plans for going ahead with the work, and he told her what they were doing for her father by giving him employment. He marched straight up to the matter in hand without flinching.

"Molly," he began without batting his eyes, "here is where you come in. That fellow Brownwell was up here this morning. Oh, you needn't shiver--I know all about it. You had the honour of refusing him last night." To her astonished, hurt face he paid no heed, but went on: "Now he's going to leave town on account of you and pull out four thousand dollars he's got in the bank. If he does that, we can't pay our guarantee. You've got to call him back." She flared up as if to stop him, but he went on: "Oh, I know, Molly Culpepper--but this is no game of London Bridge. It's bad enough, but it's business--cold clammy business, and sometimes we have to do things in this world for

the larger good. That roan simply can't leave this town and you must
bold him. It's ruin and perhaps prison to Bob and his father if he
goes; and as for your own father and mother--it makes them paupers,
Molly. There's no other way out of it." He paused a moment.

The girl's face blanched, and she looked at the floor and spoke, "And
Bob--when can he come back?"

"I don't know, Molly--but not now--he never was needed there as he
is now. It's a life-and-death matter, Molly Culpepper, with every
creature on earth that's nearest and dearest to you--it makes or
breaks us. It's a miserable business, I know well--but your duty is
to act for the larger good. You can't afford to send Bob to jail and
your people to the poorhouse just because--"

The girl looked up piteously and then cried out: "Oh, John--don't,
don't--I can't. It's awful, John--I can't."

"But, Molly," he replied as gently as he could, "you must. You can't
afford to be squeamish about this business. This is a woman's job,
Molly, not a child's."

She rose and looked at him a fleeting moment as if in search of some
mercy in his face. Then she looked away. He stood beside her, barring
her way to the door. "But you'll try, Molly, won't you--you'll try?"
he cried. She looked at him again with begging eyes and stepped around
him, and said breathlessly as she reached the door: "Oh, I don't know,
John--I don't know. I must think about it."

She felt her way down the stairs, and stopped a minute to compose
herself before she crossed the street and walked wearily up the hill.

That night at supper Colonel Culpepper addressed the assembled family expansively. "The ravens, my dears, the ravens. Behold Elijah fed by the sacred birds. By Adrian P. Brownwell, to be exact. This morning I went down town with the sheriff selling the roof over our heads. This afternoon who should come to me soliciting the pleasure of lending, me money--who, I say, but Adrian P. Brownwell?"

"Well, I hope you didn't keep him standing," put in Buchanan.

"My son," responded the colonel, as he whetted the carving knife on the steel--a form which was used more for rhetorical effect than, culinary necessity, as there were pork chops on the platter, "my son, no true gentleman will rebuke another who is trying to lend him money. Always remember that." And the colonel's great body shook with merriment, as he proceeded to fill up the plates. But one plate went from the table untouched, and Molly Culpepper went about her work with a leaden heart. For the world had become a horrible phantasm to her, a place of longing and of heartache, a place of temptation and trial, lying under the shadow of tragedy. And whose world was it that night, as she sat chattering with her father and the man she feared, whose world was it that night, if this is a real world, and not the shadow of a dream? Was it the colonel's gay world, or John's golden world, or Ward's harmonious world, or poor little Molly's world--all askew with miserable duties and racking heartaches, and grinning sneering fears, with the relentless image of the Larger Good always before her? Surely it was not all their worlds, for there is only one world. Then whose was it? God who made it and set it in the heavens in His great love and mercy only knows. Watts McHurdie once wrote some query like this, and the whole town smiled at his fancy. In that portion of his "Complete Poetical and Philosophical Works" called "Fragments" occur these lines:--

"The wise men say
This world spins 'round the universe of which it is a part;

But anyway--
The only world I know about is spun from out my heart."

And perhaps Watts, sewing away in his harness shop, had deciphered one letter in the riddle of the Sphinx.

CHAPTER XII

"If I ever get to be a Turk or anything like that," said Watts McHurdie, in October, two months after the events recorded in the last chapter had occurred, as he sat astraddle of his bench, sewing on a bridle, "I'm going to have one red-headed wife--but not much more'n one."

Colonel Culpepper dropped a "Why?" into the reflections of the poet.

Watts replied, "Oh, just to complete the set!"

The colonel did not answer and Watts chuckled: "I figure out that women are a study. You learn this one and pat yourself on the breast-bone and say, 'Behold me, I'm on to women.' But you ain't. Another comes along and you have to begin at the beginning and learn 'em all over. I wonder if Solomon who had a thousand--more or less--got all his wisdom from them."

The colonel shook his head, and said sententiously, "Watts--they hain't a blame thing in it--not a blame thing." The creaking of the treadle on Watt's bench slit the silence for a few moments, and the colonel went on: "There can be educated fools about women, Watts

McHurdie, just as there are educated fools about books. There's nothing in your theory of a liberal education in women. On the contrary, in all matters relating to and touching on affairs of the heart--beware of the man with one wife."

McHurdie flashed his yellow-toothed smile upon his friend and replied, "Or less than one?"

"No, sir, just one," answered Colonel Culpepper. "A man with a raft of wives, first and last, is like a fellow with good luck--the Lord never gives him anything else. And I may say in point of fact, that the man with no wife is like a man with bad luck--the Lord never gives him anything else, either!" The colonel slapped his right hand on his knee and exclaimed: "Watts McHurdie--what's the matter with you, man? Don't you see Nellie's all ready and waitin'--just fairly honin', and longin', I may say, for a home and a place to begin to live?"

McHurdie gave his treadle a jam and swayed forward over his work and answered, "Marry in haste--repent at leisure."

But nevertheless that night Watts sat with Nellie Logan on the front porch of the Wards' house, watching the rising harvest moon, while Mrs. Ward, inside, was singing to her baby. Nellie Logan roomed with the Wards, and was bookkeeper in Dorman's store. It was nearly ten o'clock and the man rose to go. "Well," he said, and hesitated a moment, "well, Nellie, I suppose you're still waiting?" It was a question rather than an assertion.

The woman put her hands gently on the man's arms and sighed. "I just can't--not yet, Watts."

"Well, I thought maybe you'd changed your mind." He smiled as he continued, "You know they say women do change sometimes."

She looked down at him sadly. "Yes, I know they do, but some way I don't."

There was a long pause while Watts screwed up his courage to say, "Still kind of thinking about that preacher?"

The woman had no animation in her voice as she replied, "You know that by now--without asking."

The man sat down on the step, and she sat on a lower step. He was silent for a time. Then he said, "Funny, ain't it?" She knew she was not to reply; for in a dozen years she had learned the man's moods. In a minute, during which he looked into his hat absent-mindedly, he went on: "As far as I've been able to make it out, love's a kind of a grand-right-and-left. I give my right hand to you, and you give yours to the preacher, and he gives his to some other girl, and she gives hers to some one else, like as not, who gives his to some one else, and the fiddle and the horn and the piano and the bass fid screech and toot and howl, and away we go and sigh under our breaths and break our hearts and swing our partners, and it's everybody dance." He looked up at her and smiled at his fancy. For he was a poet and thought his remarks had some artistic value.

She smiled back at him, and he leaned on his elbows and looked up at her as he said quietly: "I'd like awful well, Nellie--awful well if you'd be my partner for the rest of this dance. It's lonesome down there in the shop."

The woman patted his hand, and they sat quietly for a while and then she said, "Maybe sometime, Watts, but not to-night."

He got up, and stood for a moment beside her on the walk. "Well," he said at length, "I suppose I must be moving along--as the wandering Jew said." He smiled and their eyes met in the moonlight. Watts dropped his instantly, and exclaimed, "You're a terrible handsome girl, Nellie--? did you know it?" He repeated it and added, "And the Lord knows I love you, Nellie, and I've said it a thousand times." He found her hand again, and said as he put on his hat, "Well, good-by, Nellie--good-by--if you call that gone." His handclasp tightened and hers responded, and then he dropped her hand and turned away.

The woman felt a desire to scream; she never knew how she choked her desire. But she rushed after him and caught him tightly and sobbed, "Oh, Watts--Watts--Watts McHurdie--are you never going to have any more snap in you than that?"

As he kicked away the earth from under him, Watts McHurdie saw the light in a window of the Culpepper home, and when he came down to earth again five minutes later, he said, "Well, I was just a-thinking how nice it would be to go over to Culpeppers' and kind of tell them the news!"

"They'll have news of their own pretty soon, I expect," replied Nellie. And to Watts' blank look she replied: "The way that man Brownwell keeps shining around. He was there four nights last week, and he's been there two this week already. I don't see what Molly Culpepper can be thinking of."

So they deferred the visit to the Culpeppers', and in due time Watts McHurdie flitted down Lincoln Avenue and felt himself wafted along Main Street as far in the clouds as a mortal may be. And though it was nearly midnight, he brought out his accordion and sat playing it, beating time with his left foot, and in his closed eyes seeing visions that by all the rights of this game of life should come only to youth.

And the guests in the Thayer House next morning asked, "Well, for heaven's sake, who was that playing 'Silver Threads among the Gold' along there about midnight?--he surely must know it by this time."

And Adrian Brownwell, sitting on the Culpepper veranda the next night but one, said: "Colonel, your harness-maker friend is a musical artist. The other night when I came in I heard him twanging his lute--'The Harp that once through Tara's Hall'; you know, Colonel."

And John Barclay closed his letter to Bob Hendricks: "Well, Bob, as I sit here with fifty letters written this evening and ready to mail, and the blessed knowledge that we have 18,000 acres of winter wheat all planted if not paid for, I can hear old Watts wheezing away on his accordion in his shop down street. Poor old Watts, it's a pity that man hasn't the acquisitive faculty--he could turn that talent into enough to keep him all his days. Poor old Watts!"

And Molly Culpepper, sitting in her bedroom chewing her penholder, finally wrote this: "Watts McHurdie went sailing by the house to-night, coming home from the Wards', where he was making his regular call on Nellie. You know what a mouse-like little walk he has, scratching along the sidewalk so demurely; but to-night, after he passed our place I heard him actually break into a hippety-hop, and as I was sitting on the veranda, I could hear him clicking clear down to the new stone walk in front of the post-office." Oho, Molly Culpepper, you said "as I was sitting on the veranda"; that is of course the truth, but not the whole truth; what you might have said was "as we were sitting on the veranda," and "as we were talking of what I like" and "what you like," and of "what I think" and "what you think," and as "I was listening to war tales from a Southern soldier," and as "I was finding it on the whole rather a tiresome business "; those things you might have written, Molly Culpepper, but you did not. And was it a twinge or a prick or a sharp reproachful stab of your conscience that made you chew the tip of your penholder into shreds and then madly write down this:--

"Bob, I don't know what is coming over me; but some way your letters seem so far away, and it has been such a long time since I saw you, a whole lonesome year, and Bob dear, I am so weak and so unworthy of you; I know it, oh, I know it. But I feel to-night that I must tell you something right from my heart. It is this, dear: no matter what may happen, I want you to know that I must always love you better than any one else in all the world. I seem so young and foolish, and life is so long and the world is so big--so big and you are so far away. But, Bob dear, my good true boy, don't forget this that I tell you to-night, that through all time and all eternity the innermost part of my heart must always be yours. No matter what happens to you and me in the course of life in the big world--you must never forget what I have written here to-night."

And these words, for some strange reason, were burned on the man's soul; though she had written him fonder ones, which passed from him with the years. The other words of the letter fell into his eyes and were consumed there, so he does not remember that she also wrote that night: "I have just been standing at my bedroom window, looking out over the town. It is quiet as the graveyard, save for the murmur of the waters falling over the dam. And I cannot tell whether it is fancy or whether it is real, but now and then there comes to me a faint hint of music,--it sounds almost like Watts' accordion, but of course it cannot be at this unholy hour, and the tune it makes me think of some way is 'Silver Threads among the Gold.' Isn't it odd that I should hear that song, and yet not hear it, and have it running through my mind?"

And thus the town heard Watts McHurdie's song of triumph--the chortle that every male creature of the human kind instinctively lets out when

he has found favour in some woman's eyes, that men have let out since
Lemech sang of victory over the young man to Adah and Zillah! And in
all the town no one knew what it meant. For the accordion is not
essentially an instrument of passion. So the episode ended, and
another day came in. And all that is left to mark for this world that
night of triumph--and that mark soon will bleach into oblivion--are
the verses entitled "Love at Sunset," of which Colonel Martin
Culpepper, the poet's biographer, writes in that chapter "At Hymen's
Altar," referred to before: "This poem was written October 14, 1874,
on the occasion of the poet's engagement to Miss Nellie Logan, who
afterward became his wife. By many competent critics, including no
less a personage than Hon. John Barclay, president of the National
Provisions Company, this poem is deemed one of Mr. McHurdie's noblest
achievements, ranking second only to the great song that gave him
national fame."

And it should be set down as an integral part of this narrative that
John Barclay first read the verses "Love at Sunset" in the ***Banner***,
two weeks after the night of their composition, as he was finishing a
campaign for the Fifth Parallel bonds. He picked up the ***Banner*** one
evening at twilight in a house in Pleasant township, and seeing Watts'
initials under some verses, read them at first mechanically, and then
reread them with real zest, and so deeply did they move the man from
the mooring of the campaign that seeing an accordion on the table of
the best room in which he was waiting for supper, Barclay picked it up
and fooled with it for half an hour. It had been a dozen years since
he had played an accordion, and the tunes that came into his fingers
were old tunes in vogue before the war, and he thought of himself as
an old man, though he was not yet twenty-five. But the old tunes
brought back his boyhood from days so remote that they seemed a long
time past. And that night when he addressed the people in the Pleasant
Valley schoolhouse, he was half an hour getting on to the subject of
the bonds; he dwelt on the old days and spoke of the drouth of '60 and

of the pioneers, and preached a sermon, with their lives for texts, on the value of service without thought of money or hope of other reward than the joy one has in consecrated work. Then he launched into the bond proposition, and when the votes were counted Pleasant township indorsed Barclay's plan overwhelmingly. For he was a young man of force, if not of eloquence. His evident sincerity made up for what he lacked in oratorical charm, and he left an impression on those about him. So when the bonds carried in Garrison County, the firm of Ward and Barclay was made local attorneys for the road, and General Ward, smarting under the defeat of his party in the state, refused to accept the railroad's business, and the partnership was dissolved.

"John," said Ward, as he put his hands on the young man's shoulders and looked at him a kindly moment, before picking up his bushel basket of letters and papers, to move them into another room and dissolve the partnership, "John," the elder man repeated, "if I could always maintain such a faith in God as you maintain in money and its power, I could raise the dead."

Barclay blinked a second and replied, "Well, now, General, look here--what I don't understand is how you expect to accomplish anything without money."

"I can't tell you, John--but some way I have faith that I can--can do more real work in this world without bothering to get money, than I can by stopping to get money with which to do good."

"But if you had a million, you could do more good with it than you are doing now, couldn't you?" asked Barclay.

"Yes, perhaps I could," admitted the general, as he eyed his miserable little pile of worldly goods in the basket. "I suppose I could," he repeated meditatively.

"All right then, General," cut in Barclay. "I have no million, any more than you have; but I'm going to get one--or two, maybe a dozen if I can, and I want to do good with it just as much as you do. When I get it I'll show you." Barclay rose to lend the general a hand with his basket. As they went awkwardly through the door with the load, the general stopping to get a hold on the basket that would not twist his hand, he put the load down in the hall and said: "But while you're getting that million, you're wasting God's ten talents, boy. Can't you see that if you would use your force, your keenness, and persistence helping mankind in some way--teaching, preaching, lending a hand to the poor, or helping to fight organized greed, you would get more of God's work done than you will by squeezing the daylights out of your fellow-men, making them hate money because of your avarice, and end by doling it out to them in charity? That's my point, boy. That's why I don't want your railroad job."

They had dropped the basket in the bare room. The general had not so much as a chair or a desk. He looked it over, and Barclay's eyes followed his. "What are you going to do for furniture?" asked the younger man.

The general's thin face wrinkled into a smile. "Well," he replied, "I suppose that if a raven can carry dry-goods, groceries, boots and shoes and drugs, paints and oils,--and certainly the ravens have been bringing those things to the Wards for eight years now, and they're all paid for,--the blessed bird can hump itself a little and bring some furniture, stoves, and hardware."

Barclay limped into his room, while the general rubbed the dust off the windows. In a minute John came stumbling in with a chair, and as he set it down he said, "Here comes the first raven, General, and now if you'll kindly come and give the ravens a lift, they'll bring you a table." And so the two men dragged the table into the office, and as they finished, Ward saw General Hendricks coming up the stairs, and when the new room had been put in order,--a simple operation, --General Ward hurried home to help Mrs. Ward get in their dahlia roots for the winter.

As they were digging in the garden, covering the ferns and wrapping the magnolia tree they had lately acquired, and mulching the perennials, Mrs. Mary Barclay came toward them buffeting the wind. She wore the long cowlish waterproof cloak and hood of the period--which she had put on during the cloudy morning. Her tall strong figure did not bend in the wind, and the schoolbooks she carried in her hand broke the straight line of her figure only to heighten the priestess effect that her approaching presence produced.

"Well, children," she said, as she stood by the Wards at their work, "preparing your miracles?" She looked at the bulbs and roots, and smiled. "How wonderful that all the beauty of the flowers should be in those scrawny brown things; and," she added as she brushed away the brown hair of her forties from her broad brow, "God probably thinks the same thing when He considers men and their souls."

"And when the gardener puts us away for our winter's sleep?" Ward asked.

She turned her big frank blue eyes upon him as she took the words from his mouth, "'And the last Adam was made a quickening spirit.'" Then she smiled sadly and said, "But it is the old Adam himself that I seem to be wrestling with just now."

"In the children--at school?" asked the Wards, one after the other. She sighed and looked at the little troopers straggling along the highway, and replied, "Yes, partly that, too," and throwing her unnecessary hood back, turned her face into the wind and walked quickly away. The Wards watched her as she strode down the hill, and finally as he bent to his work the general asked:--

"Lucy, what does she think of John?"

Mrs. Ward, who was busy with a geranium, did not reply at once. But in a moment she rose and, putting the plant with some others that were to go to the cellar, replied: "Oh, Phil--you know a mother tries to hope against hope. She teaches her school every day, and keeps her mind busy. But sometimes, when she stops in here after school or for lunch, she can't help dropping things that let me know. I think her heart is breaking, Phil."

"Does she know about the wheat deal--I mean about the way he has made the farmers sign that mortgage by cutting them off from borrowing money at the bank?"

"Not all of it--but I think she suspects," replied the wife.

"Did you know, dear," said the general, as he put the plants in the barrow to wheel them to the cellar, "that I ran across something to-day--it may be all suspicion, and I don't want to wrong John--but Mart Culpepper, God bless his big innocent heart, let something slip--well, it was John, I think, who arranged for that loan of ten thousand from Brownwell to Mart. Though why he didn't get it at the bank, I don't know. But John had some reason. Things look mighty crooked there at the bank. I know this--Mart says that Brownwell lent him the money, and Mart lent it to the bank for a month there in August, while he was holding the Chicago fellow in the air."

Mrs. Ward sat down on the front steps of the porch, and exclaimed:--

"Well, Phil Ward--that's why the Culpeppers are so nice to Brownwell. Honestly, Phil, the last time I was over Mrs. Culpepper nearly talked her head off to me and at Molly about what a fine man he is, and told all about his family, and connections--he's related to the angel Gabriel on his mother's side," she laughed, "and he's own cousin to St. Peter through the Brownwells."

"Oh, I guess they're innocent enough about it--they aren't mercenary," interrupted the general.

"Oh, no," replied Mrs Ward, "never in the world; but he's been good to them and he's of their stock--and it's only natural."

"Yes, probably," replied the general, and asked, "Does she intend to marry him, do you think?" Mrs. Ward was sorting some dahlia roots on the wheelbarrow and did not reply at once. "Do you suppose they're engaged?" repeated the general.

"I often wonder," she returned, still at her task. Then she rose, holding a bulb in her hands, and said: "It's a funny kind of relation. Her father and mother egging her on--and you know that kind of a man; give him an inch and he'll take an ell. I wonder how far he has got." She took the bulb to a pile near the rear of the house. "Those are the nice big yellow ones I'm saving for Mrs. Barclay. But I'm sure of one thing, Molly has no notion of marrying Brownwell." She continued: "Molly is still in love with Bob. She was over here last week and had a good cry and told me so."

"Well, why doesn't she send this man about his business?" exclaimed the general.

Mrs. Ward sighed a little and replied, "Because--there is only one perfect person in all the world, and that's you." She smiled at him and continued: "The rest of us, dear, are just flesh and blood. So we make mistakes. Molly knows she should; she told me so the other day. And she hates herself for not doing it. But, dearie--don't you see she thinks if she does, her father and mother will lose the big house, and Bob will be involved in some kind of trouble? They keep that before her all of the time. She says that John is always insisting that she be nice to Brownwell. And you know the Culpeppers think Brownwell is--well, you know what they think."

They worked along for a while, and the general stopped and put his foot on his spade and cried: "That boy--that boy--that boy! Isn't he selling his soul to the devil by bits? A little chunk goes every day. And oh, my dear, my dear--" he broke out, "what profiteth a man if he gain the whole world, and lose his own soul? Poor, poor John." He fell to his work again, sighing, "Poor John, poor John!" So they talked on until the afternoon grew old.

And while they were talking, John and General Hendricks were in Barclay's office going over matters, and seeing where they stood.

"So he says seventy thousand is too much for the company and me to owe?" said John, at the end of half an hour's conference.

The general was drumming his fingers on the table nervously. "Yes--he says we've got to reduce that in thirty days, or he'll close us up. Haven't you got any political influence, somewhere in the East, John,--some of those stockholders,--that will hold this matter up till you can harvest your crop next June?"

Barclay thought a moment, with his hand in his chin, and then slowly shook his head. A bank inspector from Washington was several degrees higher in the work of politics than Barclay had gone.

"Let me see--" droned Barclay; "let me see. We can at least try scattering it out a little; cut off, say, fifty thousand from me and the company and put it in the name of Lige--"

"He's on to Lige, we've got a hat full of Lige's notes in there," interrupted the general.

"All right, then, drop Lige and put in the colonel--he'll do that for me, and I'll see if I can't get the colonel to get Brownwell to accommodate us. He's burning a good bit of the colonel's stove wood these nights." Barclay smiled, and added, "And I'll just put Bob in for a few thousand."

"But what'll we do about those taxes?" asked the general, anxiously. "You know they've got to be paid before the first of the year, and that's only six weeks off."

Barclay rose and paced the rug, and replied: "Yes, that's so. I was going to make another note for them. But I suppose we oughtn't to do it even under cover; for if he found out you had exceeded our loan right now--you know those fellows get ugly sometimes." The young man screwed up his face and stood looking out of the window in silence for a long minute. Then he limped over to his chair and sat down as one who has a plan. "Say now, General; you know Gabe Carnine's coming in as county treasurer right after the first of the year, and we will make him help us. You make your personal check for the nine thousand, and give it to the old cuss who's in the county treasurer's office now, with the descriptions of the land, and get the tax receipts; he'll bring the check back to the bank; you give him credit on his pass-book with the other checks, and just hold your own check out in the drawer as cash. If my check was in there, the inspector might drop in and see it, and cause a disturbance. When Gabe comes in, I'll make him carry the matter over till next summer."

The transaction would cover only a few days, Barclay explained; and finally he had his way. So the Larger Good was accomplished.

And later Adrian Brownwell came into the office to say:--

"Mr. Barclay, our friend, Colonel Culpepper, confessed to me after some transparent attempts at subterfuge that my signing an accommodation note would help you, and do I understand this also will help our young friend, Robert Hendricks, whom I have never seen, and enable him to remain at his post during the winter?"

John Barclay took a square hard look at Brownwell, and got a smile and a faint little shrug in return, whereupon, for the Larger Good, he replied "Yes," and for the Larger Good also, perhaps, Adrian Brownwell answered:

"Well, I shall be delighted--just make my note for thirty days--only thirty days, you understand; and then--well, of course if circumstances justify it, I'll renew it." Barclay laughed and asked, "Well, Mr. Brownwell, as between friends may I ask how 'circumstances' are getting on?"

Brownwell shrugged his shoulders and smiled blandly as he answered: "Just so-so; I go twice a week. And--" he waved his gloves airily and continued, "What is it the immortal Burns says: 'A man's a man, for a' that and a' that!' And I'm a man, John Barclay, and she's a woman. And I go twice a week. You know women, sir, you know women--they're mostly all alike. So I think--" he smirked complacently as he concluded--"I think what I need is time--only time."

"Luck to you," said Barclay. "I'll just make the note thirty days, as you say, and we can renew it from time to time."

Then Brownwell put on his hat, twirled his cane effusively, and bade Barclay an elaborate adieu.

And ten days later, Molly Culpepper, loathing herself in her soul, and praying for the day of deliverance when it should be all over, walked slowly from the post-office up the hill to the house, the stately house, with its impressive pillars, reading this: "My darling Girl: John has sent me some more mortgages to sell, and they have to be sold now. He says that father has to have the money, and he and father have laid out work for me that will keep me here till the middle of January. John says that the government inspector has been threatening us with serious trouble in the bank lately, and we must have the money. He says the times have forced us to do certain things that were technically wrong--though I guess they were criminally wrong from what he says, and we must have this money to make things good. So I am compelled to stay here and work. Father commands me to stay in a way that makes me fear that my coming home now would mean our ruin. What a brick John is to stay there and shoulder it all. But, oh, darling, darling, darling, I love you."

There was more, of course, and it was from a man's heart, and the strange and sad part of this story is that when Molly Culpepper read the rest of the letter, her heart burned in shame, and her shame was keener than her sorrow that her lover was not coming home.

So it happened naturally that Molly Culpepper went to the Christmas dance with Adrian Brownwell, and when Jane Barclay, seeing the proprietary way the Alabaman hovered over Molly, and his obvious jealousy of all the other men who were civil to her, asked John why he did not let Bob come home for the holidays, as he had promised, for the Larger Good John told her the facts--that there were some mortgages that had just come in, and they must be sold, so that the

company could reduce its indebtedness to the bank. But the facts are
not always the truth, and in her heart, which did not reason but only
felt, Molly Culpepper, knowing that Brownwell and John Barclay were in
some kind of an affair together, feared the truth. And from her heart
she wrote to her lover questioning John's motives and pleading with
him to return, and he, having merely the facts, did not see the truth,
and replied impatiently--so impatiently that it hurt, and there was
temper in her answer, and then for over a week no letter came, and for
over a week no reply went back to that. And so the Larger Good was
doing its fine work in a wicked world.

CHAPTER XIII

The spring sun of 1875 that tanned John Barclay's face gave it a
leathery masklike appearance that the succeeding years never entirely
wore off. For he lived in the open by day, riding among his fields in
three townships, watching the green carpet of March rise and begin to
dimple in April, and billow in May. And at night he worked in his
office until the midnight cockcrow. His back was bowed under a score
of burdens. But his greatest burden was the bank; for it gave him
worry; and worry weighed upon him more than work. It was in
April--early April when the days were raw and cloudy, and the nights
blustery and dreary--that Barclay sat in his office one night after a
hard day afield, his top-boots spattered with mud, his corduroy coat
spread out on a chair to dry, and his wet gray soft hat on his desk
beside him. Jane was with her parents in Minneola, and Barclay had
come to his office without eating, from the stable where he left his
team. The yellow lights in the street below were reflected on the
mists outside his window, and the dripping eaves and cornices above

him and about him seemed to mark the time of some eery music too fine for his senses, and the footfalls in the street below, hurrying footfalls of people shivering through the mists, seemed to be the drum beats of the weird symphony that he could not hear.

Barclay drew a watch from, the pocket of his blue flannel shirt, and looked at it and stopped writing and stood by the box-stove. He was looking at the door when he heard a thud on the stairs. It was followed by a rattling sound, and in a moment Adrian Brownwell and his cane were in the room. After the rather gorgeous cadenza of Brownwell's greeting had died away and Barclay had his man in a chair, Barclay opened the stove door and let the glow of the flames fight the shadows in the room.

"Well," said Barclay, turning toward his visitor brusquely, "why won't you renew that accommodation paper for me again?"

The Papins and the Dulangpres shrugged their shoulders and waved their hands through Brownwell rather nastily as he answered, "Circumstances, Mr. Barclay, circumstances!"

"You're not getting along fast enough, eh?" retorted Barclay.

"Yes--and no," returned Brownwell.

"What do you mean?" asked Barclay, half divining the truth.

"Well--it is after all our own affair--but since you are a friend I will say this: three times a week--sometimes four times a week I go out to pay my respects. Until November I stayed until nine, at Christmas we put on another hour; now it is ten-thirty. I am a man, John Barclay--as you see. She--she is an angel. Very good. In that way, yes. But," the Papins and Dulangpres came back to his face, and he shook his head. "But otherwise--no. There we stand still. She will not say it."

Barclay squinted at the man who sat so complacently in the glow of the firelight, with his cane between his toes and his gloves lightly fanning the air. "So I take it," said John, "that you are like the Memorial Day parade, several hours passing a given point!"

"Exactly," smiled back Brownwell. He drew from his pocket a diamond ring. "She will look at it; she will admire it. She will put it on a chain, but she will not wear it. And so I say, why should I put my head in a noose here in your bank--what's the use? No, sir, John Barclay--no, sir. I'm done, sir."

Barclay knew wheedling would not move Brownwell. He was of the mulish temperament. So Barclay stretched out in his chair, locked his hands back of his head, and looked at the ceiling through his eyelashes. After a silence he addressed the cobwebs above him: "Supposing the case. Would a letter from me to you, setting forth the desperate need of this accommodation paper, not especially for me, but for Colonel Culpepper's fortunes and the good name of the Hendricks family--would that help your cause--a letter that you could show; a letter," Barclay said slowly, "asking for this accommodation; a letter that you could show to--to--well, to the proper parties, let us say, to-night; would--that kind of a letter help--" Barclay rose suddenly to an upright position and went on: "Say, Mr. Man, that ought to pretty nearly fix it. Let's leave both matters open, say for two hours, and then at ten o'clock or so--you come back here, and I'll have the note for you to sign--if you care to. How's that?" he asked as he turned to his desk and reached for a pen.

"Well," replied Brownwell, "I am willing to try."

And so Barclay sat writing for five minutes, while the glow of the flames died down, and the shadows ceased fighting and were still.

"Read this over," said Barclay at length. "You will see," he added, as he handed Brownwell the unfolded sheets, "that I have made it clear that if you refuse to sign our notes, General Hendricks will be compelled to close the bank, and that the examination which will follow will send him to prison and jeopardize Bob, who has signed a lot of improper notes there to cover our transactions, and that in the crash Colonel Culpepper will lose all he has, including the roof over his head--if you refuse to help us." ("However," snarled Barclay, at his conscience, "I've only told the truth; for if you take your money and go and shut down on the colonel, it would make him a pauper.")

With a flourishing crescendo finale Adrian Brownwell entered the dark stairway and went down into the street. Barclay turned quickly to his work as if to avoid meditation. The scratch of his pen and the murmur of the water on the roof grew louder and louder as the evening waxed old. And out on the hill, out on Lincoln Avenue, the rain descended, and the floods came, and the winds blew and beat upon that house--that stately house of a father's pride and--

At ten o'clock John Barclay heard a light footstep and a rattling cane upon the stair, and Brownwell, a human whirligig of gay gestures, came tripping into the room. "A pen, a pen,"--he cried, "my kingdom for a pen." He was tugging at his gloves as he spoke, and in the clatter that he made, Barclay found the blank note and pushed it toward the table's edge to Brownwell, who put his ornate copy-book signature upon it with a flourish.

When he had gone, Barclay wrote a note to Jane telling her of Molly's engagement to Brownwell, and then he sat posting his books, and figuring up his accounts. It was after midnight when he limped down

the stairs, and the rain had ceased. But a biting wind like a cruel
fate came out of the north, and he hurried through the deserted
street, under lowering clouds that scurried madly across the stars.
But John Barclay could not look up at the stars, he broke into a
limping run and head downward plunged into the gale. And never in all
his life could he take a square look at Molly Culpepper's diamond
ring.

As the spring deepened Bob Hendricks felt upon him at his work the
pressure of two distinct troubles. One was his sweetheart's attitude
toward him, and the other was the increasing weakness of his father.
Molly Culpepper's letters seemed to be growing sad; also they were
failing in their length and frequency--the young man felt that they
were perfunctory. His father's letters showed a physical breakdown.
His handwriting was unsteady, and often he repeated himself in
successive letters. The sister wrote about her father's weakness, and
seemed to think he was working too hard. But the son suspected that it
was worry rather than work, and that things were not going right in
the bank. He did not know that the Golden Belt Wheat Company had
sapped the money of the bank and had left it a husk, which at any time
might crumble. The father knew this, and after the first of the year
every morning when he opened the bank he feared that day would be the
last day of its career.

And so it fell out that "those that look out of the windows" were
darkened, and General Hendricks rose up with the voice of the bird and
was "afraid of that which was high" and terrors were in the way. So on
his head, the white blossom of the almond tree trembled; and one noon
in March the stage bore to this broken, shaking old man a letter from
Kansas City that ran the sword of fear into his heart and almost
stopped it forever. It ran:--

"Dear General: I have just learned from talking with a banker here that an inspector is headed our way. He probably will arrive the day after this reaches you. Something must be done about that tax check of yours. The inspector should not find it in the drawer again. Once was all right, but you must get it out now. Put it in the form of a note. Make it Carnine's note. He is good for twice that. Don't bother him with it, but make it out for ninety days, and by that time we can make another turn. But that note must be in there. Your check won't do any longer. The inspector has been gossiping about us up here--and about that check of yours. For God's sake, don't hesitate, but do this thing quick."

The letter was not signed, but it came in Barclay's envelope, and was addressed by Barclay's hand.

The general fumbled with the pad of blank notes before him for a long time. He read and reread Barclay's letter. Then he put away the pad and tore the letter into bits and started for the front door. But a terror seized him, and he walked behind the counter and put his palsied hand into the box where he kept cancelled checks, and picked out one of Gabriel Carnine's checks. He folded it up, and started for the door again, but turned weakly at the threshold, and walked to the back room of the bank.

When it was done, and had been worked through the books, General Hendricks, quaking with shame and fear, sat shivering before his desk with jaws agape and the forged name gashed into his soul. And "the strong men" bowed themselves as he shuffled home in the twilight. The next day when the inspector came, "all the daughters of music were brought low" and the feeble, bent, stricken man piped and wheezed and stammered his confused answers to the young man's questions, and stood paralyzed with unspeakable horror while the inspector glanced at the Carnine note and asked some casual question about it. When the bank closed that night, General Hendricks tried to write to his son and

tell him the truth, but he sat weeping before his desk and could not
put down the words he longed to write. Bob Hendricks found that
tear-stained letter half finished in the desk when he came home, and
he kept it locked up for years. And when he discovered that the date
on the letter and the date on the forged note were the same, the son
knew the meaning of the tears. But it was all for the Larger Good, and
so John Barclay won another game with Destiny.

But the silver cord was straining, and morning after morning the old
pitcher went to the fountain, to be battered and battered and
battered. His books, which he kept himself, grew spotted and dirty,
and day by day in the early spring the general dreaded lest some
depositor would come into the bank and call for a sum in cash so large
that it would take the cash supply below the legal limit, and that an
inspector would suddenly appear again and discover the deficiency.
Except Barclay the other directors knew nothing of the situation. They
signed whatever reports the general or Barclay put before them; there
came a time in April when any three of a dozen depositors could have
taken every penny out of the bank. When the general was unusually low
in spirits, Barclay sent Colonel Culpepper around to the bank with his
anthem about times being better when the spring really opened, and for
an hour the general was cheerful, but when the colonel went, the
general always saw the axe hanging over his head. And then one morning
late in April--one bright Sunday morning--the wheel of the cistern
was broken, and they found the old man cold in his bed with his face
to the wall.

John Barclay was on a horse riding to the railroad--four hours away,
before the town was up for late Sunday morning breakfast. That
afternoon he went into Topeka on a special engine, and told a Topeka
banker who dealt with the bank of Sycamore Ridge the news of the
general's death, and asked for five thousand dollars in silver to
allay a possible run. At midnight he drove into the Ridge with the

money, and the bank opened in the morning at seven o'clock instead of nine, so that a crowd might not gather, and depositors who came, saw back of Barclay a great heap of silver dollars, flanked by all the gold and greenbacks in the vault, and when a man asked for his money he got it in silver, and when Oscar Fernald presented a check for over three thousand dollars, Barclay paid it out in silver, and in the spirit of fun, Sheriff Jake Dolan, who heard of the counting and recounting of the money while it was going on, brought in a wheelbarrow and Oscar wheeled his money to his hotel, while every loafer in town followed him. At noon Fernald came back with his money, and Barclay refused to take it. The town knew that also. Barclay did not step out of the teller's cage during the whole day, but Lige Bemis was his herald, and through him Barclay had Dolan refuse to give Fernald protection for his money unless Fernald would consent to be locked up in jail with it. In ten minutes the town knew that story, and at three o'clock Barclay posted a notice saying the bank would remain open until nine o'clock that night, to accommodate any depositors who desired their money, but that it would be closed for three days following until after the funeral of the president of the bank.

The next day he sat in the back room of the bank and received privately nearly all the money that had been taken out Monday, and several thousand dollars besides that came through fear that Fernald's cash would attract robbers from the rough country to the West who might loot the town. To urge in that class of depositors, Barclay asked Sheriff Dolan to detail a guard of fifty deputies about the bank day and night, and the day following the cash began coming in with mildew on it, and Adrian Brownwell appeared that night with a thousand dollars of old bank-notes, issued in the fifties, that smelled of the earth. Thursday John limped up and down the street inviting first one business man and then another into the bank to help him count cash and straighten out his balance. And each of a dozen men believed for years that he was the man who first found the balance in the books of the Exchange National Bank of Sycamore Ridge, after John Barclay had got them tangled. And when Barclay was a great and powerful man in the world, these men, being interviewed by reporters about the personality of Barclay, took pride in telling this story of his blundering. But when Bob Hendricks reached Sycamore Ridge Thursday noon, confidence in the safety of the bank was founded upon a rock.

So when the town closed its stores that afternoon and took the body of the general, its first distinguished citizen to die, out upon the Hill, and laid it to rest in the wild prairie grass, John Barclay and Jane, his wife, rode in the carriage with the mourners, and John stood by his friend through the long service, and when the body was lowered into the grave, the most remote thought in all the world from John's mind was that he was responsible for the old man's death.

Bob Hendricks saw Molly Culpepper for the first time in twenty months, standing by her father with those who gathered about the general's grave, and as soon as he could leave the friends who came home with him and his sister, he hurried to the Culpeppers'. As he left his home, he could see Molly sitting on the veranda behind one of the pillars of great pride. She moved down the steps toward the gate to meet him. It was dusk,--deep dusk,--but he knew her figure and was thrilled with joy. They walked silently from the gate toward the veranda, and the youth's soul was moved too deeply for words. So deeply indeed was his being stirred, that he did not notice in his eagerness to bring their souls together how she was holding him away from her heart.

The yellow roses were blooming, and the pink roses were in bud. They strayed idly to the side of the house farthest from the street, and there they found the lilacs, heavy with blooms; they were higher than the girl's head,--a little thicket of them,--and behind the thicket was a rustic seat made of the grape-vines. He stepped toward the chair, pulling her by the hand, and she followed. He tried to gather her into his arms, but she slid away from him and cried, "No--no, Bob--no!"

"Why--why--why! what's wrong?" gasped the youth.

The girl sank on the seat and covered her face with her hands. He touched her shoulder and her hair with his finger-tips, and she shivered away from him. "Oh, Bob--Bob, Bob!--" she cried in agony, still looking at the grass before her.

The young man looked at her in perplexity. "Why, dear--why--why, darling--why, Molly," he stammered, "why--why--"

She rose and faced him. She gripped herself, and he could feel the unnatural firmness in her voice as she spoke.

"Bob, I am not the little girl you left." He put out his arms, but she shrank back among the lilacs; their perfume was in her face, and she was impressed with that odd feeling one sometimes has of having had some glimpse of it all before. She knew that she would say, "I am not worthy--not worthy any more--Bob, do you understand?"

And when he had stepped to ward her again with piteous pleading face,--a face that she had never seen before, yet seemed always to have known,--she felt that numb sense of familiarity with it all, and it did not pain her as she feared it would when he cried, "Oh--God, Molly--nothing you ever could do would make you unworthy of me--Molly, Molly, what is it?" The anguish in his face flashed back from some indefinite past to her, and then the illusion was gone, and the drama was all new. He caught her, but she fought herself away.

"Don't--don't!" she cried; "you have no right--now." She dropped into the seat, while he stood over her with horror on his face. She answered the question of his eyes, rocking her body as she spoke, "Bob--do you understand now?" He shook his head, and she went on, "We aren't engaged--not any more, Bob--not any more--never!" He started to speak, but she said: "I'm going to marry Mr. Brownwell. Oh, Bob--Bob, I told you I was unworthy--now do you understand?"

The man turned his face starward a second, and then dropped his head. "Oh," he groaned, and then sat down beside her at the other end of the bench. He folded his hands on his knees, and they sat silent for a time, and then he asked in a dead voice, "You know I love you--still, don't you, Molly?"

She answered, "Yes, that's what makes it hard."

"And do you love me?" he cried with eagerness.

She sat for a minute without replying and then answered, "I am a woman now, Bob--a grown woman, and some way things are different."

They sat without speaking; then he drew a deep breath and said, "Well, I suppose I ought to go." His head rested on his hand which was supported by an arm of the chair. He did not offer to rise.

She rose and went to him, kneeling before him. She put her hands upon his shoulders, and he put them aside, and she felt him shudder. She moaned, and looked up at him. Her face was close to his, but he did not come closer. He stared at her dumbly, and kept shaking his head as if asking some mute question too deep for words. Then he put out his hand and took hers. He put it against his cheek and held it in both his own. She did not take her eyes from his face, but his eyes began to wander.

"I will never see you again, Bob--I mean like this." She paused.

There was no life in his hands, and hers slipped away unrestrained. "How sweet the lilacs smell to-night," he said as he drew in a deep breath. He leaned back that he might breathe more freely, and added as he sighed, "I shall smell them through eternity--Molly." Then he rose and broke off a spray. He helped her rise and said, "Well--so this is the way of it." His handsome fair face was white in the moonlight, and she saw that his hair was thinning at the temples, and the strange flash of familiarity with it all came again as she inhaled the fragrance of the lilacs.

She trembled with some chill of inner grief, and cried vehemently, "Oh, Bob--my boy--my boy--say you hate me--for God's love, say you hate me." She came so close to him that she touched him, then she crumpled against the side of the seat in a storm of tears, but he looked at her steadily and shook his head.

"Come on, Molly. It's too cool for you out here," he said, and took her hand and walked with her to the steps. She was blinded by her weeping, and he helped here to the veranda, but he stopped on a lower step where his face was on a level with hers, and dropping her hand, he said, "Well, good night, Molly--good night--" and as he half turned from her, he said in the same voice, "Good-by."

He went quickly down the walk--a tall stalwart figure, and he carried his hat in his hand, and wiped his forehead as he went. At the gate he looked back and saw her standing where he had left her; he could still hear the pitiful sobs, but he made no sign to her, and she heard him walking away under the elms into the night. When his steps had ceased she ran on tiptoe, holding her breath to silence her sobs, through the hall, up the stairs of the silent home to her room, and locked the door. When she could not pray, she lay sobbing and groaning through a long night.

CHAPTER XIV

The next morning John Barclay gave Robert Hendricks the keys to the bank. Barclay watched the town until nine o'clock and satisfied himself that there would be no run on the bank, for during the early part of the morning young Hendricks was holding a reception in his office; then Barclay saddled a horse and started for the wheat fields. After the first hours of the morning had passed, and the townspeople had gone from the bank, Robert Hendricks began to burrow into the books. He felt instinctively that he would find there the solution of the puzzle that perplexed him. For he was sure Molly Culpepper had not jilted him wantonly. He worked all the long spring afternoon and into the night, and when he could not sleep he went back to the bank at midnight, following some clew that rose out of his under-consciousness and beckoned him to an answer to his question.

The next morning found him at his counter, still worrying his books as a ferret worries a rat. They were beginning to mean something to him, and he saw that the bank was a worm-eaten shell. When he discovered that Brownwell's notes were not made for bona fide loans, but that they were made to cover Barclay's overdrafts, he began to find the truth, and then when he found that Colonel Culpepper had lent the money back to the bank that he borrowed from Brownwell,--also to save John's overdrafts,--Bob Hendricks' soul burned pale with rage. He found that John had borrowed far beyond the limit of his credit at the bank to buy the company's stock, and that he had used Culpepper and

Brownwell to protect his account when it needed protection. Hendricks went about his work silently, serving the bank's customers, and greeting his neighbours pleasantly, but his heart was full of a lust to do some bodily hurt to John Barclay. When John came back, he sauntered into the bank so airily that Hendricks could not put the hate into his hands that was in his breast. John was full of a plan to organize a commission company, buy all of the wheat grown by the Golden Belt Wheat Company and make a profit off the wheat company for the commission company. He had bargained with the traffic officers of the railroad company to accept stock in the commission company in return for rate concessions on the Corn Belt Railroad, which was within a few months' building distance of Sycamore Ridge.

As John unfolded his scheme, Bob eyed his partner almost without a word. A devil back in some recess of his soul was thirsting for a quarrel. But Bob's sane consciousness would not unleash the devil, so he replied:--

"No--you go ahead with your commission company, and I'll stick to the wheat proposition. That and the bank will keep me going."

The afternoon was late, and a great heap of papers of the bank and the company lay before them that needed their time. Bob brushed his devil back and went to work. But he kept looking at Barclay's neck and imagining his fingers closing upon it. When the twilight was falling, Barclay brought the portmanteau containing the notes into the back room and turning to the "C's" pulled out a note for nine thousand dollars signed by Gabriel Carnine, who was then county treasurer. Barclay put it on the table before Hendricks and looked steadily at him a minute before saying, "Bob--see that note?" And when the young man answered, the other returned: "We had to do that, and several other things, this spring to tide us over. I didn't bother you with it--but we just had to do it--or close up, and go to pieces with the wheat scheme."

Hendricks picked up the note, and after examining it a moment, asked quickly, "John, is that Gabe's signature?"

"No--I couldn't get Gabe to sign it--and we had to have it to make his account balance."

"And you forged his note,--and are carrying it?" cried Hendricks, rising.

"Oh, sit down, Bob--we did it here amongst hands. It wasn't exactly my affair, the way it got squared around."

Hendricks took the note to the window. He was flushed, and the devil got into his eyes when he came back, and he cried, "And you made father do it!"

Barclay smiled pacifically, and limped over to Hendricks and took the note from him and put it back into the portmanteau. Then Barclay replied: "No, Bob, I didn't make your father--the times made your father. It was that or confess to Gabe Carnine, who swelled up on taking his job, that we hadn't paid the taxes on the company's land, though our check had been passed for it. When it came in, we gave the county treasurer credit on his daily bank-book for the nine thousand, but we held out the check. Do you see?"

"Yes, that far," replied Hendricks.

"Well, it's a long story after that, but when I found Gabe wouldn't accommodate us for six months by giving us his note to carry as cash until we could pay it,--the inspectors wouldn't take mine or your father's,--and our books had to show the amount of gross cash that the treasurer deposited before Gabe came in, your father thought it unwise to keep holding checks that had already been paid in the drawer as cash for that nine thousand, so we--well, one day he just put this note in, and worked it through the books."

Hendricks had his devil well in hand as he stared at Barclay, and then said: "John--this is mighty dangerous business. Are we carrying his account nine thousand short on our books, and making his pass-book balance?"

"That's it, only--"

"But suppose some one finds it out?" asked Hendricks.

"Oh, now, Bob, keep your shirt on. I fixed that. You know they keep two separate accounts,--a general maintenance account and a bond account, and Gabe has been letting us keep the paid-off bonds in the vault and look after their cancelling, and while he was sick, I was in charge of the treasurer's office and had the run of the bank, and I squared our account at the Eastern fiscal agency and in the bond account in the treasurer's office, and fixed up the short maintenance account all with nine thousand dollars' worth of old bonds that were kicking around the vault uncancelled, and now the job is hermetically sealed so far as the treasurer and the bank are concerned."

"So we can't pay it back if we want to? Is that the way, John?" asked Hendricks, his fingers twitching as he leaned forward in his chair.

"Ah, don't get so tragic about it. Some day when Gabe has calmed down, and wants a renomination, I'll take him in the back room and show him the error that we've both made, and we'll just quietly put back the money and give him the laugh." There was a pause, and Barclay tilted his chair back and grinned. "It's all right, Bob--we were where we had to do it; the books balance to a 'T' now--and we'll square it with Gabe sometime."

"But if we can't--if Gabe won't be--be--well, be reasonable? What then?" asked Hendricks.

"Oh, well," returned John, "I've thought of that too. And you'll find that when, the county treasury changes hands in '79, you'll have to look after the bond account and the treasurer's books and make a little entry to satisfy the bonds when they really fall due; then--I'll show you about it when we're over at the court-house. But if we can't get the money back with Gabe or the next man, the time will come when we can."

And Bob Hendricks looked at the natty little man before him and sighed, and began working for the Larger Good also. And afterwards as the months flew by the Golden Belt Wheat Company paid the interest on the forged note, and the bank paid the Golden Belt Wheat Company interest on a daily ledger balance of nine thousand, and all went happily. The Larger Good accepted the sacrifices of truth, and went on its felicitous way.

After Barclay left the bank that night, Hendricks found still more of the truth. And the devil in the background of his soul came out and glared through the young man's sleepless eyes as he appeared in Barclay's office in the morning and said, before he had found a chair, "John, what's your idea about those farmers' mortgages? Are you going to let them pay them, or are you going to make them sell under that option that you've got in them?"

"Why," asked Barclay, "what's it to us? Haven't the courts decided that that kind of an option is a sale--clear through to the United States Supreme Court?"

"Well, what are you going to do about it?" persisted Hendricks.

Barclay squinted sidewise at his partner for a few seconds and said, "Well, it's no affair of ours; we've sold all the mortgages anyway."

Hendricks wagged his head impatiently and exclaimed, "Quit your dodging and give me a square answer--what have you got up your sleeve about those options?"

Barclay rose, limped to the window, and looked out as he answered: "Well, I've always supposed we'd fix it up some way to buy back those mortgages and then take the land we want for ourselves--for you and me personally--and give the poor land back to the farmers if they pay the money we lent them."

"Well," returned Hendricks, "just count me out on that. Whatever I make in this deal, and you seem to think our share will be plenty, goes to getting those farmers back their land. So far as I'm concerned that money we paid them was rent, not a loan!"

Barclay dropped his hands in astonishment and gaped at Hendricks.

"Well, my dear Miss Nancy," he exclaimed, "when did you get religion?"

The two men glared at each other a moment, and Hendricks grappled his devil and drew a long breath and replied: "Well, you heard what I said." And then he added: "I'm pretty keen for money, John, but when it comes to skinning a lot of neighbours out of land that you and every one says is going to raise thirty dollars' worth of wheat to the acre this year alone, and only paying them ten dollars an acre for the title to the land itself--" He did not finish. After a pause he added: "Why, they'll mob you, man. I've got to live with those farmers." Barclay sneered at Hendricks without speaking and Hendricks stepped over to him and drew back his open hand as he said angrily, "Stop it--stop it, I say." Then he exclaimed: "I'm not what you'd call nasty nice, John--but I'm no robber. I can't take the rent of that land for nothing, raise a thirty-dollar crop on every acre of it, and make them pay me ten dollars an acre to get back the poor land and steal the good land, on a hocus-pocus option."

"'I do not use the nasty weed, said little Robert Reed,'" replied Barclay, with a leer on his face. Then, he added: "I've held your miserable little note-shaving shop up by main strength for a year, by main strength and awkwardness, and now you come home with your mouth all fixed for prisms and prunes, and want to get on a higher plane. You try that," continued Barclay, and his eyes blazed at Hendricks, "and you'll come down town some morning minus a bank."

Then the devil in Bob Hendricks was freed for an exultant moment, as his hands came out of his pockets and clamped down on Barclay's shoulders, and shook him till his teeth rattled.

"Not with me, John, not with me," he cried, and he felt his fingers clutching for the thin neck so near them, and then suddenly his hands went back to his pockets. "Now, another thing--you got Brownwell to lend the colonel that money?" Hendricks was himself.

Barclay nodded.

"And you got Brownwell to sign a lot of accommodation paper there at the bank?"

"Yes--to cover our own overdrafts," retorted Barclay. "It was either that or bust--and I preferred not to bust. What's more, if we had gone under there at one stage of the game when Brownwell helped us, we

could have been indicted for obtaining money under false
pretences you and I, I mean. I'm perfectly willing to stick my head
inside the jail and look around," Barclay grinned, "but I'll be damned
if I'm going clear inside for any man--not when I can find a way to
back out." Barclay tried to laugh, but Hendricks would not let him.

"And so you put up Molly to bail you out." Barclay did not answer and
Hendricks went on bitterly: "Oh, you're a friend, John Barclay, you're
a loyal friend. You've sold me out like a dog, John--like a dog!"

Barclay, sitting at his desk, playing with a paper-weight, snarled
back: "Why don't you get in the market yourself, if you think I've
sold you out? Why don't you lend the old man some money?"

"And take it from the bank you've just got done robbing of everything
but the wall-paper?" Hendricks retorted.

"No," cried Barclay, in a loud voice. "Come off your high horse and
take the profits we'll make on our wheat, pay off old Brownwell and
marry her."

"And let the bank bust and the farmers slide?" asked Hendricks, "and
buy back Molly with stolen money? Is that your idea?"

"Well," Barclay snapped, "you have your choice, so if you think more
of the bank and your old hayseeds than you do of Molly, don't come
blubbering around me about selling her."

"John," sighed Hendricks, after a long wrestle--a final contest with
his demon, "I've gone all over that. And I have decided that if I've
got to swindle seventy-five or a hundred farmers--most of them old
soldiers on their homesteads--out of their little all, and cheat five
hundred depositors out of their money to get Molly, she and I wouldn't

be very happy when we thought of the price, and we'd always think of the price." His demon was limp in the background of his soul as he added: "Here are some papers I brought over. Let's get back to the settlement--fix them up and bring them over to the bank this morning, will you?" And laying a package carefully on the table, Hendricks turned and went quickly out of the room.

After Hendricks left the office that May morning, Barclay sat whistling the air of the song of the "Evening Star," looking blankly at a picture of Wagner hanging beside a picture of Jay Gould. The tune seemed to restore his soul. When he had been whistling softly for five minutes or so, the idea flashed across his mind that flour was the one thing used in America more than any other food product and that if a man had his money invested in the manufacture and sale of flour, he would have an investment that would weather any panic. The idea overcame him, and he shut his eyes and his ears and gripped his chair and whistled and saw visions. Molly Culpepper came into the room, and paused a moment on the threshold as one afraid to interrupt a sleeper. She saw the dapper little man kicking the chair rounds with his dangling heels, his flushed face reflecting a brain full of blood, his eyes shut, his head thrown far back, so that his Adam's apple stuck up irrelevantly, and she knew only by the persistence of the soft low whistle that he was awake, clutching at some day-dream. When she cleared her throat, he was startled and stared at her foolishly for a moment, with the vision still upon him. His wits came to him, and he rose to greet her.

"Well--well--why--hello, Molly--I was just figuring on a matter," he said as he put her in a chair, and then he added, "Well--I wasn't expecting you."

Even before she could speak his lips were puckering to pick up the tune he had dropped. She answered, "No, John, I wanted to see you--so

I just came up."

"Oh, that's all right, Molly--what is it?" he returned.

"Well--" answered the young woman, listlessly, "it's about; father. You know he's badly in debt, and some way--of course he sells lots of land and all, but you know father, John, and he just doesn't--oh, he just keeps in debt."

Barclay had been lapsing back into his revery as she spoke, but he pulled himself out and replied: "Oh, yes, Molly--I know about father all right. Can't you make him straighten things out?"

"Well, no. John, that's just it. His money comes in so irregularly, this month a lot and next month nothing, that it just spoils him. When he gets a lot he spends it like a prince," she smiled sadly and interjected: "You know he is forever giving away--and then while he's waiting he gets in debt again. Then we are as poor as the people for whom he passes subscription papers, and that's just what I wanted to see you about."

Barclay took his eyes off Jay Gould's picture long enough to look at the brown-eyed girl with an oval face and a tip of a chin that just fitted the hollow of a man's hand; there were the smallest brown freckles in the world across the bridge of her nose, and under her eyes there was the faintest suggestion of dark shading. Youth was in her lips and cheeks, and when she smiled there were dimples. But John's eyes went back to Jay Gould's solemn black whiskers and he said from his abstraction, "Well, Molly, I wish I could help you."

"Well, I knew you would, John, some way; and oh, John, I do need help so badly." She paused a moment and gazed at him piteously and repeated, "So badly." But his eyes did not move from the sacred whiskers of his joss. The vision was flaming in his brain, and with his lips parted, he whistled "The Evening Star" to conjure it back and keep it with him. The girl went on:--

"About that money Mr. Brownwell loaned father, John." She flushed and cried, "Can't you find some way for father to borrow the money and pay Mr. Brownwell--now that your wheat is turning out so well?"

The young man pulled himself out of his day-dream and said, "Well--why--you see, Molly--I--Well now, to be entirely frank with you, Molly, I'm going into a business that will take all of my credit--and every cent of my money."

He paused a moment, and the girl asked, "Tell me, John, will the wheat straighten things up at the bank?"

"Well, it might if Bob had any sense--but he's got a fool notion of considering a straight mortgage that those farmers gave on their land as rent, and isn't going to make them redeem their land,--his share of it, I mean,--and if he doesn't do that, he'll not have a cent, and he couldn't lend your father any money." Barclay was anxious to get back to his "Evening Star" and his dream of power, so he asked, "Why, Molly, what's wrong?"

"John," she began, "this is a miserable business to talk about; but it is business, I guess." She stopped and looked at him piteously. "Well, John, father's debt to Mr. Brownwell--the ten-thousand-dollar loan on the house--will be due in August." The young man assented. And after a moment she sighed, "That is why I'm to be married in August." She stood a moment looking out of the window and cried, "Oh, John, John, isn't there some way out--isn't there, John?"

Barclay rose and limped to her and answered harshly: "Not so long as

Bob is a fool--no, Molly. If he wants to go mooning around releasing those farmers from their mortgages--there's no way out. But I wouldn't care for a man who didn't think more of me than he did of a lot of old clodhoppers."

The girl looked at the hard-faced youth a moment in silence, and turned without a word and left the room. Barclay floated away on his "Evening Star" and spun out his dream as a spider spins his web, and when Hendricks came into the office for a mislaid paper half an hour later, Barclay still was figuring up profits, and making his web stronger. As Hendricks, having finished his errand, was about to go, Barclay stopped him.

"Bob, Molly's been up here. As nearly as I can get at it, Brownwell has promised to renew the colonel's mortgage in August. If he and Molly aren't married by then--no more renewals from him. Don't be a fool, Bob; let your sod-busters go hang. If you don't get their farms, some one else will!"

Hendricks looked at his partner a minute steadily, grunted, and strode out of the room. And the incident slipped from John Barclay's mind, and the web of the spider grew stronger and stronger in his brain, but it cast a shadow that was to reach across his life.

After Hendricks went from his office that morning, Barclay bounded back, like a boy at play, to the vision of controlling the flour market. He saw the waving wheat of Garrison County coming to the railroad, and he knew that his railroad rates were so low that the miller on the Sycamore could not ship a pound of flour profitably, and Barclay's mind gradually comprehended that through railroad rates he controlled the mill, and could buy it at his leisure, upon his own terms. Then the whole scheme unfolded itself before his closed eyes as he sat with his head tilted back and pillowed in his hands. If his railroad concession made it possible for him to underbid the miller at the Ridge, why could he not get other railroad concessions and underbid every miller along the line of the Corn Belt road, by dividing profits with the railroad officials? As he spun out his vision, he could hear the droning voices of General Ward and Colonel Culpepper in the next room; but he did not heed them.

They were discussing the things of the day,--indeed, the things of a fortnight before, to be precise,--the reception given by the Culpeppers to celebrate their silver wedding anniversary. The windows were open, and Barclay could hear the men's voices, and he knew vaguely that they were talking of Lige Bemis. For Barclay had tactfully asked the colonel as a favour to invite Mr. and Mrs. Bemis to the silver wedding reception. So the Bemises came. Mrs. Bemis, who was rather stout, even for a woman in her early forties, wore black satin and jet ornaments, including black jet ear bobs of tremendous size. And Watts McHurdie was so touched by the way ten years under a roof had tamed the woman whom he had known of old as "Happy Hallie," that he wrote a poem for the **Banner** about the return of the "Prodigal Daughter," which may be found in Garrison County scrap-books of that period. As for Mr. Bemis, he went slinking about the outskirts of the crowd, showing his teeth considerably, and making it obvious that he was there.

So as John Barclay rode his "Evening Star" to glory, in the next room General Ward turned to the colonel, who stood puffing in the doorway of the general's law-office. "Martin, did John Barclay make you invite that woman to your house--that Bemis woman?"

The colonel got his breath slowly after climbing the stair, and he did not reply at once. But he smiled, and stood with his arms akimbo a few seconds before he spoke. "Well now, General--since you ask it, I may as well confess it pointedly--I am ashamed to say he did!"

Ward motioned the colonel to a seat and asked impatiently, "Ashamed?"

"Well," responded Culpepper, as he put his feet in the window ledge, "she's as good as I am--if you come down to that! Why shouldn't I, who pretend to be a gentleman,--a Virginia gentleman, I may say, sir,--why shouldn't I be ashamed, disgraced, sir, disgraced in point of fact, that I had to be forced to invite any person in all God's beautiful world to my home?"

Ward looked at the colonel coldly a moment and then blurted out: "Ah, shucks, sir--stuff and nonsense! You know what she was before the war--Happy Hally! My gracious, Martin, how could you?"

Martin Culpepper brought his chair down with a bang and turned squarely to Ward. "General, the war's over now. I knew Happy Hally--and I knew the Red Legs she trained with. And we're making senators and governors and state officers and indeed, I may say, prominent citizens out of them. Why not give Hally her show? You damn cold-nosed Yankee Brahmins--you have Faith and you have Hope, but you have no more Charity than a sausage-grinder." The colonel rose, and cried with some asperity, "General, if you'd preach about the poor less, and pray with 'em more, you'd know more about your fellow-men, sir!"

Perhaps this conversation should not have been set down here; for it has no direct relation to the movement of this narrative. The narrative at this point should be hurrying along to tell how John Barclay and Bob Hendricks cleared up a small fortune on their wheat deal, and how that autumn Barclay bought the mill at Sycamore Ridge by squeezing its owner out, and then set about to establish four branches of the Golden Belt Wheat Company's elevator service along the line of the new railroad, and how he controlled the wheat output of three counties the next year through his enterprise. These facts carry John Barclay forward toward his life's goal. And while these two middle-aged gentlemen--the general and the colonel--were in the next room wrangling over the youthful love affairs of a middle-aged lady, a great dream was shaping in Barclay's head, and he did not heed them. He was dreaming of controlling the wheat market of the Golden Belt Railroad, through railroad-rate privileges, and his fancy was feeling its way into flour, and comprehending what might be done with wheat products.

It was a crude dream, but he was aflame with it, and yet--John Barclay, aged twenty-five, was a young man with curly hair and flattered himself that he could sing. And there was always in him that side of his nature, so the reader must know that when Nellie Logan came to his office that bright summer morning and found him wrapped in his day-dream of power, she addressed herself not to the Thane of Wheat who should be King hereafter, but to the baritone singer in the Congregational choir, and the wheat king scampered back to the dream world when John replied to Nellie's question.

"So it's *your* wedding, is it, Nellie--your wedding," he repeated. "Well, where does Watts come in?" And then, before she answered, he went on, "You bet I'll sing at your wedding, and what's more, I'll bring along my limping Congregational foot, and I'll dance at your wedding."

"Well, I just knew you would," said the young woman.

"So old Watts thought I wouldn't, did he?" asked Barclay. "The old skeezicks--Well, well! Nellie, you tell him that the fellow who was with Watts when he was shot ten miles from Springfield isn't going to desert him when he gets a mortal wound in the heart." Then Barclay added: "You get the music and take it down to Jane, and tell her to teach me, and I'll be there. Jane says you're going to put old Watts through all the gaits."

He leaned back in his swivel chair and smiled at his visitor. He had a slow drawl that he used in teasing, and one who heard that voice and afterward heard the harsh bark of the man in driving a bargain or browbeating an adversary would have to look twice to realize that the same man was talking. A little over an hour before in that very room he had looked at Bob Hendricks from under wrinkled brows with the vertical line creased between his eyes and snarled, "Well, then, if you think she's going to marry that fellow because I got him to lend the colonel some money, why don't you go and lend the colonel some more money and get her back?"

But there was not a muscle twitching in his face as he talked to Nellie Logan, not a break in his voice, not a ruffle of a hair, to tell her that John Barclay had broken with the friend of his boyhood and the partner of his youth, and that he had closed and bolted the Door of Hope on Molly Culpepper. He drawled on: "Jane was saying that you were going to have Bob and Molly for best man and bridesmaid. Ought you to do that? You know they--"

He did not finish the sentence, but she replied: "Oh, yes, I know about that. I told Watts he ought to have Mr. Brownwell; but he's as stubborn as a mule about just that one thing. Everything else--the flower girls and the procession and the ring service and all--he's so nice about. And you know I just had to have Molly."

John slapped the arms of his chair and laughed. "As old Daddy Mason says, 'Now hain't that just like a woman!' Well, Nellie, it's your wedding, and a woman is generally not married more than once, so it's all right. Go it while you're young."

And so he teased her out of the room, and when Sycamore Ridge packed itself into the Congregational Church one June night, to witness the most gorgeous church wedding the town ever had seen, John opened the ceremonies by singing the "Voice that breathed o'er Eden" most effectively, and Sycamore Ridge in its best clothes, rather stuffed and uncomfortable thereby, was in that unnatural attitude toward the world where it thought John Barclay's voice, a throaty baritone, with much affectation in the middle register, a tendency to flat in the upper register, and thick fuzz below "C," was beautiful, though John often remembered that night with unalloyed shame. He saw himself as he stood there, primped to kill, like a prize bull at a fair, bellowing out a mawkish sentiment in a stilted voice, and he wondered how the Ridge ever managed to endure him afterwards.

But this is a charitable world, and his temperament was such that he did not realize that no one paid much attention to him, after the real ceremony started. When the bride and the bridesmaid came down the aisle, Nellie Logan radiant in the gown which every woman in the church knew had come from Chicago and had been bought of the drummer at wholesale cost, saving the bride over fifteen dollars on the regular price--what did the guests care for a dapper little man singing a hymn tune through his nose, even if he was the richest young man in town? And when Molly Culpepper--dear little Molly Culpepper--came after the bride, blushing through her powder, and looking straight at the floor for fear her eyes would wander after her heart and wondering if the people knew--it was of no consequence that John Barclay's voice frazzled on "F"; for if the town wished to notice a man at that wedding, there was Watts McHurdie in a paper collar, with a white embroidered bow tie and the first starched shirt the town had ever seen him wear, badly out of step with the procession, while the best man dragged him like an unwilling victim to the altar; and of course there was the best man,--and a handsome best man as men go,--fair-skinned, light-haired, blue-eyed, with a good glow on his immobile face and rather sad eyes that, being in a man's head, went boldly where they chose and where all the women in the town could see them go. So there were other things to remember that night besides John Barclay's singing and the festive figure he cut at that wedding: there was the wedding supper at the Wards', and the wedding reception at the Culpeppers', and after it all the dance in Culpepper Hall. And all the town remembers these things, but only two people remember a moment after the reception when every one was hurrying away to the dance and when the bridesmaid--such a sweet, pretty little bridesmaid--was standing alone in a deserted room with a tall groomsman--just for a moment--just for a moment before Adrian Brownwell came up bustling and bristling, but long enough to say, "Bob--did you take my gloves there in the carriage as we were coming home from the church?" and long enough for him to answer, "Why, did you lose them?" and then to get a good square look into her eyes. It was only a few seconds in the long evening--less than a second that their eyes met; but it was enough to be remembered forever; though why--you say! It was all so commonplace; there was nothing in it that you would have thought worth remembering for a moment. "Bob, did you take my gloves?" "Why, did you lose them?" and then a glance of the eyes. Surely there are more romantic words than these. But when a man and a woman go in for collecting antiques in their dialogues, Heaven only knows what old rubbish you will find in their attics, scoured off and rebuilt and polished with secret tears until the old stuff glows like embers.

And that is why, when the music was silent in Culpepper Hall, and the tall young man walked slowly home alone, as he clicked his own gate behind him, he brought from his pocket two little white gloves,--just two ordinary white gloves,--and held them to his lips and lifted his arms in despair once and let them drop as he stood before his doorstep. And that is why a girl, a little girl with the weariest face in the town, looked out of her bedroom window that night and whispered over and over to herself the name she dared not speak. And all this was going on while the town was turning over in its bed, listening to the most tumultuous charivari that Sycamore Ridge has ever known.

Night after night that summer faithful Jake Dolan walked the streets of Sycamore Ridge with Bob Hendricks. By day they lived apart, but at night the young man often would look up the elder, and they would walk and walk together, but never once did Hendricks mention Molly's name nor refer to her in any way; yet Jake Dolan knew why they walked abroad. How did he know? How do we know so many things in this world that are neither seen nor heard? And the Irish--they have the drop of blood that defies mathematics; the Irish are the only people in the world whom kind Providence permits to add two and two together to make six. "You say 'tis four," said Dolan, one night, as he and Hendricks stood on the bridge listening to the roar from the dam. "I say 'tis six. There is this and there is that and you say they make the other. Not at all; they make something else entirely different. You take your two and your two and make your four and try your four on the world, and it works--yes, it works up to a point; but there is something left over, something unexplained; you don't know what. I do. It's the other two. Therefore I say to you, Mr. Robert Hendricks, that two and two make six, because God loves the Irish, and for no other reason on earth."

So much for the dreams of Molly, the memories of Bob, and the vagaries of Mr. Dolan. They were as light as air. But in John Barclay's life a vision was rising--a vision that was real, palpable, and vital; a vision of wealth and power,--and as the days and the months passed, the shadow of that vision grew big and black and real in a score of lives.

CHAPTER XV

As June burned itself gloriously into July, Robert Hendricks no longer counted the weeks until Molly Culpepper should be married, but counted the days. So three weeks and two days, from the first of July, became three weeks, then two weeks and six days, and then one week and six days, and then six days, five days, four days, three days; and then it became seventy-two hours. And the three threshing machines of the Golden Belt Wheat Company were pouring their ceaseless stream into the company's great bins. The railroad was only five miles away, and Hendricks was sitting in his office in the bank going over and over his estimates of the year's crop which was still lying in the field,--save the crop from less than two thousand acres that was harvested and threshed. From that he judged that there would be enough to redeem his share of the farmers' mortgages, which in Hendricks' mind could be nothing but rent for the land, and to pay his share of the bank's fraudulent loans to the company--and leave nothing more.

The fact that John expected to buy back the mortgages from Eastern investors who had bought them, and then squeeze the farmers out of their land by the option to buy hidden in the contract, did not move Hendricks. He saw his duty in the matter, but as the golden flood rose higher in the bins, and as hour after hour rolled by bringing him nearer and nearer to the time when Molly Culpepper should marry Adrian Brownwell, a temptation came to him, and he dallied with it as he sat figuring at his desk. The bank was a husk. Its real resources had been sold, and a lot of bogus notes--accommodation paper, they called it--had taken the place of real assets. For Hendricks to borrow money of any other institution as the officer of the Exchange National Bank of Sycamore Ridge would be a crime. And yet he knew that ten thousand dollars would save her, and his brain was wrought with a madness. And so he sat figuring while the hours slipped by, trying to discount his future income from the wheat to justify himself in taking the money from the bank's vaults. His figures did not encourage him. They showed him that to be honest with the farmers he might hope for no profit from that year's crop, and with two years of failure behind him, he knew that to discount the next year's crop would be nothing less than stealing. Then, strong and compelling, came the temptation to let the farmers fight it out with the Eastern investors. The temptation rocked the foundations of his soul. He knew it was wrong; he knew he would be a thief, if he did it, no matter what the law might say, no matter what the courts might adjudge. To Barclay what was legal was right, and what the courts had passed upon--that was legal. But Hendricks sat with his pencil in his hand, going over and over his figures, trying to silence his conscience.

It was a hot afternoon that he sat there, and idly through his mind went the computation that he had but sixty-six more hours of hope, and as he looked at the clock he added, "and thirty-eight minutes and twenty-seven seconds," when Martin Culpepper came ambling into the back room of the bank.

"Robert," began the colonel, with his eyes on the floor and his hands deep in his trousers pockets, "I've just been talking to John." The colonel rubbed his neck absent-mindedly and went on, "John's a Yankee, Robert--the blue stripe on his belly is fast blue, sir; it won't fade, change colour, or crock, in point of fact, not a damned bit, sir, not till the devil covers it with a griddle stripe, sir, I may say." The colonel slouched into a chair and looked into Hendricks' face with a troubled expression and continued, "That John certainly is Yankee, Robert, and he's too many for me. Yes, sir, certainly he's got me up in the air, sir--up in the air, and as I may say a mile west, on that wheat deal." Hendricks leaned forward unconsciously, and the colonel dropped both hands to his knees and leaned toward Hendricks.

"Robert Hendricks," asked the colonel, as he bored his deep black eyes into the younger man, "did you know about that option in the wheat land mortgage? Answer me, sir!"

"Not at the time, Colonel," returned Hendricks, and began, "but I--"

"Well, neither did I. And I got half of those mortgages myself. Lige and I did it all, sir. And Lige knew--Lige, he says it's legal, but I say it's just common stealing." Hendricks moistened his lips and sat with mute face gazing at the colonel. The colonel went on, "And now the farmers have found it out, and the devil's to pay, sir, with no pitch hot!"

Hendricks cleared his throat and began, "Well, Colonel--I don't know; of course I--"

The elder man rose to his full height and glared at the younger, and cried, "Ah, Robert, Robert, fire in the mountain, snakes in the grass--you do know--you do know, sir. You know that to hold up the farmers of this county in the midst of what amounted to a famine, not to let them borrow a dollar in the county except on a gouging mortgage, and then to slip into that mortgage a blind option to sell for ten dollars an acre land that is worth three times that, is stealing, and so does John Barclay know that, and, worst of all, so does Martin Culpepper know that, and the farmers are finding it out--my neighbours and comrades that I helped to swindle, sir--to rob, I may say--they know what it is."

The colonel's voice was rising, and he stood glaring and puffing before the young man, shaking his head furiously. Young Hendricks was engaged in swallowing his Adam's apple and blinking unsteadily, and just as he started to reply, the colonel, who had caught his temper by the horn and was shaking it into submission, cried: "Yes, sir, Robert, that's what I said, sir; those were my very words in point of fact. And," he began as he sat down and sighed, "what galls me most of all, Robert, is that John laughs at me. Here you've been gagging and gulping and sputtering, boy, to keep down your conscience, and so I know--yes, Robert, I'm dead sure, I may say, that you're all right; but John giggles--giggles, sir, snickers in point of fact, as though he had done something smart in getting me to go out among my old soldier friends and rob 'em of their homesteads. He doesn't care for my good name any more than for his own."

Hendricks drummed with his fingers on the desk before him. His blue eyes looked into nothing, and his mind's eye saw the house of cards he had been dallying with totter and fall. He drew a deep breath before he looked up at the colonel, and said rather sadly: "Well, Colonel, you're right. I told John the day after I came home that I wouldn't stand it." He drummed with his fingers for a moment before continuing, "I suppose you got about half of those contracts, didn't you?"

The colonel pulled from his pocket a crumpled paper and handed it to Hendricks, "Here they are, sir--and every one from a soldier or a soldier's widow, every one a homestead, sir."

Hendricks walked to the window, and stood looking out with his eyes cast down. He fumbled his Masonic watch-charm a moment, and then glancing at it, caught the colonel's eye and smiled as he said: "I'm on the square, Colonel, in this matter. I'll protect you." He went to the elder man and put his hands on his shoulder as he said: "You go to your comrades and tell them this, Colonel, that between now and snowfall every man will have his land clear. But," he added, picking up the list of the colonel's contracts, "don't mention me in the matter." He paused and continued, "It might hurt the bank. Just tell them you'll see that it's taken care of."

The colonel put out his hand as he rose. When their hands met he was saying: "Blood tells, Robert Hendricks, blood tells. Wasn't your sainted father a Democrat, boy, a Democrat like me, sir,--a Union Democrat in point of fact?" The colonel squeezed the younger man's hand as he cried: "A Union Democrat, sir, who could shoot at his party, sir, but never could bring himself to vote against it--not once, sir--not once. And Robert Hendricks, when I see you acting as you've acted just now, sir, this very minute in point of fact, I may say, sir, that you're almost honest enough to be a Democrat, sir--like your sainted father." The colonel held the young man's hand affectionately for a time and then dropped it, sighing, "Ah, sir--if it wasn't for your damned Yankee free schools and your damned Yankee surroundings, what a Democrat you would have made, Robert--what a grand Democrat!" The colonel waved his silver tobacco box proudly and made for the door and left Hendricks sitting at his desk, drumming on the board with one hand, and resting his head in the other, looking longingly into the abyss from which he had escaped; for the lure of the danger still fluttered his soul.

Strength had come to him in that hour to resist the temptation. But the temptation still was there. For he was a young man, giving up for an intangible thing called justice the dearest thing in his life. He had opened the door of his life's despair and had walked in, as much like a man as he could, but he kept looking back with a heavy heart, hungering with his whole body and most of his soul for all that he had renounced. And so, staring at the light of other days, and across the shadow of what might have been, he let ten long minutes tick past toward the inevitable hour, and then he rose and put his hand to the plough for the long furrow.

They are all off the stage now, as Bob Hendricks is standing in the front door of the bank that August night with his watch in his hand reckoning the minutes--some four thousand three hundred of them--until Molly Culpepper will pass from him forever, and as the stage is almost deserted, we may peep under the rear curtain for a minute. Observe Sycamore Ridge in the eighties, with Hendricks its moving spirit, controlling its politics, dominating its business,--for John Barclay's business has moved to the City and Bob Hendricks has become the material embodiment of the town. And the town there on the canvas is a busy town of twenty thousand people. Just back of that scene we find a convention spread on the canvas, a political convention wherein Robert Hendricks is struggling for good government and clean politics. Observe him a taciturn, forceful man, with his hands on the machinery of his party in the state, shaping its destinies, directing its politics, seeking no office, keeping himself in the background, desiring only to serve, and not to advertise his power. So more and more power comes to him, greater and wider opportunities to serve his state. His business grows and multiplies, and he becomes a strong man among men; always reserved, always cautious, a man whose self-poise makes people take him for a cynic, though his heart is full of hope and of the joy of life to the very last. Let us lift up one more rag--one more painted rag in the scenery of his life--and see him a reformer of national fame; see him with an unflinching hand pull the wires that control a great national policy of his party, and watch in that scene wherein he names a president--even against the power and the money and the organization of rich men, brutally rich men like John Barclay. Hendricks' thin hair is growing gray in this scene, and his skin is no longer fresh and white; but his eyes have a twinkle in them, and the ardour of his soul glows in a glad countenance. And as he sits alone in his room long after midnight while the bands are roaring and the processions cheering and the great city is ablaze with excitement, Robert Hendricks, turning fifty, winds his watch--the same watch that he holds in his hand here while we pause to peek under the canvas behind the scenes--and wonders if Molly will be glad that his side won. He has not seen her for months, nor talked with her for years, and yet as he sits there winding his watch after his great strategic victory in national politics, he hopes fondly that perhaps Molly will know that he played a clean hand and won a fair game.

Now let us crawl out from under this rubbish of the coming years, back into Sycamore Ridge. And while the street is deserted, let us turn the film of events forward, letting them flit by unnoticed past the wedding of Molly Culpepper and Adrian Brownwell until we come to the August day when the railroad came to Sycamore Ridge.

Jacob Dolan, sheriff in and for Garrison County for four years, beginning with 1873, remembered the summer of 1875 to his dying day, as the year when he tore his blue soldier coat, and for twenty-five years, after the fight in which the coat was torn, Dolan never put it on for a funeral or a state occasion, that he did not smooth out the seam that Nellie Logan McHurdie made in mending the rent place, and recall the exigencies of the public service which made it necessary to tear one's clothes to keep the peace.

"You may state to the court in your own way," said the judge at the trial of the sheriff for assault, "just how the difficulty began."

"Well, sir," answered Dolan, "there was a bit of a celebration in town, on August 30, it being the day the railroad came in, and in honour of the occasion I put on my regimentals, and along about--say eleven o'clock--as the crowd began to thicken up around the bank corner, and in front of the hardware store, I was walking along, kind of shoving the way clear for the ladies to pass, when some one behind me says, 'General Hendricks was an old thief, and his son is no better,' and I turned around and clapt my eye on this gentleman here. I'd never seen him before in my whole life, but I knew by the bold free gay way he had with his tongue that he was from Minneola and bent on trouble. 'Keep still,' says I, calm and dignified like, bent on preserving the peace, as was my duty. 'I'll not,' says he. 'You will,' says I. 'Tis a free country,' says he, coming toward me with one shoulder wiggling. 'But not for cowards who malign the dead,' says I. 'Well, they were thieves,' says he, shaking his fist and getting more and more into contempt of court every minute. 'You're a liar,' says I, maintaining the dignity of my office. 'And you're a thief too,' says he. 'A what?' says I. 'A thief,' says he. 'Whack,' says I, with my stick across his head, upholding the dignity of the court. 'Biff,' says he, with a brick that was handy, more and more contemptuous. 'You dirty, mangy cur,' says I, grabbing him by the ears and pounding his head against the wall as I spoke, hoping to get some idea of the dignity of the court into his rebellious head. 'Whoop,' says he, and, as he tore my coat, 'Yip yip,' says I, and may it please the court it was shortly thereafter that the real trouble started, though I misremember just how at this time." And as there were three "E" Company men on the jury, they acquitted Dolan and advised the court to assess a fine on the prosecuting witness for contributory negligence in resisting an officer.

But the coat--the blue coat with brass buttons, with the straps of a lieutenant on the shoulders, was mended and even in that same summer did active service many times. For that was a busy summer for Sycamore Ridge, and holidays came faster than the months. When the supreme court decided the Minneola suit to enjoin the building of the court-house, in favour of Syeamore Ridge, there was another holiday, and men drew John Barclay around in the new hack with the top down, and there were fireworks in the evening. For it was John Barclay's lawsuit. Lige Bemis, who was county attorney, did not try to claim credit for the work, and when the last acre of the great wheat crop of the Golden Belt Wheat Company was cut, and threshed, there was a big celebration and the elevator of the Golden Belt Wheat Company was formally turned over to the company, and John Barclay was the hero of another happy occasion. For the elevator, standing on a switch by the railroad track, was his "proposition." And every one in town knew that the railroad company had made a rate of wheat to Barclay and his associates, so low that Minneola could not compete, even if she hauled her wheat to another station on the road, so Minneola teams lined up at Barclay's elevator. That autumn Minneola, without a railroad, without a chance for the county-seat, and without a grain market, began to fag, and during the last of September, the Mason House came moving out over the hill road, from Minneola to Sycamore Ridge, surrounded by a great crowd of enthusiastic men from the Ridge. Every evening, of the two weeks in which the house was moving, people drove out from Sycamore Ridge to see it, and Lycurgus Mason, sitting on the back step smoking,--he could not get into the habit of using the front steps even in his day of triumph,--was a person of considerable importance.

Money was plentiful, and the Exchange National Bank grew with the country. The procession of covered wagons, that had straggled and failed the year before, began to close ranks in the spring; and in place of "Buck" and "Ball" and "Star," and "Bright" and "Tom" and "Jerry," who used to groan under the yoke, horses were hitched to the wagons, and stock followed after them, and thus Garrison County was settled, and Sycamore Ridge grew from three to five thousand people in three years. In the spring of '75 the ***Banner*** began to publish a daily edition, and Editor Brownwell went up and down the railroad on his pass, attending conventions and making himself a familiar figure in the state. Times were so prosperous that the people lost interest in the crime of '73, and General Ward had to stay in his law-office, but he joined the teetotalers and helped to organize the Good Templars and the state temperance society. Colonel Culpepper in his prosperity took to fancy vests, cut extremely low, and the Culpepper women became the nucleus of organized polite society in the Ridge.

The money that John Barclay made in that first wheat transaction was the foundation of his fortune. For that money gave him two important things needed in making money--confidence in himself, and prestige. He was twenty-five years old then, and he had demonstrated to his community thoroughly that he had courage, that he was crafty, and that he went to his end and got results, without stopping for overnice scruples of honour. Sycamore Ridge and Garrison County, excepting a few men like General Ward, who were known as cranks, regarded John as the smartest man in the county--smarter even than Lige Bemis. And the whole community, including some of the injured farmers themselves, considered Hendricks a sissy for his scruples, and thought Barclay a shrewd financier for claiming all that he could get. Barclay got hold of eight thousand acres of wheat land, in adjacent tracts, and went ahead with his business. In August he ploughed the ground for another crop. Also he persuaded his mother to let him build a new home on the site of the Barclay home by the Sycamore tree under the ridge, and when it was done that winter Mr. and Mrs. John Barclay moved out of their rooms at the Thayer House and lived with John's mother. The house they built cost ten thousand dollars when it was finished, and it may still be seen as part of the great rambling structure that he built in the nineties. John put five hundred dollars' worth of books into the new house--sets of books, which strangely enough he forced himself to wade through laboriously, and thus he cultivated a habit of reading that always remained with him. In those days the books with cracked backs in his library were Emerson, Browning, and Tennyson. And after a hard day's work he would come home to his poets and his piano. He thought out the whole plan of the Barclay Economy Car Door Strip about midnight, sitting in his night clothes at the piano after reading "Abt Vogler," and the central idea for the address on the "Practical Transcendentalist," which he delivered at the opening of the state university the next year, came to him one winter night after he had tried to compose a clanging march as an air to fit Emerson's "The Sphinx." After almost a quarter of a century that address became the first chapter of Barclay's famous book, which created such ribaldry in the newspapers, entitled "The Obligations of Wealth."

It was in 1879 that Barclay patented his Economy Door Strip, and put it in his grain cars. It saved loss of grain in shipping, and Barclay, being on terms of business intimacy with the railroad men, sold the Economy Strip to the railroads to use on every car of grain or flour he shipped. And Lycurgus Mason, taken from the kitchen of the Mason House, hired a room over McHurdie's harness shop, and made the strips there. His first day in his new shop is impressed upon his memory by an incident that is the seed of a considerable part of this story.

He always remembers that day, because, when he got to the Thayer House, he found John there in the buggy waiting for him, and a crowd of men sitting around smoking cigars. In the seat by Barclay was a cigar-box, and Lycurgus cut in, before John could speak, with, "Well, which is it?"

And John returned, "A girl--get in; Mother Mason needs you."

Lycurgus fumbled under the box lid for a cigar as he got into the buggy, and repeated: "Mother needs me, eh? Well, now, ain't that just like a woman, taking a man from his work in the middle of the day? What are you going to name her?"

"How do you like Jeanette?" asked Barclay, as he turned the horse. "You know we can't have two Janes," he explained.

"Well," asked the elder man, tentatively, "how does mother stand on Jeanette?"

"Mother Mason," answered Barclay, "is against it."

"All right," replied Lycurgus, "I vote aye. What does she want?" he asked.

"Susan B.," returned Barclay.

"Susan B. Anthony?" queried the new grandfather.

"Exactly," replied the new father.

The two rode down the street in silence; as they turned into the Barclay driveway Lycurgus chuckled, "Well--well--Susan B. Wants to put breeches on that child before she gets her eyes open." Then he turned on Barclay with a broad grin of fellowship, as he pinched the young man's leg and laughed, "Say--John--honest, ain't that just like a woman?"

And so Jeanette Thatcher Barclay came into this world, and what with her Grandmother Barclay uncovering her to look at the Thatcher nose, and her Grandmother Mason taking her to the attic so that she could go upstairs before she went down, that she might never come down in the world, and what with her Grandfather Mason rubbing her almost raw with his fuzzy beard before the women could scream at him, and what with her father trying to jostle her on his knee, and what with all the different things Mrs. Ward, the mother of six, would have done to her, and all the things Mrs. Culpepper, mother of three, would have done to her, and Mrs. McHurdie, mother of none, prevented the others from doing, Jeanette had rather an exciting birthday. And Jeanette Barclay as a young woman often looks at the scrap-book with its crinkly leaves and reads this item from the ***Daily Banner***: "The angels visited our prosperous city again last Thursday, June 12, and left a little one named Jeanette at the home of our honoured townsman, John Barclay. Mother and child progressing nicely." But under this item is a long poem clipped from a paper printed a week later,--Jeanette has counted the stanzas many times and knows there are seventeen, and each one ends with "when the angels brought Jeanette." Her father used to read the verses to her to tease her when she was in her teens, and once when she was in her twenties, and Jeanette had the lonely poet out to dinner one Sunday, she sat with him on the sofa in the library, looking at the old scrap-book. Their eyes fell upon the verses about the angels bringing Jeanette, and the girl noticed the old man mumming it over and smiling.

"Tell me, Uncle Watts," she asked, "why did you make such a long poem about such a short girl?"

The poet ran his fingers through his rough gray beard, and went on droning off the lines, and grinning as he read. When he had finished, he took her pretty hand in his gnarly, bony one and patted the white firm flesh tenderly as he peered back through the years. "U-h-m, that was years and years ago, Jeanette--years and years ago, and Nellie had just bought me my rhyming dictionary. It was the first time I had a chance to use it." The lyrical artist drummed with his fingers on the mahogany arm of the sofa. "My goodness, child--what a long column there was of words rhyming with 'ette.'" He laughed to himself as he mused: "You know, my dear, I had to let 'brevet' and 'fret' and 'roulette' go, because I couldn't think of anything to say about them. You don't know how that worries a poet." He looked at the verses in the book before him and then shook his head sadly: "I was young then--it seems strange to think I could write that. Youth, youth," he sighed as he patted the fresh young hand beside him, "it is not by chance you rhyme with truth."

His eyes glistened, and the girl put her cheek against his and squeezed the thin, trembling hand as she cried, "Oh, Uncle Watts, Uncle Watts, you're a dear--a regular dear!"

"In his latter days," writes Colonel Culpepper, in the second edition

of the Biography, "those subterranean fires of life that flowed so
fervently in his youth and manhood smouldered, and he did not write
often. But on occasion the flames would rise and burn for a moment
with their old-time ardour. The poem 'After Glow' was penned one night
just following a visit with a young woman, Jeanette, only daughter of
Honourable and Mrs. John Barclay, whose birth is celebrated elsewhere
in this volume under the title 'When the Angels brought Jeanette.' The
day after the poem 'After Glow' was composed I was sitting in the
harness shop with the poet when the conversation turned upon the
compensations of age. I said: 'Sir, do you not think that one of our
compensations is that found in the freedom and the rare intimacy with
which we are treated by the young women? They no longer seem to fear
us. Is it not sweet?' I asked. Our hero turned from his bench with a
smile and a deprecating gesture as he replied softly, 'Ah,
Colonel--that's just it; that's just the trouble.' And then he took
from a box near by this poem, 'The After Glow,' and read it to me. And
I knew the meaning of the line--

"'Oh, drowsy blood that tosses in its sleep.'

"And so we fell to talking of other days. And until the twilight came
we sat together, dreaming of faded moons."

CHAPTER XVI

Colonel Martin Culpepper was standing with, one foot on the window
ledge in the office of Philemon R. Ward one bright spring morning
watching the procession of humanity file into the post-office and out
into the street upon the regular business of life. Mrs. Watts

McHurdie, a bride of five years and obviously proud of it, hurried by, and Mrs. John Barclay drove down the street in her phaeton; Oscar Fernald, with a pencil behind his ear, came out of his office licking an envelope and loped into the post-office and out like a dog looking for his bone; and then a lank figure sauntered down the street, stopping here and there to talk with a passerby, stepping into a stairway to light a cigar, and betimes leaning languidly against an awning post in the sun and overhauling farmers passing down Main Street in their wagons.

"He's certainly a gallus-looking slink," ejaculated the colonel.

The general, writing at his desk, asked, "Who?"

"Our old friend and comrade in arms, Lige Bemis." At the blank look on the general's face the colonel shook his head wearily. "Don't know what a gallus-looking slink is, do you? General, the more I live with you damn Yankees and fight for your flag and die for your country, sir, the more astonished I am at your limited and provincial knowledge of the United States language. Here you are, a Harvard graduate, with the Harvard pickle dripping off your ears, confessing such ignorance of your mother-tongue. General, a gallus-looking slink is four hoss thieves, three revenue officers, a tin pedler, and a sheep-killing dog, all rolled into one man. And as I before remarked, our beloved comrade, Lige Bemis, is certainly a gallus-looking slink."

"Far be it from me," continued the colonel, "residing as I may say in a rather open and somewhat exposed domicile--a glass house in fact--to throw stones at Elijah Westlake Bemis,--far be it." The colonel patted himself heroically on the stomach and laughed. "Doubtless, while I haven't been a professional horse thief, nor a cattle rustler, still, probably, if the truth was known, I've done a number of things equally distasteful--I was going to say

obnoxious--in the sight of Mr. Bemis, so we'll let that pass." The
colonel stretched his suspenders out and let them flap against the
plaits of his immaculate shirt. "But I will say, General, that as I
see it, it will be a heap handier for me to explain to St. Peter at
the gate the things I've done than if he'd ask me about Lige's
record."

The general scratched along, without answering, and the colonel looked
meditatively into the street; then he began to smile, and the smile
glowed into a beam that bespread his countenance and sank into a mood
that set his vest to shaking "like a bowl full of jelly." "I was just
thinking," he said to nobody in particular, "that if Lige was jumped out
of his grave right quick by Gabriel and hauled up before St. Peter and
asked to justify my record, he'd have some trouble too--considerable
difficulty, I may say. I reckon it's all a matter of having to live with
your sins till you get a good excuse thought up."

The general pushed aside his work impatiently and tilted back in his
chair. "Come, Martin Culpepper, come, come! That won't do. You know
better than that. What's the use of your pretending to be as bad as
Lige Bemis? You know better and I know better and the whole town knows
better. He's little, and he's mean, and snooping, and crooked as a
dog's hind leg. Why, he was in here yesterday--actually in here to
see me. Yes, sir--what do you think of that? Wants to be state
senator."

"So I hear," smiled the colonel.

"Well," continued the general, "he came in here yesterday as pious as
a deacon, and he said that his friends were insisting on his running
because his enemies were bringing up that 'old trouble' on him. He
calls his horse stealing and cattle rustling 'that old trouble.'
Honestly, Martin, you'd think he was being persecuted. It was all I

could do to keep from sympathizing with him. He said he couldn't afford to retreat under fire, and then he told me how he had been trying to be a better man, and win the respect of the people--and I couldn't stand it any longer, and I rose up and shook my fist in his face and said: 'Lige Bemis, you disreputable, horse-stealing cow thief, what right have you to ask my help? What right have you got to run for state senator, anyway?' And, Martin, the brazen whelp reared back and looked me squarely in the eye and answered without blinking, 'Because, Phil Ward, I want the job.' What do you think of that for brass?"

The colonel slapped his campaign hat on his leg and laughed. There was always, even to the last, something feminine in Martin Culpepper's face when he laughed--a kind of alternating personality of the other sex seemed to tiptoe up to his consciousness and peek out of his kind eyes. As he laughed with Ward the colonel spoke: "Criminy, but that's like him. He's over there talking to Gabe Carnine on the corner now. I know what he's saying. He has only one speech, and he gets it off to all of us. He's got his cigar chawed down to a rag, stuck in one corner of his mouth, and he's saying, 'Gabe--this is the fight of my life. This is the last time I'm going to ask my friends for help.' General, I've heard that now, off and on, first and last, from old Lige at every city, state, county, and lodge election since the war closed, and I can see how Gabe is twisting and wiggling trying to get away from it. He's heard it too. Now Lige is saying: 'Gabe, I ain't going to lie to you; you know me, and you know I've made mistakes--but they were errors of judgment, and I want to get a chance to live 'em down. I want to show the young men of this state that Lige Bemis of the Red Legs is a man--even if he was wild as a young fellow; it'll prove that a man can rise.' Poor old Gabe--Lige has got him by the coat front, now. That's the third degree. When he gets him by the neck and begins to whisper, he's giving him the work in the uniform rank. He's saying: 'Gabe, I've got to have you with me.

I can't win without you, and I would rather lose than win with you against me. You stand for all that's upright in this county, and if you'll come to my aid, I can win.' Here, General--look--Lige's got him by the neck and the hand. Now for the password right from the grand lodge, 'Gabe, you'd make a fine state treasurer--I can land it for you. Make me state senator, and with my state acquaintance, added to the prestige of this office, I can make a deal that will land you.' Oh, I know his whole speech," laughed the colonel. "Bob Hendricks is to be secretary of state, John Barclay is to be governor, Oscar Fernald is to be state auditor, and the boys say that Lycurgus Mason has the refusal of warden of the Penitentiary." The colonel chuckled as he added: "So far as the boys have been able to learn, Lige still has United States senator, president, and five places in the cabinet to go on, but Minneola township returns ain't all in yet, and they may change the result. By the way, General, what did you get?"

The general flushed and replied, "Well, to be perfectly honest with you, Mart--he did promise me to vote for the dram-shop law."

And in the convention that summer Lige Bemis strode with his ragged cigar sticking from the corner of his mouth, with his black eyes blazing, and his shock of black hair on end, begging, bulldozing, and buying delegates to vote for him. He had the river wards behind him to a man, and he had the upland townships where the farmers needed a second name on their notes at the bank; and in the gentleman's ward--the silk-stocking ward--he had Gabriel Carnine, chairman of the first ward delegation, casting the solid vote of that ward for Bemis ballot after ballot. And when Bemis got Minneola township for fifty dollars,--and everybody in the convention knew it,--he was declared the nominee of the party with a whoop.

But behind Bemis was the sinister figure of young John Barclay working for his Elevator Company. He needed Bemis in politics, and Bemis needed Barclay in business. And there the alliance between Barclay and Bemis was cemented, to last for a quarter of a century. Barclay and Bemis went into the campaign together and asked the people to rally to the support of the party that had put down the rebellion, that had freed four million slaves, and had put the names of Lincoln and of Grant and Garfield as stars in the world's firmament of heroes. And the people of Garrison County responded, and State Senator Elijah Westlake Bemis did for Barclay in the legislature the things that Barclay would have preferred not to do for himself, and the Golden Belt Elevator Company throve and waxed fat. And Lige Bemis, its attorney, put himself in the way of becoming a "general counsel," with his name on an opaque glass door. For as Barclay rose in the world, he found the need of Bemis more and more pressing every year. In politics the favours a man does for others are his capital, and Barclay's deposit grew large. He was forever helping some one. His standing with the powers in the state was good. He was a local railroad attorney, and knew the men who had passes to give, and who were responsible for the direction which legislation took during the session. Barclay saw that they put Bemis on the judiciary committee, and by manipulating the judiciary committee he controlled a dozen votes through Bemis. He changed a railroad assessment law, secured the passage of a law permitting his Elevator Company to cheat the farmers by falsely grading their wheat, and prevented the passage of half a dozen laws restricting the powers of railroads. So at the close of the legislative session his name appeared under a wood-cut picture in the *Commonwealth* newspaper, and in the article thereunto appended Barclay was referred to as one of the "money kings of our young state." That summer he turned his wheat into his elevator early and at a low price, and borrowed money on it, and bought five new elevators and strained his credit to the limit, and before the fall closed he had ten more, and controlled the wheat in twenty counties. Strangers riding through the state on the Corn Belt Railroad saw the words, "The Golden Belt Elevator Company" on elevators all along the line. But few people knew then that the "Company" had become a partnership between John Barclay of Sycamore Ridge and less than half a dozen railroad men, with Barclay owning seventy-five per cent of the partnership and with State Senator Bemis the attorney for the company.

That year the railroad officials who were making money out of the Golden Belt Elevator Company were obliging, and Barclay made a contract with them to ship all grain from the Golden Belt Company's elevators in cars equipped with the Barclay Economy Rubber Strip, and he sold these strips to the railroads for four dollars apiece and put them on at the elevators. He shipped ten thousand cars that year, and Lycurgus Mason hired two men to help him in the strip factory. And John Barclay, in addition to the regular rebate, made forty thousand dollars that he did not have to divide. The next year he leased three large mills and took over a score of elevators and paid Lycurgus twenty dollars a week, and Lycurgus deposited money in the bank in his own name for the first time in his life.

As the century clanged noisily into its busy eighties, Adrian P. Brownwell creaked stiffly into his forties. And while all the world about him was growing rich,--or thought it was, which is the same thing,--Brownwell seemed to be struggling to keep barely even with the score of life. The ***Banner*** of course ran as a daily, but it was a miserable, half-starved little sheet, badly printed, and edited, as the printers used to say, with a pitchfork. It looked shiftless and dirty-faced long before Brownwell began to look seedy. Editor Brownwell was forever going on excursions--editorial excursions, land-buyers' excursions, corn trains, fruit trains, trade trains, political junkets, tours of inspection of new towns and new fields, and for consideration he was forever writing grandiloquent accounts of his adventures home to the ***Banner***. But from the very first he ostentatiously left Molly, his wife, at home. "The place for a woman," said Brownwell to the assembled company on the Barclay veranda one evening, when Jane had asked him why he did not take Molly to the opening of the new hotel at Garden City, "the place for woman is in the sacred precincts of home, 'far from the madding crowd's ignoble throng.' The madame and I," with a flourish of his cane, "came to that agreement early, eh, my dear, eh?" he asked, poking her masterfully with his cane. And Molly Brownwell, wistful-eyed and fading, smiled and assented, and the incident passed as dozens of other incidents passed in the Ridge, which made the women wish they had Adrian Brownwell, to handle for just one day. But the angels in that department of heaven where the marriages are made are exceedingly careful not to give to that particular kind of women the Adrian Brownwell kind of men, so the experiment which every one on earth for thousands of years has longed to witness, still remains a theory, and Adrian Brownwell traipsed up and down the earth, in his lavender gloves, his long coat and mouse-coloured trousers, his high hat, with his twirling cane, and the everlasting red carnation in his buttonhole. His absence made it necessary for Molly Brownwell to leave the sacred precincts of the home many and many a Saturday afternoon, to go over the books at the *Banner* office, make out bills, take them out, and collect the money due upon them and pay off the printers who got out the paper. But Adrian Brownwell ostentatiously ignored such services and kept up the fiction about the sacred precincts, and often wrote scorching editorials about the "encroachment of women" and grew indignant editorially at the growth of sentiment for woman's suffrage. On one occasion he left on the copy-hook a fervid appeal for women to repulse the commercialism which "was sullying the fair rose of womanhood," and taking "from woman the rare perfume of her chiefest charm," and then he went away on a ten days' journey, and the foreman of the *Banner* had to ask Mrs. Brownwell to collect enough money from the sheriff and a delinquent livery-stable keeper to pay the freight charges on the paper stock needed for that week's issue of the paper.

The town came to know these things, and so when Brownwell, who, since his marriage, had taken up his abode at the Culpeppers', hinted at his "extravagant family," the town refused to take him seriously. And the strutting, pompous little man, who referred grandly to "my wife," and then to "the madame," and finally to "my landlady," in a rather elaborate attempt at jocularity, laughed alone at his merriment along this line, and never knew that no one cared for his humour.

So in his early forties Editor Brownwell dried up and grew yellow and began to dye his mustaches and his eyebrows, and to devote much time to considering his own importance. "Throw it out," said Brownwell to the foreman, "not a line of it shall go!" He had just come home from a trip and had happened to glance over the proof of the article describing the laying of the corner-stone of Ward University.

"But that's the only thing that happened in town this week, and Mrs. Brownwell wrote it herself."

"Cut it out, I say," insisted Brownwell, and then threw back his shoulders and marched to his desk, snapping his eyes, and demonstrating to the printers that he was a man of consequence. "I'll teach 'em," he roared. "I'll teach 'em to make up their committees and leave me out."

He raged about the office, and finally wrote the name of Philemon R. Ward in large letters on the office blacklist hanging above his desk. This list contained the names which under no circumstances were to appear in the paper. But it was a flexible list. The next day John Barclay, who desired to have his speech on the laying of the corner-stone printed in full, gave Brownwell twenty dollars, and a most glowing account of the event in question appeared in the *Banner*, and eloquence staggered under the burden of praise which Brownwell's language loaded upon the shoulders of General Ward.

It is now nearly a generation since that corner-stone was laid. Boys and girls who then were children have children in the university, and its alumni include a brigadier in the army, a poet, a preacher of national renown, two college presidents, an authority upon the dynamics of living matter, and two men who died in the American mission at Foo Chow during the uprising in 1900. When General Ward was running for President of the United States on one of the various seceding branches of the prohibition party, while Jeanette Barclay was a little girl, he found the money for it; two maiden great-aunts on his mother's side of the family had half a million dollars to leave to something, and the general got it. They willed it to him to hold in trust during his lifetime, but the day after the check came for it, he had transferred the money to a university fund, and had borrowed fifty dollars of Bob Hendricks to clean up his grocery bills and tide him over until his pension came. But he was a practical old fox. He announced that he would give the money to a college only if the town would give a similar sum, and what with John Barclay's hundred-thousand-dollar donation, and Bob Hendricks' ten thousand, and what with the subscription paper carried around by Colonel Culpepper, who proudly headed it with five thousand dollars, and after the figure wrote in red ink "in real estate," much to the town's merriment, and what with public meetings and exhortations in the churches, and what with voting one hundred thousand dollars in bonds by Garrison County for the privilege of sending students to the college without tuition, the amount was raised; and as the procession wheeled out of Main Street to attend the ceremonies incident to laying the corner-stone that beautiful October day, it is doubtful which was the prouder man--Martin Culpepper, the master of ceremonies, in his plumed hat, flashing sword, and red sash, or General Philemon Ward, who for the first time in a dozen years heard the crowd cheer his name when the governor in his speech pointed at the general's picture--his campaign picture that had been hooted with derision and spattered with filth on so many different occasions in the town. The governor's remarks were of course perfunctory; he devoted five or ten minutes to the praise of

General Ward, of Sycamore Ridge, of John Barclay, and of education in
general, and then made his regular speech that he used for college
commencements, for addresses of welcome to church conferences, synods,
and assemblies, and for conclaves of the grand lodge. General Ward spoke
poorly, which was to his credit, considering the occasion, and Watts
McHurdie's poem got entangled with Juno and Hermes and Minerva and a
number of scandalous heathen gods,--who were no friends of Watts,--and
the crowd tired before he finished the second canto. But many
discriminating persons think that John Barclay's address, "The Time of
True Romance," was the best thing he ever wrote. It may be found in his
book as Chapter XI. "The Goths," he said, "came out of the woods, pulled
the beards of the senators, destroyed the Roman state, murdered and
pillaged the Roman people, and left the world the Gothic arch; the
Vikings came over the sea, roaring their sagas of rapine and slaughter;
the conquerors came to Europe with spear and sword and torch and left
the outlines of the map, the boundaries of states. Luther married his
nun, and set Christendom to fighting over it for a hundred years, but he
left a free conscience. Cromwell thrust his pikes into the noble heads
of England, snapped his fingers at law, and left civil liberty.
Organized murder reached its sublimity in the war that Lincoln waged,
and in that murdering and pillage true romance came to mankind in its
flower. Murder for the moment in these piping times has become impolite.
But true romance is here. Our heroes rob and plunder, and build cities,
and swing gayly around the curves of the railroads they have stolen, and
swagger through the cities they have levied upon the people to build. Do
we care to-day whether Charlemagne murdered his enemies with a sword or
an axe; do we ask if King Arthur used painless assassination or burned
his foes at the stake? Who cares to know that Caesar was a rake, and that
William the Conqueror was a robber? They did their work and did it well,
and are snugly sitting on their monuments where no moralist can reach
them. So those searching for true romance to-day, who regard the
decalogue as mere persiflage, and the moral code as a thing of archaic
interest, will get their day's work done and strut into posterity in

bronze and marble. They will cheat and rob and oppress and grind the faces off the poor, and do their work and follow their visions, and live the romance in their hearts. To-morrow we will take their work, disinfect it, and dedicate it to God's uses."

There was more of it--four thousand words more, to be exact, and when General Ward went home that night he prayed his Unitarian God to forgive John Barclay for his blasphemy. And for years the general shuddered when his memory brought back the picture of the little man, with his hard tanned face, his glaring green eyes, his brazen voice trumpeting the doctrine of materialism to the people.

"John," said the general, the next day, as he sat in the mill, going over the plans of the college buildings with Barclay, who was chairman of the board of directors, "John, why are you so crass, so gross a materialist? You have enough money--why don't you stop getting it and do something with it worth while?"

"Because, General, I'm not making money--that's only an incident of my day's work. I'm organizing the grain industry of this country as it is organized in no other country on this planet." Barclay rose as he spoke and began limping the length of the room. It was his habit to walk when he talked, and he knew the general had come to catechize him.

"Yes, but then, John--what then?"

"What then?" repeated Barclay, with his hands in his pockets and his eyes on the floor. "Coffee, maybe--perhaps sugar, or tobacco. Or why not the whole food supply of the people--let me have meat and sugar where I will have flour and grain, and in ten years no man in America can open his grocery store in the morning until he has asked John Barclay for the key." He snapped his eyes good naturedly at the general, challenging the man's approval.

The general smiled and replied: "No, John, you'll get the social bug and go around in knee-breeches, riding a horse after a scared fox, or keeping a lot of hussies on a yacht. They all get that way sooner or later."

Barclay leaned over Ward, stuck out his hard jaw and growled: "Well, I won't. I'm going to be a tourist-sleeper millionaire. I stick to Sycamore Ridge; Jeanette goes to the public schools; Jane buys her clothes at Bob Hendricks' or Dorman's, or at the most of Marshall Field in Chicago; I go fishing down at Minneola when I want rest." Ward started to protest, but Barclay headed him off. "I made a million last year. What did I do with it? See any yachts on the Sycamore? Observe any understudies for Jane around the place? Have you heard of any villas for the Barclays in Newport? No--no, you haven't, but you may like to know that I have control of a railroad that handles more wheat than any other hundred miles in the world, and it is the key to the lake situation. And I've put the price of my Economy Door Strip up to ten dollars, and they don't dare refuse it. What's more, I'm going to hire a high-priced New York sculptor to make a monument for old Henry Schnitzler, who fell at Wilson's Creek, and put it in the cemetery. But I am giving none of my hard-earned cash to cooks and florists and chorus ladies. So if I want to steal a mill or so every season, and gut a railroad, I'm going to do it, but no one can rise up and say I am squandering my substance on riotous living."

Barclay shook his head as he spoke and gesticulated with his hands, and the general, seeing that he could not get the younger man to talk of serious things, brought out the plans for the college buildings, and the men fell to the work in hand with a will.

Barclay's spirit was the spirit of his times--growing out of a condition which, as Barclay said in his speech, was like Emersonian optimism set to Wagnerian music. In Sycamore Ridge factories rose in the bottoms near the creek, and shop hands appeared on the streets at night; new people invaded Lincoln Avenue, and the Culpeppers, to maintain their social supremacy, had to hire a coloured man to open the door for an afternoon party, and for an evening reception it took two, one for the door and one to stand at the top of the stairs.

Those were the palmy days of the colonel's life. Money came easily, and went easily. The Culpepper Mortgage Company employed fifty men, who handled money all over the West, and one of the coloured men who opened the door at the annual social affair at the Culpepper home also took care of the horses, and drove the colonel down to his office in the Barclay block every morning, and drove him home in the evening.

"Well," said Watts McHurdie to Gabriel Carnine as the two walked down the hill into the business section of the town, a few days after the corner-stone of Ward College was laid, "old Phil has got his college started and Mart's got his church a-going."

"You mean the East End Mission? Yes, and I don't know which, of 'em is happier over his work," replied Carnine.

"Well, Mart certainly is proud; he's been too busy to loaf in the shop for six months," said McHurdie.

Carnine smiled, and stroked his chestnut beard reflectively before he added: "Probably that's why he hasn't been in to renew his last two notes. But I guess he does a lot of good to the poor people over there along the river. Though I shouldn't wonder if he was encouraging them to be paupers." Carnine paused a moment and then added, "Good old Mart--he's got a heart just like a woman's."

They were passing the court-house square, and Bailiff Jacob Dolan, with a fist full of legal papers, caught step with Carnine and McHurdie. "We were talking about Mart Culpepper and his Mission Church," said Carnine. "Don't you suppose, Jake, that Mart, by circulating down there with his basket so much, encourages the people to be shiftless? We were just wondering."

"Oh, you were, were you?" snapped Dolan. "There you go, Gabe Carnine; since you've moved to town and got to be president of a bank, you're mighty damn scared about making paupers. When Christ told the young man to sell his goods and give them to the poor, He didn't tell him to be careful about making them paupers. And Mr. Gabriel Carnine, Esquire, having the aroma of one large morning's drink on my breath emboldens me to say, that if you rich men will do your part in giving, the Lord will manage to keep His side of the traces from scraping on the wheel. And if I had one more good nip, I'd say, which Heaven forbid, that you fellows are asking more of the Lord by expecting Him to save your shrivelled selfish little souls from hell-fire because of your squeeze-penny charities, than you would be asking by expecting Him to keep the poor from becoming paupers by the dribs you give them. And if Mart Culpepper can give his time and his money every day helping them poor devils down by the track, niggers and whites, good and bad, male and female, I guess the Lord will put in lick for lick with Mart and see that his helping doesn't hurt them." Dolan shook his head at the banker, and then smiled at him good-naturedly as he finished, "Put that in your knapsack, you son of a gun, and chew on it till I see you again." Whereupon he turned a corner and went his way.

Carnine laughed rather unnaturally and said to McHurdie, "That's why he's never got on like the other boys. Whiskey's a bad partner."

McHurdie agreed, and went chuckling to his work, when Carnine turned into the bank. Later in the forenoon Bailiff Dolan came in grinning, and took a seat by the stove in McHurdie's shop and said as he reached into the waste-basket for a scrap of harness leather, and began whittling it, "What did Gabe say when I left you this morning?" and without waiting for a reply, went on, "I've thought for some time Gabe needed a little something for what ails him, and I gave it to him, out of the goodness of my heart."

McHurdie looked at Dolan over his glasses and replied, "Speech is silver, but silence is golden."

"The same," answered Dolan, "the same it is, and by the same authority apples of gold in pictures of silver is a word fitly spoken to a man like Gabe Gamine." He whittled for a few minutes while the harness maker worked, and then sticking his pocket-knife into the chair between his legs, said: "But what I came in to tell you was about Lige Bemis; did you know he's in town? Well, he is. Johnnie Barclay wired him to leave the dump up in the City and come down here, and what for, do you think? 'Tis this. The council was going to change the name of Ellen Avenue out by the college to Garfield, and because it was named for that little girl of Mart's that died right after the war, don't you think Johnnie's out raising hell about it, and brought Lige down here to beat the game. He'll be spending a lot of money if he has to. Now you wouldn't think he'd do that for old Mart, would you? He's too many for me--that Johnny boy is. I can't make him out." The Irishman played with his knife, sticking it in the chair and pulling it out for a while, and then continued: "Oh, yes, what I was going to tell you was the little spat me and Lige had over Johnnie. Lige was in my room in the court-house waiting to see a man in the court, and was bragging to me about how smart John was, and says Lige, 'He's found some earth over in Missouri--yellow clay,' he says, 'that's just as good as oatmeal, and he ships it all over the country to his oatmeal mills and mixes it with the real stuff and sells it.' I says: 'He does, does he? Sells mud mixed with oatmeal?' and Lige says, 'Yes, sir, he's got a whole mountain of it, and he's getting ten dollars a ton net for it, which is better than a gold mine.' 'And you call that smart?' says I. 'Yes,' says he, 'yes, sir, that's commercial instinct; it's perfectly clean mud, and our chemist says it won't harm any one,' says he. 'And him president of the Golden Belt Elevator Co.?' says I. 'He is,' says Lige. 'And don't need the money at all?' says I. 'Not a penny of it,' says he. 'Well,' says I, 'Lige Bemis,' says I, 'when Johnnie gets to hell,--and he'll get there as sure as it doesn't freeze over,' says I, 'may the devil put him under that mountain of mud and keep his railroad running night and day dumping more mud on while he eats his way out as a penance,' says I. And you orto heard 'em laugh." Dolan went on cutting curly-cues from the leather, and McHurdie kept on sewing at his bench. "It is a queer world--a queer world; and that Johnnie Barclay is a queer duck. Bringing Lige Bemis clear down here to help old Mart out of a little trouble there ain't a dollar in; and then turning around and feeding the American people a mountain of mud. Giving the town a park with his mother's name on it, and selling little tin strips for ten dollars apiece to pay for it. He's a queer duck. I'll bet it will keep the recording angel busy keeping books on Johnnie Barclay."

"Oh, well, Jake," replied McHurdie, after a silence, "maybe the angels will just drop a tear and wipe much of the evil off."

"Maybe so, Watts McHurdie, maybe so," returned Dolan, "but there won't be a dry eye in the house, as the papers say, if they keep up with him." And after delivering himself of this, Dolan rose and yawned, and went out of the shop singing an old tune which recited the fact that he had "a job to do down in the boulevard."

Looking over the years that have passed since John Barclay and Sycamore Ridge were coming out of raw adolescence into maturity, one sees that there was a miracle of change in them both, but where it was

and just how it came, one may not say. The town had no special
advantages. It might have been one of a thousand dreary brown
unpainted villages that dot the wind-swept plain to-day, instead of
the bright, prosperous, elm-shaded town that it is. John Barclay in
those days of his early thirties might have become a penny-pinching
dull-witted "prominent citizen" of the Ridge, with no wider sphere of
influence than the Sycamore Valley, or at most the Corn Belt Railroad.
But he and the town grew, and whether it was destiny that guided them,
or whether they made their own destiny, one cannot say. The town
seemed to be struggling and fighting its way to supremacy in the
Sycamore Valley; and the colonel and the general and Watts McHurdie,
sitting in the harness shop a score of years after those days of the
seventies, used to try to remember some episode or event that would
tell them how John fought his way up. But they could not do so. It was
a fight in his soul. Every time his hand reached out to steal a mill
or crush an opponent with the weapon of his secret railroad rebates,
something caught his hand and held it for a moment, and he had to
fight his way free. At first he had to learn to hate the man he was
about to ruin, and to pretend that he thought the man was about to
ruin him. Then he could justify himself in his greedy game. But at
last he worked almost merrily. He came to enjoy the combat for its own
sake. And sometimes he would play with a victim cat-wise, and after a
victory in which the mouse fought well, John would lick his chops with
some satisfaction at his business prowess. Mill after mill along the
valley and through the West came under his control. And his skin grew
leathery, and the brass lustre in his eyes grew hard and metallic.
When he knew that he was the richest man in Garrison County, he saw
that there were richer men in the state, and in after years when he
was the richest man in the state, and in the Missouri Valley, the rich
men in other states moved him by their wealth to work harder. But
before he was thirty, his laugh had become a cackle, and Colonel
Martin Culpepper, who would saunter along when Barclay would limp by
on Main Street, would call out after him, "Slow down, Johnnie, slow

down, boy, or you'll bust a biler." And then the colonel would pause and gaze benignly after the limping figure bobbing along in the next block, and if there was a bystander to address, the colonel would say, "For a flat-wheel he does certainly make good time." And then if the bystander looked worth the while, the colonel, in seven cases out of ten, would pull out a subscription paper for some new church building, or for some charitable purpose, and proceed to solicit the needed funds.

BOOK II

BEING NO CHAPTER AT ALL, BUT AN INTERLUDE FOR THE ORCHESTRA

And so the years slipped by--monotonous years they seem now, so far as this story goes. Because little happened worth the telling; for growth is so still and so dull and so undramatic that it escapes interest and climax; yet it is all there is in life. For the roots of events in the ground of the past are like the crowded moments of our passing lives that are recorded only in our under-consciousnesses, to rise in other years in character formed, in traits established, in events fructified. And in the years when the evil days came not, John Barclay's tragedy was stirring in the soil of his soul.

And now, ladies and gentlemen, on behalf of the management, let us thank you for your kind attention, during the tedious act which has closed. We have done our best to please you with the puppets and have cracked their heads together in fine fashion, and they have danced and cried and crackled, while we pulled the strings as our mummers mumbled. But now they must have new clothes on. Time, the great costumer, must change their make-up. So we will fold down the curtain. John Barclay, a Gentleman, must be painted yellow with gold. Philemon Ward, a Patriot, must be sprinkled with gray. Martin Culpepper's Large White Plumes must be towsled. Watts McHurdie, a Poet, must be bent a little at the hips and shoulders. Adrian Brownwell, a Gallant, must creak as he struts. Neal Dow Ward, an Infant, must put on long trousers. E. W. Bemis, a Lawyer, must be dignified; Jacob Dolan, an Irishman and a Soldier, must grow unkempt and frowsy. Robert Hendricks, Fellow Fine, must have his blond hair rubbed off at the temples, and his face marked with maturity. Lycurgus Mason, a Woman Tamer, must get used to wearing white shirts. Gabriel Carnine, a Money Changer, must feel his importance; and Oscar Fernald, a Tavern Keeper, must be hobbled by the years. All but the shades must be refurbished. General Hendricks and Elmer, his son, must fade farther into the mists of the past, while Henry Schnitzler settles comfortably down in storied urn and animated bust.

There they hang together on the line, these basswood folk, and beside them wave their womankind. These also must be repaired and refitted throughout, as Oscar Fernald's letter-heads used to say of the Thayer House. Jane Barclay, Wife of John, must have the "star light, star bright" wiped out of her eyes. Mary Barclay, Mother of the Same, must have her limbs trimmed gaunt, and her face chiselled strong and indomitable. Jeanette Barclay, a Toddler, must grow into dresses. Molly Culpepper, a Dear, must have her heart taken out, and her face show the shock of the operation. Nellie Logan, a poet's Wife, must join all the lodges in the Ridge to help her husband in politics. Trixie Lee, little Beatrix Lee, daughter of J. Lord and Lady Lee, must have her childish face scarred and her eyes glazed. Mrs. Hally Bemis, a Prodigal, must be swathed in silk. Elizabeth Cady Stanton Ward and

all her sisters must be put in the simple garb of school-teachers.
Miss Hendricks, a Mouse, must hide in the dusky places; and Ellen
Culpepper, a Memory, must come to life.

And so, ladies and gentlemen, while we have been diverting you, Time
has been at work on the little people of the passing show, and now
before we draw back the curtain to let them caper across your hearts,
let us again thank you one and all for your courtesy in staying, and
hope that what you see and hear may make you wiser and kinder and
braver; for this is a moral entertainment, good people, planned to
show you that yesterday makes to-day and they both make to-morrow, and
so the world spins round the sun.

CHAPTER XVII

The rumble of the wheels in the great stone mill across the Sycamore
and the roar of the waters over the dam seem to have been in Jeanette
Barclay's ears from the day of her birth; for she was but a baby when
the stone mill rose where the little red mill had stood, and beside
the stone mill there had grown up the long stone factory wherein
Lycurgus Mason was a man of consequence. As the trains whirled by
strangers could see the signs in mammoth letters, "The Golden Belt
Mills" on the larger building and on the smaller, "The Barclay Economy
Door Strip Factory." Standing on the stone steps of her father's house
the child could read these signs clear across the mill-pond, and from
these signs she learned her letters. For her father had more pride in
that one mill on the Sycamore than in the scores of other mills that
he controlled. And even in after years, when he controlled mills all
over the West, and owned railroads upon which to take his flour to the

sea, and ships in which to carry his flour all over the world, the
Golden Belt Mill at Sycamore Ridge was his chief pride. The rumble of
the wheels and the hoarse voice of the dam that seemed to Jeanette
like the call of the sea, were so sweet to her father's ears that when
he wearied of the work of the National Provisions Company, with its
two floors of busy offices in the Corn Exchange Building in the great
city, he would come home to Sycamore Ridge, and go to his private
office in the mill. The child remembers what seemed like endless days,
but what in truth were only a few hours in a few days in a few years,
when Daddy Barclay carried her on his shoulders across the bridge and
sat her down barefooted and bareheaded to play upon the dam, while he
in his old clothes prodded among the great wheels near by or sat
beside her telling her where he caught this fish or that fish or a
turtle or a water moccasin when he was a little boy. At low water, she
remembers that he sometimes let her wade in the clear stream, while he
sat in his office near by watching her from the window. That was when
she was only four years old, and she always had the strangest memory
of a playfellow on the dam, a big girl, who fluttered in and out of
the shadows on the stones. Jeanette talked with her, but no one else
could see her, and once the big girl, who could not talk herself,
stamped her feet and beckoned Jeanette to come away from a rock on
which she was playing, and her father, looking out of a window, turned
white when he saw a snake coiled beside the rock. But Jeanette saw the
snake and was frightened, and told her father that Ellen saw it too,
and she could not make him understand who Ellen was. So he only
trembled and hugged his little girl to him tightly, and mother would
not let the child play on the dam again all that summer.

She made songs to fit the rhythmic murmur of the wheels. And always
she remembered the days she had spent with Daddy Mason in the factory
where the machines thumped and creaked, and where the long rubber
sheets were cut and sewed, and the clanking rolls of tin and zinc
curled into strips, and Daddy Mason made her a little set of dishes

and all the things she needed in her playhouse from the scraps of tin
and rubber, and she learned to twist the little tin strips on a stick
and make the prettiest bright shiny tin curls for her dolls that a
little girl ever saw in all the world. And once Ellen came from among
the moving shadows of the wheels and drew Jeanette from beneath a
great knife that fell at her feet, and when Daddy Mason saw what had
happened he fainted, poor man, and made her promise never, never, so
long as she lived, to tell Grandma Mason. And then he drove her up
town, and they had some ice-cream, and she was sent to bed without her
lunch because she would not tell Grandma Mason why grandpa bought
ice-cream for her.

It was such a beautiful life, so natural and so exactly what a little
girl should have, that even though she went to the ocean and crossed
it as a child with her mother and grandmother, and even though she
went to the mountains many times, her childish heart always was
homesick for the mill, and at night in her dreams her ears were filled
with the murmur of waters and the wordless song of ceaseless wheels.
And once when she came back a big girl,--an exceedingly big girl with
braids down her back, a girl in the third reader in fact, who could
read everything in the fourth reader, because she had already done so,
and who could read Eugene Aram in the back of the sixth, only she
never did find out what "gyves upon his wrists" meant,--once when she
came back to the dam and was sitting there looking at the sunset
reflected in the bubbling, froth-flecked water at her feet, Ellen came
suddenly, under the noise of the roaring water, and frightened
Jeanette so that she screamed and jumped; and Ellen, who was much
older than Jeanette--four or five and maybe six years older--ran
right over the slippery, moss-covered ridge of the dam, and was gone
before Jeanette could call her back. The child never saw her playmate
again, though often Jeanette would wonder where Ellen lived and who
she was. As the years went by, Jeanette came to remember her playmate
as her dream child, and once when she was a young miss of eighteen,

and something in her hurt to be said, she tried to make a little poem about her dream-child playmate, but all she ever got was:--

"O eyes, so brown and clear like water sparkling over mossy stones."

So she gave it up and wrote a poem about a prince who carried away a maiden, and then she tore up the prince and the maiden, and if it were not for that line about the eyes in the back of her trigonometry, with a long list of words under it rhyming with "stones," she would have forgotten about her playfellow, and much of the memory of the dam and the pride she took as a child in the great letters upon the high stone walls of the mills, and of the word "Barclay" on the long low walls of the factory, might have passed from her consciousness altogether. By such frail links does memory bind us to our past; and yet, once formed, how like steel they hold us! What we will be, grows from what we are, and what we are has grown from what we were. If Jeanette Barclay, the only child of a man who, when she was in her twenties, was to be one of the hundred richest men in his country,--so far as mere money goes,--had been brought up with a governess and a maid, and with frills and furbelows and tucks and Heaven knows what of silly kinks and fluffy stuff in her childish head, instead of being brought up in the Sycamore Ridge public schools, with Grandmother Barclay to teach her the things that a little girl in the fourth reader should know, and with a whole community of honest, hard-working men and women about her to teach her what life really is, indeed she would have lived a different life, and when she was ready to marry--But there we go looking in the back of the book again, and that will not do at all; and besides, a little blue-eyed girl in gingham aprons, sitting on a cool stone with moss on its north side, watching the bass play among the rocks in a clear, deep, sun-mottled pool under a great elm tree, has a right to the illusions of her childhood and should not be hustled into long dresses and love affairs until her time has come.

But the recollection of those days, so vivid and so sweet, is one of her choicest treasures. Of course things were not as she saw them. Jake Dolan was only in his forties then, and considered himself a young man. But the child remembers him as a tall, brown-eyed man whom she saw on state occasions in his faded blue army clothes, and to her he has always been the picture of a veteran. Some one must have told her--though she cannot remember who it was--that as Jake Dolan gently descended the social and political scale, he sloughed off his worldly goods, and as he moved about in the court-house from the sheriff's office to the deputy's office, and from the deputy's to the bailiff's, and from the bailiff's to the constable's, and from the constable's to the janitor's room in the basement, he carried with him the little bundle that contained all his worldly goods, the thin blue uniform, spotless and trim, and his lieutenant's commission, and mustering-out papers from the army. It is odd, is it not, that this prosaic old chap, who smoked a clay pipe, and whose only accomplishment was the ability to sing "The Hat me Father Wore," under three drinks, and the "Sword of Bunker Hill," under ten, should have epitomized all that was heroic in this child's memory. As for General Philemon Ward,--a dear old crank who, when Jeanette was born, was voting with the Republican party for the first time since the war, and who ran twice for President on some strange issue before she was in long dresses,--General Ward, whose children's ages could be guessed by the disturbers of the public peace, whose names they bore,--Eli Thayer, Mary Livermore, Elizabeth Cady Stanton, Frances Willard, Neal Dow, Belva Lockwood, and Helen Gougar,--General Ward, who scorned her father's offer of ten thousand dollars a year as state counsel for the National Provisions Company, and went out preaching fiat money and a subtreasury for the farmers' crops, trusting to God and the flower garden about his little white house, to keep the family alive--it is odd that Jeanette's childish impression was that General Ward was a man of consequence in the world. Perhaps his white necktie, his long black coat, and his keen lean face, or his prematurely gray hair, gave her some sort of a notion of his dignity, but whatever gave her that notion she kept it, and though in her later life there came a passing time when she hated him, she did not despise him. And what with the song that she heard the bands playing all over the country, the song that the bands sometimes played for Americans in Europe, very badly, as though it was being translated from English into broken French or Italian, what with Watts McHurdie's fame and with his verses that appeared in the *Banner* on formal occasions, the girl built a fancy of him as one of the world's great poets--some one like Shakespeare or Milton; and she was well into her teens before she realized the truth, that he was an excellent harness maker who often brought out of his quaint little dream world odd-shaped fancies in rhyme,--some grotesque, some ridiculous, and some that seemed pretty for a moment,--and who under the stress of a universal emotion had rhymed one phase of our common nature and set it to a simple tune that moved men deeply without regard to race or station. So she lived in her child world--a world quite different from the real world--a world gilded by the sunrise of consciousness; and because the angels loved her and kept her heart clean, the gilding never quite wore off her heroes. And nothing that Heaven gives us in this world is so blessed as to have the gilding stick to the images of our youth. In Jeanette's case even Lige Bemis--Judge Bemis, she had been taught to call him--never showed the tar under the gilding to her eyes. Her first memory of him was in her father's office in the big City. He was a tall man, with gray hair that became him well, with sharp black eyes, and enough flesh on his bones to carry the frock-coats he always wore and give him a corporosity just escaping the portly. She remembers seeing the name "E. W. Bemis" in gold letters on the door of his room, and not being able to figure out how a man whose name began with "E" or "W" could be called Lige. He was General Counsel of the Corn Belt Railroad in those days, when her father was president of the road, and she knew that he was a man always to be considered. And when, as a woman grown, she learned the truth about Lige Bemis, it was hard to believe, for all she could find against him was his everlasting smile.

It is a curious and withal a beautiful thing to see a child come into the worn and weary world that we grownups have made, and make it over into another world altogether. Perhaps the child's eye and the child's heart, fresh from God, see and feel more clearly and more justly than we do. For this much is sure--Jeanette was right in keeping to the end the image of Colonel Martin Culpepper as a knight-errant, who needed only a bespangled steed, a little less avoirdupois, and a foolish cause to set him battling in the tourney. As it was, in this humdrum world, the colonel could do nothing more heroic than come rattling down Main Street into the child's heart, sitting with some dignity in his weather-beaten buggy, while instead of shining armour and a glistening helmet he wore nankeen trousers, a linen coat, and a dignified panama hat. Moreover, it is stencilled into her memory indelibly that the colonel was the first man in this wide world to raise his hat to her.

Now it should not be strange that this world was a sad jumble of fiction and of facts to a child's eyes; for to many an older pair of eyes it has all seemed a puzzle. Even the shrewd, kind brown eyes of Jacob Dolan often failed to see things as they were, and what his eyes did see sometimes bewildered him. By day Dolan saw Robert Hendricks, president of the Exchange National Bank, president and manager of the Sycamore Ridge Light, Heat, and Power Company, proprietor of the Hendricks Mercantile Company, treasurer and first vice-president of the new Western Wholesale Grocery, and chairman of his party's congressional central committee, and Dolan's eyes saw a hard, busy man--a young man, it is true; a tall, straight, rather lean, rope-haired young man in his thirties, with frank blue eyes, that turned rather suddenly upon one as if to frighten out a secret. The man seemed real enough to Dolan, from the wide crown of his slightly bald, V-shaped head, to his feet with the hard click in the heels; and yet that man paid no particular attention to Dolan. It was "Hello, Jake," with a nod, as they passed, maybe only an abstracted stare and a grunt. But at night, as they walked together over the town under the stars or moon, a lonely soul rose out of the tall body and spread over the face.

Dolan kept to his pipe and Hendricks to his cigar. But these were the only marks of caste between them. One night Hendricks led the way across the bridge down the river road and into the fields. They walked far up the stream and their conversation had consisted largely of "Watch out," "All right," "I see," "This is the best way." They loitered down a dark lane shaded by hedgerows until they came to a little wooden bridge and sat down. Dolan looked at the stars, while a pipe and a cigar had burned out before Hendricks spoke, "Well, chatterbox?"

"I was bothered with a question of mistaken identity," replied Dolan. To the silence he answered: "Me myself. I'm the man. Do you happen to know who I am?" Hendricks broke a splinter from the wood under him, and Dolan continued: "Of course you don't, and neither do I. For example, I go down into Union township before election and visit with the boys. I bring a box of cigars and maybe a nip under the buggy seat, and maybe a few stray five-dollar bills for the lads that drive the wagons that haul the voters to the polls. I go home, and I says to myself: 'I have that bailiwick to a man. No votes there against Jake.' But the morning after election I see Jake didn't get but two votes in the township. Very well. Now who did they vote against? Surely not against the genial obliging rollicking Irish lad whose face I shave every other morning. What could they possibly have against him? No--they voted against that man Dolan, who got drunk, at the Fair and throwed the gate receipts into the well, and tried to shoo the horses off the track into the crowd at the home-stretch of the trotting race.

He's the man they plugged. And there's another one--him that confesses to Father Van Sandt." Dolan shook his head sadly and sighed. "He's a black-hearted wretch. If you want to see how a soul will look in its underwear, get an Irishman to confess to a Dutchman." The chirp of crickets arose in the silence, and after a time Dolan concluded, "And now there abideth these three, me that I shave, me that they vote against, and me that the Father knows; and the greatest of these is charity--I dunno."

The soul beside him on the bridge came back from a lilac bower of other years, with a girl's lips glowing upon his and the beat of a girl's heart throbbing against his own. The soul was seared with images that must never find spoken words, and it moved the lips to say after exhaling a deep breath from its body, "Well, let's go home." There, too, was a question of identity. Who was Robert Hendricks? Was he the man chosen to lead his party organization because he was clean above reproach and a man of ideals; was he the man who was trusted with the money of the people of his town and county implicitly; or was he the man who knew that on page 234 of the cash ledger for 1879 in the county treasurer's office in the Garrison County court-house there was a forgery in his own handwriting to cover nine thousand dollars of his father's debt? Or was he the man who for seven years had crept into a neighbour's garden on a certain night in April to smell the lilac blossoms and always had found them gone, and had stood there rigid, with upturned face and clenched fists, cursing a fellow-man? Or was he the man who in the county convention of his party had risen pale with anger, and had walked across the floor and roared his denunciation of Elijah W. Bemis as a boodler and a scoundrel squarely to the man's gray, smirking face and chattering teeth, and then had reached down, and grabbed the trapped bribe-giver by the scruff of the neck and literally thrown him out of the convention, while the crowd went mad with applause? As he went home that night following the convention, walking by the side of Dolan in silence, he wondered which of all his *aliases* he really was. At the gate of the Hendricks home the two men stopped. Hendricks smiled quizzically as he asked: "Well, I give it up, Jake. By the way, did you ever meet me?"

The brown eyes of the Irishman beamed an instant through the night, before he hurried lightly down the street.

And so with all of this hide-and-seek of souls, now peering from behind eyes and now far away patting one--two--three upon some distant base, with all these queer goings-on inside of people here in this strange world, it is no wonder that when the angels brought Jeanette to the Barclays, they left her much to learn and many things to study about. So she had to ask questions. But questions often reveal more than answers. At least once they revealed much, when she sat on the veranda of the Barclay home a fine spring evening with all the company there. Aunt Molly was there; and Uncle Bob Hendricks was there, the special guest of Grandma Barclay. Uncle Adrian was away on a trip somewhere; but Uncle Colonel and Grandma Culpepper and all the others were there listening to father's new German music-box, and no one should blame a little girl, sitting shyly on the stone steps, trying to make something out of the absurd world around her, if she piped out when the talk stopped:--

"Mother, why does Aunt Molly cut off her lilac buds before they bloom?"

And when her mother assured her that Aunt Molly did nothing of the kind, and when Uncle Bob Hendricks looked up and saw Aunt Molly go pale under her powder, and when Aunt Molly said, "Why, Jane--the child must have dreamed that," no one in this wide world must blame a little girl for opening her eyes as wide as she could, and lifting her little voice as strongly as she could, and saying: "Why, Aunt Molly, you know I saw you last night--when I stayed with you. You know I

did, 'cause I looked out of the window and spokened to you. You know I
did--don't you remember?" And no one must blame the mother for
shaking her finger at Jeanette, and no one must blame Jeanette for
sitting there shaking a protesting head, and screwing up her little
face, trying to make the puzzle out.

And when, later in the evening, Daddy Barclay went over to the mill
with his work, and Uncle Bob left in the twilight, and Aunt Molly and
mother were alone in mother's room, how should a little girl know what
the crying was all about, and how should a little girl understand when
a small woman, looking in a mirror, and dabbing her face with a powder
rag, said to mother, who knows everything in the world, and all about
the angels that brought you here: "Oh, Jane, Jane, you don't
know--you don't understand. There are things that I couldn't make you
understand--and I mustn't even think of them."

Surely it is a curious world for little girls--a passing curious
world, when there are things in it that even mothers cannot
understand.

So Jeanette turned her face to the wall and went to sleep, leaving
Aunt Molly powdering her nose and asking mother, "Does it look all
right now--" and adding, "Oh, I'm such a fool." In so illogical a
world, the reader must not be allowed to think that Molly Brownwell
lamented the folly of mourning for a handsome young gentleman in blue
serge with white spats on his shoes and a Byronic collar and a fluffy
necktie of the period. Far be it from her to lament that sentiment as
folly; however, when she looked at her eyes in the mirror and saw her
nose, she felt that tears were expensive and reproached herself for
them. But so long as these souls of ours, whatever they may be, are
caged in our bodies, our poor bodies will have to bear witness to
their prisoners. If the soul smiles the body shines, and if the soul
frets the body withers. And Molly Brownwell saw in the looking-glass

that night more surely than ever before that her face was beginning to slump. Her cheeks were no longer firm, and at her eyes were the stains of tears that would not wipe off, but crinkled the skin at the temples and deepened the shadows into wide salmon-coloured lines that fell away from each side of the nose so that no trick could hide them. Moreover, the bright eyes that used to flash into Bob Hendricks' steady blue eyes had grown tired, and women who did not know, wondered why such a pretty girl had broken so.

The Culpeppers had remained with the Barclays for dinner, and the hour was late for the Ridge--after nine o'clock, and as the departing guests went down the long curved walk of Barclay pride to the Barclay gate, they saw a late April moon rising over the trees by the mill. They clanged the tall iron gate behind them, and stood a moment watching the moon. For the colonel never grew too old to notice it. He put his arms about his wife and his daughter tenderly, and said before they started up the street, "It never grows old--does it?" And he pressed his wife to him gently and repeated, "Does it, my dear--it's the same old moon; the one we used to have in Virginia before the war, isn't it?"

His wife smiled at him placidly and said, "Now, pa--"

Whereupon the colonel squeezed his daughter lustily, and exclaimed, "Well, Molly still loves me, anyway. Don't you, Molly?" And the younger woman patted his cheek, and then they started for home.

"Papa, how much money has John?" asked the daughter, as they walked along.

A man always likes to be regarded as an authority in financial matters, and the colonel stroked his goatee wisely before replying: "U-h-m-m, let me see--I don't exactly know. Bob and I were talking about it the other day--after I bought John's share in College Heights--last year, to be exact. Of course he's got the mill and it's all paid for--say a hundred thousand dollars--and that old wheat land he got back in the seventies--he's cleaned all of that up. I should say that and the mill were easily worth half a million, and they're both clear. That's all in sight." The colonel ruminated a moment and then continued: "About the rest--it's a guess. Some say a million, some say ten. All I know in point of fact, my dear, to get right down to bed-rock, is that Lycurgus says they are turning out two or three car-loads of the strips a year. I wouldn't believe Lycurgus on a stack of Bibles as high as his head, but little Thayer Ward, who works down there in the shipping department, told the general the same thing, and Bob says he knows John gets ten dollars apiece for them now, so that's a million dollars a year income he's got. He handles grain and flour way up in Minnesota, and back as far as Ohio, and west to California. But what he actually owns,--that is, whether he rents the mills or, to be exact, steals them,--I haven't any idea--not the slightest notion in the world, in point of fact--not the slightest notion."

As they passed through Main Street it was deserted, save in the billiard halls, and as no one seemed inclined to talk, the colonel took up the subject of Barclay: "Say we call it five million--five million in round numbers; that's a good deal of money for a man to have and haggle a month over seventy-five dollars the way he did with me when he sold me his share of College Heights. But," added the colonel, "I suppose if I had that much I'd value it more." The women were thinking of other things, and the colonel addressed the night: "Man gets an appetite for money just as he does for liquor--just like the love for whiskey, I may say." He shook his sides as he meditated aloud: "But as for me--I guess I've got so I can take it or let it alone. Eh, ma?"

"I didn't catch what you were saying, pa," answered his wife. "I was just thinking whether we had potatoes enough to make hash for breakfast; have we, Molly?"

As the women were discussing the breakfast, two men came out of a cross street, and the colonel, who was slightly in advance of his women, hailed the men with, "Hello there, Bob--you and Jake out here carrying on your illicit friendship in the dark?"

The men and the Culpeppers stopped for a moment at the corner. Molly Brownwell's heart throbbed as they met, and she thought of the rising moon, and in an instant her brain was afire with a hope that shamed her. Three could not walk abreast on the narrow sidewalk up the hill, and when she heard Hendricks say after the group had parleyed a moment, "Well, Jake, good night; I'll go on home with the colonel," she managed the pairing off so that the young man fell to her, and the colonel and Mrs. Culpepper walked before the younger people, and they all talked together. But at Lincoln Avenue, the younger people disconnected themselves from the talk of the elders, and finally lagged a few feet behind. When they reached the gate the colonel called back, "Better come in and visit a minute, Bob," and Molly added, "Yes, Bob, it's early yet."

But what she said with her voice did not decide the matter for him. It was her eyes. And what he said with his voice is immaterial--it was what his eyes replied that the woman caught. What he said was, "Well, just for a minute, Colonel," and the party walked up the steps of the veranda, and Bob and Molly and the colonel sat down.

Mrs. Culpepper stood for a moment and then said, "Well, Bob, you must excuse me--I forgot to set my sponge, and there isn't a bit of bread in the house for Sunday." Whereupon she left them, and when the colonel had talked himself out he left them, and when the two were alone there came an awkward silence. In the years they had been apart a thousand things had stirred in their hearts to say at this time, yet all their voices spoke was, "Well, Molly?" and "Well, Bob?" The moon was in their faces as it shone through the elm at the gate. The man turned his chair so that he could look at her, and after satisfying his eyes he broke the silence with, "Seven years."

And she returned, "Seven years the thirteenth of April."

The man played a tune with his fingers and a foot and said nothing more. The woman finally spoke. "Did you know it was the thirteenth?"

"Yes," he replied, "father died the ninth. I have often counted it up." He added shortly after: "It's a long time--seven years! My! but it has been a long time!"

"I have wondered if you have thought so," a pause, "too!"

Their hearts were beating too fast for thoughts to come coherently. The fever of madness was upon them, and numbed their wills so that they could not reach beneath the surface of their consciousnesses to find words for their emotions. Then also there was in each a deadening, flaming sense of guilt. Shame is a dumb passion, and these two, who in the fastnesses of a thousand nights had told themselves that what they sought was good and holy, now found in each other's actual presence a gripping at the tongue's root that held them dumb.

"Yes, I--" the man mumbled, "yes, I--I fancied you understood that well enough."

"But you have been busy?" she asked; "very busy, Bob, and oh, I've been so proud of all that you've done." It was the woman's tongue that first found a sincere word.

The man replied, "Well--I--I am glad you have."

It seemed to the woman a long time since her father had gone. Her conscience was making minutes out of seconds. She said, "Don't you think it's getting late?" but did not rise.

The man looked at his watch and answered, "Only 10.34." He started to rise, but she checked him breathlessly.

"Oh, Bob, Bob, sit down. This isn't enough for these long years. I had so many things to say to you." She hesitated and cried, "Why are we so stupid now--now when every second counts?"

He bent slightly toward her and said in a low voice, "So that's why your lilacs have never bloomed again."

She looked at her chair arm and asked, "Did you know they hadn't bloomed?"

"Oh, Molly, of course I knew," he answered, and then went on: "Every thirteenth of April I have slipped through the fence and come over here, rain or shine, at night, to see if they were blooming. But I didn't know why they never bloomed!"

The woman rose and walked a step toward the door, and turned her head away. When she spoke it was after a sob, "Bob, I couldn't bear it--I just couldn't bear it, Bob!"

He groaned and put his hands to his forehead and rested his elbow on the chair arm. "Oh, Molly, Molly, Molly," he sighed, "poor, poor little Molly." After a pause he said: "I won't ever bother you again. It doesn't do any good." A silence followed in which the woman turned her face to him, tear-stained and wretched, with the seams of her heart all torn open and showing through it. "It only hurts," the man continued, and then he groaned aloud, "Oh, God, how it hurts!"

She sank back into her chair and buried her face in the arm farthest from him and her body shook, but she did not speak. He stared at her dry-eyed for a minute, that tolled by so slowly that he rose at the end of it, fearful that his stay was indecorously long.

"I think I should go now," he said, as he passed her.

"Oh, no!" she cried. "Not yet, not just yet." She caught his arm and he stopped, as she stood beside him, trembling, haggard, staring at him out of dead, mad eyes. There was no colour in her blotched face, and in the moonlight the red rims of her eyes looked leaden, and her voice was unsteady. At times it broke in sobbing croaks, and she spoke with loose jaws, as one in great terror. "I want you to know--" she paused at the end of each little hiccoughed phrase--"that I have not forgotten--" she caught her breath--"that I think of you every day--" she wiped her eyes with a limp handkerchief--"every day and every night, and pray for you, though I don't believe--" she whimpered as she shuddered--"that God cares much about me."

He tried to stop her, and would have gone, but she put a hand upon his shoulder and pleaded: "Just another minute. Oh, Bob," she cried, and her voice broke again, "don't forget me. Don't forget me. When I was so sick last year--you remember," she pleaded, "I raved in delirium a week." She stopped as if afraid to go on, then began to shake as with a palsy. "I raved of everything under God's sun, and through it all, Bob--not one word of you. Oh, I knew that wouldn't do." She swayed upon his arm. "I kept a little corner of my soul safe to guard you." She sank back into her chair and chattered, "Oh, I guarded you."

She was crying like a child. He stood over her and touched her dishevelled hair with the tips of his fingers and said: "I oughtn't to stay, Molly."

And she motioned him away with her face hidden and sobbed, "No--I know it."

He paused a moment on the step before her and then said, "Good-by, Molly--I'm going now." And she heard him walking down the yard on the grass, so that his footsteps would not arouse the house. It seemed to them both that it was midnight, but time had moved slowly, and when the spent, broken woman crept into the house, and groped her way to her room, she did not make a light, but slipped into bed without looking at her scarred, shameful face.

CHAPTER XVIII

In the sunshine of that era of world-wide prosperity in the eighties, John Barclay made much hay. He spent little time in Sycamore Ridge, and his private car might be found in Minnesota to-day and at the end of the week in California. As president of the Corn Belt Road and as controlling director in the North Lake Line, he got rates on other railroads for his grain products that no competitor could duplicate. And when a competitor began to grow beyond the small fry class, Barclay either bought him out or built a mill beside the offender and crushed him out. Experts taught him the value of the chaff from the grain. He had a dozen mills to which he shipped the refuse from his flour and heaven only knows what else, and turned the stuff into various pancake flours and breakfast foods. He spent hundreds of thousands of dollars in advertising--in a day when large appropriations for advertising were unusual. And the words "Barclay's Best" glared at the traveller from crags in the Rocky Mountains and from the piers of all the great harbour bridges. He used Niagara to glorify the name of Barclay, and "Use Barclay's Best" had to be washed off the statue of the Goddess of Liberty in New York Harbour. The greenish brown eyes of the little man were forever looking into space, and when he caught a dream, instead of letting it go, he called a stenographer and made it come true. In those days he was beginning to realize that an idea plus a million dollars will become a fact if a man but says the word, whereas the same idea minus a million remains a dream. The great power of money was slowly becoming part of the man's consciousness. During the years that were to come, he came to think that there was nothing impossible. Any wish he had might be gratified. Such a consciousness drives men mad.

But in those prosperous days, while the millions were piling up, Barclay kept his head. All the world was buying then, but wherever he could Barclay sold. He bought only where he had to, and paid cash for what he bought. He did not owe a dollar for anything. He had no equities; his titles were all good. And as he neared his forties he believed that he could sell what he had at forced sale for many millions. He was supposed to be much richer than he was, but the one thing that he knew about it was that scores of other men had more than he. So he kept staring into space and pressing the button for his stenographer, and at night wherever his work found him, whether in Boston or in Chicago or in San Francisco, he hunted up the place where he could hear the best music, and sat listening with his eyes closed. He always kept his note-book in his hand, when Jane was not with him, and when an idea came to him inspired by the music, he jotted it down, and the next day, if it stood the test of a night's sleep, he turned the idea into an event.

In planning his work he was ruthless. He learned that by bribing men in the operating department of any railroad he could find out what his competitors were doing. And in the main offices of the National Provisions Company two rooms full of clerks were devoted to considering the duplicate way-bills of every car of flour or grain or grain product not shipped by the Barclay companies. Thus he was able to delay the cars of his competitors, and get his own cars through on time. Thus he was able to bribe buyers in wholesale establishments to push his products. And with Lige Bemis manipulating the railroad and judiciary committees in the legislatures of ten states, no laws were enacted which might hamper Barclay's activities.

"Do you know, Lucy," said General Ward to his wife one night when they were discussing Barclay and his ways and works, "sometimes I think that what that boy saw at Wilson's Creek,--the horrible bloodshed, the deadly spectacle of human suffering at the hospital wagon, some way blinded his soul's eye to right and wrong. It was all a man could stand; the picture must have seared the boy's heart like a fire."

Mrs. Ward, who was mending little clothes in the light of the dining-room lamp, put down her work a moment and said: "I have always thought the colonel had some such idea. For once when he was speaking of the way John stole that wheat land, he said, 'Well, poor John, he got a wound at Wilson's Creek that never will heal,' and when I asked if he meant his foot, the colonel smiled like a woman and said gently, 'No, Miss Lucy, not there--not there at all; in his heart, my dear, in his heart!'"

And the general's eyes met the eyes of a mother wandering toward a boy of nine sleeping, tired out, on a couch near by; he was a little boy with dark hair, and red tanned cheeks, and his mouth--such a soft innocent mouth--curved prettily, like the lips of children in old pictures, and as he slept he smiled, and the general, meeting the mother's eyes coming back from the little face, wiped his glasses and nodded his head in understanding; in a moment they both rose and stood hand in hand over their child, and the mother said in a trembling voice, "And his mother prayed for him, too--she has told me so--so many times."

But the people of Sycamore Ridge and of the Mississippi Valley did not indulge in any fine speculations upon the meaning of life when they thought of John Barclay. He had become considerable of a figure in the world, and the Middle West was proud of him. For those were the days of tin cornices, false fronts, vain pretences, and borrowed plumes bought with borrowed money. Other people's capital was easy to get, and every one was rich. Debt was regarded as an evidence of prosperity, and the town ran mad with the rest of the country. It is not strange then that Mrs. Watts McHurdie, she who for four years during the war dispensed "beefsteak--ham and eggs--breakfast bacon--tea--coffee--iced tea--or--milk" at the Thayer House, and for ten years thereafter sold dry-goods and kept books at Dorman's store, should have become tainted with the infection of the times. But it is strange that she could have inoculated so sane a little man as Watts. Still, there were Delilah and Samson, and of course Samson was a much larger man than Watts, and Nellie McHurdie was considerably larger than Delilah; and you never can tell about those things, anyway. Also it must not be forgotten that Nellie McHurdie since her marriage had become Grand Preceptress in one lodge, Worthy Matron in another, Senior Vice Commander in a third, and Worshipful Benefactress in a fourth, to say nothing of positions as corresponding secretary, delegate to the state convention, Keeper of the Records and Seals, Scribe,--and perhaps Pharisee,--in half a dozen others, all in the interests of her husband's political future; and with such obvious devotion before him, it is small wonder after all that he succumbed.

But he would not run for office. He had trouble every spring persuading her, but he always did persuade her, that this wasn't his year, that conditions were wrong, and that next year probably would be better. But he allowed her to call their home "The Bivouac," and have the name cut in stone letters on the horse-block; and he sat by meekly for many long years at lodges, at church entertainments, at high school commencement exercises, at public gatherings of every sort, and heard her sing a medley of American patriotic songs which wound up with the song that made him famous. It was five drinks in Jake Dolan that stopped the medley, when the drinks aforesaid inspired him to rise grandly from his chair at the front of the hall at an installation of officers of Henry Schnitzler Post of the Grand Army, and stalk majestically out of the room, while the singing was in progress, saying as he turned back at the door, before thumping heavily down the stairs, "Well, I'm getting pretty damn tired of that!" Mrs. McHurdie insisted that Watts should whip Dolan, and it is possible that at home that night Watts did smite his breast and shake his head fiercely, for in the morning the neighbours saw Mrs. McHurdie walk to the gate with him, talking earnestly and holding his arm as if to restrain him; moreover, when Watts had turned the corner of Lincoln Avenue and had disappeared into Main Street, she hurried over to the Culpeppers' to have the colonel warn Dolan that Watts was a dangerous man. But when Dolan, sober, walked into the harness shop that afternoon to apologize, the little harness maker came down the aisle of saddles in his shop blinking over his spectacles and with his hand to his mouth to strangle a smile, and before Dolan could speak, Watts said, "So am I--Jake Dolan--so am I; but if you ever do that again, I'll have to kill you."

It happened in the middle eighties--maybe a year before the college was opened--maybe a year after, though Gabriel Carnine, talking of it some twenty years later, insists that it happened two years after the opening of the college. But no one ever has mentioned the matter to Watts, so the exact date may not be recorded, though it is an important date in the uses of this narrative, as will be seen later. All agree--the colonel, the general, Dolan, Fernald, and perhaps two dozen old soldiers who were at the railroad station waiting for the train to take them to the National Encampment of the Grand Army of the Republic,--that it was a fine morning in September. Of course John Barclay contributed the band. He afterwards confessed to that, explaining that Nellie had told him that Watts never had received the attention he should receive either in the town or the state or the nation, and so long as Watts was a National Delegate for the first time in his life, and so long as she had twice been voted for as National President of the Ladies' Aid, and might get it this time, the band would be, as she put it, "so nice to take along"; and as John never forgot the fact that Nellie asked him to sing at her wedding, he hired the band. Thus are we bound to our past. But the band was not what caused the comrades to gasp, though its going was a surprise. And when they heard it turn into Main Street far up by Lincoln Avenue, playing the good old tune that the town loved for Watts' sake and for the sake of the time and the place and the heroic deeds it celebrated,--when they heard the band, the colonel asked the general, "Where's Watts?" and they suspected that the band might be bringing him to the depot.

Heaven knows the town had bought uniforms and new horns for the band often enough for it to do something public-spirited once in a while without being paid for it. So the band did not come to the town as a shock in and of itself. Neither for that matter did the hack--the new glistening silver-mounted hack, with the bright spick-and-span hearse harness on the horses; in those bustling days a quarter was nothing, and you can ride all over the Ridge for a quarter; so when the comrades at the depot, in their blue soldiers' clothes their campaign hats, and their delegates' badges, saw the band followed by the hack, they were of course interested, but that was all. And when some of the far-sighted ones observed that the top of the hack was spread back

royally, they commented upon the display of pomp, but the comment was
not extraordinary. But when from the street as the band stopped, there
came cheers from the people, the boys at the station felt that
something unusual was about to come to them. So they watched the band
march down the long sheet-iron-covered station walk, and the hack move
along beside the band boys; and the poet's comrades-in-arms saw him
sitting beside the poet's wife,--the two in solemn state. And then
the old boys beheld Watts McHurdie,--little Watts McHurdie, with his
grizzled beard combed, with his gold-rimmed Sunday glasses far down on
his nose so that he could see over them, and--wonder of wonders, they
saw a high shiny new silk hat wobbling over his modest head.

He stumbled out of the open hack with his hand on the great stiff
awkward thing, obviously afraid it would fall off, and she that was
Nellie Logan, late of the Thayer House and still later of Dorman's
store, and later still most worshipful, most potent, most gorgeous and
most radiant archangel of seven secret and mysterious covenants,
conclaves, and inner temples, stood beaming at the pitiful sight,
clearly proud of her shameless achievement. Watts, putting his hand to
his mouth to cover his smile, grabbed the shiny thing again as he
nodded cautiously at the crowd. Then he followed her meekly to the
women's waiting room, where the wives and sisters of the comrades were
assembled--and they, less punctilious than the men, burst forth with
a scream of joy, and the agony was over.

And thus Watts McHurdie went to his greatest earthly glory. The
delegation from the Ridge, with the band, had John Barclay's private
car; that was another surprise which Mrs. McHurdie arranged, and when
they got to Washington, where the National Encampment was, opinions
differ as to when Watts McHurdie had his high tide of happiness. The
colonel says that it was in the great convention, where the Sycamore
Ridge band sat in front of the stage, and where Watts stood in front
of the band and led the great throng,--beginning with his cracked

little heady tenor, and in an instant losing it in the awful diapason of ten thousand voices singing his old song with him; and where, when it was over, General Grant came down the platform, making his way rather clumsily among the chairs, and at last in front of the whole world grasped Watts McHurdie's hands, and the two little men, embarrassed by the formality of it all, stood for a few seconds looking at each other with tears glistening in their speaking eyes.

But Jake Dolan, who knows something of human nature, does not hold to the colonel's view about the moment of McHurdie's greatest joy. "We were filing down the Avenue again, thousands and ten thousands of us, as we filed past the White House nearly twenty years before. And the Sycamore Ridge band was cramming its lungs into the old tune, when up on the reviewing stand, beside all the big bugs and with the President there himself, stood little Watts, plug hat in hand, bowing to the boys. 'Twas a lovely sight, and he had been there for two mortal hours before we boys got down--there was the Kansas boys and the Iowa boys and some from Missouri, carrying the old flag we fought under at Wilson's Creek. Watts saw us down the street and heard the old band play; a dozen other bands had played that tune that day; but Billy Dorman's tuba had its own kind of a rag in it, and Watts knew it. I seen him a-waving his hat at the boys, almost as soon as they saw him, and as the band came nearer and nearer I saw the little man's face begin to crack, and as he looked down the line and saw them Kansas and Iowa soldiers, I seen him give one whoop, and throw that plug hat hellwards over the crowd and jump down from that band stand like a wild man and make for the gang. He was blubbering like a calf when he caught step with me, and he yelled so as to reach my ears above the roar of the crowds and the blatting of the bands--yelled with his voice ripped to shreds that fluttered out ragged from the torn bosom of him, 'Jake--Jake--how I would like to get drunk--just this once!' And we went on down the avenue together--him bareheaded, hay-footing and straw-footing it the same as in the old days."

Jake always paused at this point and shook his head sorrowfully, and then continued dolefully: "But 'twas no use; he was caught and took away; some says it was to see the pictures in the White House, and some says it was to a reception given by the Relief Corps to the officers elect of the Ladies' Aid, where he was pawed over by a lot of old girls who says, 'Yes, I'm so glad--what name please--oh, --McHurdie, surely not *the* McHurdie; O dear me--Sister McIntire, come right here, this is *the* McHurdie--you know I sang your song when I was a little girl'--which was a lie, unless Watts wrote it for the Mexican War, and he didn't. And then some one else comes waddling up and says, 'O dear me, Mr. McHurdie--you don't know how glad I am to see the author of "Home, Sweet Home,"' and Watts blinks his eyes and pleads not guilty; and she says, 'O dear, excuse the mistake; well, I'm sure you wrote something?' And Watts, being sick of love, as Solomon says in his justly celebrated and popular song, Watts looks through his Sunday glasses and doesn't see a blame thing, and smiles and says calmly, 'No, madam, you mistake--I am a simple harness maker.' And she sidles off looking puzzled, to make room for the one from Massachusetts, who stares at him through her glasses and says, 'So you're Watts McHurdie--who wrote the--' 'The same, madam,' says Watts, courting favour. 'Well,' says the high-browed one, 'well--you are not at all what I imagined.' And 'Neither are you, madam,' returns Watts, as sweet as a dill pickle; and she goes away to think it over and wonder if he meant it that way. No--that's where Nellie made her mistake. It wouldn't have hurt him--just once. But what's done's done, and can't be undone, as the man said when he fished his wife out of the lard vat."

Now this all seems a long way from John Barclay--the hero of this romance. Yet the departure of Watts McHurdie for his scene of glory was on the same day that a most important thing happened in the lives of Bob Hendricks and Molly Brownwell. That day Bob Hendricks walked one end of the station platform alone. The east-bound train was half an hour late, and while the veterans were teasing Watts and the women railing at Mrs. McHurdie, Hendricks discovered that it was one hundred and seventy-eight steps from one end of the walk to the other, and that to go entirely around the building made the distance fifty-four steps more. It was almost train time before Adrian Brownwell arrived. When the dapper little chap came with his bright crimson carnation, and his flashing red necktie, and his inveterate gloves and cane, Hendricks came only close enough to him to smell the perfume on the man's clothes, and to nod to him. But when Hendricks found that the man was going with the Culpeppers as far as Cleveland, as he told the entire depot platform, "to report the trip," Hendricks sat on a baggage truck beside the depot, and considered many things. As he was sitting there Dolan came up, out of breath, and fearful he should be late.

"How long will you be gone, Jake?" asked Hendricks.

"The matter of a week or ten days, maybe," answered Dolan.

"Well, Jake," said Hendricks, looking at Dolan with serious eyes, yet rather abstractedly, "I am thinking of taking a long trip--to be gone a long time--I don't know exactly how long. I may not go at all--I haven't said anything to the boys in the store or the bank or out at the shop about it; it isn't altogether settled--as yet." He paused while a switch engine clanged by and the crowd surged out of the depot, and ebbed back again into their seats. "Did you deliver my note this morning?"

"Yes," replied Dolan, "just as you said. That's what made me a little late."

"To the lady herself?"

"To the lady herself," repeated Dolan.

"All right," acquiesced Hendricks. "Now, Jake, if I give it out that I'm going away on a trip, there'll be a lot of pulling and hauling and fussing around in the bank and in the store and at the shop and--every place, and then I may not go. So I've gone over every concern carefully during the past week, and have set down what ought to be done in case I'm gone. I didn't tell my sister even--she's so nervous. And, Jake, I won't tell any one. But if, when you get back from Washington, I'm not here, I'm going to leave this key with you. Tell the boys at the bank that it will open my tin box, and in the tin box they'll find some instructions about things." He smiled, and Dolan assented. Hendricks uncoiled his legs from the truck, and began to get down. "I won't mix up with the old folks, I guess, Jake. They have their own affairs, and I'm tired. I worked all last night," he added. He held out his hand to Dolan and said, "Well, good-by, Jake--have a good time."

The elder man had walked away a few steps when Hendricks called him back, and fumbling in his pockets, said: "Well, Jake, I certainly am a fool; here--" he pulled an envelope marked "Dolan" from his inside pocket--"Jake, I was in the bank this morning, and I found a picture for you. Take it and have a good time. It's a long time till pension day--so long."

The Irishman peeped at the bill and grinned as he said, "Them holy pictures from the bank, my boy, have powerful healing qualities." And he marched off with joy in his carriage.

Hendricks then resumed his tramp; up and down the long platform he went, stepping on cracks one way, and avoiding cracks the next, thinking it all out. He tried to remember if he had been unfair to any

one; if he had left any ragged edges; if he had taken a penny more
than his honest due. The letter to the county treasurer, returning the
money his father had taken, was on top of the pile of papers in his
tin box at the bank. He had finally concluded, that when everything
else was known, that would not add much to his disgrace. And then it
would be paid, and that page with the forged entry would not always be
in his mind. There were deeds, each witnessed by a different notary,
so that the town would not gossip before he went, transferring all of
his real estate to his sister, and the stock he had sold to the bank
was transferred, and the records all in the box; then he went over the
prices again at which he had disposed of his holdings to the bank, and
he was sure he had made good bargains in every case for the bank. So
it was all fair, he argued for the thousandth time--he was all square
with the world. He had left a deposit subject to his check of twenty
thousand dollars--that ought to do until they could get on their feet
somewhere; and it was all his, he said to himself--all his, and no
one's business.

And when he thought of the other part, the voice of Adrian Brownwell
saying, "Well, come on, old lady, we must be going," rose in his
consciousness. It was not so much Brownwell's words, as his air of
patronage and possession; it was cheerful enough, quite gay in fact,
but Hendricks asked himself a hundred times why the man didn't whistle
for her, and clamp a steel collar about her neck. He wondered
cynically if at the bottom of Brownwell's heart, he would not rather
have the check for twelve thousand dollars which Hendricks had left
for Colonel Culpepper, to pay off the Brownwell note, than to have his
wife. For seven years the colonel had been cheerfully neglecting it,
and now Hendricks knew that Adrian was troubling him about the old
debt.

As he rounded the depot for the tenth time he got back to their last
meeting. There stood General Ward with his arm about the girlish waist

of Mrs. Ward, the mother of seven. There was John Barclay with Jane beside him, and they were holding hands like lovers. The Ward children were running like rabbits over the broad lawn under the elms, and there, talking to the wide, wide world, was Adrian Brownwell, propounding the philosophy of the ***Banner***, and quoting from last week's editorials. And there sat Bob and Molly by the flower bed that bordered the porch.

"I am going to the city to hear Gilmore," he said. That was simple enough, and her sigh had no meaning either. It was just a weary little sigh, such as women sometimes bring forth when they decide to say something else. So she had said: "I'll be all alone next week. I think I'll visit Jane--if she's in town."

Then something throbbed in his brain and made him say:--

"So you'd like to hear Gilmore, too?"

She coloured and was silent, and the pulse of madness that was beating in her made her answer:--

"Oh--I can't--you know the folks are going to Washington to the encampment, and Adrian is going as far as Cleveland with the delegation to write it up."

An impulse loosened his tongue, and he asked:--

"Why not? Come on. If you don't know any one up there, go to the Fifth Avenue; it's all right, and I'll get tickets, and we'll go every night and both matinees. Come on!" he urged.

She was aflame and could not think. "Oh--don't, Bob, don't--not now. Please don't," she begged, in as low a tone as she dared to use.

Adrian was thundering on about the tariff, and the general was wrangling with him. The Barclays were talking to themselves, and the children were clattering about underfoot, and in the trees overhead. Bob's eyes and Molly's met, and the man shuddered at what he saw of pathos and yearning, and he said: "Well, why not? It's no worse to go than to want to go. What's wrong about it--Molly, do you think--"

He did not finish the sentence, for Adrian had ceased talking, and Molly, seeing his jealous eyes upon her, rose and moved away. But before they left that night she found occasion to say, "I've been thinking about it, Bob, and maybe I will."

In the year that had passed since Hendricks had left her sobbing in the chair on the porch of the Culpepper home, a current between them had been reestablished, and was fed by the chance passing in a store, a smile at a reception, a good morning on the street, and the current was pulsing through their veins night and day. But that fine September morning, as she stood on the veranda of her home with a dust-cap on her head, cleaning up the litter her parents had made in packing, she was not ready for what rushed into her soul from the letter Dolan left her, as he hurried away to overtake the band that was turning from Lincoln Avenue into Main Street. She sat in a chair to read it, and for a moment after she had read it, she held it open in her lap and gazed at the sunlight mottling the blue grass before her, through the elm trees. Her lips were parted and her eyes wide, and she breathed slowly. The tune the band was playing--McHurdie's song--sank into her memory there that day so that it always brought back the mottled sunshine, the flowers blooming along the walk, and the song of a robin from a lilac bush near by. She folded the letter carefully, and put it inside her dress, and then moving mechanically, took it out and read it again:--

"MY DARLING, MY DARLING: There is no use struggling any more. You must come. I will meet you in the city at the morning train, the one that leaves the Ridge here at 2.35 A.M. We can go to the parks to-morrow and be alone and talk it all out, before the concert--and then--oh, Molly, core of my soul, heart of my heart, why should we ever come back!   BOB."

All that she could feel as she sat there motionless was a crashing "no." The thing seemed to drive her mad by its insistence--a horrible racking thing that all but shook her, and she chattered at it: "Why not? Why not? Why not?" But the "no" kept roaring through her mind, and as she heard the servant rattling the breakfast dishes in the house, the woman shivered out of sight and ran to her room. She fell on her knees to pray, but all she could pray was, "O God, O God, O God, help me!" and to that prayer, as she said it, the something in her heart kept gibbering, "Why not? Why not? Why not?" From an old box hidden in a closet opening out of her mother's room she took Bob Hendricks' picture,--the faded picture of a boy of twenty,--and holding it close to her breast, stared open-lipped into the heart of an elm tree-top. The whistle of the train brought her back to her real world. She rose and looked at herself in the mirror, at the unromantic face with its lines showing faintly around her eyes, grown quiet during the dozen years that had settled her fluffy hair into sedate waves. She smiled at the changes of the years and shook her head, and got a grip on her normal consciousness, and after putting away the picture and closing the box, she went downstairs to finish her work.

On the stairs she felt sure of herself, and set about to plan for the next day, and then the tumult began, between the "no" and her soul. In a few minutes as she worked the "no" conquered, and she said, "Bob's crazy." She repeated it many times, and found as she repeated it that it was mechanical and that her soul was aching again. So the morning wore away; she gossiped with the servant a moment; a neighbour came in

on an errand; and she dressed to go down town. As she went out of the
gate, she wondered where she would be that hour the next day, and then
the struggle began again. Moreover, she bought some new
gloves--travelling gloves to match her gray dress.

In the afternoon she and Jane Barclay sat on the wide porch of the
Barclay home. "Gilmore's going to be in the city all this week," said
Jane, biting a thread in her sewing.

"Is he?" replied Molly. "I should so like to hear him. It's so poky up
at the house."

"Why don't you?" inquired Jane. "Get on the train and go on up."

"Do you suppose it would be all right?" replied Molly.

"Why, of course, girl! Aren't you a married woman of lawful age? I
would if I wanted to."

There was a pause, and Molly replied thoughtfully, "I have half a
notion to--really!"

But as she walked home, she decided not to do it. People from the
Ridge might be there, and they wouldn't understand, and her
finger-tips chilled at the memory of Adrian Brownwell's jealous eyes.
So as she ate supper, she went over the dresses she had that were
available. And at bedtime she gave the whole plan up and went upstairs
humming "Marguerite" as happily as the thrush that sang in the lilacs
that morning. As she undressed the note fell to the floor. When she
picked it up, the flash of passion came tearing through her heart, and
the "no" crashed in her ears again, and all the day's struggle was for
nothing. So she went to bed, resolved not to go. But she stared
through the window into the night, and of a sudden a resolve came to

her to go, and have one fair day with Hendricks--to talk it all out forever, and then to come home, and she rose from her bed and tiptoed through the house packing a valise. She left a note in the kitchen for the servant, saying that she would be back for dinner the next evening, and when she struck a match in the front hall to see what time it was, she found that it was only one o'clock. For an hour she sat in the chill September air on the veranda, thinking it all over--what she would say; how they would meet and part; and over and over again she told herself that she was doing the sensible thing. As the clock struck two she picked up her valise--it was heavier than she thought, and it occurred to her that she had put in many unnecessary things, and that she had time to lighten it. But she stopped a moment only, and then walked to the gate and down a side street to the station. It was 2.20 when she arrived, and the train was marked on the blackboard by the ticket window on time. She kept telling herself that it was best to have it out; that she would come right back; but she remembered her heavy valise, and again the warning "no" roared through her soul. She walked up and down the long platform, and felt the presence of Bob Hendricks strong and compelling; she knew he had been there that very day, and wondered where he sat. Then she thought perhaps she would do better not to go. She looked into the men's waiting room, and it was empty save for one man; his back was turned to her, but she recognized Lige Bemis. A tremble of guilt racked and weakened her. And with a thrill as of pain she heard the faint whistle of a train far up the valley. The man moved about the room inside. Apparently he also heard the far-off whistle. She shrank around the corner of the depot. But he caught sight of her dress, and slowly sauntered up and down the platform until he passed near enough to her to identify her in the faint flicker of the gas. He spoke, and she returned his greeting. The train whistled again--much nearer it seemed to her, but still far away, and her soul and the "no" were grappling in a final contest. Suddenly it came over her that she had not bought her ticket. Again the train whistled, and far up the tracks she could see a speck of light. She hurried into the waiting room to buy the ticket. The noise of the train was beginning to sound in her ears, She was frightened and nervous, and she fumbled with her purse and valise. Nearer and nearer came the train, and the "no" fairly screamed in her ears, and her face was pallid, with the black wrinkles standing out upon it in the gaslight. The train was in the railroad yards, and the glare of the headlight was in the waiting room. Bemis came in and saw her fumbling with her ticket, her pocket book, and her valise.

"You'll have to hurry, Mrs. Brownwell, this is the limited--it only stops a minute. Let me help you."

He picked up the valise and followed her from the room. The rush of the incoming train shattered her nerves. They pulsed in fear of some dreadful thing, and in that moment she wondered whether or not she would ever see it all again--the depot, the familiar street, the great mill looming across the river, and the Barclay home half a mile above them. In a second she realized all that her going meant, and the "no" screamed at her, and the "why not" answered feebly. But she had gone too far, she said to herself. The engine was passing her, and Bemis was behind her with the heavy valise. She wondered what he would say when Bob met her at the train in the city. All this flashed across her mind in a second, and then she became conscious that the rumbling thing in front of her was not the limited but a cattle train, and the sickening odour from it made her faint. In the minute while it was rushing by at full speed she became rigid, and then, taking her valise from the man behind her, turned and walked as fast as she could up the hill, and when she turned the corner she tried to run. Her feet took her to the Barclay home. She stood trembling in terror on the great wide porch and rang the bell. The servant admitted the white-faced, shaking woman, and she ran to Jane Barclay's room.

"Oh, Jane," chattered Molly, "Jane, for God's love, Jane, hold me--hold me tight; don't let me go. Don't!" She sank to the floor and put her face in Jane's lap and stuttered: "I--I--have g-g-got to t-t-tell you, Jane. I've g-g-ot to t-t-t-ell you, J-J-Jane." And then she fell to sobbing. "Hold me, don't let me go out there. When it whistles ag-g-gain h-h-hold me t-t-tight."

Jane Barclay's strong kind hands stroked the dishevelled hair of the trembling woman. And in time she looked up and said quietly, "You know--you know, Jane, Bob and I--Bob and I were going to run away!" Molly looked at Jane a fearful second with beseeching eyes, and then dropped her head and fell to sobbing again, and lay with her face on the other woman's knees.

When she was quiet Jane said: "I wouldn't talk about it any more, dear--not now." She stroked the hair and patted the face of the woman before her. "Shall we go to bed now, dear? Come right in with me." And soon Molly rose, and her spent soul rested in peace. But they did not go to bed. The dawn found the two women talking it out together--clear from the beginning.

And when the day came Molly Brownwell went to Jane Barclay's desk and wrote. And when Bob Hendricks came home that night, his sister handed him a letter. It ran:--

"MY DEAR BOB: I have thought it all out, dear; it wouldn't do at all. I went to the train, and something, I don't know what, caught me and dragged me over to Jane's. She was good--oh, so good. She knows; but it was better that she should than--the other way.

"It will never do, Bob. We can't go back. The terrible something that I did stands irrevocably between us. The love that might have made both our lives radiant is broken, Bob--forever broken. And all the king's horses and all the king's men cannot ever put it together again. I know it now, and oh Bob, Bob, it makes me sadder than the pain of unsatisfied love in my heart.

"It just can't be; nothing ever can make it as it was, and unless it could be that way--the boy and girl way, it would be something dreadful. We have missed the best in the world, Bob; we cannot enjoy the next best together. But apart, each doing his work in life as God wills it, we may find the next best, which is more than most people know.

"I have found during this hour that I can pray again, Bob, and I am asking God always to let me hope for a heaven, into which I can bring a few little memories--of the time before you left me. Won't you bring yours there, too, dear? Until then--good-by.

"MOLLY."

The springs that move God's universe are hidden,--those that move the world of material things and those that move the world of spiritual things, and make events creep out of the past into the future so noiselessly that they seem born in the present. It is all a mystery, the half-stated equation of life that we call the scheme of things. Only this is sure, that however remote, however separated by time and space, the tragedy of life has its root in the weakness of men, and of all the heart-breaking phantasms that move across the panorama of the day, somewhere deep-rooted in our own souls' weakness is the ineradicable cause. Even God's mercy cannot separate the punishment that follows sin, and perhaps it is the greatest mercy of His mercy that it cannot do so. For when we leave this world, our books are clear. If our souls grow--we pay the price in suffering; if they shrivel, we go into the next world, poorer for our pilgrimage.

So do not pity Molly Brownwell nor Robert Hendricks when you learn that as she left the station at Sycamore Ridge that night, Lige Bemis went to a gas lamp and read the note from Robert Hendricks that in her confusion she had dropped upon the floor. Only pity the miserable creature whose soul was so dead in him that he could put that note away to bide his time. In this wide universe, wherein we are growing slowly up to Godhood, only the poor leprous soul, whitened with malice and hate, deserves the angels' tears. The rest of us,--weak, failing, frail, to whom life deals its sorrows and its tears, its punishments and its anguish,--we leave this world nearer to God than when we came here, and the journey, though long and hard, has been worth the while.

CHAPTER XIX

Back in the days when John Barclay had become powerful enough to increase the price of his door strips to the railroad companies from five dollars to seven and a half, he had transferred the business of the factory that made the strips from Hendricks' Exchange National to the new Merchants' State Bank which Gabriel Carnine was establishing. For Carnine and Barclay were more of a mind than were Barclay and Hendricks; Carnine was bent on getting rich, and he had come to regard Barclay as the most remarkable man in the world. Hendricks, on the other hand, knew Barclay to the core, and since the quarrel of the seventies, while they had maintained business relations, they were merely getting along together. There were times when Barclay felt uncomfortable, knowing that Hendricks knew much about his business, but the more Carnine knew, the more praise Barclay had of him; and so, even though Jane kept her own account with Hendricks, and though John himself kept a personal account with Hendricks, the Economy Door Strip Company and the Golden Belt Wheat Company did business with Carnine, and Barclay became a director of the Merchants' State Bank, and greatly increased its prestige thereby. And Bob Hendricks sighed a sigh of relief, for he knew that he would never become John Barclay's fence and be called upon to dispose of stolen goods. So Hendricks went his way with his eyes on a level and his jaw squared with the world. And when he knew that Jane knew the secret of his soul, about the only comfort he had in those black days was the exultation in his heart that John--whatever he might know--could not turn it into cash at the Exchange National Bank.

As he walked alone under the stars that first night after Molly Brownwell's note came to him, he saw his life as it was, with things squarely in their relations. Of course this light did not stay with him always; at times in his loneliness the old cloud of wild yearning would come over him, and he would rattle the bars of his madhouse until he could fight his way out to the clean air of Heaven under the stars. And at such times he would elude Dolan, and walk far away from the town in fields and meadows and woods struggling back to sanity--sometimes through a long night. But as the years passed, this truth came to be a part of his consciousness--that in some measure the thing we call custom, or law, or civilization, or society, with all its faults, is the best that man, endowed as he is to-day, can establish, and that the highest service one can pay to man or to God is found in conforming to the social compact, at whatever cost of physical pain, or mental anguish, if the conformation does not require a moral breach. That was the faith he lived by, that by service to his fellows and by sacrifice to whatever was worthy in the social compact, he would find a growth of soul that would pay him, either here or hereafter. So he lent money, and sold light, and traded in merchandise, and did a man's work in politics--playing each game according to the rules.

But whatever came to him, whatever of honour or of influence, or of public respect, in his own heart there was the cloud--he knew that he was a forger, and that once he had offered to throw everything he had aside and take in return--But he was not candid enough even in his own heart to finish the indictment. It made him flush with shame, and perhaps that was why on his face there was often a curious self-deprecating smile--not of modesty, not of charity, but the smile of the man who is looking at a passing show and knows that it is not real. As he went into his forties, and the flux of his life hardened, he became a man of reserves--a kind, quiet, strong man, charitable to a fault for the weaknesses of others, but a man who rarely reflected his impulses, a listener in conversation, a dreamer amid the tumult of business, whose success lay in his industry and caution, and who drew men to him not by what he promised, but by the faith we chattering daws have in the man who looks on and smiles while we prattle.

His lank bones began to take on flesh, and his face rounded at the corners, and the eagerness of youth passed from him. He always looked more of a man than John Barclay. For Barclay was a man of enthusiasms, who occasionally liked to mouth a hard jaw-breaking "damn," and who followed his instincts with womanly faith in them--so that he became known as a man of impulse. But Hendricks' power was in repression, and in Sycamore Ridge they used to say that the only reason why Bob Hendricks grew a mustache was to chew it when people expected him to talk. It wasn't much of a mustache--a little blond fuzz about as heavy as his yellow eyebrows over his big inquiring blue eyes, and he once told Dolan that he kept it for a danger signal. When he found himself pulling at it, he knew he was nervous and should get out into the open. They tell a story in the Ridge to the effect that Hendricks started to run to a fire, and caught himself pulling at his mustache, and turned around and went out to the power-house instead.

It was the only anecdote ever told of Hendricks after he was
forty--for he was not a man about whom anecdotes would hang well,
though the town is full of them about John Barclay. So Hendricks lived
a strong reticent man, who succeeded in business though he was honest,
and who won in politics by choosing his enemies from the kind of noisy
men who make many mistakes, and let every one know it. The time came
when he did not avoid Molly Brownwell; she felt that he was not afraid
to see her in any circumstances, and that made her happy. Sometimes
she went to him in behalf of one of her father's charges,--some poor
devil who could not pay his note at the bank and keep the children in
school, or some clerk or workman at the power-house who had been
discharged. At such times they talked the matter in hand over frankly,
and it ended by the man giving way to the woman, or showing her simply
that she was wrong.

Only once in nearly a score of years did a personal word pass between
them. She had come to him for his signature to a petition for a pardon
for a man whose family suffered while he was in the penitentiary.
Hendricks signed the paper and handed it back to her, and his blue
eyes were fixed impersonally upon her, and he smiled his curious,
self-deprecatory smile and sighed, "As we forgive our debtors." Then
he reached for a paper in his desk and seemed oblivious to her
presence. No one else was near them, and the woman hesitated a moment
before turning to go and repeated, "Yes, Bob--as we forgive our
debtors." She tried to show him the radiance in her soul, but he did
not look up and she went away. When she had gone, he pushed aside his
work and sat for a moment looking into the street; he began biting his
mustache, and rose, and went out of the bank and found some other
work.

That night as Hendricks and Dolan walked over the town together, Dolan
said: "Did you ever know, Robert"--that was as near familiarity as
the elder man came with Hendricks--"that Mart Culpepper owed his

son-in-law a lot of money?"

"Well," returned Hendricks, "he borrowed a lot fifteen years ago or such a matter; why?"

"Well," answered Dolan, "I served papers on Mart to-day in a suit for--I dunno, a lot of money--as I remember it about fifteen thousand dollars. That seems like a good deal."

Hendricks grunted, and they walked on in silence. Hendricks knew from Brownwell's overdraft that things were not going well with him, and he believed that matters must have reached a painful crisis in the Culpepper family if Brownwell had brought suit against the colonel.

The next morning Colonel Martin Culpepper came into the bank. He had grown into a large gray man--with gray hair, gray mustaches of undiminished size, and chin whiskers grayed and broadened with the years. His fine black eyes were just beginning to lose their lustre, and the spring was going out of his stride. As he came into the bank, Hendricks noticed that the colonel seemed to shuffle just a little. He put out his fat hand, and said:--

"Robert, will you come into the back room with me a moment? It isn't business--I just want to talk with you." He smiled apologetically and added, "Just troubles, Robert--just an old man wants to talk to some one, in point of fact."

Hendricks followed the colonel into the directors' room, and without ceremony the colonel sank heavily into a fat leather chair, facing the window, and Hendricks sat down facing the colonel. The colonel looked at the floor and fumbled his triangular watch-charm a moment, and cleared his throat, as he spoke, "I don't know just how to begin--to get at it--to proceed, as I may say, Robert." Hendricks did not reply, and the colonel went on, "I just wanted to talk to some one, that's all--to talk to you--just to you, sir, to be exact."

Hendricks looked kindly at the colonel, whose averted eyes made the younger man feel uncomfortable. Then he said gently, "Well, Colonel, don't be backward about saying what you want to to me." It was a long speech for Hendricks, and he felt it, and then qualified it with, "But, of course, I don't want to urge you."

The colonel's face showed a flush of courage to Hendricks, but the courage passed, and there was a silence, and then a little twitch under his eyes told Hendricks that the colonel was contemplating a flank attack as he spoke, "Robert, may I ask you in confidence if Adrian Brownwell is hard up?"

Hendricks believed the truth would bring matters to a head, and he answered, "Well, I shouldn't wonder, Colonel."

"Very hard up?" pressed the colonel.

Hendricks remembered Brownwell's overdraft and half a dozen past due notes to cover other overdrafts and answered, "Well, Colonel, not desperate, but you know the *Index* has been getting the best of the *Banner* for two or three years."

There was a pause, and then the colonel blurted out, "Well, Bob, he's sued me."

"I knew that, Colonel," returned Hendricks, anxious to press the matter to its core. "Jake told me yesterday."

"I was going to pay him; he's spoken about it several times--dunned me, sir, in point of fact, off and on for several years. But he knew I was good for it. And now the little coward runs off up to Chicago to attend the convention and sues me while he's gone. That's what I hate." Hendricks could see that the object of the colonel's visit was still on his mind, and so he left the way open for the colonel to talk. "You know how Mrs. Culpepper feels and how Molly feels--disgraced, sir, humiliated, shamed, to be exact, sir, in front of the whole town. What would you do, Robert? What can a man do in a time like this--I ask you, what can he do?"

"Well, I'd pay him, Colonel, if I were you," ventured the younger man.

The colonel straightened up and glared at Hendricks and exclaimed: "Bob Hendricks, do you think, sir, that Martin Culpepper would rest for a minute, while he had a dollar to his name, or a rag on his back, under the imputation of not paying a debt like that? It is paid, sir,--settled in full this morning, sir. But what am I going to do about him, sir--the contemptible scamp who publicly sued his own wife's father? That's what I came to you for, Robert. What am I going to do?"

"It'll be forgotten in a week, Colonel--I wouldn't worry about it," answered Hendricks. "We all have those little unpleasantnesses."

The colonel was silent for a time, and then he said: "Bob--" turning his eyes to meet Hendricks' for the first time during their meeting--"that scoundrel said to me yesterday morning before leaving, 'If I hadn't the misfortune of being your son-in-law, you wouldn't have the honour of owing me this money.' Then he sneered at me--you know the supercilious way he has, the damn miserable hound-pup way he has of grinning at you,--and says, 'I regarded it as a loan, even though you seemed to regard it as a bargain.' And he whirled and left me." The colonel's voice broke as he added: "In God's name, Bob, tell me--did I sell Molly? You know--you can tell me."

The colonel was on his feet, standing before Hendricks, with, his hands stretched toward the younger man. Hendricks did not reply at once, and the colonel broke forth: "Bob Hendricks, why did you and my little girl quarrel? Did she break it or did you? Did I sell her, Bob, did I sell my little girl?" He slipped back into the chair and for a moment hid his face, and shook with a great sob, then pulled himself together, and said, "I know I'm a foolish old man, Bob, only I feel a good deal depends on knowing the truth--a good deal of my attitude toward him."

Hendricks looked at the colonel for an abstracted moment, and then said: "Colonel, Adrian Brownwell is hard up--very hard up, and you don't know how he is suffering with chagrin at being beaten by the *Index*. He is quick-tempered--just as you are, Colonel." He paused a moment and took the colonel by the hand,--a fat, pink hand, without much iron in it,--and brought him to his feet. "And about that other matter," he added, as he put his arm about the colonel, "you didn't sell her. I know that; I give you my word on that. It was fifteen years ago--maybe longer--since Molly and I were--since we went together as boy and girl. That's a long time ago, Colonel, a long time ago, and I've managed to forget just why we--why we didn't make a go of it." He smiled kindly at the colonel as he spoke--a smile that the colonel had not seen in Hendricks' face in many years. Then the mask fell on his face, and the colonel saw it fall--the mask of the man over the face of the boy. A puzzled, bewildered look crept into the gray, fat face, and Hendricks could see that the doubt was still in the colonel's heart. The younger man pressed the colonel's hand, and the two moved toward the door. Suddenly tears flushed into the dimmed eyes of the colonel, and he cried, through a smile, "Bob Hendricks, I believe in my soul you're a liar--a damn liar, sir, but, boy, you're a thoroughbred--God bless you, you're a thoroughbred." And he turned and shuffled from the room and out of the bank.

When Colonel Martin Culpepper left Robert Hendricks at the door of the directors' room of the Exchange National Bank, the colonel was persuaded in his heart that his daughter had married Adrian Brownwell to please her parents, and the colonel realized that day that her parents were pleased with Brownwell as a suitor for their daughter, because in time of need he had come to their rescue with money, and incidentally because he was of their own blood and caste--a Southern gentleman of family. The colonel went to the offices of the Culpepper Mortgage and Loan Company and went over his bank-book again. The check that he drew would take all but three hundred and forty-five dollars out of the accounts of his company, and not a dollar of it was his. The Culpepper Mortgage Company was lending other people's money. It had been lending money on farm mortgages for ten years. Pay-day on many mortgages was coming due, and of the fifteen thousand dollars he checked out to pay Adrian Brownwell's debt, thirteen thousand dollars was money that belonged to the Eastern creditors of the company--men and women who had sent their money to the company for it to lend; and the money checked out represented money paid back by the farmers for the release of their mortgages. Some of the money was interest paid by farmers on their mortgages, some of it was partial payments--but none of it was Colonel Culpepper's money.

"Molly," said the colonel, as his daughter came into the office, "I've given a check for that--that money, you know, to Adrian--paid it in full, my dear. But--" the colonel fumbled with his pencil a moment and added, "I'm a trifle shy--a few thousand in point of fact, and I just thought I'd ask--would you borrow it of Bob, if you were me?"

He looked at her closely, and she coloured and shook her head vehemently as she replied: "Oh, no, father--no, can't you get it somewhere else? Not from Bob--for that! I mean--oh--I'd much rather not."

The colonel looked at his daughter a moment and drew a deep breath, and sighed, and smiled across his sigh, and took her hand and put it around his neck and kissed it, and when she was close to him he put his arm about her, and their eyes met for a fleeting instant, and they did not speak. But in a moment from across his desk the daughter spoke, "Why don't you go to John or Carnine, father?"

"Well, Gabe--you know Gabe. I'm borrowed clear to the limit there, now. And John--you know John, Molly--and the muss, the disagreeable muss,--the row, in point of fact, we had over that last seventy-five dollars settling up the College Heights business--you remember? Well, I just can't go to John. But," he added cheerfully, "I can get it elsewhere, my dear--I have other resources, other resources, my dear." And the colonel smiled so gayly that he deceived even his daughter, and she went home as happy as a woman with eyelids as red as hers were that day might reasonably expect to be.

As for the colonel, he sat figuring for an hour upon a sheet of white paper. His figures indicated that by putting all of his property except his home into the market, and reserving all of his commissions on loans that would fall due during the three years coming, he could pay back the money he had taken, little by little, and be square with the company's creditors in three years--or four at the most. So he let the check stand, and did not try to borrow money of the banks to make it good, but trusted to to-morrow's receipts to pay yesterday's debts of the company. Knowing that several mortgages of more than three thousand each would fall due in a few weeks, and that the men carrying them, expected to pay them, the colonel wrote dilatory letters to the Eastern creditors whose money he had taken, explaining that there was some delay in the payment of the notes, and that the matter would be straightened out in a few weeks. When the money came

in from the mortgages falling due the next month, he paid those
already due, and delayed the payment of Peter until Paul paid up. It
was a miserable business, and Colonel Culpepper knew that he was a
thief. The knowledge branded him as one, and bent his eyes to the
ground, and wrenched his proud neck so that his head hung loosely upon
it. Always when he spoke in public, or went among his poor on errands
of mercy, at his elbow stood the accusing spectre, and choked his
voice, and unnerved his hand. And trouble came upon the Culpeppers,
and the colonel's clothes, which, had always been immaculate, grew
shabby. As that year and the next passed and mortgages began falling
due, not only in the colonel's company but all over the county, all
over the state, all over the Missouri Valley, men found they could not
pay. The cycle of business depression moved across the world, as those
things come and go through the centuries. Moreover, General Ward was
riding on the crest of a wave of unrest which expressed in terms of
politics what the people felt in their homes. Debts were falling due;
crops brought small returns; capital was frightened; men in the mills
lost their work; men on the farms burned their corn; and Colonel
Martin Culpepper sank deeper and deeper into the mire.

Those years of the panic of the early nineties pressed all the youth
out of his step, dimmed the lustre of his eyes, and slowly broke his
heart. His keenest anguish was not for his own suffering, but because
his poor, the people at the Mission, came trooping to him for help,
and he had to turn so many away. The whole town knew that he was in
trouble, though no one knew or even suspected just what it was. For
the people had their own troubles in those days, and the town and the
county and the state and the whole world grew shabby.

One day in the summer of '93, Colonel Culpepper was sitting in his
office reading a letter from Vermont demanding a long-deferred
interest payment on a mortgage. There were three hundred dollars due,
and the colonel had but half that amount, and was going to send what

he had. Jake Dolan came into the office and saw the colonel sitting with the letter crumpled in his hands, and with worry in the dull old eyes.

"Come in, Jake, come in," cried the colonel, a little huskily. "What's the trouble, comrade--what's wrong?"

But let Dolan tell it to Hendricks three days later, as the two are sitting at night on the stone bridge across the Sycamore built by John Barclay to commemorate the battle of Sycamore Ridge. "'Well, Mart,' says I, 'I'm in vicarious trouble,' says I. 'It's along of my orphan asylum,' says I. 'What orphan asylum?' says he. 'Well, it's this way, Mart,' says I. 'You know they found Trixie Lee guilty this afternoon in the justice court, don't you?' Mart sighs and says, 'Poor Trixie, I supposed they would sooner or later, poor girl--poor girl. An' old Cap Lee of the Red Legs was her father; did you know that, Jake?' he asks. 'Yes, Mart,' says I, 'and Lady Lee before her. She comes by it honestly.' Mart sat drumming with his fingers on the table, looking back into the years. 'Poor Jim,' he says, 'Jim was a brave soldier--a brave, big-hearted, generous soldier--he nursed me all that first night at Wilson's Creek when I was wounded. Poor Jim.' 'Yes,' says I, 'and Trixie has named her boy for him--Jim Lord Lee Young; that was her husband's name--Young,' says I. 'And it's along of the boy that I'm here for. The nicest bright-eyed little chap you ever saw; and he seems to know that something is wrong, and just clings to his mother and cries--seven years old, or maybe eight--and begs me not to put his mother in jail. And,' says I to Mart, 'Mart, I just can't do it. The sheriff he's run, and so has the deputy; they can't stand the boy crying, and damn it to hell, Mart, I can't, either; so I just left 'em in the office and locked the door and come around to see you. I'd 'a' gone to see Bob, only he's out of town this week,' I says. 'I can throw up the job, Mart--though I'd have to go on the county; but Mart, they ain't a soul for the boy to go to; and it ain't right to put him in jail with the scum that's in there.'"

"Tough--wasn't it?" said Hendricks. "What did you do? Why didn't you go to Carnine or Barclay?"

"That's just what I'm a-comin' to,--the Priest or the Levite?" said Jake. "Well, Mart said, 'Where're the men they caught--won't they help?' and I says, 'They paid their tine and skipped.' 'Fine?' asks Mart, 'fine? I thought you said it was jail sentence.' 'Well,' says I, 'it amounts to the same thing; she can't pay her fine, and that damn reform judge, wanting to make a record as a Spartan, has committed her to jail till it is paid!' 'So they go free, and she goes to jail, because she is poor,' says Mart.' That's what your reform means,' says I, 'or I let her and the boy loose and lose my job. And oh, Mart,' says I, 'the screams of that little boy at the disgrace of it and the terror of the jail--man--I can't stand it!' 'How much is it?' sighs Mart. 'An even hundred fine and seventeen dollars and fifty cents costs,' says I. Mart's eyes was leaking, and he gets up and goes to the vault, and comes back with the cash and says, blubbering like a calf: 'Here, Jake Dolan, you old scoundrel, take this. I'll pass a paper and get it to-morrow--now get out of here.' And he handed me the money all cried over where he'd been slow counting it out, and said when he'd got hold of his wobbly jaw: 'Don't you tell her where you got it--I don't want her around here. I'll see her to-morrow when I'm down that way and talk to her for old Cap Lee--' And then he laughs as he stands in the door and says: 'Well, Jim,' and he points up, 'your bread cast upon the waters was a long time a-coming--but here she is;' and he says, 'Do you suppose the old villain knows?' And I turned and hunted up the justice and went around to the office, and told Trixie to 'go sin no more,' and she laughs and says, 'Well, hardly ever!' and I kissed the kid, and he fought my whiskers, and we all live happy ever after."

But the colonel, after Dolan left the office, went into the darkening room, and spread out the harsh letter from the Vermont banker demanding money long past due, and read and reread it and took up his burden, and got into the weary treadmill of his life. It rained the next day, and he did not go out with his subscription paper; he had learned that people subscribe better on bright days; and as Hendricks and Barclay were both out of town, he wrote a dilatory letter to the Vermont people--the fifth he had written about that particular transaction--and waited another rainy day and still another before starting out with his paper. But the event was past; the cry of the child was not in the people's ears; they knew that the colonel had put up the money; so it was not until Hendricks came back and heard the story from Dolan that the colonel was repaid. Then because he actually had the money--at least half of it due on that particular debt, which was one of scores of its kind--the colonel delayed another day and another, and while he was musing the fire burned. And events started in Vermont which greatly changed the course of this story.

"I wonder," he has written in that portion of the McHurdie Biography devoted to "The Press of the Years," "why, as we go farther and farther into life, invariably it grows dingier and dingier. The 'large white plumes' that dance before the eyes of youth soil, and are bedraggled. And out of the inexplicable tangle of the mesh of life come dark threads from God knows where and colour the woof of it gray and dreary. Ah for the days of the large white plumes--for the days when life's woof was bright!"

CHAPTER XX

If the reader of this tale should feel drawn to visit Sycamore Ridge, he will find a number of interesting things there, and the trip may be made by the transcontinental traveller with the loss of but half a dozen hours from his journey. The Golden Belt Railroad, fifteen years ago, used to print a guide-book called "California and Back," in which were set down the places of interest to the traveller. In that book Sycamore Ridge was described thus:--

"Sycamore Ridge, pop. 22,345, census 1890; large water-power, main industry milling; also manufacturing; five wholesale houses. Seat Ward University, 1300 students; also Garrison County High School, also Business College. Thirty-five churches, two newspapers, the *Daily Banner* and the *Index*; fifty miles of paved streets; largest stone arch bridge in the West, marking site of Battle of Sycamore Ridge, a border ruffian skirmish; home of Watts McHurdie, famous as writer of war-songs, best known of which is--" etc., etc.

But excepting Watts, who may be gone before you get there,--for he is an old man now, and is alone and probably does not always have the best of care,--the things above annotated will not interest the traveller. At the Thayer House they will tell you that three things in the town give it distinction: the Barclay home, a rambling gray brick structure which the natives call Barclay Castle, with a great sycamore tree held together by iron bands on the terraced lawn before the house--that is number one; the second thing they will advise the traveller to see is Mary Barclay Park, ten acres of transplanted elm trees, most tastefully laid out, between Main Street and the Barclay home; and the third thing that will be pointed out to the traveller is the Schnitzler fountain, in the cemetery gateway, done by St. Gaudens;

it represents a soldier pouring water from his canteen into his hand, as he bathes the brow of a dying comrade.

These things, of course,--the house, the park, and the fountain,--represent John Barclay and his money. The town is proud of them, but the reader is advised not to expect too much of them. One of the two things really worth seeing at the Ridge is the view over the wheat fields of the Sycamore Valley from the veranda of the Culpepper home on the hill. There one may see the great fields lying in three townships whereon John Barclay founded his fortune. The second thing worth seeing may be found in the hallway of the public library building, just at the turn of the marble stairway, where the morning light strikes it. Take the night train out of Chicago and get to the Ridge in the morning, to get the light on that picture.

It is a portrait of John Barclay, done when he was forty years old and painted by a Russian during the summer when the Barclays were called home from Europe before their journey was half completed, to straighten out an obstreperous congressman, one Tom Wharton by name, who was threatening to put wheat and flour on the free list in a tariff bill, unless--but that is immaterial, except that Wharton was on Barclay's mind more or less while the painter was at work, and the portrait reflects what Barclay thought of a number of things. It shows a small gray-clad man, with a pearl pin in a black tie, sitting rather on the edge of his chair, leaning forward, so that the head is thrown into the light. The eyes are well opened, and the jaw comes out, a hard mean jaw; but the work of the artist, the real work that reveals the soul of the sitter, is shown in three features, if we except the pugnacious shoulders. In the face are two of these features: the mouth, a hard, coarse, furtive mouth,--the mouth of the liar who is not polished,--the peasant liar who has been caught and has brazened it out; the mouth and the forehead, full almost to bulging, so clean and white and naked that it seems shameful to expose it, a poet's forehead, noble and full of dreams, broad over the eyes, and as delicately modelled at the temples as a woman's where the curly brown hair is brushed away from it. But the wonderful feature about the portrait is the right hand. The artist obviously asked Barclay to assume a natural attitude, and then seeing him lean forward with his hand stretched out in some gesture of impatience, persuaded him to take that pose. It is the sort of vital human thing that would please Barclay--no sham about it; but he did not realize what the Russian was putting into that hand--a long, hard, hairy, hollow, grasping, relentless hand, full in the foreground and squarely in the light--a horrible thing with artistic fingers, and a thin, greedy palm indicated by the deep hump in the back. It reaches out from the picture, with the light on the flesh tints, with the animal hair thick upon it, and with the curved, slender, tapering fingers cramped like a claw; and when one follows up the arm to the crouching body, the furtive mouth, the bold, shrewd eyes, and then sees that forehead full of visions, one sees in it more than John Barclay of Sycamore Ridge, more than America, more than Europe. It is the menace of civilization--the danger to the race from the domination of sheer intellect without moral restraint.

General Ward, who was on the committee that received the picture fifteen years after it was painted, stood looking at it the morning it was hung there on the turn of the stairs. As the light fell mercilessly upon it, the general, white-haired, white-necktied, clean-shaven, and lean-faced, gazed at the portrait for a long time, and then said to his son Neal who stood beside him, "And Samson wist not that the Lord had departed from him."

It will pay one to stop a day in Sycamore Ridge to see that picture--though he does not know John Barclay, and only understands the era that made him, and gave him that refined, savage, cunning, grasping hand.

Barclay stopped a week in Washington on his return from Europe the year that picture was painted, made a draft for fifty thousand dollars on the National Provisions Company to cover "legal expenses," and came straight home to Sycamore Ridge. He was tired of cities, he told Colonel Culpepper, who met Barclay at the post-office the morning he returned, with his arms full of newspapers. "I want to hear the old mill, Colonel," said Barclay, "to smell the grease down in the guts of her, and to get my hair full of flour again." When he had gorged himself for two days, he wired Bemis to come to the Ridge, and Barclay and Bemis sat on the dam one evening until late bedtime, considering many things. As they talked, Barclay found that a plan for the reorganization of the Provisions Company was growing in his mind, and he talked it out as it grew.

"Lige," he said, as he leaned with his elbows on a rock behind him, "the trouble with the company as it now stands is that it's too palpable. There's too much to levy on--too much in sight; too much physical property. How would it do to sell all these mills and elevators, and use the company as a kind of a cream skimmer--a profit shop--to market the products of the mills?" He paused a moment, and Bemis, who knew he was not expected to reply, flipped pebbles into the stream. Barclay changed his position slightly and began to pick stones out of the crevices, and throw the stones into the water. "That's the thing to do--go ahead and sell every dollar's worth of assets the company's got--I'll take the mill here. I couldn't get along without that. Then we'll buy the products of the mills at cost of the millers, and let them get their profits back as individual holders of our stock. Our company will handle the Door Strip--buy it and sell it--and if any long-nosed reformer gets to snooping around the mills, he'll find they are making only a living profit; and as for us--any state grain commissioner or board of commissioners who wanted to examine us could do so, and what'd he find? Simply that we're buying

our products at cost of the millers and selling at the market
price--sometimes at a loss, sometimes at a profit; and what if we do
handle all the grain and grain products in the United States? They
can't show that we are hurting anything. I tell you there's getting to
be too much snooping now in the state and federal governments. Have
you got any fellow in your office who can fix up a charter that will
let us buy and sell grain, and also sell the Barclay Economy Strip?"

Bemis nodded.

"Then, damn 'em, let 'em go on with their commissioners and boards and
legislative committees; they can't catch us. There's no law against
the railroads that ship our stuff buying the Economy Door Strip, is
there? You bet there isn't. And we're entitled to a good round
inventor's profit, ain't we? You bet we are. You go ahead and get up
that reorganization, and I'll put it through. Say, Lige--" Barclay
chuckled as a recollection flashed across his mind--"you know I've
made some of our Northwest senators promise to make you a federal
judge. That's one of the things I did last week; I thought maybe
sometime we'd need a federal judge as one of the--what do you call
it--the hereditaments thereunto appertaining of the company." Bemis
opened his eyes in astonishment, and Barclay grunted in disgust as he
went on: "Of course we can't get you appointed from this
state--that's clear--but they think we can work it through in the
City--as soon as there is a vacancy--or make a new district. How
would you like that? Judge Bemis--say, that sounds all right, doesn't
it?"

Barclay rose and stretched his legs and arms. "Well, I must be
going--Mrs. Barclay and my mother want to hear the new organ over in
the Congregational Church. It's a daisy--Colonel Culpepper, amongst
hands, skirmished up three thousand. They let me pick it out, and I
had to put up another thousand myself to get the kind I wanted. Are

you well taken care of at the hotel?" When Bemis explained that he had
the bridal chamber, the two men clambered up the bank of the stream,
crossed the bridge, and at his gate Barclay said: "Now, I'll sleep on
this to-night,--this reorganization,--and then I'll write you a
letter to-morrow, covering all that I've said, and you can fix up a
tentative charter and fire it down--and say, Lige, figure out what a
modest profit on all the grain and grain produce business of the
country would be--say about two and a half per cent, and make the
capitalization of the reorganization fit that. We'll get the real
profits out of the Door Strip, and can fix that up in the books. We'll
show the reformers a trick or two." It was a warm night, and when the
organ recital was over, John and Jane Barclay, after the custom of the
town, sat on a terrace in front of the house talking of the day's
events. Music always made John babble.

"Jane," he asked suddenly, "Jane--when does a man begin to grow old?
Here I am past forty. I used to think when a man was forty he was
middle-aged; every five years I have advanced my idea of what an old
man was; when I was fifteen, I thought a man was getting along when he
was thirty. When I was twenty-five, I regarded forty as the beginning
of the end; when I was thirty, I put the limit of activity at
forty-five; five years ago I moved it up to fifty; and to-day I have
jumped it to sixty. It seems to me, Jane, that I'm as much of a boy as
ever; all this talk about my being a man puzzles me. What's this
Provisions Company but a game? And I'm going to play another game; I'm
going to get grain and grain produce organized, and then I'm going to
tackle meat. In ten years I'll have the packing-houses where I have
the mills; but it's just play--and it's a lot of fun."

He was silent a moment. Jane did not disturb his reveries. She
understood, without exactly putting her feeling into language, that
she was being talked at, not talked to.

"Say, Jane," he exclaimed, "wasn't that 'Marche Triomphante to-night great?" He hummed a bar from the motif, "That's it--my--" he cried, hitting his chair arm with his fist, "but that's a big thing--almost good enough for Wagner to have done; big and insistent and strong. I'm getting to like music with go to it--with bang and brass. Wagner does it; honest, Jane, when I hear his trombones coming into a theme, I get ideas enough to give the whole force in the office nervous prostration for a month. To-night when that thing was swelling up like a great tidal wave of music rolling in, I worked out a big idea; I'm going to sell all the mills and factories back to the millers for our stock, and when I own every dollar of our stock, I'm going to double the price of it to them and sell it back to them; and if they haggle about it, I'll build a new mill across the track from every man-jack who tries to give me any funny business--I'll show 'em. That reorganization ought to clean up millions for us in the next year. What a lot of fun it all is! I used to think old Jay Gould was some pumpkins; but if we get this reorganization through, I'll go down there and buy the Gould outfit and sell 'em for old iron."

The current of his thoughts struck under language, as a prairie stream sometimes hides from its surface bed. After a time Jane said: "Grandma Barclay thought the 'Marche Funebre' was the best thing the man did. I heard the Wards speaking of it in the vestibule; and Molly, who held my hand through it, nearly squeezed it off--poor girl; but she looks real well these days." Jane paused a moment and added: "Did you notice the colonel? How worn and haggard he looks--he seems broken so. They say he is in trouble. Couldn't we help him?"

Her husband did not reply at once. Finally he recalled his wandering wits and answered: "Oh, I don't know, Jane. He'll pull through, I guess." Then he reverted to the music, which was still in his head. "He played the Largo well--didn't he? That was made for the organ. But some way I like the big things. The Largo is like running a little twenty-horse-power steam mill, and selling to the home grocers. But 'The Ride of the Valkyries,' with those screaming discords of brass, and those magnificent crashes of harmony--Jane, I've got an idea--Wagner's work is the National Provisions Company set to music, and I'm the first trombone." He laughed and reached for his wife's hand and kissed it; then he rose and stood before her, admiring her in the starlight, as he exclaimed: "And you are those clarinets, sweet and clear and delicious, that make a man want to cry for sheer joy. Come on, my dear--isn't it very late?" And the little man limped across the grass up the steps and into the house. The two stopped a moment while he listened to the roar of the water and the rumble of the mill, that glowed in the night like a phosphorescent spectre. He squeezed her hand and cried out in exultation, "It's great, isn't it--the finest mill on this planet, my dear--do you realize that?" And then they turned into the house.

The next morning he kept two stenographers busy; he was spinning the web of his reorganization, bringing about a condition under which men were compelled to exchange their stock in the National Provisions Company for their former property. He was a crafty little man, and his ways were sometimes devious, even though to outward view his advertised and proclaimed methods were those of a pirate. So when he had dictated a day's work to two girls, he went nosing through the mill, loafing in the engine rooms, looking at the water wheel, or running about rafters in the fifth floor like a great gray rat. As he went he hummed little tunes under his breath or whistled between his teeth, with his lips apart. After luncheon he unlocked a row-boat, and took a cane pole and rowed himself a mile up the mill-pond, and brought home three good-sized bass. Thus did he spend his idle moments around the Ridge. That night he thumped his piano and longed for a pipe organ. The things he tried to play were noisy, and his mother, sitting in the gloaming near him, sighed and said: "John, play some of the old pieces--the quieter ones; play 'The Long and Weary Day' and some of the old songs. Have you forgotten the 'Bohemian Girl' and those Schubert songs?"

His fingers felt their way back to his boyhood, and when he ceased playing, he stood by his mother a moment, and patted her cheeks as he hummed in German the first two lines of the "Lorelei," and then said, "We have come a long way since then--eh, mother?" She held his hand to her cheek and then to her lips, but she did not reply. He repeated it, "A long, long way from the little home of one room here!" After a pause he added, "Would you like to go back?"

A tear fell on the hand against her cheek. He felt her jaw quiver, and then she said, "Oh, yes, John--yes, I believe I would."

He knew she did not care for his wealth, and there were many things about his achievements that he felt she might misunderstand; her attitude often puzzled him. So he sat a moment on her chair arm, and said, "Well, mother, I have done my best." It was a question more than a protest.

"Yes, dear," she replied, "I know you have--you have done your best--your very best. But I think it is in your blood."

"What?" he asked.

"Oh, all this," she answered; "all this money-getting. I am foolish, John, but some way, I want my little boy back--the one who used to sit with me so long ago, and play on the guitar and sing 'Sleeping, I Dream, Love.' I don't like your new music, John; it's so like clanging cars, and crashing hammers, and the groans of men at toil."

"But this is a new world, mother--a new world that is different," protested the son, impatiently.

And the mother answered sadly as she looked up at him: "I know, dear--it is a new world; but the same old God moves it; and the same faith in God and love of man move men that always have moved them, and always will move them; there are as many things to live and die for now, as when your father gave up his life, John--just as many." They rocked together in silence--the boy of forty and the mother of sixty. Finally she said, "Johnnie, play me 'Ever of Thee I'm fondly Thinking,' won't you, before you go?"

He sat with his foot on the soft pedal and played the old love song, and as he played his mother wandered over hills he had never seen, through fields he had never known, and heard a voice in the song he might never hear, even in his dreams. When he finished, she stood beside him and cried with all the passion her years could summon: "Oh, John--John--it will come out some way--some day. It's in your soul, and God in His own way will bring it out." He did not understand her then, and it was many years before he prayed her prayer.

The next day he went to the City and plunged into his work, and the Ridge and its people and the prayers of his mother became to him only as a dream that comes in the night and fades in the day. Even the shabby figure of Colonel Martin Culpepper, with his market basket on his arm, waving a good-by as the Barclay private car pulled out of the Sycamore Ridge depot, disappeared from his mind, though that pathetic image haunted him for nearly a hundred miles as he rode, and he could not shake it off until he immersed himself in the roar of the great City. He could not know that he had any remote relation with the worry in the old man's eyes. Nor did Martin Culpepper try to shift his load to John. He knew where the blame was, and he tried to take it like a man. But in reckoning the colonel's account, may not something be charged off to the account of John Barclay, who to save himself and accomplish the Larger Good--which meant the establishment of his own fortunes--sent Adrian Brownwell in those days in the seventies with the money to the colonel, not so much to help the colonel as to save John Barclay? The Larger Good is a slow, vicious, accumulative poison, and heaven only knows when it will come out and kill.

It was a week after the pipe-organ recital at the church, when Mary Barclay, doing her day's marketing, ran into Colonel Culpepper standing rather forlornly in front of McHurdie's shop. He bowed to her with elaborate graciousness, and she stopped to speak with him. In a moment he was saying, "So you have not heard, are unaware, entirely ignorant, in point of fact, of my misfortunes?" She assented, and the colonel went on: "Well, madam, the end has come; I have played out my hand; I have strutted my hour upon the stage, and now I go off. Old Mart Culpepper, my dear, is no longer the leading citizen, nor our distinguished capitalist, not even the hustling real estate agent of former days--just plain old Mart Culpepper, I may say. He who was, is now a has-been,--just an old man without a business." He saw that she did not appreciate what had happened, and he smiled gently and said: "Closed up, my dear madam. A receiver was appointed a few minutes ago for the Culpepper Mortgage Company, and I gave him the key. Failure--failure--" he repeated the word bitterly--"failure is written over the door of this life."

Mary Barclay grasped his big fat hand and pressed it, and shook her head. Something in her throat choked her, and she could not speak at first. The two stood a moment in silence before the woman said emphatically, "No--no! Martin Culpepper, God is keeping your books!"

The shabby old man stood uncovered, a smile quivering about his eyes. "Maybe so, Mary Barclay, maybe so," he said. The smile fell into his countenance as he added, "That is why I have gone so long without a settlement; with my account so badly overdrawn, too." Then he turned to go and walked as lightly down the street as a man could walk, broken before his time with the weight of a humiliation upon him and a fear greater than his shame burning in his fluttering old heart.

And now if you are reading this story to be in the company of the rich Mr. Barclay, to feel the madness of his millions, to enjoy the vain delirium of his power, skip the rest of this chapter. For it tells of a shabby time in the lives of all of the threadbare people who move in this tale. Even John Barclay sees the seams and basting threads of his life here, and as for the others,--the colonel and Jake and the general and Watts, and even Molly,--what do these people mean to you, these common people, in their old clothes, with their old hearts and their rusty sins and their homely sorrows? Milord and his lady will not scamper across these pages; no rooms with rich appointments will gladden your eyes, and perhaps in the whole book you will not find a man in evening dress nor a woman in a dinner gown. And now the only thing there is to offer is Jake Dolan, aged fifty-seven, with scanty, grizzled hair, sitting in his shirt-sleeves in the basement of the court-house, with the canvas cot he sleeps on for a chair, mending his blue army coat. Beside him on the bed are his trousers, thin, almost worn through, patched as to the knees and as to other important places, but clean and without a loose thread hanging from them. Surely an old Irishman mending an old army coat under a dusty electric light bulb in the basement of a court-house, wherein he is janitor by grace of the united demand of Henry Schnitzler Post of the G.A.R. No. 432, is not a particularly inspiring picture. But he has bitten the last thread with his teeth, and is putting away the sewing outfit. And now Mr. Dolan, from the drawer of a little table beside the cot,--a table with Bob Hendricks' picture, framed in plush, sitting on the top,--now Mr. Dolan takes from the drawer a tablet of writing paper printed by the county. It is his particular pride, that writing paper. For upon it at the top is the picture of the new one-hundred-thousand-dollar court-house, and beside the court-house picture are these words: "Office of Jacob Dolan, Custodian of Public Buildings and Grounds of Garrison County." Mr. Dolan will be writing a letter, and so long as it begins with "Dear Sir," and nothing more endearing, surely we may look over his shoulder while he writes,--even though it is bad form. And as Mr. Dolan will be writing to "Robert Hendricks, care of Cook's Hotel, Cairo, Egypt,"--which he spells with an "i," but let that pass, and let some of his literary style and construction pass with it,--and as he will be writing to Mr. Hendricks, perhaps Miss Nancy may do well to go sit in the corridor and put her fingers in her ears while we read. For Mr. Dolan is an emotional man, and he is breathing hard, and by the way he grabs his pen and jabs it into the ink one can see that he is angry.

"DEAR SIR (begins Mr. Dolan): I take my pen in hand to answer yours of this date from New York and would have written you anyhow, as there is much on my mind and I would cable you, but I can't, being for the moment short of funds. I write to say, Robert, that we have Mart Culpepper in jail--right across the hall. He came in at nine o'clock to-night, and the damn Pop judge put his bail at $15,999 to cover his alleged shortage, and the stinker won't accept us old boys on the bond--Phil and Watts and Os and the Company 'C' boys I could get before the judge went to bed, and Gabe Carnine, the gut, would not sign--would not sign old Mart's bond, sir, and I hope to be in hell with a fishpole some day poking him down every time his slimy fingers get on the rim of the kettle. But we'll have him out in the morning, if every man in Garrison County has to go on the bond. They say Mart received money to pay four or five mortgages due to a Vermont Bank, and they sent a detective here about a month ago and worked up the case, and closed his business to-day and waited until to-night to arrest him. I've just come from Mart. It's hell. Hoping this will find you enjoying the same I beg my dear sir to sign myself

"Your ob't s'r'v't J. DOLAN."

When Jacob Dolan finished his letter, he addressed the envelope and hurried away to mail it. And so long as we are here in the court-house, and the custodian is gone, would you like to step in and see Martin Culpepper across the hall? It is still in the basement now, and if you are quiet, so quiet that the slipping patter of a rat's foot on the floor comes to you, a sound as of a faint whining will come to you also. There--now it comes again. No, it is not a dog; it is a man--a man in his agony. Shall we open the great iron door, and go into the cell room? Why, not even you, Miss Nancy--not even you, who love tears so? You would not see much--only a man, with his coat and vest off, an old man with a rather shaggy, ill-kept chin whisker and not the cleanest shirt in the world--though it is plaited, and once was a considerable garment. And the man wearing it, who lies prostrate upon his face, once was a considerable man. But he is old now, old and broken, and if he should look up, as you stepped in the corridor before him, you would see a great face ripped and scarred by fear and guilt, and eyes that look so piteously at you--eyes of a man who cannot understand why the blow has fallen, surprised eyes with a horror in them; and if he should speak, you will find a voice rough and mushy with asthma. The heart that has throbbed so many nights in fear and the breath that has been held for so many footsteps, at last have turned their straining into disease. No--let's not go in. He bade his daughter go, and would not see his wife, and they have sent to the City for his son,--so let us not bother him, for to-morrow he will be out on bail. But did you hear that fine, trembling, animal whine--that cry that wrenched itself out of set teeth like a living thing? Come on--let us go and find Jake, and if he is taking a drink, don't blame him too much, Miss Nancy--how would you like to sleep in that room across the corridor?

At nine o'clock the next morning two hundred men had signed the bond the judge required, and Martin Culpepper shambled home with averted eyes. They tried to carry him on their shoulders, thinking it would cheer him up; and from the river wards of the town scores came to give him their hands. But he shook himself away from them, like a great whipped dog, and walked slowly up the hill, and turned into Lincoln Avenue alone.

John Barclay heard the news of the colonel's trouble as he stepped from his private car in the Sycamore Ridge yards that morning, and Jane went to the Culpepper home without stopping at her own. That afternoon, Molly Brownwell knocked at Barclay's office door in the mill, and went in without waiting for him to open it. She was pale and haggard, and she sat down before he could speak to her.

"John," she said in a dead voice that smote his heart, "I have come for my reward now. I never thought I'd ask it, John, but last night I thought it all out, and I don't believe it's begging."

"No," he replied quietly, "it's not. I am sure--"

But she did not let him finish. She broke in with: "Oh, I don't want any of your money; I want my own money--money that you got when you sold me into bondage, John Barclay--do you remember when?" She cried the last words in a tremulous little voice, and then caught herself, and went on before he could put into words the daze in his face. "Let me tell you; do you remember the day you called me up into your office and asked me to hold Adrian in town to save the wheat company? Yes, you do--you know you do! And you remember that you played on my love for Bob, and my duty to father. Well, I saved you, didn't I?"

"Yes, you did, Molly," Barclay replied.

She stared a moment at the framed pictures of mill designs on the wall, and at the wheat samples on the long table near her, and did not speak; nor did he. She finally broke the silence: "Well, I saved you, but what about father--" her voice broke into a sob--"and Bob--Jane has told you what Bob and I have been--and what about me--what have you taken from me in these twenty years? Oh, John, John, what a fearful wreck we have made of life--you with your blind selfishness, and I with my weakness! Did you know, John, that the money that father borrowed that day, twenty years ago, of Adrian, to lend to you, is the very money that sent him to jail last night? I guess he--he took what wasn't his to pay it back." Her face twitched, and she was losing control of her voice. Barclay stepped to the door and latched it. She watched him and shook her head sadly. "You needn't be afraid, John--I'm not going to make a scene."

"It's all right, Molly," said Barclay. "I want to help you--you know that. I'm sorry, Molly--infinitely sorry."

She looked at him for a moment in silence, and then said: "Yes, John, I'll give you credit for that; I think you're as sorry as a selfish man like you can be. But are you sorry enough to go to jail a pauper, like father, or wander over the earth alone, like Bob, or come and beg for money, like me?" Then she caught herself quickly and cried: "Only it's not begging, John--it's my own; it's the price you got when you sold me into bondage; it's the price of my soul, and I need it now. Those people only want their money--that is all."

"Yes," he replied, "I suppose that is all they want." He drummed on his desk a moment and then asked, "Does your father know how much it is?"

"Yes," she answered, "I found in his desk at the house last night a paper on which he had been figuring--poor father--all the night before. All the night before--" she repeated, and then sobbed, "Poor father--all the night before. He knew it was coming. He knew the detective was here. He told me to-day that the sum he had there was

correct. It is sixteen thousand five hundred and forty-three dollars.
But he doesn't know I'm here, John. I told him I had some money of my
own--some I'd had for years--and I have--oh, I have, John
Barclay--I have." She looked up at him with the pallid face stained
with fresh tears and asked, "I have--I have--haven't I, John,
haven't I?"

He put his elbows on the desk and sank his head in his hands and
sighed, "Yes, Molly--yes, you have."

They sat in silence until the roar of the waters and the murmur of the
wheels about them came into the room. Then the woman rose to go.
"Well, John," she said, "I suppose one shouldn't thank a person for
giving her her own--but I do, John. Oh, it's like blood money to
me--but father--I can't let father suffer."

She walked to the door, he stepped to unlatch it, and she passed out
without saying good-by. When she was gone, he slipped the latch, and
sat down with his hands gripping the table before him. As he sat
there, he looked across the years and saw some of the havoc he had
made. There was no shirking anything that he saw. A footfall passing
the door made him start as if he feared to be caught in some guilty
act. Yet he knew the door was locked. He choked a little groan behind
his teeth, and then reached for the top of his desk, pulled down the
rolling cover, and limped quickly out of the room--as though he were
leaving a corpse. What he saw was the ghost of the Larger Good,
mocking him through the veil of the past, and asking him such
questions as only a man's soul may hear and not resent.

He walked over the mill for a time, and then calling his stenographers
from their room, dictated them blind and himself dumb with details of
a deal he was putting through to get control of the cracker companies
of the country. When he finished, the sunset was glaring across the

water through the window in front of him, and he had laid his ghost. But Molly Brownwell had her check, and her father was saved.

That evening the colonel sat with Watts McHurdie, on the broad veranda of the Culpepper home, and as the moon came out, General Ward wandered up the walk and Jake Dolan came singing down the street about "the relic of old dacincy--the hat me father wore." Perhaps he had one drink in him, and perhaps two, or maybe three, but he clicked the gate behind him, and seeing the three men on the veranda, he called out:--

"Hi, you pig-stealing Kansas soldiers, haven't ye heard the war is over?" And then he carolled: "Oh, can't get 'em up, Oh, can't get 'em up, Oh, can't get 'em up in the mornin'--Get up, you"--but the rest of the song, being devoted to the technical affairs of war, and ending with a general exhortation to the soldier to "get into your breeches," would give offence to persons of sensitive natures, and so may as well be omitted from this story.

There was an awkward pause when Dolan came on the veranda. The general had just tried to break the ice, but Dolan was going at too high a speed to be checked.

"Do you know," he asked, "what I always remember when I hear that call? You do not. I'll tell you. 'Twas the morning of the battle of Wilson's Creek, and Mart and me was sleeping under a tree, when the bugler of the Johnnies off somewhere on the hill he begins to crow that, and it wakes Mart up, and he rolls over on me and he says: 'Jake,' he says, or maybe 'twas me says, 'Mart,' says I--anyway, one of us says, 'Shut up your gib, you flannel-mouthed mick,' he says, 'and let me pull my dream through to the place where I find the money,' he says. And I says, 'D'ye know what I'm goin' to do when I get home?' says I. 'No,' says he, still keen for that money; 'no,' says he, 'unless it is you're going to be hanged by way of diversion,' he says. 'I'm going to hire a bugler,' says I. 'What fer--in the name of all the saints?' says he. 'Well,' says I, 'I'm going to ask him to blow his damn horn under my window every morning at five o'clock,' I says, 'and then I'm going to get up and poke my head out of the window and say: "Mister, you can get me up in the army, but on this occasion would you be obliging enough to go to hell"!' And Mart, seeing that the money was gone from his dream, he turns over and wallops me with the blanket till I was merely a palpitating mass. That was a great battle, though, boys--a great battle."

And then they shouldered arms and showed how fields were won. Boom! went Sigel's guns out of the past, and crash! came the Texas cavalry, and the whoop of the Louisiana Pelicans rang in their ears. They marched south after Hindman, and then came back with Grant to Vicksburg, where they fought and bled and died. The general left them and went east, where he "deployed on our right" and executed flank movements, and watched Pickett's column come fling itself to death at Gettysburg. And Watts McHurdie rode with the artillery through the rear of the rebel lines at Pittsburg Landing, and when the rebel officer saw the little man's bravery, and watched him making for the Union lines bringing three guns, he waved his hat and told his soldiers not to shoot at that boy. The colonel took a stick and marked out on the floor our position at Antietam, and showed where the reserves were supposed to be and how the enemy masked his guns behind that hill, and we planted our artillery on the opposite ridge; and he marched with the infantry and lay in ambush while the enemy came marching in force through the wood. In time Watts McHurdie was talking to Lincoln in the streets of Richmond, and telling for the hundredth time what Lincoln said of the song and how he had sung it. But who cares now what Lincoln said? It was something kind, you may be sure, with a tear and a laugh in it, and the veterans laughed, while their eyes grew moist as they always did when Watts told it. Then they fell to carnage again--a fierce fight against time, against the moment when they must leave their old companion alone. Up hills they charged and down dales, and the moon rose high, and cast its shadow to the eastward before they parted. First Dolan edged away, and then the general went, waving his hand military fashion; and the colonel returned the salute. When the gate had clanged, Watts rose to go. He did not speak, nor did the colonel. Arm in arm, they walked down the steps together, and halfway down the garden path the colonel rested his hand on the little man's shoulder as they walked in silence. At the gate they saw each other's tears, and the little man's voice failed him when the colonel said, "Well, good-by, comrade--good night." So Watts turned and ran, while the colonel, for the first time in his manhood, loosed the cords of his sorrow and stood alone in the moonlight with upturned face, swaying like an old tree in a storm.

CHAPTER XXI

And now those who have avoided the gray unpainted shame of these unimportant people of the Ridge may here take up again for a moment the trailing clouds of glory that shimmer over John Barclay's office in the big City. For here there is the sounding brass and tinkling cymbal of great worldly power. Here sits John Barclay, a little gray-haired, gray-clad, lynx-eyed man, in a big light room at the corner of a tower high over the City in the Corn Exchange Building, the brain from which a million nerves radiate that run all over the world and move thousands of men. Forty years before, when John was playing in the dust of the road leading up from the Sycamore, no king in all the world knew so much of the day's doings as John knows now, sitting there at the polished mahogany table with the green blotting paper upon it, under the green vase adorned with the red rose. A blight may threaten the wheat in Argentine, and John Barclay knows every cloud that sails the sky above that wheat, and when the cloud bursts into rain he sighs, for it means something to him, though heaven only knows what, and we and heaven do not care. But a dry day in India or a wet day in Russia or a cloudy day in the Dakotas are all taken into account in the little man's plans. And if princes quarrel and kings grow weary of peace, and money bags refuse them war, John Barclay knows it and puts the episode into figures on the clean white pad of paper before him.

It is a privilege to be in this office; one passes three doors to get here, and even at the third door our statesmen often cool their toes. Mr. Barclay is about to admit one now. And when Senator Myton comes in, deferentially of course, to tell Mr. Barclay the details of the long fight in executive session which ended in the confirmation by the senate of Lige Bemis as a federal judge, the little gray man waves the senator to a chair, and runs his pencil up a column of figures, presses a button, writes a word on a sheet of paper, and when the messenger appears, hands the paper to him and says, "For Judge Bemis."

"I have just dismissed a Persian satrap," expands Barclay, "who won't let his people use our binders; that country eventually will be a great field for our Mediterranean branch."

Myton is properly impressed. For a man who can make a senator out of Red River clay and a federal judge out of Lige Bemis is a superhuman creature, and Myton does not doubt Barclay's power over satraps.

When the business of the moment between the two men is done, Barclay, rampant with power, says: "Myton" (it is always "Myton," never "Senator," with Barclay; he finds it just as well to let his inferiors know their relation to the universe), "Myton, I ran across a queer thing last week when I took over that little jerkwater New England

coast line. The Yankees are a methodical lot of old maids. I find they
had been made agents of a lot of the big fellows--insurance people,
packing-houses, and transcontinental railroads--two of my lines were
paying them, though I'd forgotten about it until I looked it up--and
the good old sewing society had card-indexed the politics of the
United States--the whole blessed country, by state and congressional
districts. I took over the chap who runs it, and I've got the whole
kit in the offices here now. It's great. If a man bobs up for
something in Florida or Nebraska, we just run him down on the card
index, and there he stands--everything he ever did, every interview
he ever gave, every lawsuit he ever had, every stand he ever took in
politics--right there in the index, in an envelope ready for use, and
all the mean things ever written about him. I simply can't make a
mistake now in getting the wrong kind of fellows in. Commend me to a
Yankee or a Jap for pains. I can tell you in five minutes just what
influences are behind every governor, congressman, senator, judge,
most of the legislators in every state, the federal courts clear up to
the Supreme Court. There was a man appointed on that court less than a
dozen years ago who swapped railroad receiverships like a tin peddler
with his senator for his job, when he was on the circuit bench. And he
was considerable of a judge in the bean country for a time. Just to
verify my index, I asked Bemis about this judge. 'Lige,' I said, 'was
Judge So-and-So a pretty honest judge?' 'Oh, hell,' says Lige, and
that was all I could get out of him. So I guess they had him indexed
right." And Barclay rattles on; he has become vociferous and
loquacious, and seems to like to hear the roar of his voice in his
head. The habit has been growing on him.

But do not laugh at the blindness of John Barclay, sitting there in
his power, admiring himself, boasting in the strength of his
card-index to Senator Myton. For the tide of his power was running in,
and soon it would be high tide with John Barclay--high tide of his
power, high tide of his fame, high tide of his pride. So let us watch

the complacent smile crack his features as he sits listening to
Senator Myton: "Mr. Barclay, do you know, I sometimes think that
Providence manifests itself in minds like yours, even as in the days
of old it was manifest in the hearts of the prophets. In those days it
was piety that fitted the heart for higher things; to-day it is
business. You and a score of men like you in America are intrusted
with the destiny of this republic, as surely as the fate of the
children of Israel was in the hands of Moses and Aaron!"

Barclay closed his eyes a moment, in contemplation of the figure, and
then broke out in a roaring laugh, "Hanno is a god! Hanno is a
god!--get out of here, Henry Myton,--get out of here, I say--this
is my busy day," and he laughed the young senator out of the room. But
he sat alone in his office grinning, as over and over in his mind his
own words rang, "Hanno is a god!" And the foolish parrot of his other
self cackled the phrase in his soul for days and days!

It is our high privilege thus to stand close by and watch the wheels
of the world go around. In those days of the late nineties Barclay
travelled up and down the earth so much in his private car that Jane
used to tell Molly Brownwell that living with John was like being a
travelling man's wife. But Jane did not seem to appreciate her
privilege. She managed to stay at home as much as possible, and
sometimes he took the Masons along for company. Mrs. Mason gloried in
it, and lived at the great hotels and shopped at the highest-priced
antique stores to her heart's delight. Lycurgus' joy was in being
interviewed, and the Barclay secretaries got so that they could edit
the Mason interviews and keep out the poison, and let the old man
swell and swell until the people at home thought he must surely burst
with importance at the next town.

One day in the nineties Barclay appropriated a half-million dollars to
advertise "Barclay's Best" and a cracker that he was pushing. When the

man who placed the business in the newspaper had gone, Barclay sat looking out of the window and said to his advertising manager: "I've got an idea. Why should I pay a million dollars to irresponsible newspapers? I won't do it."

"But we must advertise, Mr. Barclay--you've proved it pays."

"Yes," he returned, "you bet it pays, and I might just as well get something out of it besides advertising. Take this; make five copies of it; I'll give you the addresses later." Barclay squared himself to a stenographer to dictate:--

"Dear Sir: I spend a million dollars a year advertising grain products; you and the packers doubtless spend that much advertising your products and by-products; the railroads spend as much more, and the Oil people probably half as much more. Add the steel products and the lumber products, and we have ten million dollars going into the press of this country. In a crisis we cannot tell how these newspapers will treat us. I think we should organize so that we will know exactly where we stand. Therefore it is necessary absolutely to control the trade advertising of this country. A company to take over the five leading advertising agencies could be formed, for half as much as we spend every year, and we could control nine-tenths of the American trade advertising. We could then put an end to any indiscriminate mobbing of corporations by editors. I will be pleased to hear from you further upon this subject."

A day or two later, when the idea had grown and ramified itself in his mind, he talked it all out to Jane and exclaimed, "How will old Phil Ward's God manage to work it out, as he says, against that proposition? Brains," continued Barclay, "brains--that's what counts in this world. You can't expect the men who dominate this country--who make its wealth, and are responsible for its prosperity, to be at the mercy of a lot of long-nosed reformers who don't know how to cash their own checks."

How little this rich man knew of the world about him! How circumscribed was his vision! With all his goings up and down the earth, with all of his great transactions, with all of his apparent power, how little and sordid was his outlook on life. For he thought he was somebody in this universe, some one of importance, and in his scheme of things he figured out a kind of partnership between himself and Providence--a partnership to run the world in the interests of John Barclay, and of course, wherever possible, with reasonable dividends to Providence.

But a miracle was coming into the world. In the under-consciousnesses of men, sown God only knows how and when and where, sown in the weakness of a thousand blind prophets, the seeds of righteous wrath at greed like John Barclay's were growing during all the years of his triumph. Men scarcely knew it themselves. Growth is so simple and natural a process that its work is done before its presence is known. And so this arrogant man, this miserable, little, limping, brass-eyed, leather-skinned man, looked out at the world around him, and did not see the change that was quickening the hearts of his neighbours.

And yet change was in everything about him. A thousand years are as but a watch in the night, and tick, tock, tick, tock, went the great clock, and the dresses of little Jeanette Barclay slipped down, down, down to her shoe-tops, and as the skirts slipped down she went up. And before her father knew it her shoe-tops sank out of sight, and she was a miss at the last of her teens. But he still gave her his finger when they walked out together, though she was head and shoulders above him.

One day when she led him to the *Banner* office to buy some fancy programmes for a party she was giving, he saw her watching young Neal

Ward,--youngest son of the general,--who was sitting at a reporter's desk in the office, and the father's quick eyes saw that she regarded the youth as a young man. For she talked so obviously for the Ward boy's benefit that her father, when they went out of the printing-office, took a furtive look at his daughter and sighed and knew what her mother had known for a year.

"Jeanette," he said that night at dinner, "where's my shot-gun?" When she told him, he said: "After dinner you get it, load it with salt, and put it in the corner by the front door." Then he added to the assembled family: "For boys--dirty-faced, good-for-nothing, long-legged boys! I'm going to have a law passed making an open season for boys in this place from January first until Christmas."

Jeanette dimpled and blushed, the family smiled, and her mother said: "Well, John, there'll be a flock of them at Jeanette's party next week for you to practise on. All the boys and girls in town are coming."

And after dessert was served the father sat chuckling and grinning and grunting, "Boys--boys," and at intervals, "Measly little milk-eyed kids," and again "Boys--boys," while the family nibbled at its cheese.

Those years when the nineteenth century was nearing its close and when the tide of his fortunes was running in, bringing him power and making him mad with it, were years of change in Sycamore Ridge--in the old as well as in the young. In those years the lilacs bloomed on in the Culpepper yard; and John Barclay did not know it, though forty years before Ellen Culpepper had guarded the first blossoms from those bushes for him. Miss Lucy, his first ideal, went to rest in those years while the booming tide was running in, and he scarcely knew it. Mrs. Culpepper was laid beside Ellen out on the Hill; and he hardly realized it, though no one in all the town had watched him growing into worldly success with so kindly an eye as she. But the tide was roaring in, and John Barclay's whole consciousness was turned toward it; the real things of life about him, he did not see and could not feel. And so as the century is old the booming tide is full, and John Barclay in his power--a bubble in the Divine consciousness, a mere vision in the real world--stands stark mad before his phantasm, dreaming that it is all real, and chattering to his soul, "Hanno is a god."

And now we must leave John Barclay for the moment, to explain why Neal Dow Ward, son of General Philemon Ward, made his first formal call at the Barclays'. It cannot be gainsaid that young Mr. Ward, aged twenty-one, a senior at Ward University, felt a tingle in his blood that day when he met Miss Jeanette Barclay, aged eighteen, and home for the spring vacation from the state university; and seeing her for the first time with her eyes and her hair and her pretty, strong, wide forehead poking through the cocoon of gawky girlhood, created a distinct impression on young Mr. Ward.

But in all good faith it should be stated that he did not make his first formal call at the Barclays' of his own accord; for his sister, Elizabeth Cady Stanton Ward, took him. She came home from the Culpeppers' just before supper, laughing until she was red in the face. And what she heard at the Culpeppers', let her tell in her own way to the man of her heart. For Lizzie was her father's child; the four other Ward girls, Mary Livermore, Frances Willard, Belva Lockwood, and Helen Gougar, had climbed to the College Heights and had gone to Ward University, and from that seat of learning had gone forth in the world to teach school. Elizabeth Cady Stanton Ward had remained in the home, after her mother's death filling her mother's vacant place as well as a daughter may.

"Well, father," said the daughter, as she was putting the evening meal on the table, addressing the general, who sat reading by the window in the dining room, "you should have been at the Culpeppers' when the colonel came home and told us his troubles. It seems that Nellie McHurdie is going to make Watts run for sheriff--for sheriff, father. Imagine Watts heading a posse, or locking any one up! And Watts has passed the word to the colonel, and he has passed it to Molly and me, and I am to see Mrs. Barclay, and she is to see Mrs. Carnine to-morrow morning, and they are all to set to work on Nellie and get her to see that it won't do. Poor Watts--the colonel says he is terribly wrought up at the prospect."

The general folded his paper and smiled as he said: "Well, I don't know; Watts was a brave soldier. He would make a good enough sheriff; but I suppose he doesn't really care for it."

"Why, no, of course not, father--why should he?" asked the daughter. "Anyhow, I want you to make Neal go down to Barclays' with me to-night to talk it over with Jane. Neal," she called to the young man who was sitting on the porch with his book on his knee, "Neal, I want you to go to Barclays' with me to-night. Come in now, supper's ready."

And so it happened that Neal Dow Ward made his first call on Jeanette Barclay with his sister, and they all sat on the porch together that fine spring evening, with the perfume of the lilacs in the air; and it happened naturally enough that the curious human law of attraction which unites youth should draw the chairs of the two young people together as they talked of the things that interest youth--the parties and the ball-games and the fraternities and sororities, and the freshman picnic and the senior grind; while the chairs of the two others drew together as they talked of the things which interest women in middle life--the affairs of the town, the troubles of Watts McHurdie, the bereavement of the Culpeppers, the scarcity of good help in the kitchen, the popularity of Max Nordau's "Social Evolution," and the fun in "David Harum." Nor is it strange that after the girl had shown the boy her Pi Phi pin, and he had shown her his Phi Delta shield, they should fall to talking of the new songs, and that they should slip into the big living room of the Barclay home, lighted by the electric lamps in the hall, and that she should sit down to the piano to show him how the new song went. And if the moonlight fell across the piano, and upon her face as she sang the little Irish folk-song, all in minors, with her high, trembling, half-formed notes in the upper register, and if she flushed and looked up abashed and had to be teased to go on,--not teased a great deal, but a little,--will you blame the young man if he forgot for a moment that her father was worth such a lot of money, and thought only that she was a beautiful girl, and said so with his eyes and face and hands in the pretty little pause that followed when she ceased singing? And if to hide her confusion when her heart knew what he thought, she put one foot on the loud pedal of the piano and began singing "O Margery, O Margery," and he sang with her, and if they thrilled just a little as their voices blended in the rollicking song--what of it? What of it? Was it not natural that lilacs should grow in April? Was it not natural that Watts McHurdie should dread the white light that beats upon the throne of the sheriff's office? Was it not natural that he should turn to women for protection against one of their sex, and that the women plotting for him should have a boy around and having a boy around where there is a girl around, and spring around and lilacs around and a moon and music and joy around,--what is more natural in all this world than that in the fire struck by the simple joy of youth there should be the flutter of unseen wings around, and when the two had finished singing, with something passing between their hearts not in the words, what is more natural than that the girl, half frightened at the thrill in her soul, should say timidly:--

"I think they will miss us out there--don't you?" as she rose from the piano.

And if you were a boy again, only twenty-one, to whom millions of money meant nothing, would you not catch the blue eyes of the girl as she looked up at you, in the twilight of the big room, and answer, "All right, Jeanette"? Certainly if you had known a girl all your life, you would call her by her first name, if her father were worth a billion, and would you not continue, emboldened some way by not being frowned upon for calling her Jeanette, though she would have been astonished if you had said Miss Barclay--astonished and maybe a little fearful of your sincerity--would you not continue, after a little pause, repeating your words, "All right, Jeanette--I suppose so--but I don't care--do you?" as you followed her through the door back to the moon-lit porch?

And as you walked home, listening to your elder sister, would you not have time and inclination to wonder from what remote part of this beautiful universe, from what star or what fairy realm, that creature came, whose hair you pulled yesterday, whose legs seem to have been covered with long skirts in the twinkling of an eye, and whose unrelated features by some magic had sloughed off, leaving a beautiful face? Would you not think these things, good kind sir, when you were twenty-one--even though to-day they seem highly improbable thoughts for any one to have who was not stark mad? But if we were not all stark mad sometimes, how would the world go round? If we were not all mad sometimes, who would make our dreams come true? How would visions
in thin air congeal into facts, how would the aspirations of the race make history? And if we were all sane all the time, how would the angels ever get babies into the world at all, at all?

CHAPTER XXII

"Speaking of lunatics," said Mr. Dolan to Mr. Hendricks one June
night, a few weeks after the women had persuaded Mrs. McHurdie not to
drag the poet into politics,--"speaking of lunatics, you may remember
that I was born in Boston, and 'twas my duty as a lad to drive the
Cambridge car, and many a time I have heard Mr. Holmes the poet and
Mr. Emerson the philosopher discussing how the world was made; whether
it was objective or subjective,--which I take it to mean whether the
world is in the universe or only in your eye. One fine winter night we
were waiting on a switch for the Boston car, when Mr. Holmes said to
Mr. Emerson: 'What,' says he, 'would you think if Jake Dolan driving
this car should come in and say, "Excuse me, gentlemen, but the moon I
see this moment is not some millions of miles away, but entirely in my
own noddle?"' 'I'd think,' says the great philosopher, never blinking,
'that Mr. Dolan was drunk,' says he. And there the discussion ended,
but it has been going on in my head ever since. Here I am a man
climbing up my sixties, and when have I seen the moon? Once walking by
this very creek here trying to get me courage up to put me arm around
her that is now Mary Carnine; once with me head poked up close to the
heads of Watts McHurdie, Gabe Carnine, and Philemon Ward, serenading
the girls under the Thayer House window the night before we left for
the army. And again to-night, sitting here on the dam, listening to
the music coming down the mill-pond. Did you notice them, Robert--the
young people--Phil Ward's boy, and John Barclay's girl, and Mary
Carnine's oldest, and Oscar Fernald's youngest, with their guitars and
mandolins, piling into the boats and rowing up stream? And now they're
singing the songs we sang--to their mothers, God bless 'em--the
other day before these children were born or thought of, and now I sit
here an old man looking at the moon."

"But is it the moon?" he went on after a long silence, puffing at his pipe. "If the moon is off there, three or thirty or three hundred million miles away in the sky, where has it been these forty years? I've not seen it. And yet here she pops out of my memory into my eye, and if I say the moon has always been in my eye, and is still in my eye, Mr. Ralph Waldo Emerson says I'm drunk. But does that settle the question of who's got the moon--me or the cosmos--as the poets call it?" After that the two men smoked in silence, and as Hendricks threw away the butt of his cigar, Dolan said, "'Tis a queer, queer world, Robert--a queer, queer world."

Now do not smile at Mr. Dolan, gentle reader, for Adam must have thought the same thing, and philosophy has been able to say nothing more to the point.

It is indeed a queer, queer world, and our blindness is the queerest thing in it. Here a few weeks, later sit John and Jane Barclay on the terrace before their house one June night, listening to singing on the water. Suddenly they realize that there is youth in the world--yet there has been singing on the mill-pond ever since it was built. It has been the habitat of lovers for a quarter of a century, this mill-pond, yet Jane and John Barclay have not known it, and not until their own child's voice came up to them, singing "Juanita," did they realize that the song had not begun anew after its twenty years' silence in their own hearts, but always had been on the summer breeze. And this is strange, too, considering how rich and powerful John Barclay is and how by the scratch of his pen, he might set men working by the thousands for some righteous cause. Yet so it is; for with all the consciousness of great power, with all the feeling of unrestraint that such power gives a man, driving him to think he is a kind of god, John Barclay was only a two-legged man, with a limp in one foot, and a little mad place in his brain, wherein he kept the sense of his relation to the rest of this universe. And as he sat, blind to the moon, dreaming of a time when he would control Presidents and dominate courts if they crossed his path, out on the mill-pond under an elm tree that spread like a canopy upon the water, a boy, letting the oars hang loosely, was playing the mandolin to a girl--a pretty girl withal, blue as to eyes, fair as to hair, strong as to mouth and chin, and glorious as to forehead--who leaned back in the boat, played with the overhanging branches, and listened and looked at the moon, and let God's miracle work unhindered in her heart. And all up and down those two miles of mill-pond were other boats and other boys and other maidens, and as they chatted and sang and sat in the moonlight, there grew in their hearts, as quietly as the growing of the wheat in the fields, that strange marvel of life, that keeps the tide of humanity ceaselessly flowing onward. And it is all so simply done before our eyes, and in our ears, that we forget it is so baffling a mystery.

Now let us project our astral bodies into the living room of the Barclay home, while Mr. and Mrs. John Barclay are away in Boston, and only John Barclay's mother and his daughter are in Sycamore Ridge; and let us watch a young man of twenty-one and a young woman of eighteen dispose of a dish of fudge together. Fudge, it may be explained to the unsophisticated, is a preparation of chocolate, sugar, and cream, cooked, cooled, and cut into squares. As our fathers and mothers pulled taffy, as our grandfathers and grandmothers conjured with maple sugar, and as their parents worked the mysterious spell with some witchery of cookery to this generation unknown, so is fudge in these piping times the worker of a strange witchery. Observe: Through a large room, perhaps forty feet one way and twenty-five feet the other way, flits a young woman in the summer twilight. She goes about humming, putting a vase in place here, straightening a picture there, kicking down a flapping rug, or rearranging a chair; then she sits down and turns on an electric light and pretends to read. But she does not read; the light shows her something else in the room that needs attention, and she turns to that. Then she sits down again, and again goes humming about the room. Suddenly the young woman rises and hurries out of the room, and a footstep is heard on the porch, outside. A bell tinkles, and a maid appears, and--

"Yes," she says. "I'll see if Miss Jeanette is at home!"

And then a rustle of skirts is heard on the stairway and Miss Jeanette enters with: "Why, Neal, you are an early bird this evening--were you afraid the worm would escape? Well, it won't; it's right here on the piano."

The young man's eyes,--good, clear, well-set, dark eyes that match his brown hair; eyes that speak from the heart,--note how they dwell upon every detail of the opposing figure, caressing with their shy surreptitious glances the girl's hair, her broad forehead, her lips; observe how they flit back betimes to those ripe red lips, like bees that hover over a flower trembling in the wind; how the eyes of the young man play about the strong chin, and the bewitching curves of the neck and shoulders, and rise again to the hair, and again steal over the face, to the strong shoulders, and again hurry back to the face lest some feature fade. This is not staring--it is done so quickly, so furtively, so deftly withal as the minutes fly by, while the lips and the teeth chatter on, that the stolen honey of these glances is stored away in the heart's memory, all unknown to him who has gathered it.

An hour has passed now, while we have watched the restless eyes at their work, and what has passed with the hour? Nothing, ladies and gentlemen--nothing; gibber, chatter, giggles, and squeals--that is all. Grandma Barclay above stairs has her opinion of it, and wonders how girls can be so addle-pated. In her day--but who ever lived long enough or travelled far enough or inquired widely enough to find one single girl who was as wise, or as sedate, or as industrious, or as meek, or as gentle, or as kind as girls were in her grandmother's day? No wonder indeed that grandmothers are all married--for one could hardly imagine the young men of that day overlooking such paragons of virtue and propriety as lived in their grandmothers' days. Fancy an old maid grandmother with all those qualities of mind and heart that girls had in their grandmothers' days!

So the elder Mrs. Barclay in her room at the top of the stairs hears what "he said," "he said he said," and what "she said she said," and what "we girls did," and what "you boys ought to do," and what "would be perfectly lovely," and what "would be a lot of fun!" and so grandmother, good soul, grows drowsy, closes her door, and goes to bed. She does not know that they are about to sit down together on a sofa--not a long, straight, cold, formal affair, but a small, rather snuggly sofa, with the dish between them. No, girls never did that in their grandmothers' days, so of course who would imagine they would do so now? Who, indeed? But there they are, and there is the dish between them, and two hands reaching into the same dish, must of course collide. Collision is inevitable, and by carefully noting the repetitions of the collisions, one may logically infer that the collisions are upon the whole rather pleasurable than otherwise; and when it comes to the last piece of fudge in the dish,--the very last piece,--the astral observer will see that there is just the slightest, the very slightest, quickest, most fleeting little tussle of hands for it, and much laughter; and then the young woman rises quickly--also note the slight pink flush in her cheeks, and she goes to her chair and folds her pretty hands in her lap, and asks:--

"Well, do you like my fudge, Neal Ward? Is it as good as Belva Lockwood's? She puts nuts in hers--I've eaten it; do you like it with nuts in it?"

"Not so well as this," says the boy.

The girl slips into the dining room, for a glass of water. See the eyes
of the youth following her. It is dusky in the dining room, and the
youth longs for dusky places, but has not developed courage enough to
follow her. But he has courage enough to steady his eyes as she comes
back with the water, so that he can look into her blue eyes while you
would count as much as one--two--three--slowly--four--slowly--five. A
long, long time, so long indeed that she wishes he would look just a
second longer.

So at the end of the evening here stand Neal, and Jeanette, even as
Adam and Eve stood in the garden, talking of nothing in particular as
they slowly move toward the door. "Yes, I suppose so," she says, as
Eve said and as Eve's daughters have said through all the centuries,
looking intently at the floor. And then Neal, suddenly finding the
language of his line back to Adam, looks up to say, "Oh, yes, I
forgot--but have you read 'Monsieur Beaucaire'?" Now Adam said, "Have
you heard the new song that the morning stars are singing together?"
and Priam asked Helen if she would like to hear that new thing of
Solomon's just out, and so as the ages have rolled by, young gentlemen
standing beside their adored but not declared ones have mixed
literature with love, and have tied wisdom up in a package of candy or
wild honey, and have taken it to the trysting place since the
beginning of time. It is thus the poets thrive. And when she was asked
about the new song of the morning stars, Eve, though she knew it as
she knew her litany, answered no; and so did Eve's daughter, standing
in the dimly lighted hallway of the Barclay home in Sycamore Ridge;
and so then and there being, these two made their next meeting sure.

In those last years of the last century John Barclay became a powerful
man in this world--one of the few hundred men who divided the
material kingdoms of this earth among them. He was a rich man who was
turning his money into great political power. Senates listened to him,

many courts were his in fee simple, because he had bought and paid for the men who named the judges; Presidents were glad to know what he thought, and when he came to the White House, reporters speculated about the talk that went on behind the doors of the President's room, and the stock market fluttered. If he desired a law, he paid for it and got it--not in a coarse illegal way, to be sure, but through the regular conventional channels of politics, and if he desired to step on a law, he stepped on it, and a court came running up behind him, and legalized his transaction. He sneered at reformers, and mocked God, did John Barclay in those days. He grew arrogant and boastful, and strutted in his power like a man in liquor with the vain knowledge that he could increase the population of a state or a group of states, or he could shrivel the prosperity of a section of the country by his whim. For by changing a freight rate he could make wheat grow, where grass had nourished. By changing the rate again, he could beckon back the wilderness. And yet, how small was his power; here beside him, cherished as the apple of his eye, was his daughter, a slip of a girl, with blue eyes and fair hair, whose heart was growing toward the light, as the hearts of young things grow, and he, with all of his power, could only watch the mystery, and wonder at it. He was not displeased at what he saw. But it was one of the few things in his consciousness over which he could find no way to assume control. He stood in the presence of something that came from outside of his realm and ignored him as the sun and the rain and the simple processes of nature ignored him.

"Jane," he said one night, when he was in the Ridge for the first time in many weeks, a night near the end of the summer when Jeanette and Neal Ward were vaguely feeling their way together, "Jane, mother says that while we've been away Neal Ward has been here pretty often. You don't suppose that--"

"Well, I've rather wondered about it myself a little," responded Jane.

"Neal is such a fine handsome young fellow."

"But, Jane," exclaimed Barclay, impatiently, as he rose to walk the rug, "Jennie is only a child. Why, she's only--"

"Nineteen, John--she's a big girl now."

"I know, dear," he protested, "but that's absurdly young. Why--"

"Yes," she answered, "I was nearly twenty when I was engaged to you, and Jennie's not engaged yet, nor probably even thinking seriously of it."

"Don't you think," cried Barclay, as he limped down the diagonal of the rug, "that you should do something? Isn't it a little unusual? Why--"

"Well, John," smiled the wife, "I might do what mother did: turn the young man over to father!" Barclay laughed, and she went on patiently: "It's not at all unusual, John, even if they do--that is, if they are--you know; but they aren't, and Jennie is too much in love with her work at school to quit that. But after all it's the American way; it was the way we did, dear, and the way our mothers and fathers did, and unless you wish to change it--to Europeanize it, and pick--"

"Ah, nonsense, Jane--of course I don't want that! Only I thought some way, if it's serious she ought to--Oh, don't you know she ought to--"

Mrs. Barclay broke her smile with, "Of course she ought to, dear, and so ought I and so ought mother when she married father and so ought my grandmother when she married grandpa--but did we? Dear, don't you see the child doesn't realize it? If it is anything, it is growing in her heart, and I wouldn't smudge it for the world, by speaking to her now--unless you don't like Neal; unless you think he's too--unless you want a different boy. I mean some one of consequence?"

"Oh, no, it isn't that, Jane--it isn't that. Neal's all right; he's clean and he is honest--I asked Bob Hendricks about him to-day, when we passed the boy chasing news for the *Banner*, and Bob gives him a fine name." Barclay threw himself into a chair and sighed. "I suppose it's just that I feel Jeanette's kind of leaving us out of it--that is all."

Jane went to him and patted his head gently, as she spoke: "That is nature, dear--the fawn hiding in the woods; we must trust to Jennie's good sense, and the good blood in Neal. My, but his sisters are proud of him! Last week Lizzie was telling me Neal's wages had been increased to ten dollars a week--and I don't suppose their father in all of his life ever had that much of a steady income. The things the family is planning to do with that ten dollars a week brought tears of joy to my eyes. Neal's going to have his mother-in-law on his side, anyway--just as you had yours. I know now how mother felt."

But John Barclay did not know how mother felt, and he did not care. He knew how father felt--how Lycurgus Mason felt, and how the father of Mrs. Lycurgus Mason felt; he felt hurt and slighted, and he could not repress a feeling of bitterness toward the youth. All the world loves a daughter-in-law, but a father's love for a son-in-law is an acquired taste; some men never get it. And John Barclay was called away the next morning to throttle a mill in the San Joaquin Valley, and from there he went to North Dakota to stop the building of a competitive railroad that tapped his territory; so September came, and with it Jeanette Barclay went back to school. The mother wondered what the girl would do with her last night at home. She was clearly nervous and unsettled all the afternoon before, and made an errand into town and

came back with a perturbed face. But after dinner the mother heard
Jeanette at the telephone, and this is the one-sided dialogue the
mother caught: "Yes--this is Miss Barclay." "Oh, yes, I didn't
recognize your voice at first." "What meeting?" "Yes--yes." "And they
are not going to have it?" "Oh, I see." "You were--oh, I don't know.
Of course I should have felt--well, I--oh, it would have been all
right with me. Of course." Then the voice cheered up and she said:
"Why, of course--come right out. I understand." A pause and then,
"Yes, I know a man has to go where he is called." "Oh, she'll
understand--you know father is always on the wing." "No--why, no, of
course not--mother wouldn't think that of you. I'll tell her how it
was." "All right, good-by--yes, right away." And Jeanette Barclay
skipped away from the telephone and ran to her mother to say, "Mother,
that was Neal Ward--he wants to come out, and he was afraid you'd
think it rude for him to ask that way, but you know he had a meeting
to report and thought he couldn't come, and now they've postponed the
meeting, and I told him to come right out--wasn't that all right?"

And so out came Neal Ward, a likely-looking young man of twenty-one or
maybe twenty-two--a good six feet in height, with a straight leg, a
square shoulder, and firm jaw, set like his father's, and clean brown
eyes that did not blink. And as Jeanette Barclay, with her mother's
height, and her father's quick keen features, and her Grandmother
Barclay's eyes and dominant figure, stood beside him in the doorway,
Mrs. Jane Barclay thought a good way ahead, and Jeanette would have
blushed her face to a cinder if the mother had spoken her thoughts.
The three, mother and daughter and handsome young man, sat for a while
together in the living room, and then Jane, who knew the heart of
youth, and did not fear it, said, "You children should go out on the
porch--it's a beautiful night; I'm going upstairs."

And now let us once more in our astral bodies watch them there in the
light of the veiled moon--for it is the last time that even we should

see them alone. She is sitting on a balustrade, and he is standing beside her, and their hands are close together on the stones. "Yes," he is saying, "I shall be busy at the train to-morrow trying to catch the governor for an interview on the railroad question, and may not see you."

"I wish you would throw the governor into the deep blue sea," she says, and he responds:--

"I wish I could." There is a silence, and then he risks it--and the thing he has been trying to say comes out, "I wonder if you will do something for me, Jeanette?"

"Oh, I don't know--don't ask me anything hard--not very hard, Neal!"

The last word was all he cared for, and by what sleight of hand he slipped his fraternity pin from his vest into her hand, neither ever knew.

"Will you?" he asks. "For me?"

She pins it at her throat, and smiles. Then she says, "Is this long enough--do you want it back now?"

He shakes his head, and finally she asks, "When?" and then it comes out:--

"Never."

And her face reddens, and she does not speak. Their hands, on the wall, have met--they just touch, that is all, but they do not hasten apart. A long, long time they are silent--an eternity of a minute; and then she says, "We shall see in the morning."

And then another eternal minute rolls by, and the youth slips the rose from her hair--quickly, and without disarranging a strand.

"Oh," she cries, "Neal!" and then adds, "Let me get you a pretty one--that is faded."

But no, he will have that one, and she stands beside him and pins it on his coat--stands close beside him, and where her elbows and her arms touch him he is thrilled with delight. In the shadow of the great porch they stand a moment, and her hand goes out to his.

"Well, Jeanette," he says, and still her hand does not shrink away, "well, Jeanette--it will be lonesome when you go."

"Will it?" she asks.

"Yes--but I--I have been so happy to-night."

He presses her hand a little closer, and as she says, "I'm so glad," he says, "Good-by," and moves down the broad stone steps. She stands watching him, and at the bottom he stops and again says:--

"Well--good-by--Jeanette--I must go--I suppose." And she does not move, so again he says, "Good-by."

               *   *   *   *   *

"Youth," said Colonel Martin Culpepper to the assembled company in the ballroom of the Barclay home as the clock struck twelve and brought in the twentieth century; "Youth," he repeated, as he tugged at the bottom of Buchanan Culpepper's white silk vest, to be sure that it met his own black trousers, and waved his free hand grandly aloft;

"Youth," he reiterated, as he looked over the gay young company at the foot of the hall, while the fiddlers paused with their bows in the air, and the din of the New Year's clang was rising in the town; "Youth,--of all the things in God's good green earth,--Youth is the most beautiful." Then he signalled with some dignity to the leader of the orchestra, and the music began.

It was a memorable New Year's party that Jeanette Barclay gave at the dawn of this century. The Barclay private car had brought a dozen girls down from the state university for the Christmas holidays, and then had made a recruiting trip as far east as Cleveland and had brought back a score more of girls in their teens and early twenties--for an invitation from the Barclays, if not of much social consequence, had a power behind it that every father recognized. And what with threescore girls from the Ridge, and young men from half a dozen neighbouring states,--and young men are merely background in any social picture,--the ballroom was as pretty as a garden. It was her own idea,--with perhaps a shade of suggestion from her father,--that the old century should be danced out and the new one danced in with the pioneers of Garrison County set in quadrilles in the centre of the floor, while the young people whirled around them in the two-step then in vogue. So the Barclays asked a score or so of the old people in for dinner New Year's Eve; and they kept below stairs until midnight. Then they filed into the ballroom, with its fair fresh faces, its shrill treble note of merriment,--these old men and women, gray and faded, looking back on the old century while the others looked into the new one. There came Mr. and Mrs. Watts McHurdie in the lead, Watts in his best brown suit, and Mrs. Watts in lavender to sustain her gray hair; General Ward, in his straight black frock coat and white tie, followed with Mrs. Dorman, relict of the late William Dorman, merchant, on his arm; behind him came the Brownwells, in evening clothes, and Robert Hendricks and his sister,--all gray-haired, but straight of figure and firm of foot; Colonel Culpepper followed with

Mrs. Mary Barclay; the Lycurgus Masons were next in the file, and in
their evening clothes they looked withered and old, and Lycurgus was not
sure upon his feet; Jacob Dolan in his faded blue uniform marched in
like a drum-major with the eldest Miss Ward; and the Carnines followed,
and the Fernalds followed them; and then came Judge and Mrs. Bemis--he a
gaunt, sinister, parchment-skinned man, with white hair and a gray
mustache, and she a crumbling ruin in shiny satin bedecked in diamonds.
Down the length of the long room they walked, and executed an
old-fashioned grand march, such as Watts could lead, while the orchestra
played the tune that brought cheers from the company, and the little old
man looked at the floor, while Mrs. McHurdie beamed and bowed and
smiled. And then they took their partners to step off the
quadrille--when behold, it transpired that in all the city orchestra,
that had cost the Barclays a thousand dollars according to town
tradition, not one man could be found who could call off a quadrille.
Then up spake John Barclay, and stood him on a chair, and there, when
the colonel had signalled for the music to start, the voice of John
Barclay rang out above the din, as it had not sounded before in nearly
thirty years. Old memories came rushing back to him of the nights when
he used to ride five and ten and twenty miles and play the cabinet organ
to a fiddle's lead, and call off until daybreak for two dollars. And
such a quadrille as he gave them--four figures of it before he sent them
to their seats. There were "cheat or swing," the "crow's nest," "skip to
my Loo,"--and they all broke out singing, while the young people clapped
their hands, and finally by a series of promptings he quickly called the
men into one line and the women into another, and then the music
suddenly changed to the Virginia reel. And so the dance closed for the
old people, and they vanished from the room, looking back at the youth
and the happiness and warmth of the place with wistful but not eager
eyes; and as Jacob Dolan, in his faded blues and grizzled hair and
beard, disappeared into the dusk of the hallway, Jeanette Barclay,
looking at her new ring, patted it and said to Neal Ward: "Well, dear,
the nineteenth century is gone! Now let us dance and be happy in this

one."

And so she danced the new year and the new century and the new life in, as happy as a girl of twenty can be. For was she not a Junior at the state university, if you please? Was she not the heir of all the ages, and a scandalous lot of millions besides, and what is infinitely more important to a girl's happiness, was she not engaged, good and tight, and proud of it, to a youth making twelve dollars every week whether it rained or not? What more could an honest girl ask? And it was all settled, and so happily settled too, that when she had graduated with her class at the university, and had spent a year in Europe--but that was a long way ahead, and Neal had to go to the City with father and learn the business first. But business and graduation and Europe were mere details--the important thing had happened. So when it was all over that night, and the girls had giggled themselves to bed, and the house was dark, Jeanette Barclay and her mother walked up the stairs to her room together. There they sat down, and Jeanette began--

"Neal said he told you about the ring?"

"Yes," answered her mother.

"But he did not show it to you--because he wanted me to be the first to see it."

"Neal's a dear," replied her mother. "So that was why? I thought perhaps he was bashful."

"No, mother," answered the girl, "no--we're both so proud of it." She kept her hand over the ring finger, as she spoke, "You know those 'Short and Simple Annals' he's been doing for the *Star*--well, he got his first check the day before Christmas, and he gave half of it to his father, and took the other twenty-five dollars and bought this ring. I think it is so pretty, and we are both real proud of it." And then she took her hand from the ring, and held her finger out for her mother's eyes, and her mother kissed it. They were silent a moment; then the girl rose and stood with her hand on the doorknob and cried: "I think it is the prettiest ring in all the world, and I never want any other." Then she thought of mother, and flushed and ran away.

And we should not follow her. Rather let us climb Main Street and turn into Lincoln Avenue and enter the room where Martin Culpepper sits writing the Biography of Watts McHurdie. He is at work on his famous chapter, "Hymen's Altar," and we may look over his great shoulder and see what he has written: "The soul caged in its prison house of the flesh looks forth," he writes, "and sees other chained souls, and hails them in passing like distant ships. But soul only meets soul in some great passion of giving, whether it be man to his fellow-man, to his God, or in the love of men and women; it matters not how the ecstasy comes, its root is in sacrifice, in giving, in forgetting self and merging through abnegation into the source of life in this universe for one sublime moment. For we may not come out of our prison houses save to inhale the air of heaven once or twice, and then go scourged back to our dungeons. Great souls are they who love the most, who breathe the deepest of heaven's air, and give of themselves most freely."

CHAPTER XXIII

The next morning, before the guests were downstairs, Barclay, reading his morning papers before the fireplace, stopped his daughter, who was going through the living room on some morning errand.

"Jeanette," said the father, as he drew her to his chair arm, "let me see it."

She brought the setting around to the outside of her finger, and gave him her hand. He looked at it a moment, patted her hand, put the ring to his lips, and the two sat silent, choked with something of joy and something of sorrow that shone through their brimming eyes. Thus Mary Barclay found them. They looked up abashed, and she bent over them and stroked her son's hair as she said:--

"John, John, isn't it fine that Jennie has escaped the curse of your millions?"

Barclay's heart was melted. He could not answer, so he nodded an assenting head. The mother stooped to kiss her son's forehead, as she went on, "Not with all of your millions could you buy that simple little ring for Jennie, John." And the father pressed his lips to the ring, and his daughter snuggled tightly into his heart and the three mingled their joy together.

Two hours later Barclay and General Ward met on the bridge by the mill. It was one of those warm midwinter days, when nature seems to be listening for the coming of spring. A red bird was calling in the woods near by, and the soft south wind had spring in it as it blew across the veil of waters that hid the dam. John Barclay's head was full of music, and he was lounging across the bridge from the mill on his way home to try his new pipe organ. He had spent four hours the day before at his organ bench, trying to teach his lame foot to keep up with his strong foot. So when General Ward overhauled him, Barclay was annoyed. He was not the man to have his purposes crossed, even when they were whims.

"I was just coming over to the mill to see you," said the general, as he halted in Barclay's path.

"All right, General--all right; what can I do for you?"

The general was as blunt a man as John Barclay. If Barclay desired no beating around the bush, the general would go the heart of matters. So he said, "I want to talk about Neal with you."

Barclay knew that certain things must be said, and the two men sat in a stone seat in the bridge wall, with the sun upon them, to talk it out then and there. "Well, General, we like Neal--we like him thoroughly. And we are glad, Jane and I, and my mother too--she likes him; and I want to do something for him. That's about all there is to say."

"Yes, but what, John Barclay--what?" exclaimed the general. "That's what I want to know. What are you going to do for him? Make him a devil worshipper?"

"Well now, General, here--don't be too fast," Barclay smiled and drawled. He put his hands on the warm rocks at his sides and flapped them like wing-tips as he went on: "Jeanette and Neal have their own lives to live. They're sensible--unusually sensible. We didn't steal Neal, any more than you stole Jeanette, General, and--"

"Oh, I understand that, John; that isn't the point," broke in the general. "But now that you've got him, what are you going to do with him? Can't you see, John, he's my boy, and that I have a right to know?"

"Now, General, will you let me do a little of this talking?" asked

Barclay, impatiently. "As I was saying, Jeanette and Neal are sensible, and money isn't going to make fools of them. When the time comes and I'm gone, they'll take the divine responsibility--"

"The divine tommyrot!" cried the general; "the divine fiddlesticks! Why should they? What have they done that they should have that thrust upon them like a curse; in God's name, John Barclay, why should my Neal have to have that blot upon his soul? Can't they be free and independent?"

Barclay did not answer; he looked glumly at the floor, and kicked the cement with his heel. "What would you have them do with the money when they get it," he growled, "burn it?"

"Why not?" snapped the general.

"Oh--I just thought I'd ask," responded Barclay.

The two men sat in silence. Barclay regarded conversation with the general in that mood as arguing with a lunatic. Presently he rose, and stood before Ward and spoke rather harshly: "What I am going to do is this--? and nothing more. Neal tells me he understands shorthand: I know the boy is industrious, and I know that he is bright and quick and honest. That's all he needs. I am going to take him into our company as a stockholder--with one share--a thousand-dollar share, to be explicit; I'm going to give that to him, and that's all; then he's to be my private secretary for three years at five thousand a year, so long as you must know, and then at the end of that time, if he and Jennie are so minded, they're going to marry; and if he has any business sense--of course you know what will happen. She is all we have, General--some one's got to take hold of things."

As Barclay spoke General Ward grew white--his face was aquiver as his trembling voice cried out: "Oh, God, John Barclay, and would you take my boy--my clean-hearted, fine-souled boy, whom I have taught to fear God, and callous his soul with your damned money-making? How would you

like me to take your girl and blacken her heart and teach her the wiles of the outcasts? And yet you're going to teach Neal to lie and steal and cheat and make his moral guide the penal code instead of his father's faith. Shame on you, John Barclay--shame on you, and may God damn you for this thing, John Barclay!" The old man trembled, but the sob that shook his frame had no tears in it. He looked Barclay in the eyes without a tremor for an angry moment, and then broke: "I am an old man, John; I can't interfere with Neal and Jeanette; it's their life, not mine, and some way God will work it out; but," he added, "I've still got my own heart to break over it--that's mine--that's mine."

He rose and faced the younger man a moment, and then walked quickly away. Barclay limped after him, and went home. There he sat on his bench and made the great organ scream and howl and bellow with rage for two hours.

When Neal Ward went to the City to live, he had a revelation of John Barclay as a man of moods. The Barclay Neal Ward saw was an electric motor rather than an engine. The power he had to perceive and to act seemed transmitted to him from the outside. At times he dictated letters of momentous importance to the young man, which Neal was sure were improvised. Barclay relied on his instincts and rarely changed a decision. He wore himself out every day, yet he returned to his work the next day without a sign of fag. The young man found that Barclay had one curious vanity--he liked to seem composed. Hence the big smooth mahogany table before him, with the single paper tablet on it, and the rose--the one rose in the green vase in the centre of the table. Visitors always found him thus accoutred. But to see him limping about from room to room, giving orders in the great offices, dictating notes for the heads of the various departments, to see him in the room where the mail was received, worrying it like a pup, was to see another man revealed. He liked to have people from Sycamore Ridge call upon him, and the man who kept door in the outer office--a fine gray-haired person, who had the manners of a brigadier--knew so many people in Sycamore Ridge that Neal used to call him the City Directory. One day Molly Brownwell called. She was the only person who ever quelled the brigadier; but when a woman has been a social leader in a country town all of her life, she has a social poise that may not be impressed by a mere brigadier. Mrs. Brownwell realized that her call was unusual, but she refused to acknowledge it to him. Barclay seemed glad to see her, and as he was in one of his mellow moods he talked of old times, and drew from a desk near the wall, which he rarely opened, an envelope containing a tintype picture of Ellen. Culpepper. He showed it to her sister, and they both sat silent for a time, and then the woman spoke.

"Well, John," she said, "that was a long time ago."

"Forty years, Molly--forty years."

When they came back to the world she said: "John, I am up here looking for a publisher. Father has written a Biography of Watts, and collected all of his poems and things in it, and we thought it might sell--Watts is so well known. But the publishers won't take it. I want your advice about it."

Barclay listened to her story, and then wheeled in his chair and exclaimed, "Can Adrian publish that book?"

"Yes," she answered tentatively; "that is, he could if it didn't take such an awful lot of money."

After discussing details with her, Barclay called Neal Ward and said:--

"Get up a letter to Adrian Brownwell asking him to print for me three thousand copies of the colonel's book, at one dollar and fifty cents a copy, and give seventy-five per cent of the profits to Colonel Culpepper. We'll put that book in every public library in this country. How's that?" And he looked at the tintype and said, "Bless her dear little heart."

"Neal," asked Barclay, as Mrs. Brownwell left the room, "how old are you? I keep forgetting." When the young man answered twenty-five, Barclay, who was putting away the tintype picture, said, "And Jeanette will be twenty-three at her next birthday." He closed the desk and looked at the youth bending over his typewriter and sighed. "Been going together off and on five or six years--I should say."

Neal nodded. Barclay put his hand on his chin and contemplated the young man a moment. "Ever have any other love affair, son?"

The youngster coloured and looked up quickly with a puzzled look and did not reply.

Barclay cut in with, "Well, son, I'm glad to find you don't lie easily." He laughed silently. "Jennie has--lots of them. When she was six she used to cry for little Watts Fernald, and they quarrelled like cats and dogs, and when she was ten there was an Irish boy--Finnegan I think his name was--who milked the cow, whom she adored, and when she was fourteen or so, it was some boy in the high school who gave her candy until her mother had to shoo him off, and I don't know how many others." He paused for a few seconds and then went on, "But she's forgotten them--that's the way of women." His eyes danced merrily as he continued, while he scratched his head: "But with us men--it's different. We never forget." He chuckled a moment, and then his face changed as he said, "Neal, I wish you'd go into the mail room and see if the noon mail has anything in it from that damn scoundrel who's trying to start a cracker factory in St. Louis--I hate to bother to smash him right now when we're so busy."

But it so happened that the damn scoundrel thought better of his intention and took fifty thousand for his first thought, and Neal Ward, being one of the component parts of an engaged couple, went ahead being sensible about it. All engaged couples, of course, resolve to be sensible about it. And for two years and a half--during nineteen one and two and part of nineteen three--Jeanette Barclay and Neal Ward had tried earnestly and succeeded admirably (they believed) in being exceedingly sensible about everything. Jeanette had gone through school and was spending the year in Europe with her mother, and she would be home in May; and in June--in June of 1904--why, the almanac stopped there; the world had no further interest, and no one on earth could imagine anything after that. For then they proposed not to be sensible any longer.

In the early years of this century--about 1902, probably--John Barclay paid an accounting company twenty-five thousand dollars--more money than General Ward and Watts McHurdie and Martin Culpepper and Jacob Dolan had saved in all their long, industrious, frugal, and useful lives--to go over his business, install a system of audits and accounts, and tell him just how much money he was worth. After a score of men had been working for six months, the accounting company made its report. It was put in terms of dollars and cents, which are fleeting and illusive terms, and mean much in one country and little in another, signify great wealth at one time and mere affluence in another period. So the sum need not be set down here. But certain

interesting details of the report may be set down to illuminate this
narrative. For instance, it indicates that John Barclay was a man of
some consequence, when one knows that he employed more men in that
year than many a sovereign state of this Union employed in its state
and county and city governments. It signifies something to learn that
he controlled more land growing wheat than any of half a dozen
European kings reign over. It means something to realize that in those
years of his high tide John Barclay, by a few lines dictated to Neal
Ward, could have put bread out of the reach of millions of his
fellow-creatures. And these are evidences of material power--these
men he hired, these lands he dominated, and this vast store of food
that he kept. So it is fair to assume that if this is a material
world, John Barclay's fortune was founded upon a rock. He and his
National Provisions Company were real. They were able to make laws;
they were able to create administrators of the law; and they were able
to influence those who interpreted the law. Barclay and his power were
substantial, palpable, and translatable into terms of money, of power,
of vital force.

And then one day, after long years of growth in the
under-consciousnesses of men, an idea came into full bloom in the
world. It had no especial champions. The people began to think this
idea. That was all. Now life reduced to its lowest terms consists of
you and him and me. Put us on a desert island together--you and him
and me--and he can do nothing without you and me--except he kill us,
and then he is alone; even then we haunt him, so our influence still
binds him. You can do nothing without him and me, and I can do nothing
without you and him. Not that you and he will hold me; not that you
will stop me; but what you think and say will bind me to your wishes
tighter than any chains you might forge. What you and he think is more
powerful than all the material forces of this universe. For what you
and he think is public opinion. It is not substantial; it is not
palpable. It may not readily be translated into terms of money, or

power, or vital force. But it crushes all these things before it. When this public opinion rises sure and firm and strong, no material force on this earth can stop it. For a time it may be dammed and checked. For a day or a week or a year or a decade it may be turned from its channel; yet money cannot hold it; arms cannot hold it; cunning cannot baffle it. For it is God moving among men. Thus He manifests Himself in this earth. Through the centuries, amid the storm and stress of time, often muffled, often strangled, often incoherent, often raucous and inarticulate with anguish, but always in the end triumphant, the voice of the people is indeed the voice of God!

Nearly a dozen years had passed since the Russian painted the picture of John Barclay, which hangs in the public library of Sycamore Ridge, and in that time the heart of the American people had changed. Barclay was beginning to feel upon him, night and day, the crushing weight of popular scorn. He called the idea envy, but it was not envy. It was the idea working in the world, and the weight of the scorn was beginning to crumple his soul; for this idea that the people were thinking was finding its way into newspapers, magazines, and books. They were beginning to question the divine right of wealth to rule, because it was wealth--an idea that Barclay could not comprehend even vaguely. The term honest wealth, which was creeping into respectable periodicals, was exceedingly annoying to him. For the very presence of the term seemed to indicate that there was such a thing as dishonest wealth,--an obvious absurdity; and when he addressed the students of the Southwestern University at their commencement exercises in 1902, his address attracted considerable attention because it deplored the modern tendency in high places toward socialism and warned the students that a nation of iconoclasts would perish from the earth. But the people went on questioning the divine right of wealth to rule. In the early part of 1903 Barclay was astounded at the action of a score of his senators and nearly a hundred of his congressmen, who voted for a national law prohibiting the giving of railroad rebates. He was assured by all of them that it was done to satisfy temporary agitation, but the fact that they voted for the law at all, as he explained to Senator Myton, at some length and with some asperity, was a breach of faith with "interests in American politics which may not safely be ignored." "And what's more," he added angrily, "this is a personal insult to me. That law hits my Door Strip."

And then out of the clear sky like a thunderbolt, not from an enemy, not from any clique or crowd he had fought, but from the government itself, during the last days of Congress came a law creating a Department of Commerce and Labour at Washington, a law giving federal inspectors the right to go through books of private concerns. Barclay was overwhelmed with amazement. He raged, but to no avail; and his wrath was heated by the rumours printed in all the newspapers that Barclay and the National Provisions Company were to be the first victims of the new law. Mrs. Barclay and Jeanette were going to Europe in the spring of 1903, and Barclay on the whole was glad of it. He wished the decks cleared for his fight; he felt that he must not have Jane at his elbow holding his hand from malice in the engagement that was coming, and when he left them on the boat, he spent a week scurrying through the East looking for some unknown enemy in high financial circles who might be back of the government's determination to move against the N.P.C. He felt sure he could uncover the source of his trouble--and then, either fight his enemy or make terms. It did not occur to Barclay that he could not find a material, palpable, personal object upon which to charge or with which to capitulate. But he found nothing, and crossed the Alleghanies puzzled.

When he got home, he learned that a government inspector, one H. S. Smith, was beginning the investigation of the Provisions Company's books in St. Paul, Omaha, Chicago, and Denver. Barclay learned that Smith had secured some bills of lading that might not easily be explained. Incidentally, Barclay learned that an attempt had been made, through proper channels, to buy Smith, and he was nonplussed to learn that Smith was not purchasable. Then to end the whole matter, Barclay wrote to Senator Myton, directing him to have Smith removed immediately. But Myton's reply, which was forwarded to Barclay at Sycamore Ridge, indicated that "the orders under which Smith is working come from a higher source than the department."

Barclay's scorn of Inspector Smith--a man whom he could buy and sell a dozen times from one day's income from his wealth--flamed into a passion. He tore Myton's letter to bits, and refreshed his faith in the god of Things As They Are by garroting a mill in Texas. While the Texas miller was squirming, Barclay did not consider Inspector Smith consciously, but in remote places in his mind always there lived the scorned person whom Barclay knew was working against him.

From time to time in the early summer the newspapers contained definite statements, authorized from Washington with increasing positiveness, that the cordon around the N.P.C. was tightening. In July Barclay's scorn of Inspector Smith grew into disquietude; for a letter from Judge Bemis, of the federal court,--written up in the Catskills,--warned him that scorn was not the only emotion with which he should honour Smith. After reading Bemis' confidential and ambiguous scrawl, Barclay drummed for a time with his hard fingers on the mahogany before him, stared at the print sketches of machinery above him, and paced the floor of his office with the roar of the mill answering something in his angry heart. He could not know that the tide was running out. He went to his telephone and asked for a city so far away that when he had finished talking for ten minutes, he had spent enough money to keep General Ward in comfort for a month. Neal Ward, sitting in his room, heard Barclay say: "What kind of a damn bunco game were you fellows putting up on me in 1900? You got my money; that's all right; I didn't squeal at the assessment, did I?" Young Ward in the pause closed his door. But the bull-like roar of

Barclay came through the wood between them in a moment, and he heard: "Matter enough--here's this fellow Smith bullying my clerks out in Omaha, and nosing around the St. Paul office; what right has he got? Who is he, anyway--who got him his job? I wrote to Myton to get him removed, or sent to some other work, and Myton said that the White House was back of him. I wish you'd go over to Washington, and tell them who I am and what we did for you in '96 and 1900; we can't stand this. It's a damned outrage, and I look to you to stop it." In a moment Ward heard Barclay exclaim: "You can't--why, that's a hell of a note! What kind of a fellow is he, anyway? Tell him I gave half a million to the party, and I've got some rights in this government that a white man is bound to respect--or does he believe in taking your money and letting you whistle?" A train rolling by the mill drowned Barclay's voice, but at the end of the conversation Ward heard Barclay say: "Well, what's a party good for if it doesn't protect the men who contribute to its support? You simply must do it. I look to you for it. You got my good money, and it's up to you to get results."

There was some growling, and then Barclay hung up the receiver. But he was mad all day, and dictated a panic interview to Ward, which Ward was to give to the Associated Press when they went to Chicago the next day. In the interview, Barclay said that economic conditions were being disturbed by half-baked politicians, and that values would shrink and the worst panic in the history of the country would follow unless the socialistic meddling with business was stopped.

The summer had deepened to its maturest splendour before Barclay acknowledged to himself his dread of the City. For he began to feel a definite discomfiture at the panorama of his pictures on the news-stands in connection with the advertising of the Sunday newspapers and magazines. The newspapers were blazoning to the whole country that the Economy Door Strip was a blind for taking railroad rebates, and everywhere he met the report of Inspector Smith that the

National Provisions Company's fifty-pound sack of Barclay's Best contained but forty-eight pounds and ten ounces; also that Barclay had been taking three ounces out of the pound cartons of breakfast food, and that the cracker packages were growing smaller, while the prices were not lowered. Even in Sycamore Ridge the reporters appeared with exasperating regularity, and the papers were filled with diverting articles telling of the Barclays' social simplicity and rehashing old stories of John Barclay's boyhood. His attempt to stop the investigation of the National Provisions Company became noised around Washington, and the news of his failure was frankly given out from the White House. This inspired a cartoon from McCutcheon in the *Chicago Tribune*, representing the President weighing a flour sack on which was printed "Barclay's Worst," with Barclay behind the President trying to get his foot on the scales.

All of his life Barclay had been a fighter; he liked to hit and dodge or get hit back. His struggles in business and in the business part of politics had been with tangible foes, with material things; and his weapons had been material things: coercion, bribery (more or less sugar-coated), cheating, and often in these later years the roar of his voice or the power of his name. But now, facing the formless, impersonal thing called public opinion, hitherto unknown in his scheme of things, he was filled with uncertainty and indecision.

One autumn day, after sending three stenographers home limp and weary with directions for his battles, Barclay strayed into McHurdie's shop. The general and Dolan were the only members of the parliament present that afternoon, besides Watts. Barclay nodded at the general without speaking, and Dolan said:--

"Cool, ain't it? Think it will freeze?"

Barclay took a chair, and when Dolan and Ward saw that he had come for a visit, they left.

"Watts," asked Barclay, after the others had gone, and the little man at the bench did not speak, "Watts, what's got into the people of this country? What have I done that they should begin pounding me this way?"

McHurdie turned a gentle smile on his visitor, knowing that Barclay would do the talking. Barclay went on: "Here are five suits in county courts in Texas against me; a suit in Kansas by the attorney-general, five or ten in the Dakotas, three in Nebraska, one or two in each of the Lake states, and the juries always finding against me. I haven't changed my methods. I'm doing just what I've done for fifteen years. I've had lots of lawsuits before, with stockholders and rival companies and partners, and millers and all that--but this standing in front of the mob and fighting them off--why? Why? What have I done? These county attorneys and attorneys-general seem to delight in it--now why? They didn't used to; it used to be that only cranks like old Phil Ward even talked of such things, and people laughed at them; and now prosecuting attorneys actually do these things, and people reelect them. Why? What's got into the people? What am I doing that I haven't been doing?"

"Maybe the people are growing honest, John," suggested the harness maker amiably.

Barclay threw back his head and roared: "Naw--naw--it isn't that; it's the damn newspapers. That's what it is! They're what's raising the devil. But why? Why? What have I done? Why, they have even bulldozed some of my own federal judges--my own men, Watts, my own men; men whose senators came into my office with their hats in their hands and asked permission to name these judges. Now why?" He was silent awhile and then began chuckling: "But I fixed 'em the other day. Did you see that article in all the papers briefed out of New York about how that professor had said that the N.P.C. was an economic necessity? I did that, Watts: and got it published in the magazines, too--and our advertising agents made all the newspapers that get our advertising print it--and they had to." Barclay laughed. After a moody silence he continued: "And you know what I could do. I could finance a scheme to buy out the meat trust and the lumber trust, and I could control every line of advertising that goes into the damn magazines--and I could buy the paper trust too, and that would fix 'em. The Phil Wards are not running this country yet. The men who make the wealth and maintain the prosperity have got to run it in spite of the long-nosed reformers and socialists. You know, Watts, that we men who do things have a divine responsibility to keep the country off the rocks. But she's drifting a lot just now, and they're all after me, because I'm rich. That's all, Watts, just because I've worked hard and earned a little money--that's why." And so he talked on, until he was tired, and limped home and sat idly in front of his organ, unable to touch the keys.

Then he turned toward the City to visit his temporal kingdom. There in the great Corn Exchange Building his domain was unquestioned. There in the room with the mahogany walls he could feel his power, and stanch the flow of his courage. There he was a man. But alas for human vanity! When he got to the City, he found the morning papers full of a story of a baby that had died from overeating breakfast food made at his mills and adulterated with earth from his Missouri clay banks, as the coroner had attested after an autopsy; and a miserable county prosecutor was looking for John Barclay. So he hid all the next day in his offices, and that evening took Neal Ward on a special train in his private car, on a roundabout way home to Sycamore Ridge.

It was a wretched homecoming for so great and successful a man as Barclay. Yet he with all his riches, with all his material power, even he longed for the safety of home, as any hunted thing longs for his lair. On the way he paced the diagonals of the little office room in his car, like a caged jackal. The man had lost his anchor; the things which his life had been built on would not hold him. Money--men envied the rich nowadays, he said, and the rich man had no rights in the courts or out of them; friends--they had gone up in the market, and he could not afford them; politics--he had found it a quicksand. So he jabbered to Neal Ward, his secretary, and pulled down the curtains of his car on the station side of every stop the train made in its long day's journey.

CHAPTER XXIV

It was nearly midnight when the special train pulled into Sycamore Ridge, and Neal Ward hurried home. He went to his room, and found there a letter and a package, both addressed in Jeanette's handwriting. The letter was only a note that read:--

"MY DEAREST BOY: I could not wait to send it for your Christmas present. So I am sending it the very day it is finished. I hope it will bring me close to you--into your very heart and keep me there. I have kissed it--for I knew that you would.

"Your loving JEANETTE."

He tore open the package and found a miniature of Jeanette done on ivory--that seemed to bring her into the room, and illumine it with her presence. The thing bloomed with life, and his heart bounded with joy as his eyes drank the beauty of it. His father called from below stairs, and the youth went down holding the note and the miniature in his hands. Before the father could speak, the son held out the picture, and Philemon Ward looked for a moment into the glowing faces--that of the picture and that of the living soul before him, and hesitated before speaking.

"I got your wire--" he began.

"But isn't it beautiful, father--wonderful!" broke in the son.

The father assented kindly and then continued: "So I thought I'd sit up for you. I had to talk with you." The son's face looked an interrogation, and the father answered, "Read that, Neal--" handing his son a letter in a rich linen envelope bearing in the corner the indication that it was written at the Army and Navy Club in Washington. The lovely face in the miniature lay on the table between them and smiled up impartially at father and son as the young man drew out the letter and read:--

"MY DEAR GENERAL WARD: This letter will introduce to you Mr. H. S. Smith, an inspector from the Bureau of Commerce and Labour, who has been working upon evidence connected with the National Provisions Company. I happened to be at luncheon this afternoon with a man of the highest official authority, whose name it would be bad faith to divulge, but whom I know you respect, even if you do not always agree with him. I mentioned your name and the part you took in the battle of the Wilderness, and my friend was at once interested, though, of course, he had known you by name and fame for forty years. One word led to another, as is usual in these cases, and my friend mentioned the fact that your son, Neal Dow Ward, is secretary to John Barclay, and in a position to verify certain evidence which the government now has in the N.P.C. matter. I happen to know that the government is exceedingly anxious to be exactly correct in every charge it makes against this Company, and hence I am writing to you. Your son can do a service to his country to-day by telling the truth when he is questioned by Inspector Smith, to my mind as important as that you did in the Wilderness. Inspector Smith has a right to question him, and will do so, and I have promised my friend here to ask you to counsel with your son, and beg him in the name of that good citizenship for which you have always stood, and for which you offered your life, to tell the simple truth. As a comrade and a patriot, I have no doubt what you will do, knowing the facts."

Neal Ward put his hand on the table, with the letter still in his fingers. "Father," he asked blankly, "do you know what that means?"

"Yes, Neal, I think I understand; it means that to-morrow morning will decide whether you are a patriot or a perjurer, my boy--a patriot or a perjurer!" The general, who was in his shirt-sleeves and collarless, rose, and putting his hands behind him, backed to the radiator to warm them.

"But, father--father," exclaimed the boy, "how can I? What I learned was in confidence. How can I?"

The father saw the anguish in his son's face, and did not reply at once. "Is it crooked, Neal?"

"Yes," replied the son, and then added: "So bad I was going to get out of it, as soon as Jeanette came home. I couldn't stand it--for a life, father. But I promised to stay three years, and try, and I think I should keep my promise."

The father and son were silent for a time, and then the father spoke. "And you love her with all your life--don't you, Nealie?" The son was gazing intently at the miniature and nodded. At length the father sighed. "My poor, poor boy--my poor, poor boy." He walked to the table on which were his books and papers, and then stood looking at the girl's face. "You couldn't explain it to her, I suppose?" he asked.

"No," replied the son. "No; she adores her father; to her he is perfect. And I don't blame her, for he is good--you can't know how good, to her." Again they stood in silence. The son looked up from the picture and said, "And you know, father, what the world would think of me--a spy, an informer--an ingrate?"

The old man did not reply, and the son shook his head and his face twitched with the struggle that was in him. Suddenly the father walked to the son and cried: "And yet you must, Neal Ward--you must. Is there any confidence in God's world so sacred as your duty to mankind? Is there any tie, even that of your wife, so sacred as that which binds you to humanity? I left your mother, my sweetheart, and went out to fight, with the chance of never seeing her again. I went out and left her for the same country that is calling you now, Neal!" The boy looked up with agony on his face. The father paused a moment and then went on: "Your soul is your soul--not John Barclay's, my boy--not Jeanette Barclay's--but yours--yours, Neal, to blight or to cherish, as you will." A moment later he added, "Don't you see, son--don't you see, Neal?" The son shook his head and looked down, and did not answer. The father put his arm about the son. "Boy, boy," he cried, "boy, you've got a a man's load on you now--a man's load. To-morrow you can run away like a coward; you can dodge and lie like a thief, or you can tell the simple truth, as it is asked of you, like a man--the simple truth like a man, Neal."

"Yes, I know, father--I see it all--but it is so hard--for her sake, father."

The old man was silent, while the kitchen clock ticked away a minute and then another and a third. Then he took his arm away from his son, and grasped the boy's hand. "Oh, little boy--little boy," he cried, "can't I make you see that the same God who has put this trial upon you will see you through it, and that if you fail in this trial, your soul will be crippled for life, and that no matter what you get in return for your soul--you will lose in the bargain? Can't you see it, Nealie--can't you see it? All my life I have been trying to live that way, and I have tried to make you see it--so that you would be ready for some trial like this."

The son rose, and the two men stood side by side, clasping hands. The boy suddenly tore himself loose, and throwing his hands in the air, wailed, "Oh, God--it is too hard--I can't, father--I can't."

And with the miniature in his hand he walked from the room, and Philemon Ward went to his closet and wrestled through the night. At dawn his son sat reading and re-reading a letter. Finally he pressed another letter to his lips, and read his own letter again. It read:--

"MY DARLING GIRL: This is the last letter I shall ever mail to you, perhaps. I can imagine no miracle that will bring us together again. My duty, as I see it, stands between us. The government inspector is going to put me under oath to-morrow--unless I run, and I won't--and question me about your father's business. What I must tell will injure him--maybe ruin him. I am going to tell your father what I am going to do before I do it. But by all the faith I have been taught in a God--and you know I am not pious, and belong to no church--I am forced to do this thing. Oh, Jeanette, Jeanette--if I loved you less, I would take you for this life alone and sell my soul for you; but I want you for an eternity--and in that eternity I want to bring you an unsoiled soul. Good-by--oh, good-by. NEAL."

The next morning when Neal Ward went out of the office at the mill, John Barclay sat shivering with wrath and horror. Every second stamped him with its indelible finger, as a day, or a month, puts its stain on other men.

Another morning, a week later, as he sat at his desk, a telegram from his office manager in the city fluttered in his hands. It read: "We are privately advised that you were indicted by the federal grand jury last night--though we do not know upon what specific charge--our friend B. will advise us later in the day."

It was a gray December day, and a thin film of ice covered the mill-pond. Barclay looked there and shuddered away from the thought that came to him. He was alone in the mill. He longed for his wife and daughter, and yet when he thought of their homecoming to disgrace, he shook with agony. Over and over again he whispered the word "indicted." The thought of his mother and her sorrow broke him down. He locked the door, dropped heavily into his chair, and bowed his head on his crossed arms. And then--

What, tears? Tears for Mr. Barclay?--for himself? Look back along the record for his life: there are many tears charged to his account, but none for his own use. Back in the seventies there are tears of Miss Culpepper, charged to Mr. Barclay, and one heart-break for General Hendricks. Again in the eighties there is sorrow for Mr. Robert Hendricks, and more tears for Mrs. Brownwell, that was Miss Culpepper--all charged to the account of Mr. Barclay; and in the early nineties there are some manly tears for Martin F. Culpepper, also charged to Mr. Barclay--but none before for his own use. Are they, then, tears of repentance? No, not tears for the recording angel, not good, man's size, soul-washing tears of repentance, but miserable, dwarf, useless, self-pitying, corroding tears--tears of shame and rage, for the proud, God-mocking, man-cheating, powerful, faithless, arrogant John Barclay, dealer in the Larger Good.

And so with his head upon his arms, and his arms upon his desk,--a gray-clad, gray-haired, slightly built, time-racked little figure,--John Barclay strained his soul and wrenched his body and tried in vain to weep.

CHAPTER XXV

Down comes the curtain. Only a minute does John Barclay sit there with his head in his arms, and then, while you are stretching your legs, or reading your programme, or looking over the house to see who may be here, up rises John Barclay, and while the stage carpenters are setting the new scene, he is behind there telephoning to Chicago, to Minneapolis, to Omaha, to Cleveland, to Buffalo,--he fairly swamps the girl with expensive long-distance calls,--trying to see if there is not some way to stop the filing of that indictment. For to him the mere indictment advertises to mankind that money is not power, and with him and with all of his caste and class a confession of weakness is equivalent to a confession of wrong. For where might makes right, as it does in his world, weakness spells guilt, and with all the people jeering at him, with the press saying: "Aha, so they have got Mr. Barclay, have they? Well, if all his money and all his power could not prevent an indictment, he must be a pretty tough customer,"--with the public peering into his private books and papers in a lawsuit, confirming as facts all that they had read in the newspapers, in short with the gold plating of respectability rubbed off his moral brass, he feels the crushing weight of the indictment, as he limps up and down his room at the mill and frets at the long-distance operator for being so slow with his calls.

But he is behind the scenes now; and so is Neal Ward, walking the streets of Chicago, looking for work on a newspaper, and finally finding it. And so are Mrs. Jane Barclay and Miss Barclay, as they sail away on their ten days' cruise of the Mediterranean. And while the orchestra plays and the man in the middle of row A of the dress circle edges out of his seat and in again, we cannot hear John Barclay sigh when the last telephone call is answered, and he finds that nothing can be done. And he is not particularly cheered by the knowledge that the Associated Press report that very afternoon is sending all over the world the story of the indictment. But late in the afternoon Judge Bemis, in whose court the indictment was found, much to his chagrin, upon evidence furnished by special counsel sent out from Washington--Judge Bemis tells him, as from one old friend to another, that the special counsellor isn't much of a lawyer. The pleasant friendly little rip-saw laugh of the judge over the telephone nearly a thousand miles away is not distinct enough to be heard across the stage even if the carpenters were not hammering, and the orchestra screaming, and the audience buzzing; but that little laugh of his good friend, Judge Bemis, was the sweetest sound John Barclay had heard in many a day. It seemed curious that he should so associate it, but that little laugh seemed to drown the sound of a clicking key in a lock--a large iron lock, that had been rattling in his mind since noon. For even in the minds of the rich and the great, even in the minds of men who fancy they are divinely appointed to parcel out to their less daring brethren the good things of this world, there is always a child's horror of the jail. So when Mr. Barclay, who was something of a lawyer himself, heard his good friend, Judge Bemis, laugh that pleasant little friendly laugh behind the scenes, the heart of Mr. Barclay gave a little pulse-beat of relief if not of joy.

But an instant later the blight of the indictment was over him again. Hammer away, and scream away, and buzz away with all your might, you noises of the playhouse; let us not hear John Barclay hastening across the bridge just before the early winter sunset comes, that he may intercept the **Index** and the **Banner** in the front yard of the Barclay home, before his mother sees them. Always heretofore he has been glad to have her read of his achievements, in the hope that she would come to approve them, and to view things as he saw them--his success and his power and his glory. But to-night he hides the paper under his gray coat and slips into the house. She and her son sit down to dinner alone. This must be a stage dinner they are eating--though it is all behind the scenes; for Mr. Barclay is merely going through the empty form of eating. "No, thank you," for the roast. "Why, Mr. Barclay did not touch his soup!" "Well," says the cook, tasting it critically, "that's strange." And "No, thank you" for the salad, and "Not any pie to-night, Clara." "What--none of the mince pie, John? Why, I went out in the kitchen and made it for you myself." "Well, a little."

Heigh-ho! We sigh, and we drum on our table-cloth with our fingers, and we are trying to find some way to tell something. We have been a bad boy, maybe--a bad little boy, and must own up; that is part of our punishment--the hardest part perhaps, even with the curtain down, even with the noise in front, even with the maid gone, even when a mother comes and strokes our head, as we sit idly at the organ bench, unable to sound a key. Shall the curtain go up now? Shall we sit gawking while a boy gropes his way out of a man's life, back through forty years, and puts his head in shame and sorrow against a mother's breast? How he stumbles and falters and halts, as the truth comes out--and it must come out; on the whole the best thing there is to say of John Barclay on that fateful December day in the year of our Lord 1903 is that he did not let his mother learn the truth from any lips but his. And so it follows naturally, because he was brave and kind, that instead of having to strengthen her, she sustained him--she in her seventies, he in his fifties.

"My poor dear child," she said, "I know--I know. But don't worry, John--don't worry. I don't mind. Jane won't mind, I am sure, and I know Jennie will understand. It isn't what even we who love you think of you, John--it is what you are that counts. Oh, Johnnie, Johnnie, maybe you could serve your country and humanity in jail--by showing the folly and the utter uselessness of all this money-getting, just as your father served it by dying. I would not mind if it made men see that money isn't the thing--if it made you see it, my boy; if you could come out of a jail with that horrible greed for money purged from you--"

But no--we will not peep behind the curtain; we will not dwell with John Barclay as he walked all night up and down the great living room of his home. And see, the footlights have winked at the leader of the orchestra, to let him know he is playing too long; observe, how quickly the music dies down--rather too quickly, for the clatter of cast iron is heard on the stage, and the sound of hurried footsteps is audible, as of some one moving rapidly about behind the curtain. The rattling iron you hear is the stove in Watts McHurdie's shop; they have just set it up, and got it red hot; for it is a cold day, that fifteenth day of December, 1903, and the footsteps you hear are those of the members of the harness shop parliament.

Ah! There goes the curtain, and there sits Watts astraddle of his bench, working with all his might, for he has an order to sew sleigh-bells on a breast strap, for some festivity or another; and here sits the colonel, and over there the general, and on his home-made chair Jacob Dolan is tilted back, warming his toes at the stove. They are all reading--all except Watts, who is working; on the floor are the Chicago and St. Louis evening papers, and the Omaha and

Kansas City morning papers. And on the first pages of all of these papers are pictures of John Barclay. There is John Barclay in the *Bee*, taken in his Omaha office by the *Bee's* own photographer--a new picture of Mr. Barclay, unfamiliar to the readers of most newspapers. It shows the little man standing by a desk, smiling rather benignly with his sharp bold eyes fixed on the camera. There is a line portrait of Mr. Barclay in the *Times*, one of recent date, showing the crow's-feet about the eyes, the vertical wrinkle above the nose, and the furtive mouth, hard and naked, and the square mean jaw, that every cartoonist of Barclay has emphasized for a dozen years. And there are other pictures of Mr. Barclay in the papers on the floor, and the first pages of the papers are filled with the news of the Barclay indictment. All over this land, and in Europe, the news of that indictment caused a sensation. In the *Times*, there on the floor, is an editorial comment upon the indictment of Barclay cabled from London, another from Paris, and a third from Berlin. It was a big event in the world, an event of more than passing note--this sudden standing up of one of the richest men of his land, before the front door of a county jail. Big business, and little business that apes big business, dropped its jaw. The world is not accustomed to think of might making wrong, so when a Charles I or a Louis XVI or a John Barclay comes to harm, the traditions of the world are wrenched. Men say: "How can these things be--if might makes right? Here is a case where might and right conflict--how about it? Jails are for the poor, not for the rich, because the poor are wrong and the rich are right, and no just man made perfect by a million should be in jail."

And so while the members of the parliament in Watts McHurdie's shop read and were disturbed at the strange twist of events, the whole world was puzzled with them, and in unison with Jacob Dolan, half the world spoke, "I see no difference in poisoning breakfast foods and poisoning wells, and it's no odds to me whether a man pinches a few ounces out of my flour sack, or steals my chickens."

And the other half of the world was replying with Colonel Culpepper, "Oh, well, Jake, now that's all right for talk; but in the realms of high finance men are often forced to be their own judges of right and wrong, and circumstances that we do not appreciate, cannot understand, in point of fact, nor comprehend, if I may say so, intervene, and make what seems wrong in small transactions, trivial matters and pinch-penny business, seem right in the high paths of commerce."

The general was too deeply interested in reading what purported to be his son's testimony before Commissioner Smith, to break into the discussion at this point, so Dolan answered, "From which I take it that you think that Johnnie down at the mill keeps a private God in his private car."

The colonel was silent for a time; he read a few lines and looked into space a moment, and then replied in a gentle husky voice: "Jake, what do we know about it? The more I think how every man differs from his neighbour, and all our sins are the result of individual weakness at the end of lonely struggles with lonely temptations--the more I think maybe there is something in what you say, and that not only John but each of us--each of us under this shining sun, sir--keeps his private God."

"You'll have to break that news gently to the Pope," returned Dolan. "I'll not try it. Right's right, Mart Culpepper, and wrong's wrong for me and for Johnnie Barclay, white, black, brown, or yellow--'tis the same."

"There's nothing in your theory, Mart," cut in the general, folding his paper across his knee; "not a thing in the world. We're all parts of a whole, and the only way this is an individual problem at all--this working out of the race's destiny--is that the whole can't

improve so long as the parts don't grow. So long as we all are like
John Barclay save in John's courage to do wrong, laws won't help us
much, and putting John in jail won't do so very much--though it may
scare the cowards until John's kind of crime grows unpopular. But what
we must have is individual--"

Tinkle goes the bell over Watts McHurdie's head--the bell tied to a
cord that connects with the front door. Down jumps Watts, and note the
play of the lights from the flies, observe that spot light moving
toward R. U. E., there by the door of the shop. Yes, all ready; enter
John Barclay. See that iron smile on his face; he has not surrendered.
He has been clean-shaven, and entering that door, he is as spick and
span as though he were on a wedding journey. Give him a hand or a hiss
as you will, ladies and gentlemen, John Barclay has entered at the
Right Upper Entrance, and the play may proceed.

"Well," he grinned, "I suppose you are talking it over. Colonel, has
the jury come to a verdict yet?"

What a suave John Barclay it was; how admirably he held his nerve; not
a quiver in the face, not a ruffle of the voice. The general looked at
him over his spectacles, and could not keep the kindness out of his
eyes. "What a brick you are!" he said to himself, and Jake Dolan,
conquered by the simplicity of it, surrendered.

"Oh, well, John, I suppose we all have our little troubles," said
Jake. Only that; the rack of the inquisitor grew limp. And Colonel
Culpepper rose and gave Barclay his hand and spoke not a word. The
silence was awkward, and at the end of a few moments the colonel found
words.

"How," he asked in his thick asthmatic voice, mushy with emotion, "how
in the world did this happen, John? How did it happen?"

Barclay looked at the general; no, he did not glare, for John Barclay had grown tame during the night, almost docile, one would say. But he did not answer at first, and Watts McHurdie, bending over his work, chuckled out: "Ten miles from Springfield, madam--ten miles from Springfield." And then John sloughed off thirty years and laughed. And the general laughed, and the colonel smiled, and Jake Dolan took John Barclay's hand from the colonel, and said:--

"The court adjudges that the prisoner at the bar pay the assembled company four of those cigars in his inside pocket, and stand committed until the same is paid."

And then there was a scratching of matches, and a puffing, and Barclay spoke: "I knew there was one place on earth where I was welcome. The mill is swarming with reporters, and I thought I'd slip away. They'll not find me here." The parliament smoked in silence, and again Barclay said, "Well, gentlemen, it's pretty tough--pretty tough to work all your life to build up an industry and in the end--get this."

"Well, John," said the general, as he rolled up his newspaper and put it away, "I'm sorry--just as sorry as Mart is; not so much for the indictment, that is all part of the inevitable consequence of your creed; if it hadn't been the indictment, it would have been something else, equally sad--don't you see, John?"

"Oh, I know what you think, General," retorted Barclay, bitterly. "I know your idea; you think it's retribution."

"Not exactly that either, John--just the other side of the equation. You have reaped what you sowed, and I am sorry for what you sowed. God gave you ten talents, John Barclay--ten fine talents, my boy, and you wrapped them in a napkin and buried them in the ground, buried them in

greed and cunning and love of power, and you are reaping envy and
malice and cruelty. You were efficient, John; oh, if I had been as
efficient as you, how much I could have done for this world--how
much--how much!" he mused wistfully.

Barclay did not reply, but his face was hard, and his neck was stiff,
and he was not moved. He was still the implacable Mr. Barclay, the
rich Mr. Barclay, and he would have no patronage from old Phil
Ward--Phil Ward the crank, who was a nation's joke. Ting-a-ling went
the bell over Watts McHurdie's head, and the little man climbed down
from his bench and hurried into the shop. But instead of a customer,
Mr. J. K. Mercheson, J. K. Mercheson representing Barber, Hancock, and
Kohn,--yes, the whip trust; that's what they call it, but it is
really an industrial organization of the trade,--Mr. J. K. Mercheson
of New York came in. No, McHurdie did not need anything at present,
and he backed into the shop. He had all of the goods in that line that
he could carry just now; and he sidled toward his seat. The members of
the parliament effaced themselves, as loafers do in every busy place
when business comes up; the colonel got behind his paper, Barclay hid
back of the stove, Dolan examined a bit of harness, and the general
busied himself picking up the litter on the floor, and folding the
papers with the pictures of Barclay inside so that he would not be
annoyed by them. But Mr. Mercheson knew how to get orders; he knew
that the thing to do is to stay with the trade.

So he leaned against the work bench and began:--

"This is a great town, Mr. McHurdie; we're always hearing from
Sycamore Ridge. When I'm in the East they say, 'What kind of a town is
that Sycamore Ridge where Watts McHurdie and your noted reformer,
Robert Hendricks, who was offered a place in the cabinet, and this man
John Barclay live?'"

Mr. Mercheson paused for effect. Mr. McHurdie smiled and went on with his work.

"Say," said Mr. Mercheson, "your man Barclay is in all the papers this morning. I was in the smoker of the sleeper last evening coming out of Chicago, and we got to talking about him--and Lord, how the fellows did roast him."

"They did?" asked Barclay, from his chair behind the stove.

"Sure," replied Mr. Mercheson; "roasted him good and brown. There wasn't a man in the smoker but me to stand up for him."

"So you stood up for the old scoundrel, did you?" asked Barclay.

"Sure," answered the travelling man. "Anything to get up an argument, you know," he went on, beginning to see which way sentiment lay in the shop. "I've been around town this morning, and I find the people here don't approve of him for a minute, any more than they did on the train."

"What do they say?" asked Barclay, braiding a four-strand whip, and finding that his cunning of nearly fifty years had not left his fingers.

"Oh, it isn't so much what they say--but you can tell, don't you know; it's what they don't say; they don't defend him. I guess they like him personally, but they know he's a thief; that's the idea--they simply can't defend him and they don't try. The government has got him dead to rights. Say," he went on, "just to be arguing, you know last evening I took a poll of the train--the limited--the Golden State Limited--swell train, swell crowd--all rich old roosters; and honest, do you know that out of one hundred and twenty-three votes polled only four were for him, and three of those were girls who said they knew his daughter at the state university, and had visited at his house. Wasn't that funny?"

Barclay laughed grimly, and answered, "Well, it was pretty funny considering that I'm John Barclay."

The suspense of the group in the shop was broken, and they laughed, too.

"Oh, hell," said Mr. Mercheson, "come off!" Then he turned to McHurdie and tried to talk trade to him. But Watts was obdurate, and the man soon left the shop, eying Barclay closely. He stood in the door and said, as he went out of the store, "Well, you do look some like his pictures, Mister."

There was a silence when the stranger went, and Barclay, whose face had grown red, cried, "Damn 'em--damn 'em all--kick a man when he is down!"

Again the bell tinkled, and McHurdie went into the shop. Evidently a customer was looking at a horse collar, for through the glass door they could see Watts' hook go up to the ceiling and bring one down.

"John," said the colonel, when Barclay had spoken, "John, don't mind it. Look at me, John--look at me! They had to put me in jail, you know; but every one seems to have forgotten it but me--and I am a dog that I don't."

John Barclay looked at the old, broken man, discarded from the playing-cards of life, with the hurt, surprised look always in his eyes, and it was with an effort that the suave Mr. Barclay kept the choke in his throat out of his voice as he replied:--

"Yes, Colonel, yes, I know I have no right to kick against the pricks."

Watts was saying: "Yes, he's in there now--with the boys; you better go in and cheer him up."

And then at the upper right-hand entrance entered Gabriel Carnine, president of the State Bank, unctuous as a bishop. He ignored the others, and walking to Barclay, put out his hand. "Well, well, John, glad to see you; just came up from the mill--I was looking for you. Couldn't find Neal, either. Where is he?"

The general answered curtly, "Neal is in Chicago, working on the *Record-Herald*."

"Oh," returned Carnine, and did not pursue the subject further. "Well, gentlemen," he said, "fine winter weather we're having."

"Is that so?" chipped in Dolan. "Mr. Barclay was finding it a little mite warm."

Carnine ignored Dolan, and Barclay grinned. "Well, John," Carnine hesitated, "I was just down to see you--on a little matter of business."

"Delighted, sir, delighted," exclaimed Dolan, as he rose to go; "we were going, anyway--weren't we, General?" The veterans rose, and Colonel Culpepper said as he went, "I told Molly to call for me here about noon with the buggy--if she comes, tell her to wait."

All of life may not be put on the stage, and this scene has to be cut; for it was at the end of half an hour's aimless, footless, foolish talk that Gabriel Carnine came to the business in hand. Round and round the bush he beat the devil, before he hit him a whack. Then he said, as if it had just occurred to him, "We were wondering--some of the directors--this morning, if under the circumstances--oh, say just for the coming six months or such a matter--it might not be wise to reorganize our board; freshen it up, don't you know; kind of get some new names on it, and drop the old ones--not permanently, but just to give the other stockholders a show on the board."

"So you want me to get off, do you?" blurted Barclay. "You're afraid of my name--now?"

The screams of Mr. Carnine, the protesting screams of that oleaginous gentleman, if they could have been vocalized in keeping with their muffled, low-voiced, whispering earnestness, would have been loud enough to be heard a mile away, but Barclay talked out:--

"All right, take my name off; and out comes my account. I don't care."

And thereupon the agony of Mr. Carnine was unutterable. If he had been a natural man, he would have howled in pain; as it was, he merely purred. But Barclay's skin was thin that day, sensitive to every touch, and he felt the rough hand of Carnine and winced. He let the old man whine and pur and stroke his beard awhile, and then Barclay said wearily, "All right, just as you please, Gabe--I'll not move my account. It's nothing to me."

In another minute the feline foot of Mr. Carnine was pattering gently toward the front door. Barclay sat looking at the stove, and Watts went on working. Barclay sighed deeply once or twice, but McHurdie paid no heed to him. Finally Barclay rose and went over to the bench.

"Watts," cried Barclay, "what do you think about it--you, your own self, what do you think way down in your heart?"

Watts sewed a stitch or two without speaking, and then put down his thread and put up his glasses and said, "That's fairly spoken, John Barclay, and will have a fair answer."

The old man paused; Barclay cried impatiently, "Oh, well, Watts, don't be afraid--nothing can hurt me much now!"

"I was just a-thinking, lad," said Watts, gently, "just a-thinking."

"What?" cried Barclay.

"Just a-thinking," returned the old man, as he put his hand on the younger man's shoulder, "what a fine poet you spoiled in your life, just to get the chance to go to jail. But the Lord knows His business, I suppose!" he added with a twinkle in his eye, "and if He thinks a poet more or less in jail would help more than one out--it is all for the best, John, all for the best. But, my boy," he cried earnestly, "if you'll be going to jail, don't whine, lad. Go to jail like a gentleman, John Barclay, go to jail like a gentleman, and serve your Lord there like a man."

"Damn cheerful you are, Watts," returned Barclay. "What a lot of Job's comforters you fellows have been this morning." He went on half bitterly and half jokingly: "Beginning with the general, continuing with your travelling salesman friend, and following up with Gabe, who wants me to get off the board of directors of his bank for the moral effect of it, and coming on down to you who bid me Godspeed to jail--I have had a--a--a rather gorgeous morning."

The door-bell tinkled, and a woman's voice called, "Father, father!"

"Yes, Molly," the harness maker answered; "he'll be here pretty soon. He said for you to wait."

"Come in, for heaven's sake, Molly," cried Barclay, "come back here and cheer me up."

"Oh, all right--it's you, John? What are you doing back here? I'm so glad to find you. I've just got the dearest letter from Jane. We won't talk business or anything--you know how I feel, and how sorry I am--so just let's read Jane's letter; it has something in it to cheer you. She said she was going to write it to you the next day--but I'll read it to you." And so Mrs. Brownwell took from her pocketbook the crumpled letter and unfolded it. "It's so like Jane--just good hard sense clear through." She turned the pages hastily, and finally the fluttering of the sheets stopped. "Oh, yes," she said, "here's the place--the rest she's told you. Let me see--Oh: 'And, Molly, what do you think?--there's a duke after Jeanette--a miserable, little, dried-up, burned-out, poverty-stricken Italian duke. And oh, how much good it did us both to cut him, and let him know how ill-bred we considered him, how altogether beneath any wholesome honest girl we thought such a fellow.' And now, John, isn't this like Jane?" interposed Mrs. Brownwell. "Listen; she says, 'Molly, do you know, I am so happy about Jeanette and Neal. We run such an awful risk with this money--such a horrible risk of unhappiness and misery for the poor child--heaven knows she would be so much happier without it. And to think, dear, that she has found the one in the world for her, in the sweet simple way that a girl should always find him, and that the money--the menacing thing that hangs like a shadow over her--cannot by any possibility spoil her life! It makes me happy all the day, and I go singing through life with joy at the thought that the money won't hurt Jennie--that it can't take from her the joy that comes from living with her lover all her life, as I have lived.' Isn't that fine, John?" asked Mrs. Brownwell, and looking up, she saw John Barclay, white-faced, with trembling jaw, staring in pain at the stove. Watts had gone into the store to wait on a customer, and the woman, seeing the man's anguish, came to him and said: "Why, John, what is it? How have I hurt you?--I thought this would cheer you so."

The man rose heavily. His colour was coming back. "Oh, God--God," he cried, "I needed that to-day--I needed that."

The woman looked at him, puzzled and nonplussed. "Why--why--why?" she stammered.

"Oh, nothing," he smiled back at her bitterly, "except--" and his jaw hardened as he snapped--"except that Neal Ward is a damned informer--and I've sent him about his business, and Jeanette's got to do the same."

Mollie Brownwell looked at him with hard eyes for a moment, and then asked, "What did Neal do?"

"Well," replied Barclay, "under cross-examination, I'll admit without incriminating myself that he gave the testimony which indicted me."

"Was it that or lie, John?" He did not reply. A silence fell, and the woman broke it with a cry: "Oh, John Barclay, John Barclay, must your traffic in souls reach your own flesh and blood? Haven't you enough without selling her into Egypt, too? Haven't you enough money now?" And without waiting for answer, Molly Brownwell turned and left him staring into nothing, with his jaw agape.

It was noon and a band was playing up the street, and as he stood by the stove in McHurdie's shop, he remembered vaguely that he had seen banners flying and some "Welcome" arches across the street as he walked through the town that morning. He realized that some lodge or conclave or assembly was gathering in the town, and that the band was a part of its merriment. It was playing a gay tune and came nearer and nearer. But as he stood leaning upon his chair, with his heart quivering and raw from its punishment, he did not notice that the band had stopped in front of the harness shop. His mind went back wearily to the old days, fifty years before, when as a toddling child in dresses he used to play on that very scrap-heap outside the back door, picking up bits of leather, and in his boyhood days, playing pranks upon the little harness maker, and braiding his whips for the town herd. Then he remembered the verses Watts had written about Bob Hendricks and him in that very room, and the music he and Watts had played together there. The old song Watts had made in his presence in the hospital at St. Louis came back to his mind. Did it come because outside the band had halted and was playing that old song to serenade Watts McHurdie? Or did it come because John Barclay was wondering if, had he made a poet of himself, or a man of spiritual and not of material power, it would have been better for him?

Heaven knows why the old tune came into his head. But when he recognized that they were serenading the little harness maker, and that so far as they thought of John Barclay and his power and his achievements, it was with scorn, he had a flash of insight into his relations with the world that illumined his soul for a moment and then died away. The great Mr. Barclay, alone, sitting in the dingy little harness shop, can hear the band strike up the old familiar tune again, and hear the crowd cheer and roar its applause at the little harness maker, who stands shamefaced and abashed, coatless and aproned, before the crowd. And he is only a poet--hardly a poet, would be a better way to say it; an exceedingly bad poet who makes bad rhymes, and thinks trite thoughts, and says silly and often rather stupid things, but who once had his say, and for that one hour of glorious liberty of the soul has moved millions of hearts to love him. John Barclay does not envy Watts McHurdie--not at all; for Barclay, with all his faults, is not narrow-gauged; he does not wish they would call for him--not to-day--not at all; he could not face them now, even if they cheered him. He says in his heart of pride, beneath his stiff neck, that it is all right; that Watts,--poor little church-mouse of a Watts, whom he could buy five times over with the money that has dropped into the Barclay till since he entered the shop--that Watts should have his due; but only--only--only--that is it--only, but only--!

CHAPTER XXVI

And now as we go out into the busy world, after this act in the dawning of John Barclay's life, let the court convene, and the reporters gather, and the honourable special counsel for the government rage, and the defendant sit nervous and fidgety as the honourable counsel reads the indictment; let the counsel for the defendant swell and strut with indignation that such indignities should be put upon honest men and useful citizens, and let the court frown, and ponder and consider; for that is what courts are for, but what do we care for it all? We have left it all behind, with the ragged programmes in the seats. So if the honourable court, in the person of the more or less honourable Elijah Westlake Bemis, after the fashion of federal judges desiring to do a questionable thing, calls in a judge from a neighbouring court--what do we care? And if the judge of the neighbouring court, after much legal hemming and judicial hawing, decides in his great wisdom--that the said defendant Barclay has been charged in the indictment with no crime, and instructs the jury to find a verdict of not guilty for said defendant John Barclay, upon the mere reading of the indictment,--what are the odds? What do

we care if the men in the packed courtroom hiss and the reporters put
down the hisses in their note-books and editors write the hisses in
headlines, and presses print the hisses all over the world? For the
fidgety little man is free now--entirely free save for fifty-four
years of selfish life upon his shoulders.

In the trial of nearly every cause it becomes necessary at some point
in the proceedings to halt the narrative and introduce certain
exhibits, records, and documents, upon which foregone evidence has
been based, and to which coming testimony may properly be attached.
That point has been reached in the case now before the reader. And as
"Exhibit A" let us submit a letter written by John Barclay, January
seventh, nineteen hundred and four, to Jane, his wife, at Naples.

"As I cabled you this afternoon, the case resulted exactly as I said
it would the day after the indictment. I had not seen or talked with
Lige since that day I talked with him over the telephone, before the
indictment was made public, but I knew Lige well enough to know how
he would act under fire. I had him out to dinner this evening, and
we talked over old times, and he tells me he wants to retire from
the bench. Jane, Lige has been my mainstay ever since this company
was organized. Sometimes I feel that without his help in
politics--looking to see that pernicious legislation was killed, and
that the right men were elected to administrative offices, and
appointed to certain judicial places--we never would have been able
to get the company to its present high standing. I feel that he has
been so valuable to us that we should settle a sum on him that will
make him a rich man as men go in the Ridge. Heaven knows that is
little enough, considering all that he has done. He may have his
faults, Jane, but he has been loyal to me.

"I hope, my dear, that Jeanette has ceased to worry about the other
matter; he is not worth her tears. Don't come home for a month or

two yet. The same conditions prevail that I spoke of in my first cable the day of the indictment. The press and the public are perfectly crazy. America is one great howling mob, and it would make you and Jennie unhappy. As for me, I don't mind it. You know me."

And that the reader may know how truthful John Barclay is, let us append herewith a letter written by Mrs. Mary Barclay, of Sycamore Ridge, to her granddaughter at Naples, January 15, 1904. She writes among other things:--

"Well, dear, it is a week now since your father's case was settled, and he was at home for the first time last night. I expected that his victory--such as it was--would cheer him up, but some way he seems worse in the dumps than he was before. He does not sleep well, and is getting too nervous for a man of his age. I have the impression that he is forever battling with something. Of course the public temper is bitter, dearie. You are a woman now, and should not be shielded and pampered with lies, so I am going to tell you the truth. The indignation of the people of this nation at your father, as he represents present business methods, is past belief. And frankly, dearie, I can't blame them. Your father and my son is a brave, sweet, loving man; none could be finer in this world, Jennie. But the head of the National Provisions Company is another person, dear; and of him I do not approve, as you know so well. I am sending you Neal Ward's statement which was published by the government the day after the case was dismissed. I have not sent it to you before, because I wanted to ask your father if it was true. Jennie, he admits that Neal told the truth, and nothing but the truth--and did not make it as bad as it was. You are entitled to the facts. You are a grown woman now, dear, and must make your own decisions. But oh, my dear little girl, I am heartsick to see your father breaking as he is. He seems to be fighting--fighting--fighting all the time; perhaps it is against the flames of public wrath, but some way I think he is fighting something inside himself--fighting it back; fighting it down--whatever it is."

Counsel also begs indulgence while he introduces and reads two clippings from the Sycamore Ridge ***Daily Banner***, of February 12, 1904. The first one reads:--

"Judge Bemis Retires

"Hon. E. W. Bemis has retired from the federal bench, and rumour has it that he is soon to return with his estimable wife to our midst. Our people will welcome the judge and Mrs. Bemis with open arms. He retires from an honourable career, to pass his declining years in the peace and quiet of the town in which he began his career over fifty years ago. For as every one knows, he came West as a boy, and before having been admitted to the bar dealt largely in horses and cattle. He has always been a good business man, having with his legal acumen the acquisitive faculty, and now he is looking for some place to invest a modest competence here in the Ridge, and rumour has it again that he is negotiating for the purchase of the Sycamore Ridge Waterworks bonds, which are now in litigation. If so, he will make an admirable head of that popular institution."

In this connection, and before introducing the other clipping from the ***Banner***, it would be entirely proper to introduce the manuscript for the above, in the typewriting of the stenographer of Judge Bemis's court, and a check for fifty dollars payable to Adrian Brownwell, signed by Judge Bemis aforesaid; but those documents would only clog the narrative and would not materially strengthen the case, so they will be thrown out.

The second clipping, found in the personal column of the ***Banner*** of the date referred to, February 12, 1904, follows:--

"Mrs. John Barclay and Miss Barclay are on the steamer *Etruria* which was sighted off Fire Island to-day. They will spend a few weeks in New York, and early in March Miss Barclay will enter the state university to do some post-graduate work in English, and Mrs. Barclay will return to Sycamore Ridge. Mr. Barclay will meet them at the pier, and they expect to spend the coming two weeks attending German opera. Mrs. Mary Barclay left to-day for the East to join them. She will remain a month visiting relatives near Haverhill, Mass."

It becomes necessary to append some letters of Miss Jeanette Barclay's, and they are set down here in the order in which they were written, though the first one takes the reader back a few weeks to December 5, 1903. It was posted at Rome, and in the body of it are found these words:--

"My dear, I know you will smile when you hear I have been reading all the Italian scientific books I can find, dealing with the human brain--partly to help my Italian, but chiefly, I think, to see if I can find and formulate some sort of a definition for love. It is so much a part of my soul, dear heart, that I would like to know more about it. And I am going to write down for you what I think it is as we know it. I have been wearing your ring nearly three years, Neal, and if you had only known it, I would have been happy to have taken it a year sooner. In those four years I have grown from a girl to a woman, and you have become a man full grown. In that time all my thoughts have centred on you. In all my schoolbooks your face comes back to me as I open them in fancy. As I think of the old room at school, of my walk up the hill, as I think of home and my room there, some thought of you is always between me and the picture. All through my physical brain are little fibres running to every centre that bring up images of you. You are woven into my life, and I know in my heart that I am woven into your life. The thing is done; it is as much apart of my being as my blood--those million fibres of my brain that from every part of my consciousness bring thoughts of you. We cannot be separated now, darling--we are united for life, whether we unite in life or not. I am yours and you are mine. It is now as inexorable as anything we call material. More than that--you have made my soul. All the aspirations of my spiritual life go to you for beginning and for being as truly as the fibres of my brain thrill to the sound of your name or the mental image of your face. My soul is your soul, because in the making the thought of you was uppermost. I know that my love for you is immortal, ineffaceable, and though I should live a hundred years, that love would still be as much a part of my life as my hands or my eyes or my body. And the best of it all is that I am so glad it is so. Divorce is as impossible with a love like that as amputation of the brain. It is big and vital in me, real and certain, and so long as I live on earth, or dwell in eternity, my soul and your soul are knit together."

Three weeks later, on December 28, 1903, Miss Barclay wrote to Mr. Ward as follows:--

"Your letter and father's letter were on my desk when we returned from our cruise. I have just finished writing to him, and I herewith return your ring and your pin."

There was neither signature nor superscription--just those words. And a month later, Miss Barclay wrote this letter to her Grandmother Barclay in Sycamore Ridge:--

"MY DEAR, DEAR GRANNY: I have told mother what you wrote of father,
and we are coming home just as soon as we can get a steamer. We are

cabling him to-day, and hope to sail within a week or ten days at the very farthest. But I cannot wait until I see you, dear, to come close into your heart. And first of all I want you to know that I share your views about the heart-break of all this money and the miserable man-killing way it is being piled up. I know the two men you speak of--father and the president of the N.P.C. But he is my father, and I must stand by him, and brace him if I can. But, oh, Granny, I don't want the old money! It has never made me happy--never for one minute. The only happiness I have ever had was when he was at home with us all, away from business--and--but you know about that other happiness, and it hurts to speak of it now. I have not read what you sent me. I can't. But I will keep it. That it is true doesn't help me any. Nothing can help me. It is just one of those awful things that I have read of coming to people, but which I thought never could possibly come to me. Oh, Granny, Granny, you who pray so much for others, now pray for me. Granny, you can't cut something out of you--right out of the heart of you, by merely saying so; it keeps growing back; it hurts, and hurts, and keeps hurting; even if you know it is cut out and thrown away. They say that men who have had legs cut off can feel them for months and even years if they are cramped when they are buried. The nerves of the old dead body reach through space and hurt. It is that way with me. The old dead thing in my heart that is buried and gone keeps cramping and hurting. You are the only one I can come to, Granny. It hurts mother too much, and she is not strong this winter. I think it is worry. She is growing thin, and her heart doesn't act right. I am terribly worried about her; but she made me promise to say nothing to father, and you must not, either; for he will see for himself soon."

A few letters from Neal Ward to Jeanette Barclay, and a document some twenty years old, which the reader may have forgotten, but which one person connected with this narrative has feared would come to light every day in that time--and then this tedious business of introducing documentary evidence will be over. The letter from Neal Ward to Jeanette Barclay is one of hundreds that he wrote and never mailed. They were dated, sealed, addressed, and put away. This one was written at midnight as the bells and whistles and pistols and fireworks were welcoming the year 1904. It begins:--

"MY VERY DEAREST: Here I am sitting at the old desk again, in the old office of the *Banner*. I could only scribble you a little note on the train last night to tell you that my heart still was with you, and I did not have the time to explain why I was coming. It is a dead secret, little woman, and perhaps I shouldn't tell even you, but I feel that I must bring everything to you. Bob Hendricks wired me to come down. He has a mortgage on the *Banner*, and he feels that things are not being properly managed, so he persuaded Mr. Brownwell to give me a place as sort of manager of the paper at twenty dollars a week--a sum that seems princely considering that I was making only eighteen dollars in Chicago, and that it costs so much less to live here. Hendricks guarantees my wages, so that Adrian cannot stand me off. Hendricks has another motive for wanting me to come here. The waterworks franchise will come up for renewal June first of this year, and Mr. Hendricks is for municipal ownership. Carnine and the State Bank are against municipal ownership, because the water company does business with them, and as they control the *Index*, they are preparing to make a warm fight for the renewal of the old franchise. So there will be a hot time in the old town this spring. But the miserable part of it is this. The growth of the town has made it dangerous to use the present supply station. The water must not come out of the mill-pond any longer, as the town is tilted so that all the surface drainage goes into it, and the sewers that drain into it, while they drain a few hundred yards below the intake of the waterworks, cannot help tainting the whole pond. Mr. Hendricks has had an expert here who declared that both the typhoid and diphtheria epidemics here last fall were due directly to the water supply, and Mr. Hendricks is going to make the fight of his life to have the city buy the waterworks plant, and move the intake six miles above town, where there is plenty of clean water. Of course it will mean first a city election to get decent councilmen, and then a bond election to vote money to buy the old plant; the waterworks company are going to move heaven and earth to get an anti-Hendricks council elected and to renew the franchise and let things go as they are. So that is why I am here, dear heart, and oh, my darling, you do not know how painful it all seems to be here and not have you--I mean--you know what I mean. All my associations with the work here in the office and on the street are with my heart close to yours. Everything in the old town tells me of you. 'Saint Andrews by the Northern sea, a haunted city is to me.' To-night I hear the music of the New Year's dance, and I can shut my eyes and feel you with me there. Oh, sweetheart, I have kept you so close, by writing to you every night. I come and lay my heart and all its thoughts at your shrine, and put all my day's work before you for your approval, just as I used to do. It is so sweet a privilege.

"Last night I dreamed about you. It was so real and your voice sounded so clearly, crying to me, that you have been with me all day. I wonder if while we sleep, we whose souls would struggle to meet through eternity, if through the walls of space they may not find each other, and speak to each other through our dreams. It is midnight here now, and you are just waking, perhaps, or just sleeping that sleep of early morning wherein the soul sinks to unknown depths. Oh--oh--oh, if I could but speak to you there, my dear! I am going to sit here and close my eyes and try."

The next letter in the exhibit was written six weeks later and is dated February 12, 1904. It says in part:--

"I must tell you what a bully fellow Bob Hendricks is. Judge Bemis sent a highly laudatory article about himself to the office to-day with a check for fifty dollars. In the article it develops that he is going to retire from the federal bench and come down here and buy the waterworks plant--on the theory that he will get a bargain because of the expiring franchise and the prospective fight. That fifty dollars looked as big as a barn to poor Adrian, so he trotted off with the letter and the check to Hendricks. Of course, the letter and the check together, just framed and put in the bank window, would make great sport of the judge; but Bob is a thoroughbred, and probably Bemis knows it, and figures on that in his dealings with him. I was in the bank when Adrian came in with the letter. He showed the check and the article to Hendricks, and you could almost see Adrian wag his tail and hear him whine to keep the check; Bob looked at the poor fellow's wistful eyes and handed it back with a quizzical little smile and said, 'Oh, I guess I'd run it; it can't hurt anything.' The light that came into Adrian's eyes was positively beatific, and he shook Bob by the hand, and twirled his cane, and waved his gloves in a sort of canine ecstasy, and trotted to the cashier's window with the check like a dog with a bone. It is the largest piece of real money he has had in six months, the boys say, and he has spent it for clothes. To-morrow he will hurry off to the first convention in the city like a comet two centuries behind time. But that is beside the point; the thing I don't like is the coming of Bemis. I know him; the things I have seen him do in your father's business and when he was on the bench, make me shudder for decent politics in this town. He is shrewd, unscrupulous, and without any restraint on earth.

"I feel closer to you than I have felt since I put the barrier between us. For you are in this country to-night--I could go to the telephone there five feet away and reach you if I would. I looked to-day in the papers and saw that they would be giving Lohengrin at the Metropolitan Opera House, and knowing your father as I do, I think he will take you there. I can hear the music rising and see you drinking in the harmony, and as it swells into exquisite pain, and thrills through the holy places of your soul where are old memories of our love, sweetheart, maybe your spirit will go forth in God's strange universe where we all dwell neighbours, loosed from those material chains that bind our bodies, and will seek the heart that is searching for you out there in the highway of heaven. I seem to feel you now, dear soul--did the music fling your spirit free for a second till it touched my own? I am so happy, Jeanette--even to love you and to know that you have loved me, and must always love me while you are you and I am I."

And now let us consider the final exhibit. It will be necessary to turn back the action of this story a month and a half and sit with John Barclay and his friend, former federal judge Elijah Westlake Bemis, before the fire in the wide fireplace in the Barclay home, one cold January night, a week after Barclay had gone free from the court and the world had hissed him. They were talking of the judge's business future, and the judge was saying:--

"John, how did Bob Hendricks ever straighten out that affair in the treasurer's office in connection with the first year's taxes of the old Wheat Company? What did he do with it finally?"

Barclay looked at the fire and then turned his searchlight eyes into Bemis's. There was not a quiver. The man sat there without a muscle of his parchment face moving. His eyes were squinted up, looking at the tip of his long cigar.

"Why?" asked Barclay.

"Well," responded Bemis, impassive as an ox, "it would help me in my business to know. Tell me."

He spoke the last two words as one in authority.

"Well," answered Barclay, "one day back in the seventies, I was appointed to check up the treasurer's book, and I found where he had fixed it on the county books--apparently between two administrations. I recognized his hand; and it made the balance for the first time."

Bemis smoked awhile. "What time in the seventies?" he asked.

There was a pause. "In January, 1879."

Bemis grinned a wicked, mean little grin and said: "That settles it. I believe I am safe in buying the waterworks."

"What are you going to do to Bob?" Barclay asked.

"Nothing, nothing--absolutely nothing, if he has any sense and drops this municipal ownership tommyrot. Absolutely nothing."

Again the grin came over his face, and at the end of a pause Barclay said:--

"Well, if not, what then?"

Bemis shut his eyes and crossed his gaunt legs, and began: "Think back twenty years ago--more or less. Do you remember when I brought your car down here for Watts McHurdie and his crowd to go to Washington in, to the G.A.R. celebration? All right; do you remember that I came to the office and told you I saw Bob Hendricks waiting for some one at the Union Station, when the train got into the city that morning?"

"Yes," said Barclay, "you were so mysterious and funny about it, I remember."

"Well," said Bemis, as he got up and poked a log that was annoying him in the fireplace, "well, I have a little document in my desk at home, that I got the night before in the Ridge, which will convince Bobbie, if he has any sense, that this municipal ownership business isn't all it's cracked up to be."

Barclay, who knew from Jane something of the truth, guessed the rest, but he did not question Bemis further. "Oh, I don't know, Lige," he began; "it seems to me I wouldn't drag that into it."

Bemis turned his old face, full of malicious passion, toward Barclay and cried, "Maybe you wouldn't, John Barclay--you forget things; but I never do; and you're a coward sometimes, and I am not."

The blaze of his wrath went out in a moment, and Barclay's mind went back to that afternoon in the seventies when Hendricks picked Bemis up and threw him bodily from the county convention and branded him as a boodler. Barclay knew argument was useless. So he said nothing.

"He has the county officers--every man-jack of them from the treasurer to Jake Dolan, the janitor--and I couldn't get hold of that book by fair means without his knowing it. But I am going to have that book, John--I'm going to have that book."

Barclay followed Bemis's mental processes, as if they were his own. "Well--what if he does know it?" asked Barclay.

"Oh, if he knew I was after the book, he'd fix me,--have it destroyed or something; he could do lots of things or beat me some way. I've got to get that book--get it out of the court-house--and there's just one way to get into the court-house, without using the doors and the windows." When Bemis had finished speaking, he gazed steadily into Barclay's eyes. And Bemis saw the fear that was in Barclay's face. "Yes, I know a way into the court-house, John--it's mine by fifty years' right of discovery. I'm going to have that book, and get an expert opinion as to the similarity of the handwriting in the book and the handwriting of my own little document. My own little document," he mused, licking his chops like a hound at the prospect.

Now we will call that little document "Exhibit I" in the case of the Larger Good **vs.** The People, and close thereby a long and tedious chapter. But we will begin another chapter in which the wheels of events spin rapidly in their courses toward that moral equilibrium that deeds must find before they stop when they are started for the Larger Good.

CHAPTER XXVII

The spring of 1904 in Sycamore Ridge opened in turmoil. The turmoil came from the contest over the purchase of the town's water system. Robert Hendricks as president of the Citizens' League was leading the forces that advocated the purchase of the system by the town, as being the only sure way to change the water supply from the polluted mill-pond to a clean source. Six months before he had leased every bill-board in town, and for the two months preceding the city election that was to decide the question of municipal purchase he had hired every available hall in town, for every vacant night during those months, and had bought half of the first page of both the ***Banner*** and the ***Index*** for those months--and all of this long before the town knew the fight was coming. He covered the bill-boards and the first pages of the newspapers with analyses of the water in the mill-pond--badly infected from the outlet of the town sewers and its surface drainage. The Citizens' League filled the halls with speakers demanding the purchase of the plant and the removal of the pumping station to a place several miles above the town, and four beyond the mill-pond. Judge Bemis, with the aid and abetment of John Barclay, who was in the game to help his old friend, put up banners denouncing Hendricks as a socialist, accusing him of being the town boss, and charged through the columns of the *Index* that Hendricks' real motive in desiring to have the city take over the waterworks system was to make money on the sale of the city's bonds. So Hendricks was the centre of the fight.

In the first engagement, a malicious contest, Hendricks lost. The town refused to vote the bonds to buy the plant. But at the same election the same people elected a city council overwhelmingly in favour of municipal ownership and in favour of compelling the operating company to move its plant from the mill-pond. The morning after the election Hendricks began a lawsuit as a taxpayer and citizen to make the waterworks company move its plant. The town could understand that issue, and sentiment rallied to Hendricks again. Judge Bemis, at the head of the company, although irritated, was not alarmed. For in the courts he could promote delays, plead technicalities, and wear out his adversary. It was an old game with him. Still, the suit disturbed the value of his bonds, and having other resources, he gleefully decided to use them.

And thus it fell out that one fine day in April, Trixie Lee, from the bedraggled outer hem of the social garment down by the banks of the Sycamore, called to the telephone Robert Hendricks of the town's purple and fine linen, who dwelt on the hill. He did not recognize her voice, the first time she called. But shrewd as Judge Bemis was, and bad as he was, he did not know it all. He did not know that when Hendricks had received the first anonymous letter three days before, he had instructed the girls in the telephone office, which he controlled, to make a record of every telephone call for his office or his house, and when the woman's voice on the telephone that day delivered Judge Bemis's message, the moment after she quit talking he knew with whom he had been talking.

"Is this Mr. Hendricks?" the voice had begun, rather pleasantly. Yes, it was Mr. Hendricks. "Well, I am your friend, but I don't dare to let you know my name now; it would be all my life is worth." And Robert Hendricks grinned pleasantly into the rubber transmitter as he realized that his trap would work. "Yes, Mr. Hendricks, I am your friend, and you have a powerful enemy." What with the insinuations in the *Index* and the venom that Lige Bemis had been putting into anonymous circulars during the preliminary waterworks campaign, this was no news to Mr. Hendricks; so he let the voice go on, "They want you to dismiss that suit against the waterworks company that you brought last week." There was a pause for a reply; but none came; then the voice said, "Are you there, Mr. Hendricks--do you hear me?" And Mr. Hendricks said that he heard perfectly. "And," went on the voice, "as your friend I wish you would, too. Do you remember a letter you once wrote to a woman, asking her to elope with you--a married woman, Mr. Hendricks?" There was a pause for a reply, and again the voice asked, "Do you hear, Mr. Hendricks?" and Mr. Hendricks heard; heard in his soul and was afraid, but his voice did not quaver as he replied, "Yes, I hear perfectly." Then the voice went on, "Well, they have that letter--a little note--not over one hundred words, and with no date on it, and the man who has it also has a photograph of page 234 of a certain ledger in the county treasurer's office for 1879, and there is an entry there in your handwriting, Mr. Hendricks; and he has had them both enlarged to show that the handwriting of the note and of the county book are the same; isn't that mean, Mr. Hendricks?" Hendricks coughed into the transmitter, and she knew that he was there, so she continued: "As your friend in this matter, I have got them to promise that if you will come to the Citizens' League meeting that you have called for to-morrow night at Barclay Hall and tell the people that you think we need harmony in the Ridge worse than we need this everlasting row, if you will merely say to Mr. Barclay as you pass into the meeting, 'Well, John, I believe I'll dismiss that suit,' you can have your letter back. He hasn't got the letter, but he will be sure to tell the news to a friend who has." Here the voice faltered, and said unconsciously, "Wait a minute, I've lost my place; oh, here it is; all right. And if you don't come to the meeting and say that, I believe they are going to spring those documents on the meeting to put you in bad odour."

"Is that all?" asked Hendricks.

"Well--" a pause and then finally--"yes," came the voice.

"Well, my answer is no," said Hendricks, and while he was trying to get central the voice called again and said:--

"Just one word more: if you still maintain your present decision, a copy of that letter you wrote will be put into the hands of Mr. Brownwell of the ***Banner*** before the meeting; I tell you this to protect you. He and Mrs. Brownwell and Mrs. Barclay will be in town to morrow evening on the Barclay car from the West on No. 6; you will have until then to reconsider your decision; after that you act at your own risk."

Again the voice ceased, and Hendricks learned from central who had been talking with him. It was after banking hours, and he sat for a time looking the situation squarely in the face. The reckoning had come. He had answered "no" with much bravery over the telephone--but in his heart a question began to rise, and his decision was clouded.

Hendricks walked alone under the stars that night, and as he walked he turned the situation over and over as one who examines a strange puzzle. He saw that his "no" could not be his own "no." Molly must be partner in it. For to continue his fight for clean water he must risk her good name. He measured Bemis, and remembered the old quarrel. The hate in the face of the bribe-giver, thrown out of the county convention a quarter of a century before, came to Hendricks, and he knew that it was no vain threat he was facing. So he turned up the other facet of the puzzle. There was Adrian. For an hour he considered Adrian Brownwell, a vain jealous old man with the temper of a beast. To see Molly, tell her of their common peril, get her decision, and be with it at the meeting before Adrian saw the note, all in the two hours between the arrival of the train bearing the Brownwells and Mrs. Barclay, and the time of the meeting in Barclay Hall, was part of Hendricks' puzzle. He believed that by using the telephone to make an appointment he could manage it. Then he turned the puzzle over and saw that to save Molly Brownwell's good name and his father's, human lives must be sacrificed by permitting the use of foul water in the town. And in the end his mind set. He knew that unless she forbade it, the contest must go on to a righteous finish, through whatever perils, over any obstacles. Yet as he walked back to the bank, determined not to take his hand from the plough, he saw that he must prepare to go into the next day as though it were his last. For in his consciousness on the other side of the puzzle--always there was the foolish Adrian, impetuous at best, but stark mad in his jealousy and wrath.

And Elijah Westlake Bemis, keeping account of the man's movements, chuckled as he felt the struggle in the man's breast. For he was a wise old snake, that Lige Bemis, and he had seduced many another man after the brave impulsive "no" had roared in his face. Just before midnight when he saw the electric light flash on in the private office of the president of the Exchange National Bank, Lige Bemis, libertine with men, strolled home and counted the battle won. "He's writing his speech," he said to Barclay over the telephone at midnight. And John Barclay, who had fought the local contest in the election with Bemis to be loyal to a friend, and to help one who was in danger of losing the profit on half a million dollars' investment in the Sycamore Ridge waterworks, laughed as he walked upstairs in his pajamas, and said to himself, "Old Lige is a great one--there is a lot of fight in the old viper yet." It was nothing to Barclay that the town got its water from a polluted pond. That phase of the case did not enter his consciousness, though it was placarded on the bill-boards and had been printed in the *Banner* a thousand times during the campaign. To him it was a fight by the demagogues against property interests, and he was with property, even a little property--even a miserable little dribble of property like half a million dollars' worth of waterworks bonds.

And Robert Hendricks--playfellow of John Barclay's boyhood, partner of his youth--sat working throughout the night, a brave man, going into battle without a tremor. He went through his books, made out statements of his business relations, prepared directions for the heads of his different concerns, as a man would do who might be going on a long journey. For above everything, Robert Hendricks was foresighted. He prepared for emergencies first, and tried to avoid them afterwards. And with the thought of the smallness of this life in his soul, he looked up from his work to see the hard gray lines of the dawn in the street outside of his office, bringing the ugly details from the shadows that hid them during the day, and he sighed as he wondered in what bourne he should see the next dawn break.

It was a busy day for Robert Hendricks, that next day, and through it all his mind was planning every moment of the time how he could protect Molly Brownwell. Did he work in the bank, behind his work his mind was seeking some outlet from his prison. If he went over the power-house at the electric plant, always he was looking among the wheels for some way of refuge for Molly. When he spent an hour in the office of the wholesale grocery house, he despatched a day's work, but never for a second was his problem out of his head. He spent two hours with his lawyers planning the suit against the water company, pointing out new sources of evidence, and incidentally leaving a large check to pay for the work. But through it all Molly Brownwell's good name was ever before him, and when he thought how twenty years before he had walked through another day planning, scheming, and contriving, all to produce the climax of calamity that was hovering over her to-day, he was sick and faint with horror and self-loathing.

But as the day drew to its noon, Hendricks began to feel a persistent detachment from the world about him. It floated across his consciousness, like the shadow anchor of some cloud far above him. He began to watch the world go by. He seemed not to be a part of it. He became a spectator. At four o'clock he passed Dolan on the street and said, absently, "I want you to-night at the bank at seven o'clock sharp--don't forget, it's very important."

As he walked down Main Street to the bank, the shadow anchor of the cloud had ceased to flit across his consciousness. Life had grown all gray and dull, and he was apart from the world. He saw the handbills announcing the meeting that night as one who sees a curious passing show; the men he met on the street he greeted as creatures from another world. Yet he knew he smiled and spoke with them casually. But it was not he who spoke; the real Robert Hendricks he knew was separated from the pantomime about him. When he went into the bank at five o'clock, the janitor was finishing his work. Hendricks called up the depot on the telephone and found that No. 6 was an hour late. With the realization that a full hour of his fighting time had been taken from him and that the train would arrive only a scant hour before the meeting, the Adrian face of his puzzle turned insistently toward Hendricks. It was not fear but despair that seized him. The cloud was over him. And for want of something to do he wrote. First he wrote abstractedly and mechanically to John Barclay, then to Neal Ward--a note for the ***Banner***--and as the twilight deepened in the room, he squared his chair to the table and wrote to Molly Brownwell; that letter was the voice of his soul. That was real. Six o'clock struck. Half-past six clanged on the town clock, and as Jake Dolan opened the bank door, Hendricks heard the roar of the train crossing at the end of Main Street.

"There goes Johnnie's private car, switching on the tail of her," said Dolan, standing in the doorway.

Hendricks sent Dolan to a back room of the bank, and at seven-twenty went to the telephone. "Give me 876, central," he called. "Hello--hello--hello," he cried nervously, "hello--who is this?" The answer came and he said, "Oh, I didn't recognize your voice." Then he asked in a low tone, as one who had fear in his heart: "Do you recognize me? If you do, don't speak my name. Where is Adrian?" Then Mr. Dolan, listening in the next room, heard this: "You say Judge Bemis phoned to him? Oh, he was to meet him at eight o'clock. How long ago did he leave?" After a moment Hendricks' answer was: "Then he has just gone; and will not be back?" Hendricks cut impatiently into whatever answer came with: "Molly, I must see you within the next fifteen minutes. I can't talk any more over the telephone, but I must come up." "Yes," in a moment, "I must have your decision in a matter of great importance to you--to you, Molly." There was a short silence, then Dolan heard: "All right, I'll be there in ten minutes." Then Hendricks turned from the telephone and called Dolan in. He unlocked a drawer in his desk, and began speaking to Dolan, who stood over him. Hendricks' voice was low, and he was repressing the agitation in his heart by main strength.

"Jake," he said, talking as rapidly as he could, "I must be ungodly frank with you. It doesn't make any difference whether he is right or not, but Adrian Brownwell may be fooled into thinking he has reason to be jealous of me." Hendricks was biting his mustache. "He's a raging maniac of jealousy, Jake, but I'm not afraid of him--not for myself. I can get him before he gets me, if it comes to that, but to do it I'll have to sacrifice Molly. And I won't do that. If it comes to her good name or my life--she can have my life." They were outside now and Dolan was unhitching the horse. He knew instinctively that he was not to reply. In a moment Hendricks went on, "Well, there is just one chance in a hundred that it may turn that way--her good name or my life--and on that chance I've written some letters here." He reached in his coat and said, "Now, Jake, put these letters in your pocket and if anything goes wrong with me, deliver them to the persons whose names are on the envelopes--and to no one else. I must trust everything to you, Jake," he said.

Driving up the hill, he met Bemis coming down town. He passed people going to the meeting in Barclay Hall. He did not greet them, but drove on. His jaw was set hard, and the muscles of his face were firm. As he neared the Culpepper home he climbed from the buggy and hitched the horse to the block in front of his own house. He hurried into the Culpepper yard, past the lilac bushes heavy with blooms, and up the broad stone steps with the white pillars looming above him. It was a quarter to eight, and at that minute Bemis was saying to Adrian Brownwell, "All right, if you don't believe it, don't take my word for it, but go home right now and see what you find."

Molly Brownwell met Hendricks on the threshold with trembling steps. "Bob, what is it?" she asked. They stood in the shadow of the great white pillars, where they had parted a generation ago.

"It's this, Molly," answered Hendricks, as he put his hand to his forehead that was throbbing with pain; "Lige Bemis has my letter to you. Yes," he cried as she gasped, "the note--the very note, and to get it I must quit the waterworks fight and go to the meeting to-night and surrender. I had no right to decide that alone. It is our question, Molly. We are bound by the old life--and we must take this last stand together."

The woman shrank from Hendricks with horror on her face, as he personified her danger. She could not reply at once, but stood staring at him in the dusk. As she stared, the feeling that she had seen it all before in a dream came over her, and the premonition that some awful thing was impending shook her to the marrow.

"Molly, we have no time to spare," he urged. "I must answer Bemis in ten minutes--I can do it by phone. But say what you think."

"Why--why--why--Bob--let me think," she whispered, as one trying to speak in a dream, and that also seemed familiar to her. "It's typhoid for my poor who died like sheep last year," she cried, "or my good name and yours, is it, Bob? Is it, Bob?" she repeated.

He put his hand to his forehead again in the old way she remembered so well--to temples that were covered with thin gray hair--and answered, "Yes, Molly, that's our price."

Those were the last words that she seemed to have heard before; after that the dialogue was all new to her. She was silent a few agonized seconds and then said, "I know what you think, Bob; you are for my poor; you are brave." He did not answer, fearing to turn the balance. As she sank into a porch chair a rustling breeze moved the lilac plumes and brought their perfume to her. From down the avenue came the whir of wheels and the hurrying click of a horse's hoofs. At length

she rose, and said tremulously: "I stand with you, Bob. May God make
the blow as light as He can."

They did not notice that a buggy had drawn up on the asphalt in front
of the house. Hendricks put out his hand and cried, "Oh,
Molly--Molly--Molly--" and she took it in both of hers and pressed
it to her lips, and as Adrian Brownwell passed the lilac thicket in
the gathering darkness that is what he saw. Hendricks was halfway down
the veranda steps before he was aware that Brownwell was running up
the walk at them, pistol in hand, like one mad. Before the man could
fire, Hendricks was upon him, and had Brownwell's two hands gripped
tightly in one of his, holding them high in the air. The little man
struggled.

"Don't scream--for God's sake, don't scream," cried Hendricks to the
woman in a suppressed voice. Then he commanded her harshly, "Go in the
house--quick--Molly--quick."

She ran as though hypnotized by the force of the suggestion. Hendricks
had his free hand over Brownwell's mouth and around his neck. The
little old man was kicking and wriggling, but Hendricks held him. "Not
here, you fool, not here. Can't you see it would ruin her, you fool?
Not here." He carried and dragged Brownwell across the grass through
the shrubbery and into the Hendricks yard. No one was passing, and the
night had fallen. "Now," said Hendricks, as he backed against a pine
tree, still holding Brownwell, "I shall let you go if you'll promise
to listen to me just a minute until I tell you the whole truth. Molly
is innocent, man--absolutely innocent, and I'll show you if you'll
talk for a moment. Will you promise, man?"

Brownwell nodded his assent; Hendricks looked at him steadily for a
second and then said, "All right," and set the little man on his feet.
The glare of madness came into Brownwell's eyes, and as he turned he

came at Hendricks with his pistol drawn. An instant later there was a shot. Brownwell saw the amazement flash into Hendricks' eyes, and then Hendricks sank gently to the foot of the pine tree.

And Molly Brownwell, with the paralysis of terror still upon her, heard the shot and then heard footsteps running across the grass. A moment later her husband, empty-handed, chattering, shivering, and white, stumbled into the room. Rage had been conquered by fear. For an agonized second the man and woman stared at one another, speechless--then the wife cried:--

"Oh--oh--why--why--Adrian," and her voice was thick with fear.--

The man was a-tremble--hands, limbs, body--and his mad eyes seemed to shrink from the woman's gaze. "Oh, God--God--oh, God--" he panted, and fell upon his face across the sofa. They heard a hurrying step running toward the Hendricks house, there came a frightened, choked cry of "Help!" repeated twice, another and another sound of pattering feet came, and five minutes after the quaking man had entered the door the whole neighbourhood seemed to be alive with running figures hurrying silently through the gloom. The thud of feet and the pounding of her heart, and the whimpering of the little man who lay, face down, on the sofa, were the only sounds in her ears. She started to go with the crowd. But Adrian screamed to her to stay.

"Oh," he cried, "he sank so softly--he sank so softly--he sank so softly! Oh, God, oh, God--he sank so softly!"

And the next conscious record of her memory was that of Neal Ward bursting into the room, crying, "Aunt Molly--Aunt Molly--do you know Mr. Hendricks has committed suicide? They've found him dead with a pistol by his side. I want some whiskey for Miss Hendricks. And they need you right away."

But Molly Brownwell, with what composure she could, said, "Adrian is sick, Neal--I can't--I can't leave him now." And she called after Neal as he ran toward the door, "Tell them, Neal, tell them--why I can't come." There was a hum of voices in the air, and the sound of a gathering crowd. Soon the shuffle and clatter of a thousand feet made it evident that the meeting at Barclay Hall had heard the news and was hurrying up the hill. The crowd buzzed for an hour, and Molly and Adrian Brownwell waited speechless together--he face downward on the sofa, she huddled in a chair by the window. And then the crowd broke, slowly, first into small groups that moved away together and then turned in a steady stream and tramped, tramped, tramped down the hill.

When the silence had been unbroken a long time, save by the rumble of a buggy on the asphalt or by the footsteps of some stray passerby, the man on the sofa lifted his head, looked at his wife and spoke, "Well, Molly?"

"Well, Adrian," she answered, "this is the end, I suppose?"

He did not reply for a time, and when he did speak, it was in a dead, passionless voice: "Yes--I suppose so. I can't stay here now."

"No--no," she returned. "No, you should not stay here."

He sat up and stared vacantly at her for a while and then said, "Though I don't see why I didn't leave years and years ago; I knew all this then, as well as I do now." The wife looked away from him as she replied: "Yes, I should have known you would know. I knew your secret and you--"

"My secret," said Adrian, "my secret?"

"Yes--that you came North with your inherited money because when you were in the Confederate army you were a coward in some action and could not live among your own people."

"Who told you," he asked, "who told you?"

"The one who told you I have always loved Bob; life has told me that, Adrian. Just as life has told you my story." They sat without speaking for a time, and then the woman sighed and rose. "Two people who have lived together twenty-five years can have no secrets from each other. In a thousand, ways the truth comes out."

"I should have gone away a long time ago," he repeated, "a long time ago; I knew it, but I didn't trust my instincts."

"Here comes father," she said, as the gate clicked.

They stood together, listening to the slow shuffle of the colonel coming up the walk, and the heavy fall of his cane. The wife put out her hand and said gently, "I think I have wronged you, Adrian, more than any one else."

He did not take her hand but sighed, and turned and went up the wide stairway. He was an old man then, and she remembered the years when he tripped up gayly, and then she looked at her own gray hair in the mirror and saw that her life was spent too.

As the colonel came in gasping asthmatically, he found his daughter waiting for him. "Is Adrian better?" he asked excitedly. "Neal said Adrian was sick."

"Yes, father, he's upstairs packing. He is going out on the four o'clock train."

"Oh," said the colonel, and then panted a moment before asking, "Has any one told you how it happened?"

"Yes," she replied, "I know everything. I think I'll run over there now, father." As she stood in the doorway, she said, "Don't bother Adrian--he'll need no help."

And so Molly Brownwell passed the last night with her dead lover. About midnight the bell rang and she went to the door.

"Ah, madam," said Jacob Dolan, as he fumbled in his pockets, and tried to breathe away from her to hide the surcease of his sorrow, "Ah, madam," he repeated, as he suddenly thought to pull off his hat, "I did not come for you--'twas Miss Hendricks I called for; but I have one for you, too. He gave the bundle to me the last thing--poor lad, poor lad." He handed her the letter addressed to Mrs. Brownwell, and then asked, "Is the sister about?"

And when he found she could not be seen he went away, and Molly Brownwell sat by the dead man's body and read:--

"My darling--my darling--they will let a dead man say that to you--won't they? And yet, so far as any thought of mine could sin against you, I have been dead these twenty years. Yet I know that I have loved you all that time, and as I sit alone here in the bank, and take the bridle off my heart, the old throb of joy that we both knew as children comes back again. It is such a strange thing--this life--such a strange thing." Then there followed a burst of passionate regret from the man's very heart, and it is so sacred to a manly love that curbed itself for a score of years, that it must not be set down here.

Over and over Molly Brownwell read the letter and then crept out to her lilac thicket and wept till dawn. She heard Adrian Brownwell go, but she could not face him, and listened as his footsteps died away, and he passed from her life.

And John Barclay kept vigil for the dead with her. As he tossed in his bed through the night, he seemed to see glowing out of the darkness before him the words Hendricks had written, in the letter that Dolan gave Barclay at midnight. Sometimes the farewell came to him:--

"It is not this man of millions that I wish to be with a moment to-night, John--but the boy I knew in the old days--the boy who ran with me through the woods at Wilson's Creek, the boy who rode over the hill into the world with me that September day forty years ago; the boy whose face used to beam eagerly out of yours when you sat playing at your old melodeon. I wish to be near him a little while to-night. When you get this, can't you go to your great organ and play him back into consciousness and tell him Bob says good-by?"

At dawn Barclay called Bemis out of bed, and before sunrise he and Barclay were walking on the terrace in front of the Barclay home.

"Lige," began Barclay, "did you tell Adrian of that note last night?" Bemis grinned his assent.

"And he went home, found Bob there conferring with Mrs. Brownwell about his position in the matter, and Adrian killed him."

"That's the way I figured it out myself," replied Bemis, laconically, "but it's not my business to say so."

"I thought you promised me you would just bluff with that note and not go so far, Lige Bemis," said Barclay.

"Did he just bluff with me when he called me a boodler and threw me downstairs in the county convention?"

"Then you lied to me, sir," snapped Barclay.

"Oh, hell, John--come off," sneered Bemis. "Haven't I got a right to lie to you if I want to?"

The two men stared at each other like growling dogs for a moment, and then Barclay turned away with, "What is there in the typhoid talk?"

"Demagogery--that's all. Of course there may be typhoid in the water; but let 'em boil the water."

"But they won't."

"Well, then, if they eat too much of your 'Old Honesty' or drink too much of my water unboiled, they take their own risk. You don't make a breakfast food for hogs, and I can't run my water plant for fools."

"But, Lige," protested Barclay, "couldn't we hitch up the electric plant--"

"Hitch up the devil and Tom Walker, John Barclay. When the wolves got after you, did I come blubbering to you to lay down and take a light sentence?" Barclay did not answer. Bemis continued: "Brace up, John--what's turned you baby when we've got the whole thing won? We didn't kill Hendricks, did we? Are you full of remorse and going to turn state's evidence?"

Barclay looked at the ground for a time, and said: "I believe, Lige, we did kill Bob--if it comes to that; and we are morally responsible for--"

"Oh, bag your head, John; I'm going home. When you can talk some sense, let me know."

And Bemis left Barclay standing in the garden looking at the sunrise across the mill-pond. Presently the carrier boy with a morning paper came around, and in it Barclay read the account of Hendricks' reported suicide, corroborated by his antemortem statement, written and delivered to Jacob Dolan an hour before he died.

"When I took charge of the Exchange National Bank," it read, "I found that my father owed Garrison County nine thousand dollars for another man's taxes, which he, my father, had agreed to pay, but had no money to do so. The other man insisted on my father forging a note to straighten matters up. It seemed at that time that the bank would close and the whole county would be ruined if my father had not committed that deed. I could not put the money back into the treasury without revealing my father's crime, so I let the matter run for a few years, renewing the forged note, and then, as it seemed an interminable job of forgery, I forged the balance on the county books, one afternoon between administrations in 1879. Mr. E. W. Bemis, who is trying to force polluted water on Sycamore Ridge, has discovered this forgery and has threatened to expose me in that and perhaps other matters. So I feel that my usefulness in the fight for pure water in the town is ended. I leave funds to fight the matter in the courts, and I feel sure that we will win."

Barclay sat in the warm morning sun, reading and re-reading the statement. Finally Jane Barclay, thin, broken and faded, on whom the wrath of the people was falling with crushing weight, came into the veranda, and put her hands on her husband's shoulders.

"Come in, John, breakfast is ready."

The woman whom the leprosy of dishonest wealth was whitening, walked dumbly into the great house, and ate in silence. "I am going to Molly," she said simply, as the two rose from their meal. "I think she needs me, dear; won't you come, too?" she asked.

"I can't, Jane--I can't," cried Barclay. And when his wife had pressed him, he broke forth: "Because Lige Bemis made Adrian kill Bob and I helped--" he groaned, and sank into his chair, "and I helped."

When Neal Ward came to the office the next morning, he found Dolan waiting for him. Ward opened the envelope that Dolan gave him, and found in it the mortgage Hendricks had owned on the *Banner* office, assigned to Ward, and around the mortgage was a paper band on which was written: "God bless you, my boy--keep up the fight; never say die."

Then Ward read Adrian Brownwell's valedictory that was hanging on a copy spike before him. It was the heart-broken sob of an old man who had run away from failure and sorrow, and it need not be printed here.

On Memorial Day, when they came to the cemetery on the hill to decorate the soldiers' graves, men saw that the great mound of lilacs on Robert Hendricks' grave had withered. The seven days' wonder of his passing was ended. The business that he had left prospered without him, or languished and died; within a week in all but a dozen hearts Hendricks' memory began to recede into the past, and so, where there had been a bubble on the tide, that held in its prism of light for a brief bit of eternity all of God's spectacle of life, suddenly there was only the tide moving resistlessly toward the unknown shore. And thus it is with all of us.

CHAPTER XXVIII

In the summer of 1904, following the death of Robert Hendricks, John Barclay spent much time in the Ridge, more time than he had spent there for thirty years. For in the City he was a marked man. Every time the market quivered, reporters rushed to get his opinion about the cause of the disturbance; the City papers were full of stories either of his own misdeeds, or of the wrong-doings of other men of his caste. His cronies were dying all about him of broken hearts or wrecked minds, and it seemed to him that the word "indictment" was in every column of every newspaper, was on every man's lips, and literally floated in the air.

So he remained in Sycamore Ridge much of the time, and every fair afternoon he rowed himself up the mill-pond to fish. He liked to be alone; for when he was alone, he could fight the battle in his soul without interruption. The combat had been gathering for a year; a despair was rising in him, that he concealed from his womenkind--who were his only intimate associates in those days--as if it had been a crime. But out on the mill-pond alone, casting minnows for bass, he could let the melancholy in his heart rage and battle with his sanity, without let or hindrance. His business was doing well; the lawsuits against the company in a dozen states were not affecting dividends, and the department in charge of his charities was forwarding letters of condolence and consolation from preachers and college presidents, and men who under the old regime had been in high walks of life. Occasionally some conservative newspaper or magazine would praise him and his company highly; but he knew the shallowness of all the patter of praise. He knew that he paid for it in one way or another, and he grew cynical; and in his lonely afternoons on the river, often he laughed at the whole mockery of his career, smiled at the thought of organized religion, licking his boots for money like a dog for bones, and then in his heart he said there is no God. Once, to relieve the pain of his soul's woe, he asked aloud, who is God, anyway, and then laughed as he thought that the bass nibbling at his minnow would soon think he, John Barclay, was God. The analogy pleased him, and he thought that his own god, some devilish fate, had the string through his gills at that moment and was preparing to cast him into the fire. Up in the office in the city, they went on making senators and governors, and slipping a federal judge in where they could, but he had little hand in it, for his power was a discarded toy. He sat in his boat alone, rowing for miles and miles, from stump to stump, and from fallen tree-top to tree-top, hating the thing he called God, and distrusting men.

But when he appeared in the town, or at home, he was cheerful enough; he liked to mingle with the people, and it fed his despair to notice what a hang-dog way they had with him. He knew they had been abusing him behind his back, and when he found out exactly what a man had said, he delighted in facing the man down with it.

"So you think John Barclay could have saved Bob Hendricks' life, do you, Oscar?" asked Barclay, as he overhauled Fernald coming out of the post-office.

"Who said so?" asked Fernald, turning red.

"Oh," chuckled Barclay, "I got it from the hired girls' wireless news agency. But you said it all right--you said it, Oscar; you said it over to Ward's at dinner night before last." And Barclay grinned maliciously.

Fernald scratched his head, and said, "Well, John, to be frank with you, that's the talk all over town--among the people."

"The people--the people," snapped Barclay, impatiently, "the people take my money for bridges and halls and parks and churches and statues and then call me a murderer--oh, damn the people! Who started this story?"

"See Jake Dolan, John--it's up to him. He can satisfy you," said Fernald, and turned, leaving Barclay in the street.

Up the hill trudged the gray-clad little man, with his pugnacious shoulders weaving and his bronzed face set hard and his mean jaw locked. On the steps of the court-house he found Jake Dolan, smoking a morning pipe with the loafers in the shade of the building.

"Here you, Jake Dolan," called Barclay, "what do you mean by accusing me of murdering Bob Hendricks? What did I have to do with it?"

"Easy, easy, Johnnie, my boy," returned Dolan, knocking the ashes from his pipe on the steps between his feet. "Gentlemen," said Dolan, addressing the crowd, "you've heard what our friend says. All right--come with me to my office, Johnnie Barclay, and I'll show you." Barclay followed Dolan into the basement of the court-house, with the crowd at a respectful distance. "Right this way--" and Dolan switched on an electric light. "Do you see that break in the foundation, Mr. Barclay? You do? And you know in your soul that it opens into the cave that leads to the cellar of your own house. Well, then, Mr. Johnnie Barclay--the book that contained the evidence against Bob Hendricks did not go out of this court-house by the front door, as you well know, but through that hole--stolen at night when I was out; and the man who stole it was the horse thief that used to run the cave--your esteemed friend, Lige Bemis."

The crowd was gaping at the rickety place in the foundation, and one man pulled a loose stone out and let the cold air of the cave into the room.

"Lige Bemis came to your house, Mr. Johnnie Barclay, got into the cave from your cellar, broke through this wall, and stole the book that contained the forgery made to cover General Hendricks' disgrace. And who caused that disgrace but the overbearing, domineering John Barclay, who made that old man steal to pay John Barclay's taxes, back in the grasshopper year, when the sheriff and the jail were almost as familiar to him as they are now,--by all counts. Ah, John Barclay," said the Irishman, turning to the crowd, "John Barclay, John Barclay--you're a brave little man sometimes; I've seen you when I was most ungodly proud of you; I've seen you do grand things, my little man, grand things. But you're a coward too, Johnnie; sitting in your own house while your horse-thief friend used your cellar to work out the disgrace of the man who gave his good name to save your own--that was a fine trick--a damn fine trick, wasn't it, Mr. Barclay?"

Barclay started to go, but the crowd blocked his way. Dolan saw that Barclay was trying to escape. "Turn tail, will you, my little man? Wait one minute," cried Dolan. "Wait one minute, sir. For what was you conniving against the big man? I know--to win your game; to win your miserable little game. Ah, what a pup a man can be, Johnnie, what a mangy, miserable, cowardly little pup a man can be when he tries--and a decent man, too. Money don't mean anything to you--you got past that, but it's to win the game. Why, man, look at yourself--look at yourself--you'd cheat your own mother playing cards with matches for counters--just to win the game." Dolan waved for the crowd to break. "Let him out of here, and get out yourselves--every one of you. This is public property you're desecrating."

Dolan sat alone in his office, pale and trembling after the crowd had gone. Colonel Culpepper came puffing in and saw the Irishman sitting with his head in his hands and his elbows on the table.

"What's this, Jake--what's this I hear?" asked the colonel.

"Oh, nothing," answered Dolan, and then he looked up at the colonel with sad, remorseful eyes. "What a fool--what a fool whiskey in a man's tongue is--what a fool." He reached under his cot for his jug, and repeated as he poured the liquor into a glass, "What a fool, what a fool, what a fool." And then, as he gulped it down and made a wry face, "Poor little Johnnie at the mill; I didn't mean to hit him so hard--not half so hard. What a fool, what a fool," and the two old men started off for the harness shop together.

Neal Ward that night, in the *Banner* office alone, wrote to his sweetheart the daily letter that was never mailed.

"How sweet it is," he writes, "to have you at home. Sometimes I hear your voice through the old leaky telephone, talking to Aunt Molly; her phone and ours are through the same board, and your voice seems natural then, and unstrained, not as it is when we meet. But I know that some way we are meeting--our souls--in the infinite realm outside ourselves--beyond our consciousness--either sleeping or waking. Last night I dreamed a strange dream. A little girl, like one of the pictures in mother's old family photograph album, seemed to be talking with me,--dressed so quaintly in the dear old fashion of the days when mother taught the Sycamore Ridge School. She seemed to be playing with me in some way, and then she said: 'Oh, yes, I am your telephone; she knows all about it. I tell her every night as we play together.' And then she was no longer a little girl but a most beautiful soul and she said with great gentleness: 'In her heart she loves you--in her heart she loves you. This I know, only she is proud--proud with the Barclay pride; but in her heart she loves you; is not that enough?' What a strange dream! I wonder where we are--we who animate our bodies, when we sleep. What is sleep, but the proof that death is but a sleep? Oh, Jeanette, Jeanette, come into my soul as we sleep."

He folded the letter, sealed and addressed it, and dated the envelope, and put it in his desk--the desk before which Adrian Brownwell had sat, eating his heart out in futile endeavour to find his place in the world. Neal Ward had cleaned out one side of the desk, and was using that for his own. Mrs. Brownwell kept her papers in the other side, and one key locked them both. As he walked home that night under the stars, his heart was full of John Barclay's troubles. Neal knew Barclay well enough to know that the sensitive nature of the man, with his strongly developed instinctive faculty for getting at the truth, would be his curse in the turmoil or criticism through which he was going. So a day or two later Neal was not surprised to find a long statement in the morning press despatches from Barclay explaining and defending the methods of the National Provisions Company. He proved carefully that the notorious Door Strip saved large losses in transit of the National Provisions Company's grain and grain produce, and showed that in paying him for the use of these strips the railroad companies were saving great sums for widowed and orphaned stockholders of railroads--sums which would be his due for losses in transit if the strips were not used.

Neal Ward knew what it had cost Barclay in pride to give out that statement; so the young man printed it on the first page of the **Banner** with a kind editorial about Mr. Barclay and his good works. That night when the paper was off, and young Ward was working on the books of his office, he was called to the telephone.

"Is this you, Nealie Ward?" asked a woman's voice--the strong, clear, deep voice of an old woman. And when he had answered, the voice went on: "Well, Nealie, I wish to thank you for that editorial about John to-night in the paper; I'm Mary Barclay. It isn't more than half true, Nealie; and if it was all true, it isn't a fraction of what the truth ought to be if John did what he could, but it will do him a lot of good--right here in the home paper, and--Why, Jennie, I'm speaking with Nealie Ward,--why, do you think I am not old enough to talk with Nealie without breeding scandal?--as I was saying, my dear, it will cheer John up a little, and heaven knows he needs something. I'm--Jennie, for mercy sakes keep still; I know Nealie Ward and I knew his father when he wasn't as old as Nealie--did his washing for him; and boarded his mother four winters, and I have a right to say what I want to to that child." The boy and the grandmother laughed into the telephone. "Jennie is so afraid I'll do something improper," laughed Mrs. Barclay. "Oh, yes, by the way--here's a little item for your paper to-morrow: Jennie's mother is sick; I think it's typhoid, but you can't get John to admit it. So don't say typhoid." Then with a few more words she rang off.

When the *Banner* printed the item about Mrs. Barclay's illness, the town, in one of those outbursts of feeling which communities often have, seemed to try to show John Barclay the affection that was in their hearts for the man who had grown up among them, and the family that had been established under his name. Flowers--summer flowers--poured in on the Barclays. Children came with wild flowers, prairie flowers that Jane Barclay had not seen since she roamed over the unbroken sod about Minneola as a girl; and Colonel Culpepper came marching up the walk through the Barclay grounds, bearing his old-fashioned bouquet, as grandly as an ambassador bringing a king's gift. Jane Barclay sent word that she wished to see him.

"My dear," said the colonel, as he held the flowers toward her, "accept these flowers from those who have shared your bounty--from God's poor, my dear; these are God's smiles that they send you from their hearts--from their very hearts, my dear, from their poor hearts wherein God's smiles come none too often." She saw through glistening eyes the broken old figure, with his coat tightly buttoned on that July day to hide some shabbiness underneath. But she bade the colonel sit down, and they chatted of old times and old places and old faces for a few minutes; and the colonel, to whom any sort of social function was a rare and sweet occasion, stayed until the nurse had to beckon him out of the room over Mrs. Barclay's shoulder.

General Ward sent a note with a bunch of monthly blooming roses.

"MY DEAR JANE (he wrote): These roses are from slips we got from John's mother when we planted our little yard. This red one is from the very bush on which grew the rose John wore at his wedding. Pin it on the old scamp to-night, and see how he will look. He was a dapper little chap that night, and the years have hardly begun their work on him; or perhaps he is such a tough customer that he dulls the chisel of time. I do not know, and so long as it is so, you do not care, but we both know, and are both glad that of all the many things God has sent you in thirty years, he has sent you nothing so fine as the joy that came with the day John wore this rose for you--a joy that has grown while the rose has faded. And may this rose renew your joy for another thirty years."

John read the note when he came in from the mill that evening, and Jane watched the years slip off his face. He looked into the past as it spread itself on the carpet near the bed.

"Well, well, well," he said, as he smiled into the picture he saw, "I remember as well the general bringing that rose down to the office that morning, wrapped in blue tissue paper from cotton batting rolls!

The package was tied with fancy red braid that used to bind muslin bolts." He laughed quietly, and asked, "Jane, do you remember that old red braid?" The sick woman nodded. "Well, with the little blue package was a note from Miss Lucy, which said that my old teacher could not give me a present that year--times were cruelly hard then, you remember--but that she could and did put the blessing of her prayers on the rose, that all that it witnessed at my wedding would bring me happiness." He sat for a moment in silence, and, as the nurse was gone, he knelt beside the sick woman and kissed her. And as the wife stroked his head she whispered, "How that prayer has been answered, John--dear, hasn't it?" And the great clock in the silent hall below ticked away some of the happiest minutes it had ever measured.

But when he passed out of the sick room, the world--the maddening press of affairs, and the combat in his soul--snapped back on his shoulders with a mental click as though a load had fallen into its old place. He stood before his organ, and could not press the keys. As he sat there in the twilight made by the shaded electric lamps, the struggle rose in his heart against the admission of anything into his scheme of life but material things, and the conflict raged unchecked. What a silliness, he said, to think that the mummery of a woman over a rose could affect a life. Life is what the succession of the days brings. The thing is or is not, he said to himself, and the gibber about prayer and the moral force that moves the universe is for the weak-minded. So he took his hell to bed with him as it went every night, and during the heavy hours when he could not sleep, he tiptoed into the sick room, and looked at the thin face of his wife, sleeping a restless, feverish sleep, and a great fear came into his heart.

Once as the morning dawned he asked the nurse whom he met in the hall, "Is it typhoid?"

She was a stranger to the town, and she said to him, "What does the doctor tell you?"

"That's not the point," he insisted. "What do you think?"

She looked at him for an undecided moment and replied, "I'm not paid to think, Mr. Barclay," and went past him with her work. But he knew the truth. He went to his bed, and threw himself upon it, a-tremble with remorse and fear, and the sneer in his heart stilled his lips and he could not look outside himself for help. So the morning came, and another day, bringing its thousand cares, faced him, like a jailer with his tortures.

Time dragged slowly in the sick room and at the mill. One doctor brought another, and the Barclay private car went far east and came flying back with a third. The town knew that Mrs. John Barclay was dangerously sick. There came hopeful days when the patient's mind was clear; on one of these days Mrs. McHurdie called, and they let her see the sick woman. She brought some flowers.

"In the flowers, Jane," she said, "you will find something from Watts." Mrs. McHurdie smiled. "You know he sat up till 'way after midnight last night, playing his accordion. Oh, it's been years since he has touched it. And this morning when I got up, I found him sitting by the kitchen table, writing. It's a poem for you." Mrs. McHurdie looked rather sheepish as she said: "You know how Watts is, Jane; he just made me bring it. You can read it when you get well."

They hurried Mrs. McHurdie out, and when Jane Barclay went to sleep, they found tears on her pillow, and in her hand the verses,--the limping, awkward verses of an old man, whose music only echoed back from the past. The nurses and the young doctor from Boston had a good laugh at it. Each of the four stanzas began with two lines that asked: "Oh, don't you remember the old river road, that ran through the sweet-scented wood?" To them it was a curious parody on something old and quaint that they had long since forgotten. But to the woman who lay murmuring of other days, whose lips were parched for the waters of brooks that had surrendered to the plough a score of years ago, the halting verses of Watts McHurdie were laden with odours of grape blossoms, of wild cucumbers and sumach, of elder blossoms, and the fragrance of the crushed leaves of autumn. And the music of distant ripples played in her feverish brain and the sobbing voice of the turtle dove sang out of the past for her as she slept. All through the day and the night and for many nights and days she whispered of the trees and the running water and the wild grass and the birds.

And so one morning when it was still gray, she woke and said to John, who bent over her, "Why, dear, we are almost home; there are the lights across the river; just one more hill, dearie, and then--" And then with the water prattling in her ears at the last ford she turned to the wall and sank to rest.

Day after day, until the days and nights became a week and the week repeated itself until nearly a month was gone, John Barclay, dry-eyed and all but dumb, paced the terrace before his house by night, and by day roamed through the noisy mill or wandered through his desolate house, seeking peace that would not come to him. The whole foundation of his scheme of life was crumbling beneath him. He had built thirty-five years of his manhood upon the theory that the human brain is the god of things as they are and as they must be. The structure of his life was an imposing edifice, and men called it great and successful. Yet as he walked his lonely way in those black days that followed Jane's death, there came into his consciousness a strong, overmastering conviction, which he dared not accept, that his house was built on sand. For here were things outside of his plans, outside of his very beliefs, coming into his life, bringing calamity, sorrow, and tragedy with them into his own circle of friends, into his own

household, into his own heart. As he walked through the dull, lonely
hours he could not escape the vague feeling, though he fought it as
one mad fights for his delusion, that all the tragedies piling up
about him came from his own mistakes. Over and over again he threshed
the past. Molly Brownwell's cry, "You have sold me into bondage, John
Barclay," would not be stilled, though at times he could smile at it;
and the broken body and shamed face of her father haunted him like an
obsession. Night after night when he tried to sleep, Robert Hendricks'
letter burned in fire before his eyes, and at last so mad was the
struggle in his soul that he hugged these things to him that he might
escape the greater horror: the dreadful red headlines in the
sensational paper they had sent him from the City office which
screamed at him, "John Barclay slays his wife--Aids a water
franchise grab that feeds the people typhoid germs and his own wife
dies of the fever." He had not replied to the letter from the law
department of the Provisions Company which asked if he wished to sue
for libel, and begged him to do so. He had burned the paper, but the
headlines were seared into his brain.

Over and over he climbed the fiery ladder of his sins: the death of
General Hendricks, the sacrifice of Molly Culpepper, the temptation
and fall of her father, the death of his boyhood's friend, and then
the headlines. These things were laid at his door, and over and over
again, like Sisyphus rolling the stones uphill, he swept them away
from his threshold, only to find that they rolled right back again.
And with them came at times the suspicion that his daughter's
unhappiness was upon him also. And besides these things, a hundred
business transactions wherein he had cheated and lied for money rose
to disturb him. And through it all, through his anguish and shame, the
faith of his life kept battling for its dominion.

Once he sent for Bemis and tried to talk himself into peace with his
friend. He did not speak of the things that were corroding his heart,

but he sat by and heard himself chatter his diabolic creed as a drunkard watches his own folly.

"Lige," he said, "I'm sick of that infernal charities bureau we've got. I'm going to abolish it. These philanthropic millionaires make me sick at the stomach, Lige. What do they care for the people? They know what I know, that the damn people are here to be skinned." He laughed viciously and went on: "Sometimes I think we filthy rich are divided into two classes: those of us who keep mistresses, and those of us who have harmless little entanglements with preachers and college presidents. Neither the lemon-haired women nor the college presidents interfere with our business; they don't hamper us--not the slightest. They just take our money, and for a few idle hours amuse us, and make us feel that we are good fellows. As for me, I'll have neither women nor college presidents purring around my ankles. I'm going to cut out the philanthropy appropriation to-day."

And he was as good as his word. But that did not help. The truth kept wrenching his soul, and his feet blindly kept trying to find a path to peace.

It was late one night in August, and a dead moon was hanging in the south, when, treading the terrace before his house, he saw a shadow moving down the stairway in the hall. At first his racked nerves quivered, but when he found that it was his mother, he went to meet her, exclaiming as he mounted the steps to the veranda, "Why, mother, what is it--is anything wrong?"

Though it was past midnight, Mary Barclay was dressed for the day. She stood in the doorway with the dimmed light behind her, a tall, strong woman, straight and gaunt as a Nemesis. "No, John--nothing is wrong--in the house." She walked into the veranda and began as she approached a chair, "Sit down, John; I wish to talk with you."

"Well, mother--what is it?" asked the son, as he sat facing her.

She paused a moment looking earnestly at his face and replied, "The time has come when we must talk this thing out, John, soul to soul."

He shrank from what was coming. His instinct told him to fight away the crisis. He began to palaver, but his mother cut him short, as she exclaimed:--

"Why don't you let Him in, John?"

"Let who in?" asked her son.

"You know Whom, John Barclay; that was your grandfather speaking then, the old polly foxer. You know, my boy. Don't you remember me bending over the town wash-tub when you were a child, Johnnie? Don't you remember the old song I used to sing--of course you do, child--as I rubbed the clothes on the board: 'Let Him in, He is your friend, let Him in, He is your friend; He will keep you to the end--let--Him--in!' Of course you remember it, boy, and you have been fighting Him with all your might for six months now, and since Jane went, the fight is driving you crazy--can't you see, John?"

The son did not reply for a moment, then he said, "Oh, well, mother, that was all right in that day, but--"

"John Barclay," cried the mother sternly, as she leaned toward him, "the faith that bore your father a martyr to the grave, sustained me in this wilderness, and kept me happy as I scrubbed for your bread, shall not be scoffed in my presence. We are going to have this thing out to-night. I, who bore you, and nursed you, and fed you, and staked my soul on your soul, have some rights to-night. Here you are, fifty-four years old, and what have you done? You've killed your friend and your friend's father before him--I know that, John. You've wrecked the life of the sister of your first sweetheart, and put fear and disgrace in her father's face forever--forever, John Barclay, as long as he lives. I know that too; I haven't been wrapped in pink cotton all these years, boy--I've lived my own life since you left my wing, and made my own way too, as far as that goes. And now you are trying to quench the fires of remorse in your soul because your wife died a victim of your selfish, ruthless, practical scheme of things. More than that, my son--more than that, your child is suffering all the agony that a woman can suffer because of your devilish system of traffic in blood for money. You know what I mean, John. That boy told the truth, as you admit, and he could either run or lie, and for being a man you have broken up a God-sent love merely to satisfy your own vanity. Oh, John--John," she cried passionately, "my poor, blind, foolish boy--haven't you found the ashes in the core of your faith yet--aren't you ready to quit?"

He began, "Don't you think, mother, I have suffered--"

"Suffered, boy? Suffered? Of course you have suffered, John," she answered, taking his hands in hers. "I have seen the furnace fires smoking your face, and I know you have suffered, Johnnie; that's why I am coming to you--to ask you to quit suffering. Look at it, my boy--what are you suffering for? Is it material power you want? Well, you have never had it. The people are going right along running their own affairs in spite of you. All your nicely built card houses are knocked over. In the states and in the federal government, in spite of your years of planning and piecing out your little practical system, at the very first puff of God's breath it goes to pieces. The men whom you bought and paid for don't stay bought--do they, my boy? Oh, your old mother knows, John. Men who will sell are never worth buying; and the house that relies on them, falls. You have built a sand dam, son--like the dams you used to build in the spring stream when you were a child. It melts under pressure like straw. You have no worldly power. In this practical world you are a failure, and good old Phil Ward, who went out into the field and scattered seeds of discontent at your system--he is seeing his harvest ripen in his old age, John," she cried. "Can't you see your failure? Look at it from a practical standpoint: what thing in the last thirty years have you advocated, and Philemon Ward opposed, that to-day he has not realized and you lost? His prescription for the evils may have been wrong many times, but his diagnosis of them was always right, and they are being cured, in spite of all your protest that they did not exist. Which of you has won his practical fight in this practical world--his God or your God; the ideal world or the material world, boy? Can't you see it?" The old woman leaned forward and looked in her son's dull, unresponsive face. "Can't you see how you have failed?" she pleaded.

They rose together and began to pace the long floor of the veranda. "Oh, mother," he cried, as he put his arm about her, "I am so lonely--so tired, so sick in the heart of me."

They didn't speak for a time, but walked together in silence. At length the mother began again. "John," she said, as they turned at the end of the porch, "I suppose you are saying that you have your money--that it is material--solid, substantial, and undeniable. But is it? Isn't it all a myth? Leave it where it is--in the shape of securities and stocks and credits--what will it do? Will it bring Jane back? Will it give Jeanette her heart's desire, and make her happy all her life? You know, dear, that it will only make me miserable. Has it made you happy, John? Turn it into gold and pile it up in the front yard--and what will it buy that poor Phil Ward has not had all of his life--good food, good clothing--good enough, at least--a happy family, useful children, and a good name? A good name, John, is rather to be chosen than great riches--than all your money, my son--rather to be chosen than all your money. Can you buy that with your millions piled on millions?"

They were walking slowly as she spoke, and they turned into the terrace. There they stood looking at the livid moon sinking behind the great house.

"Is there more joy in this house than in any other house in town, John--answer me squarely, son--answer me," she cried. He shook his head sadly and sighed. "A mother, whose heart bleeds every hour as she sees her son torturing himself with footless remorse; that is one. A heart-broken, motherless girl, whose lover has been torn away from her by her father's vanity and her own pride, and whose mother has been taken as a pawn in the game her father played with no motive, no benefit, nothing but to win his point in a miserable little game of politics; that is number two. And a man who should be young for twenty years yet, who should have been useful for thirty years--and now what is he? powerless, useless, wretched, lonely, who spends his time walking about fighting against God, that he may prove his own wisdom and nothing more."

"Mother," cried Barclay, petulantly, "I can't stand this--that you should turn on me--now." He broke away from her, and stood alone. "When I need you most, you reproach me. When I need sympathy, you scorn all that I have done. You can't prove your God. Why should I accept Him?"

The gaunt old woman stretched out her arms and cried: "Oh, John Barclay, prove your god. Tell him to come and give you a moment's happiness--set him to work to restore your good name; command him to make Jeanette happy. These things my God can do! Let your Mammon," she cried with all the passion of her soul, "let your Mammon come down and do one single miracle like that." Her voice broke and she sobbed.

"What a tower of Babel--an industrial Babel, you are building, John--you and your kith and kind. The last century gave us Schopenhauers and Kants, all denying God, and this one gives us Railroad Kings and Iron Kings and Wheat Kings, all by their works proclaiming that Mammon has the power and the glory and the Kingdom. O ye workers of iniquity!" she cried, and her voice lifted, "ye wicked and perverse--"

She did not finish, but broken and trembling, her strength spent and her faith scorned, she sank on her knees by a marble urn on the terrace and sobbed and prayed. When she rose, the dawn was breaking, and she looked for a moment at her son, who had been sitting near her, and cried: "Oh, my boy, my little boy that I nursed at my breast--let Him in, He is your friend--and oh, my God, sustain my faith!"

Her son came to her side and led her into the house. But he went to his room and began the weary round, battling for his own faith.

As he stood by his open window that day at the mill, he saw Molly Brownwell across the pond, going into his home. He watched her idly and saw Jeanette meet her at the door, and then as his memory went back to the old days, he tried to find tears for the woman who had died, but he could only rack his soul. Tears were denied to him.

He was a rich man--was John Barclay; some people thought that, taking his wealth as wealth goes, all carefully invested in substantial things--in material things, let us say--he was the richest man in the Mississippi Valley. He bought a railroad that day when he looked through the office window at Molly Brownwell--a railroad three thousand miles long. And he bought a man's soul in a distant city--a man whom he did not know even by name, but the soul was thrown in "to boot" in a bargain; and he bought a woman's body whose face he had never seen, and that went as part of another trade he was making and he did not even know they had thrown it in. And he bought a child's life, and he bought a city's prosperity in another bargain, and bought the homage of a state, and the tribute of a European kingdom, as part of the day's huckstering. But with all his wealth and power, he could not buy one tear--not one little, miserable tear to moisten his grief-dried heart. For tears, just then, were a trifle high. So Mr. Barclay had to do without, though the man whose soul he bought wept, and the woman whose body came with a trade, sobbed, and the dead face of the child was stained with a score of tears.

They went to Jeanette Barclay's room,--the gray-haired woman and the girl,--and they sat there talking for a time--talking of things that were on their lips and not in their hearts. Each felt that the other understood her. And each felt that something was to be said. For one day before the end Jeanette's mother had said to her: "Jennie, if I am not here always go to Molly--ask her to tell you about her girlhood." The mother had rested for a while, and then added, "Tell her I said for you to ask her, and she'll know what I mean."

"Jeanette," said Molly Brownwell, "your mother and I were girls together. Your father saw more of her at our house than he did at her own home, until they married. Did you know that?" Jeanette nodded assent. "So one day last June she said to me, 'Molly, sometime I wish you would tell Jennie all about you and Bob.'"

Mrs. Brownwell paused, and Jeanette said, "Yes, mother told me to ask you to, Aunt Molly." Tears came into the daughter's eyes, and she added, "I think she knew even then that- "

And then it all came back, and after a while the elder woman was saying, "Well, once upon a time there lived a princess, my dear. All good stories begin so--don't they? She was a fat, pudgy little princess who longed to grow up and have hoop-skirts like a real

sure-enough woman princess, and there came along a tall prince--the
tallest, handsomest prince in all the wide world, I think. And he and
the princess fell in love, as princesses and princes will, you know,
my dear,--just as they do now, I am told. And the prince had to go
away on business and be gone a long, long time, and while he was gone
the father of the princess and the friend of the prince got into
trouble--and the princess thought it was serious trouble. She thought
the father of the prince would have to go to jail and maybe the prince
and his friend fail. My, my, Jeanette, what a big word that word fail
seemed to the little fat princess! So she let a man make love to her
who could lend them all some money and keep the father out of jail and
the prince and his friend from the awful fate of failure. So the man
lent the money and made love, and made love. And the little princess
had to listen; every one seemed to like to have her listen, so she
listened and she listened, and she was a weak little princess. She
knew she had wronged the prince by letting the man make love to her,
and her soul was smudged and--oh, Jeanette, she was such a foolish,
weak, miserable little princess, and they didn't tell her that there
is only one prince for every princess, and one princess for every
prince--so she took the man, and sent away the prince, and the man
made love ever so beautifully--but it was not the real thing, my
dear,--not the real thing. And afterwards when she saw the
prince--so young and so strong and so handsome, her heart burned for
him as with a flame, and she was not ashamed; the wicked, wicked
princess, she didn't know. And so they walked together one night right
up to the brink of the bad place, dearie--right up to the brink; and
the princess shuddered back, and saved the prince. Oh, Jeanette,
Jeanette, Jeanette," sobbed the woman, in the girl's arms, "right in
this room, in this very room, which was your mother's room in the old
house, I came out of the night, as bad a woman as God ever sent away
from Him. And your mother and I cried it out, and talked it out, and I
fought it out, and won. Oh, I won, Jeanette--I won!"

The two women were silent for a time, and then the elder went on: "That's what your mother wished you to know--that for every princess there is just one real prince, and for every prince there is just one real princess, my dear, and when you have found him, and know he is true, nothing--not money, not friends, not father nor mother--when he is honest, not even pride--should stand between you. That is what your mother sent you, dearie. Do you understand?"

"I think I do, Aunt Molly--I think so," repeated the girl. She looked out of the window for a moment, and then cried, "Oh, Aunt Molly--but I can't, I can't. How could he, Aunt Molly--how could he?" The girl buried her face in the woman's lap, and sobbed.

After a time the elder woman spoke. "You know he loves you, don't you, dear?"

The girl shook her head and cried, "But how could he?" and repeated it again and again.

"And you still love him--I know that, my dear, or you could not--you would not care, either," she added.

And so after a time the tears dried, as tears will, and the two women fell back into the pale world of surfaces, and as Molly Brownwell left she took the girl's hand and said: "You won't forget about the little pudgy princess--the dear, foolish, little weak princess, will you, Jeanette? And, dearie," she added as she stood on the lower steps of the porch, "don't--don't always be so proud--not about that, my dear--about everything else in the world, but not about that." And so she went back into the world, and ceased to be a fairy godmother, and took up her day's work.

John Barclay went to the City that night for the first time in two months, and Jeanette and her Grandmother Barclay kept the big house alone. In ten days he came back; his face was still hard, and the red rims around his eyes were dry, and his voice was sullen, as it had been for many weeks. His soul was still wrestling with a spirit that would not give up the fight. That night his daughter tried to sit with him, as she had tried many nights before. They sat looking at the stars in silence as was their wont. Generally the father had risen and walked away, but that night he turned upon her and said:--

"Jeanette, don't you like to be rich? I guess you are the richest girl in this country. Doesn't that sound good to you?"

"No, father," she answered simply, and continued, "What can I do with all that money?"

"Marry some man who's got sense enough to double it, and double it," cried Barclay, harshly. "Then there'll be no question but that you'll be the richest people in the world."

"And then what?" asked the girl.

"Then--then," he cried, "make the people in this world stand around--that's what."

"But, father," she said as she put her hand on his arm, "what if I don't want them to stand around? Why should I have to bother about it?"

"Oh," he groaned, "your grandmother has been filling you full of nonsense." He did not speak for a time, and at length she rose to go to bed. "Jeanette," he cried so suddenly that it startled her, "are you still moping after Neal Ward? Do you love him? Do you want me to go and get him for you?"

The girl stood by her father's chair a moment and then answered colourlessly: "No, father, I don't want you to get him for me. I am not moping for him, as you call it."

Her desolate tone reached some chord in his very heart, for he caught her hand, and put it to his cheek and said softly, "But she loves him--my poor little girl loves him?"

She tried to pull away her hand and replied, in the same dead voice: "Oh, well--that doesn't matter much, I suppose. It's all over--so far as I am concerned." She turned to leave him, and he cried:--

"My dear, my dear--why don't you go to him?"

She stopped a moment and looked at her father, and even in the starlight she could see his hard mouth and his ruthless jaw. Then she cried out, "Oh, father, I can't--I can't--" After a moment she turned and looked at him, and asked, "Would you? Would you?" and walked into the house without waiting for an answer.

The father sat crumpled up in his chair, listening to the flames crackling in his heart. The old negation was fighting for its own, and he was weary and broken and sick as with a palsy of the soul. For everything in him trembled. There was no solid ground under him. He had visited his material kingdom in the City, and had seen its strong fortresses and had tried all of its locks and doors, and found them firm and fast. But they did not satisfy his soul; something within him kept mocking them; refusing to be awed by their power, and the eternal "yes" rushed through his reason like a great wind.

As he sat there, suddenly, as from some power outside, John Barclay felt a creaking of his resisting timbers, and he quit the struggle.

His heart was lead in his breast, and he walked through the house to
his pipe organ, that had stood silent in the hall for nearly a year.
He stood hesitatingly before it for a second, and then wearily lay him
down to rest, on a couch beside it, where, when he had played the last
time, Jane lay and listened. He was tired past all telling, but his
soul was relaxed. He lay there for hours--until the tall clock above
his head chimed two. He could not sleep, but his consciousness was
inert and his mind seemed limp and empty, as one who has worked past
his limit. The hymn that the clock chimed through the quarter hours
repeated itself over and over again without meaning in his brain.
Something aroused him; he started up suddenly, and lying half on his
elbow and half on his side he stared about him, and was conscious of a
great light in the room: it was as though there was a fire near by and
he was alarmed, but he could not move. As he looked into space,
terrified by the paralysis that held him, he saw across the face of
the organ, "Righteousness exalteth a Nation, but sin is a reproach to
any people."

Quick as a flash his mind went back to the time that same motto stared
meaninglessly at him from above the pulpit in the chapel at West
Point, to which he had been appointed official visitor at Commencement
many years before. But that night as he gazed at the text its meaning
came rushing through his brain. It came so quickly that he could not
will it back nor reason it in. Righteousness, he knew, was not
piety--not wearing your Sunday clothes to church and praying and
singing psalms; it was living honestly and kindly and charitably and
dealing decently with every one in every transaction; and sin--that,
he knew--was the cheating, the deceiving, and the malicious greed
that had built up his company and scores of others like it all over
the land. That, he knew--that bribery and corruption and vicarious
stealing which he had learned to know as business--that was a
reproach to any people, and as it came to him that he was a miserable
offender and that the other life, the decent life, was the right life,

he was filled with a joy that he could not express, and he let the light fail about him unheeded, and lay for a time in a transport of happiness. He had found the secret.

The truth had come to him--to him first of all men, and it was his to tell. The joy of it--that he should find out what righteousness was--that it was not crying "Lord, Lord" and playing the hypocrite--thrilled him. And then the sense of his sinning came over him, but only with joy too, because he felt he could show others how foolish they were. The clock stopped ticking; the chimes were silent, and he lay unconscious of his body, with his spirit bathed in some new essence that he did not understand and did not try to understand. Finally he rose and went to his organ and turned on the motor, and put his hands to the keys. As he played the hymn to the "Evening Star," John Barclay looked up and saw his mother standing upon the stair with her fine old face bathed in tears. And then at last--

Tears? Tears for Mr. Barclay? All these months there have been no tears for him--none, except miserable little corroding tears of rage and shame. But now there are tears for Mr. Barclay, large, man's size, soul-healing tears--tears of repentance; not for the rich Mr. Barclay, the proud Mr. Barclay, the powerful, man-hating, God-defying Mr. Barclay of Sycamore Ridge, but for John Barclay, a contrite man, the humblest in all the kingdom.

And as John Barclay let his soul rise with the swelling music, he felt the solace of a great peace in his heart; he turned his wet face upward and cried, "Oh, mother, mother, I feel like a child!" Then Mary Barclay knew that her son had let Him in, knew in her own heart all the joy there is in heaven over one sinner that repenteth.

CHAPTER XXIX

It is written in the Book that holds the wisdom of our race that one
who is reborn into the Kingdom of God, enters as a little child. It is
there in black and white, yet few people get the idea into their
consciousnesses. They expect regeneration to produce an upright man.
God knows better than that. And we should know better too when it is
written down for us. And so you good people who expect to see John
Barclay turn rightabout face on the habits of a lifetime are to be
disappointed. For a little child stumbles and falls and goes the wrong
way many times before it learns the way of life. There came days after
that summer night of 1904, when John Barclay fell--days when he would
sneak into the stenographers' room in his office in the City and tear
up some letter he had dictated, when he would send a telegram
annulling an order, when he would find himself cheating and gouging
his competitors or his business associates,--even days when he had
not the moral courage to retrace his steps although he knew he was
wrong. Shame put her brand on his heart, and his face showed to those
who watched it closely--and there were scores of fellow-gamblers at
the game with him, whose profits came from watching his face--his
face showed forth uncertainty and daze. So men said, "The old man's
off his feed," or others said, "Barclay's losing his nerve"; and still
others said, "Can it be possible that the old hypocrite is getting a
sort of belated conscience?"

But slowly, inch by inch, the child within him grew; he gripped his
soul with the iron hand of will that had made a man of him, and when
the child fell and ached with shame, Barclay's will sustained the
weakling. We are so hidden by our masks that this struggle in the
man's soul, though guessed at by some of those about him, was unknown
to the hundreds who saw him every day. But for him the universe had

changed. And as a child, amazed, he looked upon the new wonder of God's order about him and went tripping and stumbling and toppling over awkwardly through it all as one learning some new equilibrium. There were times when his heart grew sick, and he would have given it all up. There were hours when he did surrender; when he did a mean thing and gloried in it, or a cowardly thing and apologized for it. But his will rose and turned him back to his resolve. He found the big things easy, and the little things hard to do. So he kept at the big things until they had pushed him so far toward his goal that the little things were details which he repaired slowly and with anguish of humiliation in secret, and unknown even to those who were nearest to him.

And all this struggle was behind the hard face, under the broad, high forehead, back of the mean jaw, beneath the cover of the sharp brazen eyes. Even in Sycamore Ridge they did not suspect the truth until Barclay had grown so strong in his new faith that he could look at his yesterdays without shuddering.

The year of our Lord nineteen hundred and six was a slow year politically in Sycamore Ridge, so in the parliament at McHurdie's shop discussion took somewhat wider range than was usual. It may interest metaphysicians in the world at large to know that the McHurdie parliament that August definitely decided that this is not a material world; that sensation is a delusion, that the whole phantasmagoria of the outer and material world is a reaction of some sort upon the individual consciousness. Up to this point the matter is settled, and metaphysicians may as well make a record of the decision; for Watts McHurdie, Jacob Dolan, Philemon Ward, Martin Culpepper, and sometimes Oscar Fernald, know just exactly as much about it as the ablest logician in the world. It is, however, regrettable that after deciding that the external world is but a divine reaction upon the individual consciousness, the parliament was unable to reach any sort of a

decision as to whose consciousness received the picture. Mr. Dolan
maintained vigorously that his consciousness was the one actually
affected, and that the colonel and the general and Watts were mere
hallucinations of his. The general held that Jake and the others were
accessory phantasms of his own dream, and Watts and the colonel, being
of more poetical temperament, held that the whole outfit was a chimera
in some larger consciousness, whose entity it is not given us to know.
As for Oscar, he claimed the parliament was crazy, and started to
prove it, when it was thought best to shift and modify the discussion;
and, therefore, early in September, when the upper currents of the
national atmosphere were vocal with discordant allegations, denials,
accusations, and maledictions, in Watts McHurdie's shop the question
before the house was, "How many people are there in the world?" For
ten days, in the desultory debate that had droned through the summer,
the general, true to his former contention, insisted that there was
only one person in the world. Mr. Dolan, with the Celtic elasticity of
reason, was willing to admit two.

"You and me and no more--all the rest is background for us," he
proclaimed. "If the you of the moment is the colonel--well and good;
then the colonel and I for it; but if it is the general and I--to the
trees with your colonel and Watts, and the three billion
others--you're merely stage setting, and become third persons."

"But," asked McHurdie, "if I exist this minute with you, and then you
focus your attention on Mart there, the next minute, and he exists,
what becomes of me when you turn your head from me?"

Dolan did not answer. He dipped into the *Times* and read awhile; and
the colonel and the general got out the checkerboard and plunged into
a silent game. At length Dolan, after the fashion of debaters in the
parliament, came out of his newspaper and said:--

"That, Mr. McHurdie, is a problem ranging off the subject, into the theories of the essence of time and space, and I refuse to answer it."

Me Hurdie kept on working, and the hands of the clock slipped around nearly an hour. Then the bell tinkled and Neal Ward came in on his afternoon round for news to print in the next day's issue of the *Banner*.

"Anything new?" he asked.

"Mrs. Dorman is putting new awnings on the rear windows of her store--did you get that?" asked McHurdie.

The young man made a note of the fact.

"Yes," added Dolan, "and you may just say that Hon. Jacob Dolan, former sheriff of Garrison County, and a member of 'C' Company, well known in this community, who has been custodian of public buildings and grounds in and for Garrison County, state of Kansas, ss., is contemplating resigning his position and removing to the National Soldiers' Home at Leavenworth for the future."

Young Ward smiled, but did not take the item down in his note-book.

"It isn't time yet," he said.

"Why not?" asked Dolan.

"Only two months and a half since I printed that the last time. It can't go oftener than four times a year, and it's been in twice this year. Late in December will time it about right."

"What's the news with you, boy?" asked Dolan.

"Well," said the young man, pausing carefully as if to make a selection from a large and tempting assortment, but really swinging his arms for a long jump into the heart of the matter in his mind, "have you heard that John Barclay has given the town his pipe organ?"

"You don't say!" exclaimed McHurdie.

"Tired of it?" asked Dolan, as though twenty-five-thousand-dollar pipe organs were raining in the town every few days.

"It'll not be that, Jake," said Watts. "John is no man to tire of things."

"No, it's not that, Mr. Dolan," answered Neal Ward. "He has sent word to the mayor and council that he is going to have the organ installed in Barclay Hall this week at his own expense, and he accompanied the letter with fifty thousand dollars in securities to hire a permanent organist and a band-master for the band; and a band concert and an organ concert will alternate in the hall every week during the year. I gather from reading his letter that Mr. Barclay believes the organ will do more good in the hall than in his house."

The general and the colonel kept on at their game. Dolan whistled, and Watts nodded his head. "That's what I would say he did it for," said McHurdie.

"Are the securities N.P.C. stock?" asked Dolan, tentatively.

"No," replied Neal; "I saw them; they are municipal bonds of one sort and another."

"Well, well--Johnnie at the mill certainly is popping open like a chestnut bur. Generally when he has some scheme on to buy public sentiment he endows something with N.P.C. stock, so that in case of a lawsuit against the company he'd have the people interested in protecting the stock. This new tack is certainly queer doings. Certainly queer doings for the dusty miller!" repeated Dolan.

"Well, it's like his buying the waterworks of Bemis last month, and that land at the new pumping station, and giving the council money to build the new dam and power-house. He had no rebate or take back in that--at least no one can see it," said the young man.

"Nellie says," put in Watts, "that she heard from Mrs. Fernald, who got it from her girl, who got it from the girl who works in the Hub restaurant, who had it from Mrs. Carnine's girl--so it come pretty straight--that Lige made John pay a pretty penny for the waterworks, and they had a great row because John would give up the fight."

"Yes," replied Dolan, "it come to me from one of the nigger prisoners in the jail, who has a friend who sweeps out Gabe's bank, that he heard John and Lige dickering, and that Lige held John up for a hundred thousand cold dollars for his bargain."

"The Associated Press to-day," said young Ward, "has a story to the effect that there is a great boom in certain railroad stocks owing to some secret operations of Mr. Barclay. They don't know what he is doing, but things are pretty shaky. He refuses to make a statement."

"He's a queer canny little man," explained Watts. "You never know where he'll break out next."

"Well, he's up to some devilment," exclaimed Dolan; "you can depend on that. Why do you suppose he's laying off the hands at the strip factory?"

The young man shook his head. "Give it up. I asked Mr. Mason and the best I could get out of him was a parrot-like statement that 'owing to the oversupply of our commodity, we have decided to close operations for the present. We have, therefore,' he said pompously, 'given each of our employees unable to find immediate work here, a ticket for himself and family to any point in the United States to which he may desire to go, and have agreed to pay the freight on his household goods also.' That was every word I could get out of him--and you know Mr. Mason is pretty talkative sometimes."

"Queer doings for the dusty miller," repeated Dolan.

The group by the bench heard the slap of the checkerboard on its shelf, and General Ward cut into the conversation as one who had never been out of it. "The boy's got good blood in him; it will come out some day--he wasn't made a Thatcher and a Barclay and a Winthrop for nothing. Lizzie was over there the other night for tea with them, and she said she hadn't seen John so much like himself for years."

Young Ward went about his afternoon's work and the parliament continued its debate on miscellaneous public business. The general pulled the *Times* from Dolan's pocket and began turning it over. He stopped and read for a few moments and exclaimed:--

"Boys--see here. Maybe this explains something we were talking about." He began reading a news item sent out from Washington, D.C. The item stated that the Department of Commerce and Labour had scored what every one in official circles believed was the most important victory ever achieved by the government outside of a war. The item continued:--

"Within the last ten days, the head of one of the largest so-called trusts in this country called at the department, and explained that his organization, which controls a great staple commodity, was going into voluntary liquidation. The organization in question has been the subject of governmental investigation for nearly two years, and investigators were constantly hampered and annoyed by attempts of politicians of the very highest caste, outside of the White House, trying to get inspectors removed or discredited, and all along the line of its investigations the government has felt a powerful secret influence shielding the trust. As an evidence of his good faith in the disorganization, the head of the trust, while he was here, promised to send to the White House, what he called his 'political burglar's kit,' consisting of a card index, labelling and ticketing with elaborate cross references and cabinet data, every man in the United States who is in politics far enough to get to his state legislature, or to be a nominee of his party for county attorney. This outfit, shipped in a score of great boxes, was dumped at the White House to-day, and it is said that a number of the cards indicating the reputation of certain so-called conservative senators and congressmen may be framed. There is a great hubbub in Washington, and the newspaper correspondents who called at the White House on their morning rounds were regaled by a confidential glimpse into the cards and the cabinets. It is likely that the whole outfit will be filed in the Department of Commerce and Labour, and will constitute the basis of what is called around the White House to-day, a 'National Rogues' Gallery.' The complete details of every senatorial election held in the country during twelve years last past, showing how to reach any Senator susceptible to any influence whatsoever, whether political, social, or religious, are among the trophies of the chase in the hands of the Mighty Hunter for Big Game to-day."

When General Ward had finished reading, he lifted up his glasses and said: "Well, that's it, boys; John has come to his turn of the road.

Here's the rest. It says: 'The corporation in question is practically controlled by one man, the man who has placed the information above mentioned in the hands of the government. It is a corporation owning no physical property whatever, and is organized as a rebate hopper, if one may so style it. The head of the corporation stated when he was here recently that he is preparing to buy in every share of the company's stock at the price for which it was sold and then--' Jake, where is page 3 with the rest of this article on it?" asked the general.

"Why, I threw that away coming down here," responded Dolan.

"Rather leaves us in the air--doesn't it?" suggested the colonel.

"Well, it's John. I know enough to know that--from Neal," said the general.

The afternoon sun was shining in the south window of the shop. Dolan started to go. In the doorway McHurdie halted him.

"Jake," he cried, pointing a lean, smutty finger at Dolan, "Jake Dolan, if there are only two people in the world, what becomes of me when you begin talking to Mart? If you knew, you would not dodge. In philosophy no man can stand on his constitutional rights. Turn state's evidence, Jake Dolan, and tell the truth--what becomes of me?"

"'Tis an improper question," replied Dolan, and then drawing himself up and pulling down the front of his coat, he added, "'Tis not a matter that may be discussed among gentlemen," and with that he disappeared.

The front door-bell tinkled, and the parliament prepared to adjourn. The colonel helped the poet close his store and bring in the wooden horse from the sidewalk, and then Molly Brownwell came with her phaeton and drove the two old men home. On the way up Main Street they overhauled Neal Ward. Mrs. Brownwell turned in to the sidewalk and called, "Neal, can you run over to the house a moment this evening?" And when he answered in the affirmative, she let the old nag amble gently up the street.

"How pretty you are, Aunt Molly," exclaimed Neal, as the gray-haired woman who could still wear a red ribbon came into the room where he sat waiting for her. The boy's compliment pleased her, and she did not hesitate to say so. But after that she plunged into the subject that was uppermost in her heart.

"Neal," she said, as she drew her chair in front of him so that she could see his face and know the truth, no matter what his lips might say, "we're partners now, aren't we, or what amounts to the same thing?" She smiled good-naturedly. "I own the overdraft at the bank and you own the mortgage at the court-house. So I am going to ask you a plain question; and if you say it isn't any of my business, I'll attempt to show you that it is. Neal," she asked, looking earnestly into his face, "why do you write to Jeanette Barclay every day of your life and not mail the letters?"

The youth flushed. "Why--Aunt Molly--how did you know?--I never told--"

"No, Neal, you never told me; but this afternoon while you we're out I was looking for Adrian's check-book; I was sure we paid Dorman's bill last April, and that I took the check over myself. I was going through the desk, and I got on your side, thinking I might have left the check-book there by mistake, and I ran into the very midst of those letters, before I knew what I was about. Now, Neal--why?"

The young man gazed at the woman seriously for a time and then parried her question with, "Why do you care--what difference can it make to you, Aunt Molly?"

"Because," she answered quickly, "because I wish to see my partner happy. He will do better work so--if you desire to put it on a cold-blooded basis. Oh, Nealie, Nealie--do you love her that much--that you take your heart and your life to her without hope or without sign or answer every day?"

He dropped his eyes, and turned his face away. "Not every day," he answered, "not every day--but every night, Aunt Molly."

"Why don't you go to her, Neal, and tell her?" asked the woman. "Is it so hopeless as that?"

"Oh, there are many reasons--why I don't go to her," he replied. After a minute's silence he went on: "In the first place she is a very rich girl, and that makes a difference--now. When she was just a young girl of eighteen, or such a matter, and I only twenty or twenty-one, we met so naturally, and it all came out so beautifully! But we are older now, Aunt Molly," he said sadly, "and it's different."

"Yes," admitted Mrs. Brownwell, "it is different now--you are right about it."

"Yes," he continued, repeating a patter which he had said to himself a thousand times. "Yes,--and then I can't say I'm sorry--for I'm not. I'd do it again. And I know how Mr. Barclay feels; he didn't leave me in any doubt about that," smiled the boy, "when I left his office that morning after telling him what I was going to do. So," he sighed and smiled in rather hopeless good humour, "I can't see my way out. Can you?"

Molly Brownwell leaned back in her chair, and closed her eyes for a minute, and then shook her head, and said, "No, Neal, not now; but there is a way--somehow--I am sure of that."

He laughed for want of any words to express his hopelessness, and the two--the youth in despair, and the woman full of hope--sat in silence.

"Neal," she asked finally, "what do you put in those letters? Why do you write them at all?"

The young man with his eyes upon the floor began, "Well--they're just letters, Aunt Molly--just letters--such as I used to write before--don't you know." His voice was dull and passionless, and he went on: "I can't tell you more about them. They're just letters." He drew in a quick long breath and exclaimed: "Oh, you know what they are--I want to talk to some one and I'm going to. Oh, Aunt Molly," he cried, "I'm not heart-broken, and all that--I'm infinitely happy. Because I still hold it--it doesn't die. Don't you see? And I know that always it will be with me--whatever may come to her. I don't want to forget--and it is my only joy in the matter, that I never will forget. I can be happy this way; I don't want to give any other woman a warmed-over heart, for this would always be there--I know it--and so I am just going to keep it." He dropped his voice again after a sigh, and went on: "There, that's all there is to it. Do you think I'm a fool?" he asked, as the colour came into his face.

"No, Neal, I don't," said Molly Brownwell, as she stood beside him. "You are a brave, manly fellow, Neal, and I wish I could help you. I don't see how now--but the way will come--sometime. Now," she added, "tell me about the paper."

And then they went into business matters which do not concern us; for
in this story business conjures up the face of John Barclay--the
tanned, hard face of John Barclay, crackled with a hundred wrinkles
about the eyes, and scarred with hard lines about the furtive crafty
mouth; and we do not wish to see that face now; it should be hidden
while the new soul that is rising in his body struggles with that
tough, bronzed rind, gets a focus from the heart into those glaring
brass eyes, and teaches the lying lips to speak the truth, and having
spoken it to look it. And so while John Barclay in the City is daily
slipping millions of his railroad bonds into the market,--slipping
them in quietly yet steadily withal, mixing them into the daily
commerce of the country, so gently that they are absorbed before any
one knows they have left his long grasping fingers,--while he is
trading to his heart's content, let us forget him, and look at this
young man, that September night, after he left Molly Brownwell,
sitting at his desk in the office with the telephone at his elbow,
with the smell of the ink from the presses in his nostrils, with the
silence of the deserted office becalming his soul, and with his
heart--a clean, strong, manly heart--full of the picture of a
woman's face, and the vision without a hope. In his brain are recorded
a thousand pictures, and millions of little fibres run all over this
brain, conjuring up those pictures, and if there are blue eyes in the
pictures, and lips in the pictures, and the pressure of hands, and the
touch of souls in the pictures,--they are Neal Ward's pictures,
--they are Mr. Higgin's pictures, and Mrs. Wiggin's pictures, and Mr.
Stiggin's pictures, my dears, and alack and alas, they are the
pictures of Miss Jones and Miss Lewis and Miss Thomas and Miss Smith,
for that matter; and so, my dears, if we would be happy we should be
careful even if we can't be good, for it is all for eternity, and
whatever courts may say, and whatever churches may say, and whatever
comes back with rings and letters and trinkets,--there is no divorce,
and the pictures always stay in the heart, and the sum of the pictures

is life.

So that September night Neal Ward went back over the old trail as lovers always will, and then his pen began to write. Now in the nature of things the first three words are not for our eyes, and to-night we must not see the first three lines nor the first thirty, nor the last three words nor the last three lines nor the last thirty lines. But we may watch him write; we may observe how longingly he looks at the telephone, as if tempted to go to it, and tell it what is in his breast. There it sits, all shiny and metallic; and by conjuring it with a number and a word, he could have her with him. Yet he does not take it up; because--the crazy loon thinks in the soul of him, that what he writes, some way, in the great unknown system of receivers and recorders and transmitters of thought that range through this universe, is pouring into her heart, and so he writes and smiles, and smiles and writes--no bigger fool than half the other lovers on the planet who, talking to their sweethearts, holding their hands and looking squarely into their eyes, deceive themselves that what they say is going to the heart, and not going in one ear and out of the other.

And now let us put on our seven-league boots and walk from September's green and brown, through October's gold and crimson, into that season of the year 1906 when Nature is shifting her scenery, making ready for the great spring show. It is bleak, but not cold; barren, but not ugly,--for the stage setting of the hills and woods and streams, even without the coloured wings and flies and the painted trees and grass, has its fine simplicity of form and grouping that are good to look upon. Observe in the picture a small man sitting on a log in a wood, looking at the stencil work of the brown and gray branches, as its shadows waver and shimmer upon the gray earth. He is poking reflectively in the earth with his cane. His boat is tied to some tree roots, and he doesn't breathe as regularly as a man should breathe who is merely thinking of his next dinner or his last dollar. He delves into himself and almost forgets to breathe at all, so deep is his abstraction. And so he sits for five minutes--ten minutes--half an hour--and save that he edges into the sun as the shadow of the great walnut tree above catches him, an hour passes and he does not move. Poking, poking, poking his stick into the mould, he has dug up much litter in an hour, and he has seen his whole life thrown up before him. In those leaves yonder is a battle--a bloody battle, and things are blistered into his boyish heart in that battle that never heal over; that tuft of sod is a girl's face--a little girl's face that he loved as a boy; there is his first lawsuit--that ragged pile of leaves by the twig at the log's end; and the twig is his first ten thousand dollars. All of it lies there before him, his victories and his defeats, his millions come, and his millions going--going?--yes, all but gone. Yonder that deep gash in the sod at the left hides a woman's face--pale, wasted, dead on her pillow; and that clean black streak on the ebony cane--that is a tear, and in the tear is a girl's face and back of hers shimmers a boy's countenance. All of John Barclay's life and hopes and dreams and visions are spread out before him on the ground. So he closes his eyes, and braces his soul, and then, having risen, whistles as he limps lightly--for a man past fifty--down to the boat. He rows with a clean manly stroke--even in an old flat-bottomed boat--through the hazy sunset into the dusk.

"Jeanette," he said to his daughter that evening at dinner, "I wish you would go to the phone, pretty soon, and tell Molly Culpepper that I want her to come down this evening. I am anxious to see her. The colonel isn't at home, or I'd have him, mother," explained Mr Barclay.

And that is why Miss Barclay called "876, Please--yes, 8-7-6;" and then said: "Hello--hello, is this 876? Yes--is Mrs. Brownwell in? Oh, all right." And then, "54, please; yes, 5-4. Is this you, Aunt Molly? Father is in town--he came in this morning and has spent the afternoon on the river, and he told me at dinner to ask you if you could run down this evening. Oh, any time. I didn't know you worked nights at the office. Oh, is Mr. Ward out of town?--I didn't know. All right, then--about eight o'clock--we'll look for you."

And that is why at the other end of the telephone, a pretty, gray-haired woman stood, and looked, and looked, and looked at a plain walnut desk, as though it was enchanted, and then slipped guiltily over to that black walnut desk, unlocked a drawer, and pulled out a whole apronful of letters.

And so the reader may know what Molly Brownwell had in that package which she put in the buggy seat beside her when she drove down to see the Barclays, that beautiful starry November night. She put the package with her hat and wraps in Jeanette's room, and then came down to the living room where John Barclay sat by the roaring fire in the wide fireplace, with a bundle beside him also. His mother was there, and his daughter took a seat beside him.

"Molly," said Barclay, with a deep sigh, "I sent for you, first, because, of all the people in the world, it is but just that you should be here, to witness what I am doing; and second, because Jane would have had you, and I want you to be with Jeanette when I tell her some things that she must know to-night--she and mother."

He was sitting in a deep easy chair, with one foot--not his lame foot--curled under him, a wiry-looking little gray cat of a man who nervously drummed on the mahogany chair arm, or kept running his hands over the carving, or folding and unfolding them, and twirled his thumbs incessantly as he talked. He smiled as he began:--

"Well, girls, father got off the chair car at Sycamore Ridge this morning, after having had the best sleep he has had in twenty years."

He paused for the effect of his declaration to sink in. Jeanette
asked, "Where was the car?"

"What car?" teased the little gray cat.

"Why, our car?"

"My dear, we have no car," he smiled, with the cream of mystery on his
lips. Then he licked it off. "I sold the car three weeks ago, when I
left the Ridge the last time." He dropped into an eloquent silence,
and then went on: "I rode in the chair car to save three dollars. I
need it in my business."

His mother's blue eyes were watching him closely. She exclaimed,
"John, quit your foolishness. What have you done?"

He laughed as he said: "Mother, I have returned to you poor but
honest. My total assets at this minute are seventy-five million
dollars' worth of stock of the National Provisions Company, tied up in
this bundle on the floor here, and five thousand dollars in the
Exchange National Bank of Sycamore Ridge which I have held for thirty
years. I sold my State Bank stock last Monday to Gabe Carnine. I have
thirty-four dollars and seventy-three cents in my pocketbook, and that
is all."

The women were puzzled, and their faces showed it. So the little gray
cat made short work of the mice.

"Well, now, to be brief and plain," said Barclay, pulling himself
forward in his chair and thrusting out an arm and hand, as if to grip
the attention of his hearers, "I have always owned or directly
controlled over half the N.P.C. stock--representing a big pile of

money. I am trying to forget how much, and you don't care. But it was
only part of my holdings--about half or such a matter, I should say.
The rest were railroad bonds on roads necessary to the company,
mortgages on mills and elevators whose stock was merged in the
company, and all sorts of gilt-edged stuff, bank stock and insurance
company stock--all needed to make N.P.C. a dominant factor in the
commercial life of the country. You don't care about that, but it was
all a sort of commercial blackmail on certain fellows and interests to
keep them from fighting N.P.C." Barclay hitched himself forward to the
edge of his chair, and still held out his grappling-hook of a hand to
hold them as he smiled and went on: "Well, I've been kind of swapping
horses here for six months or so--trading my gilt-edged bonds and
stuff for cash and buying up N.P.C. stock. I got a lot of it
quietly--an awful lot." He grinned. "I guess that was square enough.
I paid the price for it--and a little better than the price--because
I had to." He was silent a few moments, looking at the fire. He
meditated pleasantly: "There was some good in it--a lot of good when
you come to think of it--but a fearful lot of bad! Well--I've saved
the good. I just reorganized the whole concern from top to
bottom--the whole blame rebate hopper. We had some patents, and we
had some contracts with mills, and we had some good ideas of
organization. And I've kept the good and chucked the bad. I put N.P.C.
out of business and have issued stock in the new company to our
minority whose stock I couldn't buy and have squeezed the water out of
the whole concern. And then I took what balance I had left every
cent of it, went over the books for thirty years, and made what
restitution I could." He grinned as he added: "But I found it was
nearly whittlety whet. A lot of fellows had been doing me up, while I
had been doing others up. But I made what restitution I could and then
I got out. I closed up the City office, and moved the whole concern to
St. Paul, and turned it over to the real owners--the millers and
elevator men--and I have organized an industry with a capitalization
small enough to make it possible for them to afford to be honest for

thirty years--while our patents and contracts last, anyway." He put an elbow in the hollow of his hand, and the knuckles on his knee as he sat cross-legged, and drawled: "I wonder if it will work--" and repeated: "I wonder, I wonder. There's big money in it; she's a dead monopoly as she stands, and they have the key to the whole thing in the Commerce Department at Washington. They can keep her straight if they will." He paused for a while and went on: "But I'm tired of it. The great hulk of a thing has ground the soul out of me. So I ducked. Girls," he cried, as he turned toward them, "here's the way it is; I never did any real good with money. I'm going to see what a man can do to help his fellows with his bare hands. I want to help, not with money, but just to be some account on earth without money. And so yesterday I cleaned up the whole deal forever."

He paused to let it sink in. Finally Jeanette asked, "And are we poor, father--poor?"

"Well, my dear," he expanded, "your grandmother Barclay has always owned this house. An Omaha syndicate owns the mill. I own $5,000 in bank stock, and the boy who marries you for your money right now is going to get badly left."

"You aren't fooling me, are you, John?" asked his mother as she rose from her chair.

"No, mother," answered the son, "I've got rid of every dirty dollar I have on earth. The bank stock I bought with the money the Citizens' Committee subscribed to pay me for winning the county-seat lawsuit. As near as I can figure it out, that was about the last clean money I ever earned."

The mother walked toward her son, and leaned over and kissed him again and again as she sobbed: "Oh, John, I am so happy to-night--so happy."

In a moment he asked, "Well, Jeanette, what do you think of it?"

"You know what I think, father--you know very well, don't you?"

He sighed and nodded his head. Then he reached for the package on the floor and began cutting the strings. The bundle burst open and the stock of the National Provisions Company, issued only in fifty-thousand-dollar and one-hundred-thousand-dollar shares, littered the floor.

"Now," cried Barclay, as he stood looking at the litter, "now, Molly, here's what I want you to do: Burn it up--burn it up," he cried. "It has burned the joy out of your life, Molly--burn it up! I have fought it all out to-day on the river--but I can't quite do that. Burn it up--for God's sake, Molly, burn it up."

When the white ashes had risen up the chimney, he put on another log. "This is our last extravagance for some time, girls--but we'll celebrate to-night," he cried. "You haven't a little elderberry wine, have you, mother?" he asked. "Riley says that's the stuff for little boys with curvature of the spine--and I'll tell you it put several kinks in mine to watch that burn."

And so they sat for an hour talking of old times while the fire burned. But Molly Brownwell's mind was not in the performance that John Barclay had staged. She could see nothing but the package lying on her cloak in the girl's room upstairs. So she rose to go early, and the circle broke when she left it. She and Jeanette left John standing with his arms about his mother, patting her back while she wept.

As she closed the door of Jeanette's room behind her, Molly Brownwell knew that she must speak. "Jeanette," she said, "I don't know just how to say it, dear; but, I stole those--I mean what is in that package--I took it and Neal doesn't know I have it. It's for you," she cried, as she broke the string that tied it, and tore off the wrapping.

The girl stared at her and asked: "Why, Aunt Molly--what is it? I don't understand."

The woman in pulling her wrap from the chair, tumbled the letters to the floor. She slipped into her cloak and kissed the bewildered girl, and said as she stood in the doorway: "There they are, my dear--they are yours; do what you please with them."

She hurried down the stairs, and finding John sitting alone before the fire in the sitting room, would have bidden him good night as she passed through the room, but he stopped her.

"There is one thing more, Molly," he said, as he motioned to a chair.

"Yes," she answered, "I wondered if you had forgotten it!"

He worried the fire, and renewed the blaze, before he spoke. "What about Neal--how does he feel?"

"John," replied the woman, turning upon him a radiant face, "it is the most beautiful thing in the world--that boy's love for Jennie! Why, every night after his work is done, sitting there in the office alone, Neal writes her a letter, that he never mails; just takes his heart to her, John. I found a great stack of them in his desk the other day."

Barclay's face crinkled in a spasm of pain, and he exclaimed, "Poor little kids--poor, poor children."

"John--" Molly Brown well hesitated, and then took courage and cried: "Won't you--won't you for Ellen's sake? It is like that--like you and Ellen. And," she stammered, "oh, John, I do want to see one such love affair end happily before I die."

Barclay's hard jaw trembled, and his eyes were wet as he rose and limped across the great room. At the foot of the stairs he called up, "Don't bother with the phone, Jeanette, I'm going to use it." He explained, "The branch in her room rings when we use this one," and then asked, "Do you know where he is--at home or at the office?"

"If the ten o'clock train is in, he's at the office. If not, he's not in town."

But Barclay went to the hall, and when he returned he said, "Well, I got him; he'll be right out."

Molly was standing by the fire. "What are you going to say, John?" she asked.

"Oh, I don't know. There'll be enough for me to say, I suppose," he replied, as he looked at the floor.

She gave him her hand, and they stood for a minute looking back into their lives. They walked together toward the door, but at the threshold their eyes met and each saw tears, and they parted without words.

Neal Ward found Barclay prodding the fire, and the gray little man, red-faced from his task, limped toward the tall, handsome youth, and led him to a chair. Barclay stood for a time with his back to the fire, and his head down, and in the silence he seemed to try to speak several times before the right words came. Then he exclaimed:

"Neal, I was wrong--dead wrong--and I've been too proud and mean all this time--to say so."

Neal stared open-eyed at Barclay and moistened his lips before language came to him. Finally he said: "Well, Mr. Barclay--that's all right. I never blamed you. You needn't have bothered about--that is, to tell me."

Barclay gazed at the young man abstractedly for a minute that seemed interminable, and then broke out, "Damn it, Neal, I can't propose to you--but that's about what I've got you out here to-night for."

He laughed nervously, but the young face showed his obtuseness, and John Barclay having broken the ice in his own heart put his hands in his pockets and threw back his head and roared, and then cried merrily: "All we need now is a chorus in fluffy skirts and an orchestra with me coming down in front singing, 'Will you be my son-in-law?' for it to be real comic opera."

The young man's heart gave such a bound of joy that it flashed in his face, and the father, seeing it, was thrilled with happiness. So he limped over to Neal's chair and stood beaming down upon the embarrassed young fellow.

"But, Mr. Barclay--" the boy found voice, "I don't know--the money--it bothers me."

And John Barclay again threw his head back and roared, and then they talked it all out. He told Neal the story of his year's work. It was midnight when they heard the telephone ringing, and Barclay, curled up like an old gray cat in his chair before the fire, said for old times' sake, "Neal, go see who is ringing up at this unholy hour."

And while Neal Ward steps to the telephone, let us go upstairs on one last journey with our astral bodies and discover what Jeanette is doing. After Molly's departure, Jeanette stooped to pick up what Molly had left. She saw her own name, "Jeanette Barclay," and her address written on an envelope. She picked it up. It was dated: "Written December 28," and she saw that the package was filled with letters in envelopes similarly addressed in Neal Ward's handwriting. She dropped the letter on her dressing-table and began to undo her hair. In a few minutes she stopped and picked up another, and laid it down unopened. But in half an hour she was sitting on the floor reading the letters through her tears. The flood of joy that came over her drowned her pride. For an hour she sat reading the letters, and they brought her so near to her lover that it seemed that she must reach out and touch him. She was drawn by an irresistible impulse to her telephone that sat on her desk. It seemed crazy to expect to reach Neal Ward at midnight, but as she rose from the floor with the letters slipping from her lap and with the impulse like a cord drawing her, she saw, or thought she saw, standing by the desk, a part of the fluttering shadows, a girl--a quaint, old-fashioned girl in her teens, with--but then she remembered the dream girl her lover had described in the letter she had just been reading, and she understood the source of her delusion. And yet there the vision moved by the telephone, smiling and beckoning; then it faded, and there came rushing back to her memory a host of recollections of her childhood, and of some one she could not place, and then a memory of danger,--and then it was all gone and there stood the desk and the telephone and the room as it was.

She shuddered slightly, and then remembered that she had just been through two great nervous experiences--the story of her father's changed life, and the return of her lover. And she was a level-headed, strong-nerved girl. So the joy of love in her heart was not dampened, and the cord drawing her to the desk in the window did not loosen, and she did not resist. With a gulp of nervous fear she rang the telephone bell and called, "54, please!" She heard a buzzing, and then a faint stir in the receiver, and then she got the answer. She sat a-tremble, afraid to reply. The call was repeated in her ear, and then she said so faintly that she could not believe it would be heard, "Oh, Neal--Neal--I have come back."

The young man standing in the dimly lighted hall was startled. He cried, "Is it really you, Jeanette--is it you?"

And then stronger than before the voice said, "Yes, Neal, it is I--I have come back!"

"Oh, Jeanette--Jeanette," he cried.

But she stopped him with, "We must not talk any more--now, don't you know--but I had to tell you that I had come back, Neal." And then she said, "Good night." So there they stood, the only two people in the universe, reunited lovers, each with the voice of the other sounding in his ears. For Mr. Dolan was right. There are only two people in the world, and for these two lovers earth and the stars and the systems of suns that make up this universe were only background for the play of their happiness.

As Neal Ward came back to John Barclay from the telephone, the young man's face was burning with joy.

"Who was it?" asked Barclay.

The youth smiled bashfully as he said, "Well, it was Jeanette--she was calling up another number and I cut in."

"What did she say?" asked her father.

"Oh, nothing--in particular," replied Neal.

Barclay looked up quickly, caught the young man's abashed smile, and asked, "Does she know you're here?"

"No, she thinks I'm at the office."

Barclay rose from his chair, and limped across the room, calling back as he mounted the stair, "Wait a minute."

It was more than a minute that Neal Ward stood by the fire waiting.

And now, gentle people, observe the leader of the orchestra fumbling with his music. There is a faint stir among the musicians under the footlights. And you, too, are getting restless; you are feeling for your hat instinctively, and you for your hat-pins, and you for your rubbers, while Neal Ward stands there waiting, and the great clock ticks in the long silence. There is a rustle on the stairs, at the right, and do you see that foot peeping down, that skirt, that slender girlish figure coming down, that young face tear-stained, happy, laughing and sobbing, with the arms outstretched as she nears the last turn of the stairs? And the lover--he has started toward her. The orchestra leader is standing up. And the youth, with God's holiest glory in his face, has almost reached her. And there for an instant stand Neal and Jeanette mingling tears in their kisses, for the curtain, the miserable, unemotional, awkward curtain--it has stuck and so they must stand apart, hand in hand, devouring each other's faces a moment, and then as the curtain falls we see four feet close together again, and then--and then the world comes in upon us, and we smile and sigh and sigh and smile, for the journey of those four feet is ended, the story is done.

CHAPTER XXX

BEING SOMEWHAT IN THE NATURE OF AN EPILOGUE

And now that the performance is finished and the curtain has been rung down, we desire to thank you, one and all, for your kind attention, and to express the hope that in this highly moral show you may have found some pleasure as well as profit. But though the play is ended, and you are already reaching for your hats and coats, the lights are still dim; and as you see a great white square of light appear against the curtain, you know that the entertainment is to conclude with a brief exhibition of the wonders of that great modern invention, the cinematograph of Time.

The first flickering shadows show you the interior of Watts McHurdie's shop, and as your eyes take in the dancing shapes, you discern the parliament in session. Colonel Martin F. Culpepper is sitting there with Watts McHurdie, reading and re-reading for the fourth and fifth time, in the peculiar pride that authorship has in listening to the reverberation of its own eloquence, the brand-new copy of the second edition of "The Complete Poetical and Philosophical Works of Watts McHurdie, with Notes and a Biographical Appreciation by Martin F. Culpepper, 'C' Company, Second Regiment K.V." The colonel, with his thumb in the book, pokes the fire in the stove, and sits down again to drink his joy unalloyed. Watts is working on a saddle, but his arms and his hands are not what they were in the old days when his saddlery won first prize year after year at the Kansas City Fair. So he puffs and fusses and sighs his way through his morning's work. Sometimes the colonel reads aloud a line from a verse, or a phrase from the Biography--more frequently from the Biography--and exclaims, "Genius, Watts, genius, genius!" But Watts McHurdie makes no reply. As his old eyes--quicker than his old fingers--see the sad work they are making, his heart sinks within him.

"Listen, Watts," cries the colonel. "How do you like this, you old skeezicks?" and the colonel reads a stanza full of "lips" and "slips," "eyes" and "tries," "desires" and "fires," and "darts" and "hearts."

The little white-haired old man leans forward eagerly to catch it all. But his shoulders slump, and he draws a long, tired breath when the colonel has finished.

"Man--man," he cries, "what a saddle I could make when I wrote that!" And he turns wearily to his task again.

Oscar Fernald paces in busily, and in half an hour Lycurgus Mason, who has been thrown out of the current of life, drifts into his place in the back-water, and the parliament is ready for business. They see Gabriel Carnine totter by, chasing after pennies to add to his little pile. The bell tinkles, and the postman brings a letter. McHurdie opens it and says, as he looks at the heading:

"It's from old Jake. It is to all of us" he adds as he looks at the top of the sheet of letter paper. He takes off his apron and ceremoniously puts on his coat; then seats himself, and unfolding the sheet, begins at the very top to read:--

"National Soldiers' Home,
Leavenworth, Kansas,
March 11, 1909.

"TO THE MEMBERS OF MCHURDIE'S PARLIAMENT,

"***Gents and Comrades***: I take my pen in hand this bright spring morning to tell you that I arrived here safe, this side up with care, glass, be careful, Saturday morning, and I am willing to compromise my chances for heaven, which Father Van Saudt being a Dutchman always regarded as slim, for a couple of geological ages of this. I hope you are the same, but you are not. Given a few hundred white nighties for us to wear by day, and a dozen or two dagoes playing on harps, and this would be my idea of Heaven. The meals that we do have--tell Oscar that when I realize what eating is, what roast beef can be, cut thin and rare and dripping with gravy--it makes me wonder if the days when I boarded at the Thayer House might not be counted as part of the time I must do in the fireworks. And the porcelean bath tubs, and the white clean beds, and the music of the band, and the free tobacco--here I raise my Ebenezer, as the Colonel sings down in his heretic church; here I put my standard down.

"Well, Watts, I hear the news about Nelly. We've known it was coming for a year, but that doesn't make it easier. Why don't you come up here, Comrade--we are all lonesome up here, and it doesn't make the difference. Well, John Barclay, the reformed pirate, President of the Exchange National Bank, and general all-round municipal reformer, was over in Leavenworth last week attending the Bankers' Convention, or something, and he came to see me, as though he hadn't bid me good-by at the train two days before. But he said things were going on at the Ridge about the same, and being away from home, he grew confidential, and he told me Lige Bemis had lost all his money bucking the board of trade--did you know that? If not, it isn't so, and I never told you. John showed me the picture of little John B. Ward--as likely a looking yearling as I ever saw. Well, I must close. Remember me to all inquiring friends and tell them Comrade Dolan is lying down by the still waters."

And now the screen is darkened for a moment to mark the passage of months before we are given another peep into the parliament. It is May--a May morning that every one of these old men will remember to his death. The spring rise of the Sycamore has flooded the lowlands. The odour of spring is in the air. In the parliament are lilacs in a sprinkling pot--a great armful of lilacs, sent by Molly Culpepper. The members who are present are talking of the way John Barclay has sloughed off his years, and Watts is saying:--

"Boys will be boys; I knew him forty years ago when he was at least a hundred years older, and twice as wise."

"He hasn't missed a ball game--either foot-ball or baseball--for for nearly two years now," ventures Fernald. "And yell! Say, it's something terrible."

McHurdie turns on the group with his glasses on his forehead. "Don't you know what's a-happening to John?" he asks. "Well, I know. Whoever wrote the Bible was a pretty smart man. I've found that out in seventy-five years--especially the Proverbs, and I've been thinking some of the Testament." He smiles. "There's something in it. It says, 'Except ye come as a little child, ye shall in no wise enter the Kingdom.' That's it--that's it. I don't claim to know rightly what the kingdom may be, but John's entering it. And I'll say this: John's been a long time getting in, but now that he's there, he's having the de'el of a fine time."

And on the very words General Ward comes bursting into the room, forgetful of his years, with tragedy in his face. The bustle and clatter of that morning in the town have passed over the men in the parliament. They have not heard the shouts of voices in the street, nor the sound of footsteps running towards the river. But even their dim eyes see the horror in the general's face as he gasps for breath.

"Boys, boys," he exclaims. "My God, boys, haven't you heard--haven't you heard?" And as their old lips are slow to answer, he cries out, "John's dead--John Barclay's drowned--drowned--gave his life trying to save Trixie Lee out there on a tree caught in the dam."

The news is so sudden, so stunning, that the old men sit there for a moment, staring wide-eyed at the general. McHurdie is the first to find his voice.

"How did it happen?" he says.

"I don't know--no one seems to know exactly," replies the general. And then in broken phrases he gives them the confused report that he has gathered: how some one had found Trixie Lee clinging to a tree caught in the current of the swollen river just above the dam, and calling for help, frantic with fear; how a crowd gathered, as crowds gather, and the outcry brought John Barclay running from his house near by; how he arrived to find men discussing ways of reaching the woman in the swift current, while her grip was loosening and her cries were becoming fainter. Then the old spirit in John Barclay, that had saved the county-seat for Sycamore Ridge, came out for the last time. His skiff was tied to a tree on the bank close at hand. A boy was sent running to the nearest house for a clothes-line. When he returned, John was in the skiff, with the oars in hand. He passed an end of the line to the men, and without a word in answer to their protests, began to pull out against the current. It was too strong for him, and was sweeping him past the woman, when he stood up, measured the distance with his eye, and threw the line so it fell squarely across her shoulders. Some one said that as the skiff shot over the dam, John, still standing up, had a smile on his face, and that he waved his hand to the crowd with a touch of his old bravado.

The general paused before going on with the story.

"They sent me to tell his mother--the woman who had borne him, suckled him, reared him, lost him, and found him again."

"And what did she say?" asked Watts, as the general hesitated.

The general moistened his lips and went on. "She stood staring at me for one dreadful minute, and then she asked, 'How did he die, Philemon?' 'He died saving a woman from drowning,' I told her. 'Did he save her?'--that was what she asked, still standing stiff and motionless. 'Yes,' I said. 'She was only Trixie Lee--a bad woman--a bad woman, Mrs. Barclay.' And Mary Barclay lifted her long, gaunt arms halfway above her head and cried: 'Mine eyes have seen the glory of the coming of the Lord. I must have an hour with God now, Philemon,' she said over her shoulder as she left me; 'don't let them bother me.' Then she walked unbent and unshaken up the stairs."

So John Barclay, who tried for four years and more to live by his faith, was given the opportunity to die for it, and went to his duty with a glad heart.

    *   *   *   *   *

We will give our cinematograph one more whirl. A day, a week, a month, have gone, and we may glimpse the parliament for the last time. Watts McHurdie is reading aloud, slowly and rather painfully, a news item from the ***Banner***. Two vacant chairs are formally backed to the wall, and in a third sits General Ward. At the end of a column-long article Watts drones out:--

"And there was considerable adverse comment in the city over the fact that the deceased was sent here for burial from the National Soldiers' Home at Leavenworth, in a shabby, faded blue army uniform of most ancient vintage. Surely this great government can afford better shrouds than that for its soldier dead."

Watts lays down the paper and wipes his spectacles, and finally he says:--

"And Neal wrote that?"

"And Neal wrote that," replies the general.

"And was born and bred in the Ridge," complains McHurdie.

"Born and bred in the Ridge," responds the general.

Watts puts on his glasses and fumbles for some piece of his work on the bench. Then he shakes his head sadly and says, after drawing a deep breath, "Well, it's a new generation, General, a new generation."

There follows a silence, during which Watts works on mending some bit of harness, and the general reads the evening paper. The late afternoon sun is slanting into the shop. At length the general speaks.

"Yes," he says, "but it's a fine town after all. It was worth doing. I wake up early these days, and often of a fine spring morning I go out to call on the people on the Hill."

McHurdie nods his comprehension.

"Yes," continues the general, "and I tell them all about the new improvements. There are more of us out on the Hill now than in town, Watts; I spent some time with David Frye and Henry Schnitzler and Jim Lord Lee this morning, and called on General Hendricks for a little while."

"Did you find him sociable?" asks the poet, grinning up from his bench.

"Oh, so-so--about as usual," answers the general.

"He was always a proud one," comments Watts. "Will Henry Schnitzler be stiff-necked about his monument there by the gate?" asks the little Scotchman.

"Inordinately, Watts, inordinately! The pride of that man is something terrible."

The two old men chuckle at the foolery of the moment. The general folds away the evening paper and rises to go.

"Watts," he says, "I have lived seventy-eight years to find out just one thing."

"And what will that be?" asks the harness maker.

"This," beams the old man, as he puts his spectacle case in his black silk coat; "that the more we give in this world, the more we take from it; and the more we keep for ourselves, the less we take." And smiling at his paradox, he goes through the shop into the sunset.

The air is vocal with the home-bound traffic of the day. Cars are crowded; delivery wagons rattle home; buggies clatter by on the pavements; one hears the whisper of a thousand feet treading the hot, crowded street. But Watts works on. So let us go in to bid him a formal good-by. The tinkling door-bell will bring out a bent little old man, with grimy fingers, who will put up his glasses to peer at our faces, and who will pause a moment to try to recollect us. He will talk about John Barclay.

"Yes, yes, I knew him well," says McHurdie; "there by the door hangs a whip he made as a boy. We used to play on that accordion in the case there. Oh, yes, yes, he was well thought of; we are a neighbourly people--maybe too much so. Yes, yes, he died a brave death, and the papers seemed to think his act of sacrifice showed the world a real man--and he was that,--he was surely that, was John; yes, he was a real man. You ask about his funeral? It was a fine one--a grand funeral--every hack in town out--every high-stepping horse out; and the flowers--from all over the world they came--the flowers were most beautiful. But there are funerals and funerals. There was Martin Culpepper's--not so many hacks, not so many high-stepping horses, but the old buggies, and the farm wagons, and the little nigger carts--and man, man alive, the tears, the tears!"

The Codes Of Hammurabi And Moses
W. W. Davies

QTY

The discovery of the Hammurabi Code is one of the greatest achievements of archaeology, and is of paramount interest, not only to the student of the Bible, but also to all those interested in ancient history...

Religion   ISBN: *1-59462-338-4*   **Pages:132**

MSRP $12.95

The Theory of Moral Sentiments
Adam Smith

QTY

This work from 1749. contains original theories of conscience amd moral judgment and it is the foundation for systemof morals.

Philosophy ISBN: *1-59462-777-0*   **Pages:536**

MSRP $19.95

Jessica's First Prayer
Hesba Stretton

QTY

In a screened and secluded corner of one of the many railway-bridges which span the streets of London there could be seen a few years ago, from five o'clock every morning until half past eight, a tidily set-out coffee-stall, consisting of a trestle and board, upon which stood two large tin cans, with a small fire of charcoal burning under each so as to keep the coffee boiling during the early hours of the morning when the work-people were thronging into the city on their way to their daily toil...

Pages:84

Childrens   ISBN: *1-59462-373-2*   *MSRP $9.95*

My Life and Work
Henry Ford

QTY

Henry Ford revolutionized the world with his implementation of mass production for the Model T automobile. Gain valuable business insight into his life and work with his own auto-biography... "We have only started on our development of our country we have not as yet, with all our talk of wonderful progress, done more than scratch the surface. The progress has been wonderful enough but..."

Pages:300

Biographies/   ISBN: *1-59462-198-5*   *MSRP $21.95*

www.bookjungle.com *email: sales@bookjungle.com fax: 630-214-0564 mail: Book Jungle PO Box 2226 Champaign, IL 61825*

The Art of Cross-Examination
Francis Wellman

QTY

I presume it is the experience of every author, after his first book is published upon an important subject, to be almost overwhelmed with a wealth of ideas and illustrations which could readily have been included in his book, and which to his own mind, at least, seem to make a second edition inevitable. Such certainly was the case with me; and when the first edition had reached its sixth impression in five months, I rejoiced to learn that it seemed to my publishers that the book had met with a sufficiently favorable reception to justify a second and considerably enlarged edition. ..

Pages:412

Reference   ISBN: *1-59462-647-2*   *MSRP $19.95*

On the Duty of Civil Disobedience
Henry David Thoreau

QTY

Thoreau wrote his famous essay, On the Duty of Civil Disobedience, as a protest against an unjust but popular war and the immoral but popular institution of slave-owning. He did more than write—he declined to pay his taxes, and was hauled off to gaol in consequence. Who can say how much this refusal of his hastened the end of the war and of slavery ?

Law   ISBN: *1-59462-747-9*   **Pages:48**
MSRP $7.45

Dream Psychology Psychoanalysis for Beginners
Sigmund Freud

QTY

Sigmund Freud, born Sigismund Schlomo Freud (May 6, 1856 - September 23, 1939), was a Jewish-Austrian neurologist and psychiatrist who co-founded the psychoanalytic school of psychology. Freud is best known for his theories of the unconscious mind, especially involving the mechanism of repression; his redefinition of sexual desire as mobile and directed towards a wide variety of objects; and his therapeutic techniques, especially his understanding of transference in the therapeutic relationship and the presumed value of dreams as sources of insight into unconscious desires.

Pages:196

Psychology   ISBN: *1-59462-905-6*   *MSRP $15.45*

The Miracle of Right Thought
Orison Swett Marden

QTY

Believe with all of your heart that you will do what you were made to do. When the mind has once formed the habit of holding cheerful, happy, prosperous pictures, it will not be easy to form the opposite habit. It does not matter how improbable or how far away this realization may see, or how dark the prospects may be, if we visualize them as best we can, as vividly as possible, hold tenaciously to them and vigorously struggle to attain them, they will gradually become actualized, realized in the life. But a desire, a longing without endeavor, a yearning abandoned or held indifferently will vanish without realization.

Pages:360

Self Help   ISBN: *1-59462-644-8*   *MSRP $25.45*

QTY

The Rosicrucian Cosmo-Conception Mystic Christianity by *Max Heindel*   ISBN: *1-59462-188-8*   **$38.95**
The Rosicrucian Cosmo-conception is not dogmatic, neither does it appeal to any other authority than the reason of the student. It is: not controversial, but is: sent forth in the, hope that it may help to clear...   New Age/Religion Pages 646

Abandonment To Divine Providence by *Jean-Pierre de Caussade*   ISBN: *1-59462-228-0*   **$25.95**
"The Rev. Jean Pierre de Caussade was one of the most remarkable spiritual writers of the Society of Jesus in France in the 18th Century. His death took place at Toulouse in 1751. His works have gone through many editions and have been republished...   Inspirational/Religion Pages 400

Mental Chemistry by *Charles Haanel*   ISBN: *1-59462-192-6*   **$23.95**
Mental Chemistry allows the change of material conditions by combining and appropriately utilizing the power of the mind. Much like applied chemistry creates something new and unique out of careful combinations of chemicals the mastery of mental chemistry...   New Age Pages 354

The Letters of Robert Browning and Elizabeth Barret Barrett 1845-1846 vol II   ISBN: *1-59462-193-4*   **$35.95**
by *Robert Browning* and *Elizabeth Barrett*   Biographies Pages 596

Gleanings In Genesis (volume I) by *Arthur W. Pink*   ISBN: *1-59462-130-6*   **$27.45**
Appropriately has Genesis been termed "the seed plot of the Bible" for in it we have, in germ form, almost all of the great doctrines which are afterwards fully developed in the books of Scripture which follow...   Religion/Inspirational Pages 420

The Master Key by *L. W. de Laurence*   ISBN: *1-59462-001-6*   **$30.95**
In no branch of human knowledge has there been a more lively increase of the spirit of research during the past few years than in the study of Psychology, Concentration and Mental Discipline. The requests for authentic lessons in Thought Control, Mental Discipline and...   New Age/Business Pages 422

The Lesser Key Of Solomon Goetia by *L. W. de Laurence*   ISBN: *1-59462-092-X*   **$9.95**
This translation of the first book of the "Lernegton" which is now for the first time made accessible to students of Talismanic Magic was done, after careful collation and edition, from numerous Ancient Manuscripts in Hebrew, Latin, and French...   New Age/Occult Pages 92

Rubaiyat Of Omar Khayyam by *Edward Fitzgerald*   ISBN:*1-59462-332-5*   **$13.95**
Edward Fitzgerald, whom the world has already learned, in spite of his own efforts to remain within the shadow of anonymity, to look upon as one of the rarest poets of the century, was born at Bredfield, in Suffolk, on the 31st of March, 1809. He was the third son of John Purcell...   Music Pages 172

Ancient Law by *Henry Maine*   ISBN: *1-59462-128-4*   **$29.95**
The chief object of the following pages is to indicate some of the earliest ideas of mankind, as they are reflected in Ancient Law, and to point out the relation of those ideas to modern thought.   Religiom/History Pages 452

Far-Away Stories by *William J. Locke*   ISBN: *1-59462-129-2*   **$19.45**
"Good wine needs no bush, but a collection of mixed vintages does. And this book is just such a collection. Some of the stories I do not want to remain buried for ever in the museum files of dead magazine-numbers an author's not unpardonable vanity..."   Fiction Pages 272

Life of David Crockett by *David Crockett*   ISBN: *1-59462-250-7*   **$27.45**
"Colonel David Crockett was one of the most remarkable men of the times in which he lived. Born in humble life, but gifted with a strong will, an indomitable courage, and unremitting perseverance...   Biographies/New Age Pages 424

Lip-Reading by *Edward Nitchie*   ISBN: *1-59462-206-X*   **$25.95**
Edward B. Nitchie, founder of the New York School for the Hard of Hearing, now the Nitchie School of Lip-Reading, Inc, wrote "LIP-READING Principles and Practice". The development and perfecting of this meritorious work on lip-reading was an undertaking...   How-to Pages 400

A Handbook of Suggestive Therapeutics, Applied Hypnotism, Psychic Science   ISBN: *1-59462-214-0*   **$24.95**
by *Henry Munro*   Health/New Age/Health/Self-help Pages 376

A Doll's House: and Two Other Plays by *Henrik Ibsen*   ISBN: *1-59462-112-8*   **$19.95**
Henrik Ibsen created this classic when in revolutionary 1848 Rome. Introducing some striking concepts in playwriting for the realist genre, this play has been studied the world over.   Fiction/Classics/Plays 308

The Light of Asia by *sir Edwin Arnold*   ISBN: *1-59462-204-3*   **$13.95**
In this poetic masterpiece, Edwin Arnold describes the life and teachings of Buddha. The man who was to become known as Buddha to the world was born as Prince Gautama of India but he rejected the worldly riches and abandoned the reigns of power when...   Religion/History/Biographies Pages 170

The Complete Works of Guy de Maupassant by *Guy de Maupassant*   ISBN: *1-59462-157-8*   **$16.95**
"For days and days, nights and nights, I had dreamed of that first kiss which was to consecrate our engagement, and I knew not on what spot I should put my lips..."   Fiction/Classics Pages 240

The Art of Cross-Examination by *Francis L. Wellman*   ISBN: *1-59462-309-0*   **$26.95**
Written by a renowned trial lawyer, Wellman imparts his experience and uses case studies to explain how to use psychology to extract desired information through questioning.   How-to/Science/Reference Pages 408

Answered or Unanswered? by *Louisa Vaughan*   ISBN: *1-59462-248-5*   **$10.95**
Miracles of Faith in China   Religion Pages 112

The Edinburgh Lectures on Mental Science (1909) by *Thomas*   ISBN: *1-59462-008-3*   **$11.95**
This book contains the substance of a course of lectures recently given by the writer in the Queen Street Hail, Edinburgh. Its purpose is to indicate the Natural Principles governing the relation between Mental Action and Material Conditions...   New Age/Psychology Pages 148

Ayesha by *H. Rider Haggard*   ISBN: *1-59462-301-5*   **$24.95**
Verily and indeed it is the unexpected that happens! Probably if there was one person upon the earth from whom the Editor of this, and of a certain previous history, did not expect to hear again...   Classics Pages 380

Ayala's Angel by *Anthony Trollope*   ISBN: *1-59462-352-X*   **$29.95**
The two girls were both pretty, but Lucy who was twenty-one who supposed to be simple and comparatively unattractive, whereas Ayala was credited, as her Bombwhat romantic name might show, with poetic charm and a taste for romance. Ayala when her father died was nineteen...   Fiction Pages 484

The American Commonwealth by *James Bryce*   ISBN: *1-59462-286-8*   **$34.45**
An interpretation of American democratic political theory. It examines political mechanics and society from the perspective of Scotsman James Bryce   Politics Pages 572

Stories of the Pilgrims by *Margaret P. Pumphrey*   ISBN: *1-59462-116-0*   **$17.95**
This book explores pilgrims religious oppression in England as well as their escape to Holland and eventual crossing to America on the Mayflower, and their early days in New England...   History Pages 268

www.bookjungle.com *email: sales@bookjungle.com fax: 630-214-0564 mail: Book Jungle PO Box 2226 Champaign, IL 61825*

QTY

The Fasting Cure by *Sinclair Upton*   ISBN: *1-59462-222-1* **$13.95**
In the Cosmopolitan Magazine for May, 1910, and in the Contemporary Review (London) for April, 1910, I published an article dealing with my experiences in fasting. I have written a great many magazine articles, but never one which attracted so much attention... New Age/Self Help/Health Pages 164

Hebrew Astrology by *Sepharial*   ISBN: *1-59462-308-2* **$13.45**
In these days of advanced thinking it is a matter of common observation that we have left many of the old landmarks behind and that we are now pressing forward to greater heights and to a wider horizon than that which represented the mind-content of our progenitors... Astrology Pages 144

Thought Vibration or The Law of Attraction in the Thought World   ISBN: *1-59462-127-6* **$12.95**

by *William Walker Atkinson*   Psychology/Religion Pages 144

Optimism by *Helen Keller*   ISBN: *1-59462-108-X* **$15.95**
Helen Keller was blind, deaf, and mute since 19 months old, yet famously learned how to overcome these handicaps, communicate with the world, and spread her lectures promoting optimism. An inspiring read for everyone... Biographies/Inspirational Pages 84

Sara Crewe by *Frances Burnett*   ISBN: *1-59462-360-0* **$9.45**
In the first place, Miss Minchin lived in London. Her home was a large, dull, tall one, in a large, dull square, where all the houses were alike, and all the sparrows were alike, and where all the door-knockers made the same heavy sound... Childrens/Classic Pages 88

The Autobiography of Benjamin Franklin by *Benjamin Franklin*   ISBN: *1-59462-135-7* **$24.95**
The Autobiography of Benjamin Franklin has probably been more extensively read than any other American historical work, and no other book of its kind has had such ups and downs of fortune. Franklin lived for many years in England, where he was agent... Biographies/History Pages 332

Name	
Email	
Telephone	
Address	
City, State ZIP	

☐ **Credit Card**   ☐ **Check / Money Order**

Credit Card Number	
Expiration Date	
Signature	

Please Mail to: Book Jungle
PO Box 2226
Champaign, IL 61825
or Fax to: 630-214-0564

ORDERING INFORMATION

web: *www.bookjungle.com*
email: *sales@bookjungle.com*
fax: *630-214-0564*
mail: *Book Jungle PO Box 2226 Champaign, IL 61825*
or PayPal *to sales@bookjungle.com*

Please contact us for bulk discounts

DIRECT-ORDER TERMS

**20% Discount if You Order
Two or More Books**
Free Domestic Shipping!
Accepted: Master Card, Visa,
Discover, American Express

www.ingramcontent.com/pod-product-compliance
Lightning Source LLC
Chambersburg PA
CBHW080722020726
47503CB00010B/2751